LINKED BY FATE

LINKED BY FATE

CHARLES GARVICE

WILDSIDE PRESS

Originally published in 1903.
Published by Wildside Press LLC.
wildsidepress.com

CHAPTER I
A DUEL FOR MASTERY

The moon shone in regal splendor on one of the most beautiful spots on this beautiful earth.

It was one of the islands which lie off the eastern shore of Australia. A gentle breeze stirred the foliage; the waves lapped in on the golden sands and broke gently on the rocks, making a music as soft and soothing as the breeze; the opalescent light lit up the scene and turned it into a dream of fairyland.

And a man stood on the beach, and, looking round upon this fairyland, cursed it fluently under his breath.

He was young and well made; one of those good-looking young men which the public schools and the 'varsities turn out with machine-like regularity. He was an athlete, and strong, but in the moonlight he looked wan and pale, and infinitely weary, with the weariness of doubt, anxiety, and sleepless nights.

His serge suit was tattered and torn, and shrunk by the water and sun, and his shapely head was covered by a battered hat made of leaves.

As he stood looking moodily before him, there came from a rough hut, at a little distance from the beach, another young man. He was by no means an athlete, but small, and thin, and bent, and he wore the remains of a black serge suit of a clerical cut, for he was a clergyman. He was even paler and more wan than the man on the sands, and he pressed his thin hand to his chest, and coughed, and he came along slowly and painfully.

The two men looked like characters in an old-fashioned farce; but there was tragedy here. For these two men, with sundry other persons, were all that remained of the crew and passengers of the vessel *Alpina*, which, eight days previously, had been wrecked off the coast of this uninhabited island.

The Rev. Arthur Fleming crawled to his companion's side.

"You have seen nothing, Mannering?" he asked, not as one with hope of an answer in the affirmative, but as if the question were a formula which had grown into a habit.

Vane Mannering shook his head.

"No," he said gravely; "and I'm afraid we're not likely to. In my opinion, this beastly island is one of the numerous groups which is quite out of the line of shipping. The fact that the *Alpina* lost her course proves that, I think."

"You mean that there is little hope of rescue?" said Arthur Fleming, in a low voice.

"Very little chance," assented Mannering. "Of course, I can't say for certain. If they had taught me geography at Eton or Oxford, instead of Latin and Greek, and several other still more useless things, I might give a guess as to where we are; but as it is I've no idea. If there had been any chance of our being picked up, we should have sighted a vessel before now. In all probability we shall be left to die of starvation—well, not of starvation, perhaps, say, ennui—on this cursed island."

Fleming's lips opened to murmur, "Bless and curse not"; but he refrained. It was scarcely the moment for reproof; and, indeed, his gratitude to his companion helped to check him; for the party owed their lives to Vane Mannering, whose energy, alertness, coolness, and presence of mind had brought them from the doomed ship.

"Have you seen the doctor and Miss Nina?" asked Mannering, after a pause, filled up by Fleming's hollow cough.

"She is in their hut; I saw her go in half an hour ago. The doctor is still wandering about the island. The way that girl bears up, Mannering, fills me with admiration and reverence. She is here all alone with us men; she has suffered all the privations, that terrible journey in the boat from the ship, all the dreadful uncertainties of our position, with something more than heroism; for heroism always suggests to my mind a kind of blatancy and self-assertion; but she has been not only fearless, but cheerful and self-reliant, and yet trustful. I tell you, Mannering, when I think of her my heart goes out in gratitude to God for His creation of her sex. Who would have thought that such a slim bit of a girl, who seemed all gayety and lightness of heart, would have proved such a noble character?"

Mannering nodded. "She is still keeping well? I was afraid she might get a touch of fever, such as the rest of us have had."

"She had a slight attack," said Fleming; "but she seemed to throw it off, with a courage as great as her patience and self-denial. The doctor is about the same; he is still very weak, and his mind seems cloudy, but he insisted upon going out; and he has taken his hammer with him, to knock off bits of rock, and so on."

"Let him," said Mannering briefly; "it will amuse him, and keep him from brooding on the situation. I wish I could go and knock off pieces of rock, instead of standing idling here!"

Fleming looked at him reproachfully.

"How can you talk so, my dear Mannering?" he said. "You have been our leader, our sole support; you have worked indefatigably from morning to night. But for you, we should all be lying at the bottom of the sea there; we owe our lives to your energy, your pluck, your wonderful power of endurance."

Mannering shook his head.

"I have done little enough," he said moodily. "You ought not to be out here, Fleming," he added, as Fleming's cough shook his frail figure.

"I'm all right. It's very warm in the hut; and I don't cough any more out here. We'll both turn in presently. Why don't you smoke?"

"I gave my last pipe to the doctor," Mannering replied casually. "He wanted it worse than I do."

The strident sound of a concertina floated unmusically from one of the three huts, and was followed, still more unmusically, by loud voices and laughter.

"The men seem merry to-night," remarked Fleming, with a sigh.

"Yes," said Mannering. "I gave out a tot of rum to each man this evening. I wish——" He hesitated, and Fleming looked up at him quietly—"I wish they weren't here. They are an element of danger, Fleming. Up to the present they have behaved fairly well; but how long will they continue to behave well? For instance, how long will they be content to let me deal out the rum? They know where the keg is. I could not prevent their getting at it."

"They're—they're not all bad," suggested Fleming. "They have stood by us up to now."

"No, they are not all bad; but there are one or two black sheep among them. I mistrust that Lascar and the other stoker, Munson. He is always haranguing the rest. I saw him skulking round the doctor's hut last night. If they were Englishmen, one would not have any misgiving; but——" He shrugged his shoulders. "We man our ships with the scum of the earth, Fleming, just as we fill the East End of London with aliens, to take the bread out of the mouths of our own poor." The noise from the men's hut grew louder. "I think I'd better go and see what they are doing," he said.

He and Fleming approached the hut quietly, and looked in. Some of the six men were lying full length on the ground, others were seated on stools, roughly constructed of the limbs of the pine trees. In the centre of the hut stood the keg of rum, and Munson was drawing some of the red liquor into a can. They had all been drinking freely, and were flushed and excited.

Fleming groaned as he saw the keg, and Mannering's face grew stern; but he uttered no sound, and gripped Fleming's arm to warn him to silence, for the Lascar was speaking.

"Ve are what you call 'pals,' " he was saying, in his thick voice, his black eyes rolling evilly on the faces of the listeners. "Ve are bein' played vith! It ish thish Mishter Mann'rin' that ish trickin' us; 'im and the padre, ah, and the medico, too! They hab the money. I who speak know it. I saw thish man pash the box to the medico as he got into the boat."

"The box of medicine and instruments!" whispered Fleming.

Mannering nodded grimly. He was listening intently, and scanning the faces of the men keenly.

"That's true; I saw 'em," said Munson. And some of the others muttered assentingly.

"The box wash full o' money, gold; jewels, too, perhaps. Thatsh so! You know ze laties do give their jewelry to ze purser to take care of. Eh, vhat! Thatsh box was full of dimints. An' it belongsh to us; eh, vhat you say?"

"To us; all of us, yes!" grunted Munson.

"To us who manned ze boat, who—who vorked like slaves, puttin' up zese houses; to us, ze laborers, ze brothers of toil, ze zalt of ze earth!"

"That's so," assented one of the men. "Pass round the rum again, Lasky."

The Lascar emptied the can at a draught, refilled it, and passed it to the man next him; then he leaned forward, and whispered huskily:

"It ish in the medico's tent. It ish unter the bed o' the girl. I saw Mishter Mann'rin' put it there. Ve will go, ve will all go and git it, and share it man to man!"

Some of the men sprang to their feet unsteadily; but one or two were not so prompt; and a voice said lazily:

"There's no hurry; let's have our drink first."

Mannering cautiously drew Fleming away.

"There is no time to lose," he said gravely, when they had got out of hearing.

"You will give them the box, show them that it does not contain any gold?" said Fleming, with the cough he had been repressing with difficulty.

"No," said Mannering quietly. "They would not be convinced; besides, it would be a fatal weakness. Do you think"—he paused a moment and his lips tightened—"that they would be satisfied? Some of them might, but not the Lascar and Munson. They are brutes, beasts; and you know the effect of the first taste of blood on such wild beasts. They would want more—everything, perhaps." He paused and Fleming, following Mannering's thought, pictured the young girl in the hands of these men, and shuddered.

"What will you do?" he asked, as a man asks his leader and commander.

"Show fight," said Mannering, as quickly as before. "We have the only firearms that were saved—a couple of revolvers and a gun."

"I can manage a revolver; but, oh, Mannering, if we could avoid bloodshed!" murmured Fleming.

"We'll try," said Mannering. "It rests with them. You agree with me, it would be unwise, a criminal folly, to yield to them? They would not stop—— There is Miss Nina."

Fleming nodded and bent his head.

"You are right—as you have been all through, Mannering."

They had been approaching the hut, which Mannering, with his own hands, had built for Doctor Vernon and his daughter, and he signed to Fleming to knock; but Fleming shook his head.

"No," he said; "you will do it better than I, Mannering. She looks up to you, relies on you. You will give her courage. I—I am not a coward, I hope and trust; but I should let her see the—the dread that makes me cold at this moment, and you will not. No; you!"

Mannering nodded, and knocked at the rough door of the hut. It was opened by a young girl. She was very beautiful, with a beauty which is indicated by expression as much as regularity of feature. Her eyes were of the dark gray which at times become violet, her hair was of a soft black, and the gods had given her the mouth which, when it smiles, wins men's hearts. But she was not only young, but innocent of vanity or self-consciousness, and her eyes lit up, and her lips smiled with frank pleasure, as she saw who it was.

"Oh, good evening, Mr. Mannering!" she said, with quiet cheerfulness, and her voice rang like a low note of music in the pine-perfumed air. "Will you come in? My father is out; he went out for a stroll—— Is anything the matter?"

She did not start or turn pale, but stood, in her stained and patched serge dress, calm and attentive.

Mannering knew enough of women to know that with this one, young as she was, the proper course was the direct one. His eyes rested reflectingly for a moment on her lovely face, on the small, shapely head with its soft, black hair resting on the forehead, and wound into a knot at the back, then he said:

"I am afraid there is, Miss Nina." He had grown to call her by her Christian name; shipwrecked people are apt to be slack on extreme points of etiquette. "The men are getting—impatient. They entertain the absurd idea that we have smuggled the specie and valuables from the ship, in your father's medicine chest——"

She glanced at the box under the rough bed.

"And—and they are coming for it presently, I think."

"And you will not give it to them?" she said quietly, as if she had read his face, upon which her beautiful eyes were fixed.

"No; they'd want more," he said. "And we must make a stand at the outset. There may be a little noise and—trouble, so I came to warn you. You will not be frightened? Mr. Fleming and I are armed; the men are not; and I have no doubt they will cool off, when they find we are resolute."

"I see," she said. "No, I shall not be frightened; that is, not more than I can help."

Her smile, surely the sweetest ever smiled by woman, flickered across her lips, and shone in her eyes.

"No," he said, "you have displayed such pluck, such—oh, I cannot express myself!" he broke off, as if in despair.

"Oh, but you have!" she said, with the faintest blush. "I was just making some tea. Will you have a cup?"

Mannering glanced at the meat tin on the fire, and gauged its contents.

"Thanks, no. I have just had some." Generally, Mannering, with all his faults, was a truthful man. "But Mr. Fleming—he is outside."

He beckoned Fleming in, and Nina poured out a cup of tea for him gravely. Of course she knew that Mannering had lied.

Fleming took it gratefully; it was to him as rum was to the men.

"Mr. Mannering has told you?" he said, in a low voice.

Nina nodded.

"Yes; I am sorry. But I hope it will all be over before father comes back. He is not well; he is feverish—and—he has been wandering a little in his mind. He has taken the gun. I am sorry!"

Mannering touched Fleming on the arm, and they went out and to their own hut, got and loaded their revolvers, and, returning to the beach, sat down as if for a quiet talk.

They had not to wait long.

"Take it coolly," murmured Mannering, as the six men came out of the hut. Some of them walked unsteadily, one of them was singing; but the Lascar and Munson were still sober, though evidently excited by the liquor.

Mannering rose and slowly went to meet them, walking in the direction that put him between them and the Vernons' hut.

"Good evening," he said; "want anything?"

"You ask ze polite question, sur, and ve giv you ze polite answer. It ish ze little box in ze hut zere," replied the Lascar, with a mocking bow.

Mannering raised his brows, with simulated surprise.

"Anybody ill? The box contains medicine and instruments of various kinds," he said quietly.

The Lascar showed his gleaming teeth in a sardonic smile.

"Ish zat so?" he retorted, with an incredulous jerk of his hand. "Ve vill see——"

"I think not," said Mannering, so quietly that Fleming's heart throbbed with a tribute of admiration. "You will take my word for it. I see that you have got the keg of rum—you have broken your promise——"

"To ze devil wiz your promises!" the Lascar broke in. "Vy should you keep all ze best of ze swag ve bring away from ze ship? You keep ze rum, ze box of gold, ze girl!" he leered evilly, and moved forward as if to pass Mannering. Mannering drew his revolver.

"Stop where you are!" he said grimly. There was a spot of red on his hollow cheeks, and a light in his eyes, which spoke of the just rage which had sprung up in his heart like a flame.

Fleming stepped forward and held up his hand.

"Men, I want to speak to you!" he said, fighting with his cough. "You know what Mr. Mannering has done for us. But for him——But surely you don't want me to remind you! And surely you cannot suspect that he—we— have any idea of taking any advantage of you. The chest contains only medicine and instruments, as Mr. Mannering said. You were wrong, very wrong, to take the keg of rum; you would be acting wickedly if you were to follow the advice, the leadership, of this man, who is as much indebted as the rest of us to Mr. Mannering."

Some of the men exchanged glances, but the Lascar cut in with a short, sardonic laugh.

"Ze padre speaks softly, as ze padre always do. Vell, then, let one of us go into the medico's hut——"

He moved forward, but Mannering covered him, saying:

"Not a step."

The Lascar pulled up and looked Mannering up and down.

"You speak bravely, Mishter Mann'rin'! You 'ave the gun!" He made an insolent gesture with his facile and eloquent hands. "If you had only ze little knife like zis, we would settle the matter, ah, so ker-vickly! You are ze one coward!"

Then Mannering did a foolish thing—the foolish thing which Englishmen individually and collectively so often do: He gave away his advantage. It was inexcusable; but, ah, well, let the man who has meekly borne the taunt of a Lascar, and been called a coward, pitch the first stone; I will not, and I have an idea that the reader will not.

Mannering looked into the rolling eyeballs for a moment or two; then he said:

"See here, now, men. If it's a fair fight between us and I win, will you take my word, and go back to your hut quietly, not only go back, but leave that man's lead?"

The men looked at each other and whispered. They were more or less drunk, and therefore impressionable, and they were longing for the kind of fight Mannering indicated. Don't blame them. In the House of Commons a "personal" matter will fill the benches; and any sort of duel has a fascination for every man with red blood in his veins.

"Yes, fight it out; we'll see fair play!" shouted a man thickly.

Mannering beckoned to Fleming.

"Take my revolver," he said aloud, "and shoot the first man who attempts to interfere——"

"Mannering! Mannering! You will not do it! I implore, I beseech you!" cried Fleming, with solemn earnestness.

Mannering quickly stripped off his coat and rolled up his sleeves.

"No use, Fleming; I must. Either that man or I must be master. They'll follow the victor like sheep, you'll see. It will end the trouble——"

"But, Mannering, these men, these Lascars, are adepts at the knife," urged Fleming almost frantically.

Mannering shrugged his shoulders. "I learned a trick or two when I was in Malacca," he said quickly. "Got a handkerchief?"

Fleming shook his head. The door of the Vernons' hut opened, and Nina came quickly down to them. Her face was white as death, her eyes were like "the violets steeped in dew," her lips, white as her face, were set tightly.

"Mr. Mannering, you must not! You will not!" She looked into his eyes, and saw that her appeal was hopeless. "Then—then—there is a handkerchief!"

He took it, bound his bowie knife to his wrist, and held it out to Fleming. Fleming hesitated; the girl caught the wrist and tied the knot Mannering wanted.

"Thanks," he said coolly. "Now go inside—and shut the door."

She obeyed; and, leaning against the wall, as if to still her throbbing heart, looked between the logs.

Munson had bound the Lascar's knife to his wrist, and the two men confronted each other. The moon shone down on them in placid mockery of such poor stuff as human emotions; the soft breeze wafted the perfume of the pines across the men's heated breath; the sea sang to the golden beach; the delicious night was full of beauty. To poor Fleming, even in that intense moment, as he stood, revolver in each hand, there flashed the lines:

"Where every prospect pleases, and only man is vile."

The Lascar's face seemed to glow, as if with the reflection of fire; the Englishman's was white and set, with the calm of courage and resolution.

"Come on," said Mannering; and, as he spoke, the Lascar sprang at him.

If there is anything more exciting than a "knife fight," I do not know it. It is catlike in the rapidity of its movements; it is soul-thrilling in its moments of doubt and uncertainty; it is awe-inspiring in its pauses, rushes, wrestlings. The two men crouched, sprang, caught at the wrists of the hands that held the knives, struck, parried, and avoided the gleaming blades by swift, almost imperceptible swayings and glidings of the bodies.

The Lascar was as agile as a snake, and bent, dipped, and attacked with sinuous force; but Mannering, though lacking this facility of movement, possessed the qualities of strength, endurance, and the cool eye, and by the exercise of these he parried the terrible attack.

The men, sobered now by the intense excitement, looked on in breathless excitement. Fleming, forgetting them, and clean forgotten by them, suffered the revolvers to droop in his shaking hands.

And the girl, for whom this awful fight was being fought—what a presumptuous idiot I should be if I attempted to set down her emotions!

Suddenly a short cry, a gasp, rose from the men and was echoed by Fleming; the Lascar's knife had cut a gash in Mannering's shoulder.

"Oh, stop! stop! For God's sake, stop, Mannering!" cried Fleming.

But neither the combatants nor the other spectators heeded—they probably did not hear him.

Mannering felt the cut of the sharp knife, felt the blood running down his shoulder and side; but he set his teeth and forced himself to remain calm: everything depended, he knew, upon his keeping his head; not his life only, but the girl—the sweet, innocent girl. Ah, now he must not lose his head!

He drew back a moment, and the Lascar, with a hideous smile, pressed on to him. It was what Mannering wanted. With a sudden swerve, a movement of the leg and the strong, steellike left arm, he threw his opponent to the ground, and in an instant was on top of him with a knee like iron pressing into his chest. He raised his arm, the reflected knife gleamed in the moonlight, the Lascar's wavering life hung in the balance. A shudder ran through the spectators, a cry arose from Nina—she had come to the door. While one could count ten the knife poised above the Lascar's heart. Then, before the other men could interfere, Mannering had wrenched the knife from the Lascar's grasp and flung it behind him; then he tore the bandage from his own arm and sent his knife flying with the other.

"Get up!" he said, removing his knee.

The Lascar sprang to his feet, dazed, uncertain. Mannering waited a second or two, then he said:

"Now, we'll fight it out English fashion."

The Lascar was no mean boxer—he had picked it up from his English messmates—and, with a flickering smile, he threw himself into position.

This second fight shall not be described. Suffice it that the Lascar was as a child in the hands of the man who had carried all before him with the gloves at Christchurch. Again and again the Lascar came on—let us give him his due—to receive the terrible punishment, but at last a well-aimed blow from Mannering—who was now enjoying himself amazingly—sent the Lascar to earth with the sickening thud some of us know so well.

Mannering, panting and wiping the sweat—it had flowed like water—from his swollen face, stood over him for a moment in silence; then he beckoned to the men.

"Take him to the hut," he said. Then, as they picked up the unconscious man, Mannering added, quite quietly:

"I think that settles it. If not, if any of you would like to try your hand——"

The polite and liberal offer was declined with thanks.

"That's all right, sir," said one man, the best of the bad lot. "It was a square and fair fight, and bli' me if he ain't got what he deserves."

"Well, then," said Mannering. "You understand that I'm master here—some one has to be, you know—and that if I find any man pass the line of that tree"—he pointed to one a hundred yards from the Vernons' hut—"well!"

They went off, bearing the Lascar, and Mannering turned to Fleming, who was clinging to his arm.

"Mannering! Mannering! You are hurt! You are bleeding! Oh, Mannering, how—how nobly you fought! It was wicked, very wicked, but—oh, how—how I admire you for it! God forgive me!"

CHAPTER II
DEATH OF THE DOCTOR

Nina came from the hut, not running, but with a graceful swiftness. Her face was still paler, but her eyes were glowing under their dark lashes.

"Are you—are you hurt?" she asked, in a low voice, which she was, womanfully, trying to keep steady.

"Thanks, not at all, or very little," said Mannering, going for his coat.

"Oh, Mannering, how can you say so!" exclaimed Fleming reproachfully. "He is badly cut. Look at the blood! It is of no use putting your coat on, Mannering; you must have that dreadful wound dressed."

"It is too slight to be called a wound," said Mannering casually.

"Come to the hut," said Nina, in the tone a woman uses to a man when she means to be obeyed.

They went to the Vernons' hut, and she poured some water into a tin and examined the knife-slash.

"It is an awful cut," she said, between her white, even teeth. "I—I don't know what to do."

"Oh, we'll just wash it," said Mannering lightly. "It will be all right; it is nothing."

She shuddered slightly, as she bathed the flowing blood from the wound, but her hand was quite steady, and it was only her beautiful lips that quivered.

"I—I am glad you did not kill him, though—though at one moment I almost wished——How strong you must be!" she said, in a low voice.

"I did not know you were looking," said Mannering reluctantly. "I told you to shut the door."

"I did—oh, I did! but I looked between the logs," she said, with sudden meekness.

A shadow fell across the threshold and the doctor entered. He was an old man, bent and feeble, but at that moment in a state of suppressed excitement which lent him fictitious strength and vigor.

"Nina, where is Mr. Mannering? Oh, there you are!" he said, peering at them under his white and shaggy brows. "I've got news, great news, for you, Mannering. What are you doing? What is the matter?" he broke off to inquire.

Nina lifted her eyes from her work.

"Mr. Mannering has been hurt—the men, father. They wanted to steal the chest, and—and Mr. Mannering——"

"Eh? What? No matter!" he interrupted impatiently. "Some quarrel, I suppose. Let me see."

He put the girl aside gently, and looked at the cut.

"Knife, eh? Flesh wound only. Give me a piece of linen. Tear it off the sleeve of the shirt. Why did you quarrel? At such a moment, when you need all your strength and coolness. Mannering, Fleming," he continued as he deftly stanched and bandaged the wound, "I have made the most extraordinary discovery. A pin, Nina. Tut, tut, haven't you a safety pin?" She found one and gave it to him. "Pin it here."

Her cool, soft fingers touched Mannering's arm gently, pityingly, tenderly.

"That's right. You will do very well. Next case. Eh? What? Thought I was in the ward. How did you get that hurt? No matter! Mannering, see here!"

He turned to the empty box which served as a table, and turned out the contents of his pocket upon it.

"Look at those!" he exclaimed, in a tone of suppressed excitement. "Look at them! Do you know what they are? Wait! Shut the door!"

Nina closed the door, and came back to the group; but, though the casual observer would have said that she was looking at the apparently extremely commonplace stones on the table, she was really looking, sideways, at Mannering.

"See what they are!" said the doctor, in a thick, tremulous whisper. "Take up one of them; examine it!"

Mannering mechanically took up one of the stones. He was thinking of the men, wondering how long they would remain quiescent, amenable.

"Well?" demanded the doctor impatiently. His face was flushed with excitement as well as fever, and the sweat stood in big drops on his wrinkled forehead.

Mannering raised his brows deprecatingly.

"They look like ordinary stones, doctor," he said.

Doctor Vernon uttered a cry of impatient contempt.

"Tut, man, where were you educated?" he retorted impatiently. "They are gold quartz. Gold, gold, I tell you! Hush!" He glanced anxiously toward the door. "It's gold. We are rich—beyond the dreams of avarice!"

He uttered the dear old hackneyed phrase hoarsely, unctuously.

"I found them in the valley between the ridge of hills, south by southwest. There is gold there, I tell you, gold in immense quantities! Gold!"

His bloodshot eyes peered from one to the other, with feverish excitement, and his hanging under lip trembled as if he had been struck by palsy.

Fleming and Mannering looked at each other significantly. The glance said, "He is mad!"

"In immense quantities! It lies, most of it, on the surface, in what the miners call 'placers.' It is quite easy to get. It is, I verily believe, an island of gold. And it is ours, ours! Nina, Mannering, Fleming, we are rich, millionaires, multimillionaires, as the phrase goes. It is incorrect, but no matter, the gold is there! How hot it is!" He drew his trembling hand across his wet brow and sank, almost collapsed, onto the table.

Nina went to him and laid a soothing hand on his shoulder.

"You are tired, father; you must rest, be quiet——"

"Rest! Nonsense! You—you talk like a child! You don't understand, Nina! I tell you it is gold! I cannot have made a mistake. We have been cast ashore on an Eldorado! Mr. Mannering, Fleming, you will share it with me! Indeed, it really belongs to you, Mannering, for but for you we should never have reached the island alive. Gold! Gold in practically unlimited quantities! Think of it! Nina, I—I am thirsty. I have been in the sun—water—water!"

He was gasping for breath, his face was livid and his features twitching.

Mannering ran out of the hut and brought some water, and a draught somewhat restored the old man.

"Go, now," said Nina, in a low voice. "I will get him to lie down and sleep. He will be better in the morning."

She extended her hand to Mannering, and, as he took it, she murmured:

"Good night—and thank you!"

"That's all right, Miss Nina," he said, in true Englishman's fashion.

"Do you think there is anything in the doctor's discovery?" asked Fleming hesitatingly, as he and Mannering walked toward their hut.

Mannering shrugged his broad shoulders.

"I don't know. There may be. Gold is found in all sorts of places. But it would have been more to the point if the doctor had discovered a banana tree, a boot tree, or a coat tree. What is the use of gold to us? You can't make even a decent crock out of it."

Fleming coughed violently.

"That is true. Mannering, what a lesson to some of us who spend our lives amassing useless wealth! I wish that some of our millionaires could be here to learn that lesson!"

His pious reflection was broken by the cough which shook him from top to toe.

"Turn in and get some sleep," said Mannering.

"And you? You, too, will get some sleep to-night, Mannering?"

"Yes; oh, yes! But I'll look round first."

Fleming entered their hut and dropped into the rough bed, exhausted by the physical and mental strain; but Mannering, as soon as he had assured himself that Fleming was asleep, went up to the Vernons' hut and, revolver in hand, dropped down outside the door.

Though he had firmly resolved that he would not sleep, he must have fallen into a semi-doze, for he was startled, as one is startled out of sleep, by a cry in Nina's voice.

"Mr. Mannering—my father!"

He was on his feet in a moment and followed her into the hut.

But he could do nothing. The doctor was dead. The excitement of his discovery, on the top of the fever, had proved fatal. The girl stood beside the lifeless form, her eyes dry, all her tears shut up in her bereaved heart. Mannering found himself bereft of speech, a dumb dog. With scarcely a glance at her, he went in search of Fleming.

He met him coming up from the beach, his frail figure bent, his arms hanging limply at his side, almost every step punctuated by his cough.

"Mannering," he said, in the tone of one who brings bad news, "they—they have gone!"

"Gone? Who?" asked Mannering dully.

"The men—all of them. They have taken the boat and left us."

Mannering nodded grimly.

"It is like them. The boat gone! There goes our only hope of escape. I, too, have bad news. Doctor Vernon is dead. Go up to the hut, Fleming. She wants you."

Fleming caught his breath, then, without a word, went up the beach.

Mannering stood on the edge of the sand and looked out seaward. With the boat had gone their last chance, hope, of escaping. He and Fleming and Nina were now left sole inhabitants of this lonely island. He stared out to sea, and the sea mocked him with its splendor and majesty. It seemed to him to say: "I am master; you are my slave. I laugh at you and all your efforts. I am supreme. My will is law. I have cast you here to live in a living death. There is no escape!"

How long he remained staring at the waves, as they lapped on the sand, he never knew. He was recalled to life and its exigencies by Fleming, who, crawling up weakly, said:

"Is there a spade, Mannering?"

Mannering made a mute assent, found the spade, and the two men dug the grave. They went up to the hut and carried the dead man down.

Nina followed them, her head bowed almost to her bosom; and she stood motionless, tearless, while Fleming recited the burial service in gasps.

Then, still with bent head, she went back to the hut: a girl, an orphan, with these two men as sole companions.

Fleming, as a clergyman, had offered the usual condolences, and she had accepted them meekly, with the docile humility of her sex. It was evening before he left her and met Mannering at the entrance of their hut.

Fleming was wan and pale, and his cough was like a war cry.

"How is she?" asked Mannering.

Fleming made a gesture of despair.

"Who should say? Very bad. Poor girl! oh, poor girl! It's terrible, terrible! And—and, Mannering, I've been thinking—I—I want to speak to you."

"Well, what is it?" asked Mannering dully.

Fleming had sunk upon his bed, and was gasping as if for breath.

"I—I must do my duty. I must face it, Mannering. The doctor is dead."

"Well, I know. What then?" asked Mannering doggedly.

"And—and I—I don't think I shall last long."

"Nonsense!" said Mannering brusquely.

"I don't. I'm—I've never been strong, and this place, beautiful as it is, seems to—to sap all my remaining strength. Mannering, if—if I go, you two, you and Nina, will be alone!"

He paused and fought for breath, holding his weak chest, as if he would fain hold the strength in it.

"Well?" said Mannering.

Fleming looked at him with poignant anguish.

"Alone! You and she! Mannering, for her sake, for yours, you must be——Can you not guess? Oh, help me, Mannering! You must be married!"

Mannering stared at him, at first vaguely, then with an intense anxiety and gravity.

"Married!" broke from his parched lips.

"Yes, married!" breathed Fleming.

CHAPTER III
A STRANGE PROPOSAL

Mannering sank on to the upturned box which served as a seat, and stared over Fleming's head.

"You—you had never thought of it—never thought of the situation in which she would be placed if I were to die, and you and she were left alone?" said Fleming huskily.

Mannering shook his head.

"No. You will think me selfish, inconsiderate, but——"

"No, no!" Fleming broke in eagerly. "You have had so much to think of, Mannering. The wonder is that you have not broken down under the long, the terrible strain. But I—well, the responsibility has not rested on my weak shoulders, and I have had time to think, and I"—meekly, modestly—"am a clergyman; it was my duty to think for you, and for you both. It has been in my mind ceaselessly, ever since I began to fear that the doctor might die, and I knew that I should."

"You will pull round," muttered Mannering stubbornly; but Fleming shook his head.

"Don't let us waste time arguing it," he said quietly. "My time is short—I feel it. And think how she will be placed, that helpless girl, Mannering! Let us consider it gravely——"

"A vessel might sight the signal, the beacon, any moment," put in Mannering, under his breath.

"If it did so, before I died, all would be well; but it might not. And if one came afterward, after I am gone, and found you two here, and took you off, what would be her position? You, a man of the world, know only too well, Mannering. She—oh, poor girl, poor girl!—would be compromised in the eyes of the world, always so ready to be suspicious and censorious, always so merciless and pitiless to the woman in her position."

"I know," muttered Mannering.

"But, if you were married, all would be well. No one, not the most malignant or heartless, could cast a stone. You will not hesitate, Mannering? Why should you? She is young, and beautiful, and good—the sweetest, noblest girl——"

Mannering sprang up, then sank down again.

"She is!" he said doggedly. "But what about me? You know nothing about me. You propose that this young and beautiful girl, with all her sweetness and nobility, should marry a man of whose past you know nothing. I am quite poor. I may be, probably am, worthless, a cumberer of the earth, a waste——"

Fleming shook his head, and, after a paroxysm of coughing, said emphatically:

"Poor, yes, but not worthless, and not a cumberer of the earth. You forget that we were friends on the voyage, that I have lived with you here on the island, have had opportunities of reading your character——"

"The marriage would not be valid," said Mannering.

"Yes, I think so. I am not up in the marriage laws, as I should be, but I am almost sure it would be; and if you were not fully married, in the civil sense, you would be in the spiritual, the solemn one. If you were rescued you could be married again at the first port, or on reaching England," said Fleming, with grave earnestness. "I have thought of the case in all its bearings; I am not blind to its difficulties——"

"She may refuse to—to marry me," Mannering put in, in a low voice, and with his eyes fixed on the patch of sand and sky framed by the doorway of the hut.

"I do not think she will," returned Fleming, in almost as low a tone. "You must ask her—put the case to her——"

"No, no!" Mannering exclaimed, springing to his feet and standing at the door, with his back to Fleming. "I can't. I—I should break down. I should so put it that she would have to refuse. What? Go and tell a girl—young, beautiful, noble—your words haunt me, Fleming—that I am going to take advantage of her position and chain her for life to a man who—of whom she knows nothing! I can't do it—and I won't!"

Fleming lay back on the rough pillow of sun-dried seaweed and covered his eyes with his hands.

"I see—I understand. I will tell her—ask her, Mannering. I will make it plain to her that she must—yes, *must*—consent. I will go at once, while—while I am able. Will you give me a hand?" Mannering held him up, and gave him some of the precious brandy which they had saved.

"Thanks. Half of that; only a drop or two. Thank you, thank you, Mannering! I was not wrong in my estimate of you. It is good of you to yield so soon. Some men—I fear most men—would have stood out, or refused altogether. They would have thought of themselves, and cared nothing for her—for her reputation, her future."

"Don't try to make me out an angel or a plaster saint, Fleming," Mannering said, curtly and huskily. "In fact, I've more than half a suspicion that you're wrong, and that I'm a fool for yielding to you. But—we've been pals, and when you pull out the conscience and principle stops I'm done."

"No, I am right; and you are acting like a gentleman, and an honest man," Fleming gasped.

"Well!" Mannering sighed; then he looked at him half angrily. "But doesn't it occur to you that your trust and confidence in me are rather too thick? How do you know that I am not already married?"

Fleming smiled wanly.

"You would have told me so the very first moment you heard of my proposal," he said simply.

Mannering almost groaned.

"There is no balking you. Well, go to her——Wait!" as Fleming got to his feet, slowly and feebly. "Tell her—tell her——" Mannering stopped and swore under his breath; then he went on hoarsely: "Tell her that it is your idea, not mine, mind! And that—that it is not to be a real marriage."

Fleming's blue eyes, set in their dark hollows, rested on his face patiently.

"That we will go through the form to please you, and save her from—from scandal and the rest of it; but that I—I do not intend to take advantage of it. No! I may be a bad lot, but I'm not so bad as to snare a young girl. Fleming, see that she understands that this marriage is to be one in name—form only. She—she will understand. *Make* her. Mind!"

A faint color flushed Fleming's deathlike face.

"I will tell her," he said, in a low voice. "Mannering, you are behaving nobly——"

"Oh, rot!" Mannering broke in, as if he could not restrain himself. "Did you think I was a cur, a mean hound? No one short of that would act differently. Oh, poor girl, poor girl! Here, I'll give you a hand part of the way. And if you're wrong in this business, may God forgive you, Fleming!"

"I echo your prayer, Mannering," he said solemnly.

The two men went slowly toward the hut, Fleming leaning—one would write heavily, but that word is grotesquely inapplicable, for he was but a shadow of a man—on Mannering's arm; then Mannering stopped, and, without a word, turned, strode to the beach, and stood staring out to sea.

Fleming knocked at the door of Nina's hut, though the door was open, and she called to him to come in. She was sitting on her bed mending a skirt, and she went on with her work—for there was much to do and time was valuable—as he entered. She was very pale, but with that ivory pallor which is not inconsistent with perfect health, and her eyes were dull and heavy with the tears, that had weakened, though they had relieved her. She signed to the rough chair which Mannering had made for her father, and Fleming sank into it.

"Are you—better?" he asked.

She knew that he meant was her grief less poignant, and answered "yes," in a low voice, and with a stifled sigh.

"Do you think you are strong enough to listen to something I want to say to you?" he asked. "Something very important, serious?"

"Oh, yes!" she replied; and she stopped in her work, and let her hands lie motionless on it. "Yes; but you—you are not looking well, Mr. Fleming. Is your cough worse—are you feeling weaker?"

"Yes," replied Fleming simply, "I am weaker. I am very ill. Please don't be sorry for me! I am obliged to tell you, because my condition is connected with what I have to say to you, Miss Nina. Have you thought of your position, situation, here if anything should happen to me—if, plainly, I were to die? And, I think—indeed, I know—that I am dying! Ah, no," as a low cry of pity, of sorrow escaped her, "you will not grieve for me; you will be sorry; but you will remember that for me death means a release and—a gain. But," he went on, with a slight wave of his hand, "it was not of myself that I came to speak, but of you. Miss Nina, you and I have, I hope and trust, become something like brother and sister. Of my love and respect for you, you will have no doubt."

She made a gesture of assent, and he went on in earnest tones, broken by fits of coughing and struggling for the painful breath:

"When I am gone you will be alone on this island with Mr. Mannering."

She raised her eyes for a moment to his saintlike face, then dropped them to her hands again.

"It may be that you are fated to remain here for the rest of your lives——"

Her hands shook and her lips quivered at the dreadful suggestion.

"Or God may will that a passing vessel, one drifting out of her course, may see the signal on the cliff, and come to your rescue."

He fought for breath, and she cast a look of pity and tender sympathy at him.

"In that case they will find you here with—with Mannering—will take you back to England and tell the story of your—your solitary companionship with him."

She raised her eyes, a look of comprehension, of a woman's apprehension in them.

"Ah, you understand!" he gasped. "The world would say——You know what it would say. Forgive me! You will forgive me for speaking so plainly. Alas! there is no help for it; I must speak plainly!"

"I understand," she said, in a low voice.

"If—if you were man and wife——" he went on.

She looked at him with a vague doubt on her face.

"But we are not," she said.

"But there is no reason why you should not be," he said slowly, and yet with a throbbing heart. "Indeed, Mr. Mannering has sent me to ask you——"

Her hand clutched at the skirt, but she said nothing.

"To ask you to—marry him."

"To marry him!" Her lips formed the words, but no sound came; but Fleming answered, as if he had heard her mute exclamation:

"Yes. He sees the necessity of defending you against the suspicion, the evil suspicion and calumny of the world——Wait, dear Miss Nina; do not speak until I have told you all. And I will conceal, keep back, nothing; for it is right that you should know the whole. It was I who pointed out to him how gravely you would suffer, how terribly your future would be imperiled—nay, wrecked—if—if you two were discovered here alone, and were not married. That he should not have thought of it is a proof of his purity, high-mindedness. But I am a clergyman, and it is my duty——"

"Oh, I cannot, cannot!" broke from her lips, which were white, though the scarlet burned in her cheeks.

"My dear, you must!" he said, with gentle firmness.

"To marry me—out of pity!" she said inaudibly, her eyes full of shame and womanly protest.

"No, no!" he panted, his hand pressing against his hollow chest. "You do not know him, or you would not say that—put it that way. It is true, he pities you—what man with a spark of manliness could do otherwise, my poor child?—but he sees, with me, that it is the right, the only course to pursue. Ah, no, no; you must not think that he regards you as an object of pity—that he takes a superior, a condescending view of his responsibility. On the contrary—oh, if you had heard him speak of his unworthiness, of his inferiority, of his presumption, in offering marriage to you, you would understand how he feels toward you!"

Nina, her protest uttered, sat silent, her hands tightly clinched, her eyes fixed on the ground.

"You are thinking, reflecting?" said Fleming quietly. "I would that I could give you time—a week, a month—to consider; but there is no time; there may not be many hours. My child," his voice grew solemn and tender, "I have considered prayerfully, and I take upon myself the great responsibility of advising you—if I dared say so, of exhorting you. Your future welfare is dear to me; I must, I *must* guard it for you! There is no way of rendering that future, if you are restored to the world, safe and possible, except by marrying Mr. Mannering."

There was a pause; then she looked at him—a look which Fleming would have remembered if he had lived to be a hundred.

"If—if a vessel were to come—if we were to be rescued, I—I should be his wife, bound to him, and he to me—a marriage without love! You, a clergyman, bid me——"

The color had left her face, and she was now deathly pale.

Fleming met her eyes unflinchingly.

"There is still something to tell you," he said. "I bear a message from Mr. Mannering. He bids me say that the marriage shall be one in name—form only; that you will be as free as you are now; that you will be his wife in name only. Ah, do you understand? You do not doubt his word, his promise?"

Her eyes left his face, and wandered to the open doorway. He knew, by the writhing of the white lips, the torture she was undergoing. The silence was so intense as to be an actual burden and pain. It was he who broke it.

"You decide?" he said huskily.

"Why did he—send you? Why did he not come himself?" she asked, almost inaudibly.

"Can you not understand and appreciate his feeling? He was desirous that you should be free to discuss it with me. He would not be the one to bias, persuade, you. His instinct was a right, a noble one. He is a gentleman, you know," he wound up simply.

"Yes, he was right—I suppose," she admitted, but with the faintest qualification.

"And you will decide?" said Fleming.

She wrung her hands.

"Oh, I cannot!" she answered. "Give me—give me a little time to think—only an hour or two. I have never thought—it is so sudden, so unexpected. I feel as if it were not real—as if it were a dream—a nightmare."

Fleming rose and laid his hand on her trembling ones.

"Do you think I do not know what you are suffering?" he said in a low voice. "Ah, believe me, I do! Yes; take one hour. I will come back to you."

As he crept out of the hut, Mannering, who was still standing gazing at the sea, heard him, but would not turn his head.

"Well?" he said hoarsely, his face still averted. Fleming took his arm and leaned on it.

"I have spoken to her. She is naturally much distressed——"

"I should think so!" commented Mannering grimly.

"But she is considering it. Poor girl, she saw, with the quickness of her sex, the necessity for the step. But I think she would have been better pleased, less distressed, if you had gone to her."

"Why?" demanded Mannering shortly.

Fleming shook his head.

"I do not know. She seemed to think that you were sacrificing yourself—at any rate as much as she was herself."

"Good Lord!" ejaculated Mannering. He drew his hand across his brow impatiently. "See here, Fleming, though I can see your side of the case—the gravity of the situation for her—I've still a feeling that this—this marriage must be averted. I've been thinking, and I've got a proposal. The weather is still fine. I could knock a raft together, and she and you could venture to sea on it. You could get out on the tide, and might make one of the larger islands of the group—an inhabited one. What do you say?"

"How long would it take to make the raft?" asked Fleming.

"A couple of days. I could rig up a sail. It is a chance. Will you consent?"

"Yes," gasped Fleming calmly. "The risk is terrible—for her; there is none for me. Death in any shape I do not fear, thank God!" he added devoutly. "But for her——"

"She may prefer the risk, death itself, to—to your plan," said Mannering brusquely. "She shall decide. I'll ask her."

He strode away before Fleming could stay him, and, without pausing, as if he were afraid to hesitate, reached Nina's hut.

CHAPTER IV
LINKED BY FATE

Nina heard the knock.

"So soon!" she said to herself with a start; for she thought the hour had passed, and that it was Fleming returned for her answer, the decision which she had not yet arrived at. If she had been given a week, a month, would she have been able to decide?

She sprang to her feet as Mannering entered, then sank down again, her eyes fixed on his face with, as it seemed to him, physical fear; and, at the thought, he set his teeth and frowned: that a woman should be inspired by fear at the sight of him.

"I have just left Mr. Fleming," he said, and his voice, by reason of the emotions conflicting within him, sounded harsh and almost forbidding. "He has told you—what he came to tell you. I want you to know that it is his proposal, not mine, Miss Nina."

Her lips framed an assent, and he went on constrainedly.

"While he was with you I have been thinking, and I have got an idea—a proposal that may avert the—the sacrifice he wants you to make."

She looked up quietly, and drew a breath of relief.

"It is this," he said, using almost the exact words he had used to Fleming. "The weather is fine, the wind is set, and I think for some time, from the island. I can make a raft with a sail. It could be provisioned for some time, and you and he might escape—might reach one of the larger islands—an inhabited one. It is a risk, a great risk, but—but I fancy you would prefer it to—to his proposal."

Her eyes were fixed on him with breathless earnestness while he was speaking, then they dropped.

"Does—does Mr. Fleming consent?" she asked in a low voice. "The risk is his as well as mine. I have no right to let him take it!"

"He consents," he said.

She raised her eyes again.

"And you—you would be left here alone? Alone!" She tried to repress the shudder that shook her at the idea.

"That is all right," he responded.

"And the provisions—you would be left without sufficient food——"

"I shall not starve," he said quietly. "There are plenty of birds; other things. I will keep the gun. There is the fishing——Oh, I shall do well enough!"

"You—you wish it?" she asked almost inaudibly, her eyes hidden from him by their long lashes.

"I don't know," he said almost roughly, for his nerves were on edge, his pity for her making a kind of madness in his brain. "I think anything would be better than—the thing he wishes you to do. Do you think I don't realize it? You know nothing of me. You would commit yourself to the keeping of a man who, for all you know, may be the greatest villain unhanged—would be the wife, on compulsion, against your desire and will, of one for whom you do not care. Oh, I know how it must seem to you—how you must think of it! My plan is full of risk and danger, but I fancy that you will consider it a better one than his."

For one moment she looked him full in the eyes. In hers was the question: "But *you*, you, too, realize that you would be chained to one for whom you do not care—do you wish her, for your sake, to go?"

His eyes were averted, and he did not see the interrogation in hers; his face was glowering, frowning with the strain on nerve and brain; and it is little wonder that she read an affirmative to her question.

"I will go," she said almost inaudibly.

Mannering made a slight gesture with his hands.

"I thought you would," he said in a voice almost as low as her own. "I think you are right."

He went to their hut, to which Fleming had crawled.

"She has decided," he said curtly. "She will go."

Fleming had been sitting with his head bowed in his hands. He let them fall and looked steadily at Mannering.

"Very well," he said resignedly. "But you must be quick, Mannering," he added significantly.

Mannering nodded, took up an axe, and went straight to the pine wood. He worked like a man possessed, and the trees fell before the strokes of his axe with a dull crash which reached Nina where she sat listening. He worked until nearly nightfall, then he remembered the sail wanted mending. He took it up over his shoulder, and went to her. She was cooking the evening meal, and scarcely turned her head when he stood at the door and said:

"Do you think you could mend the sail, Miss Nina? I could manage it, but I should be a long while about it, and time is short."

"Yes," she replied. "I have one of the ship's needles, and can do it. Supper is nearly ready."

"All right," he said. "You and Fleming go on; don't wait. I want to work while there's light."

He went back to the wood, dragged one of the felled pines to the beach, and got the ends behind two rocks, then strung a rope round the middle of the log, and, using it as a winch, hauled down its fellows.

It was dark when he had got the last of that felling done, and he was so giddy with exhaustion that he had to sit down and rest. But Nina's sweet, clear voice called to him, and he got up, and, assuming a cheerfulness—he even tried to hum—went toward the men's hut in which the three took their meals.

She had persuaded Fleming to take a little food, but she had not touched hers; and as she put Mannering's before him, she avoided looking at him, and went to the sail.

He was almost too tired to eat, but he forced himself to do so, his eyes fixed on his plate. But presently he looked at her, rose, and went out.

"Put this on your finger," he said, when he came back, dropping a sail-maker's thimble on her lap; "your hand will be rubbed. It is fortunate I remembered it."

"Thank you," she said simply.

Fleming, from where he lay beside the fire, which they had made every night, watched them with sad intentness.

"You forget nothing," he said, after a while. "At every turn I find some instance of your care and thoughtfulness. Is there nothing I can do?"

"Yes; go to bed," retorted Mannering cheerfully. "It's time we all turned in. Miss Nina, you can't work by this light."

"I can see quite well," she said; "but if you wish it—good night!"

After she had gone the two men were silent for a few minutes, then Mannering said:

"Has she said anything? Is she frightened? On a raft in the open sea! It is enough to alarm the bravest!"

"No, she has said not one word," replied Fleming. "She does not seem afraid."

"I don't think she knows what fear means," said Mannering with something like a groan. "And yet she must realize the danger; she is so quick, so intelligent——"

"She is the most intelligent and acute girl I have ever known," said Fleming. "Will you give me your hand, Mannering?"

He was so weak that Mannering almost carried him to their hut. Mannering would have lain awake that night, brooding over the situation, but the next day's herculean toil loomed before him, and he forced himself to sleep.

But Nina did not sleep. She went over Fleming's proposal, Mannering's words, in endless repetition; called up the expression of his face, his quick, short gestures. Rather than marry him she was going to leave him alone on this desolate island. She did not think of her own peril, on a raft on the open sea with a dying man, but of the terrible solitude of the man who had saved her life, who had worked like a slave for her comfort. Innumerable little acts, among the big ones, occurred to her, against which, small as they were, his fight with the Lascar was diminished.

My brothers, it is our little deeds, our small acts of consideration, which weigh with women. It is the wrapping of a cloak round them, the finding of a chair, the proffered hand in some small difficulty by the way, that counts with them. Heroic self-sacrifice is all very well, but, if you want to win a woman's heart, screen her from the sun, keep her feet dry, help her over the stile.

The girl lay and thought of the thousand and one little acts of kindness and consideration which Mannering had performed on her behalf, and she was so busy with the memory of them that she had not time left in which to think of her own coming peril.

And yet, how eager he must be to avoid marrying her, seeing that he was willing to let her run the risk of setting sail on a raft for an unknown destination!

The reflection stung her and made her face burn.

Mannering was up with the dawn—and, really, it was almost worth being shipwrecked to see the dawn of day on that lovely island!—but early as it was, Nina had risen, and was standing at the door of the men's hut.

"I have got your breakfast," she said simply. "How is Mr. Fleming?"

The pearly light fell like a benediction on her lovely face, and was reflected in the calm of her violet eyes, and something stirred in Mannering's bosom: perhaps the thought that very soon he would not see her in any light.

"He was asleep—at least, I think so; he is very weak," he said as he took the slice of bread and the tin of tea.

"I am afraid he is very ill," she said sadly. "I will go to him. You are felling trees?"

"Yes," he said, trying to speak in a casual way. "I have nearly finished. I hope to have made the raft by to-night. Don't worry about the sail; I can finish it when I come in."

"It will be done before that," she said, very slowly and quietly.

He went off and resumed his work. The day grew hot, and he was thirsty, and was reluctantly thinking of going to the spring for a drink of water, when Nina came toward him with a mug of lime water. He straightened his back, and, with an unconscious admiration of her grace, watched her approach.

"Is there any need to work so hard?" she asked in a low voice, her eyes half raised with, on her side, the woman's instinctive appreciation and unconscious worship of his strength. "Have you cut down all these—in so short a time? It seems impossible."

"There is no time to lose," he said, as he set down the mug. "How is Mr. Fleming getting on? I have a hope that the voyage, the effort, will do him good."

She looked beyond him gravely as she answered:

"He is much weaker, I am afraid. I have been sitting with him, mending the sail. It is finished. Is there anything else I can do?" She looked at the logs. "I am strong, very strong. It is strange, but I have grown stronger since we have been on the island. It is the air, I suppose."

Mannering nodded.

"And the exercise," he said. "You are on the move from morning to night. I have watched you. And the simple food. We eat too much over there in England."

She looked round almost wistfully.

"It is a very beautiful island. I have never seen anything half so beautiful. The colors are so lovely. If only there were more people!" she sighed, and swept the dark hair from the sun-burned brow. "Can I not help you with these?"

"No," he said, almost curtly; "they are too heavy. But you can get the provisions together—the tinned meats and condensed milk we brought with us from the wreck—into a box, and strap up the rugs in a tarpaulin. And mind and put your spare clothes in the middle of the bundle, so that they can't get wet."

The small things, my brothers!

She glanced up at him, as he stood, his bare neck tanned by the sun, his brow knit with thought of her.

"Very well," she said, and, taking up the empty mug, left him.

By nightfall Mannering had got the last of the logs down to the beach, at the edge of the high-tide mark, and he worked on in the moonlight until he had joined the logs together and constructed his raft.

When he dragged himself up the beach, Nina was standing at the door of the men's hut.

"You are late," she said in a low voice. "Supper has been waiting a long time."

"I'm sorry," he said. "I wanted to finish the raft to-night, and I have done so. You will be able to start to-morrow. Where is Mr. Fleming?" he asked, as he entered and saw that Fleming was not there.

"He was too weak to leave his bed and come down here," she replied.

"I will go to him," he said.

"Not till you have had something to eat," she said with a touch of command in her low voice. "He has taken some milk. I have been sitting with him. Have your supper, please."

"Have you packed the box with the provisions?" he asked as he sank on to a seat.

"Yes," she replied, pouring out his coffee.

"All will be ready to-morrow," he said. "I have been studying the currents. You must steer south by southwest. I will show you on the compass. If I am right in my idea of the position of the main group, you will sail and drift for it without any difficulty, and should reach it in twenty, or say, thirty, hours."

"We may find the men there," she said. "The boat may have taken them there."

He stopped, the mug on its way to his mouth, then he shook his head.

"No, thank Heaven! The wind was in the other direction when they went. No, they drifted out to the open sea. If I were not sure of that I would not let you go. Better run the risk of—marrying me than to fall into their hands. But there is no chance of that; you need not be afraid. Aren't you going to eat something?"

She came to the rough table, and poured out a cup of coffee. It was the first meal they had taken alone, he watched her under his lowered lids for a time, then rose and went down to the beach, and gazed at his raft with grim satisfaction.

At dawn the next morning he was awake, and stood over Fleming, who, Mannering thought, was asleep, but Fleming opened his eyes and smiled wanly.

"Nearly ready, Fleming," said Mannering. "How do you feel?"

Fleming smiled and moved his hand feebly, and Mannering went down to the raft. He fixed up a mast for the sail, and he was going up to Nina's hut for the provisions, when he met her coming swiftly down the beach.

"Everything is ready, I think——" he said, but she broke in upon him with an anxious cry.

"Oh, come at once! Mr. Fleming is ill—worse!"

He strode beside her, his brows knit, and they entered the hut. Fleming was lying on his back, his face white and pinched, his eyes closed.

"Is that you, Mannering?" he asked in so low a voice that Mannering could scarcely hear it.

"Yes, it's I. What's the matter, Fleming?" replied Mannering. "Are you ill—worse? The raft—everything is ready."

"Too late!" said Fleming calmly. It is wonderful how calm a dying man can be. For him all earthly turmoil, all earthly struggles, doubts, difficulties, are over. "I cannot go. I am dying. I am sorry. Where—where is Miss Nina?"

She was beside him, her hand on his wrinkled brow, her pitying eyes full of tears.

"I'm sorry, Mannering. I would have done what you wished, but there was not time. You—you will have to do as I said. My—my prayer book! Quick! My voice—my breath—are going. Nina, my child, where are you?"

Nina sank on her knees beside the bed. Mannering had got the prayer book from underneath the pillow, and Fleming almost snatched at it and pressed it to his chest.

"It is too late," he gasped. "Heaven has decided. You—you cannot resist its decree. Kneel, Mannering."

Mannering mechanically sank onto his knees beside Nina, whose face was hidden in her hands.

"What are you going to do, Fleming? Make an effort! The raft is ready, but you need not sail to-day!"

"I am dying!" said Fleming solemnly. "I felt that I could not wait—that it would be too late. Mannering, you remember our conversation? You know that I am right. You—you consent?"

"Yes, yes!" replied Mannering, scarcely conscious of what he said. "But Miss Nina——"

"She must consent!" gasped Fleming. "She cannot refuse. There is no alternative. Take—take her hand. Have you—have you anything that will serve as a ring? Anything——"

Mannering, hypnotized by the solemn earnestness of the dying man, tore the signet ring from his finger.

"There, if you must!" he said hoarsely.

Fleming had found the "Service of Holy Matrimony," and began to read it slowly, painfully, with pauses in which he struggled for breath.

As if in a dream, Nina and Mannering, prompted by the dying man, made the proper responses. Bravely, with faltering accents and heroic struggles with his death weakness, the Rev. Arthur Fleming read the marriage service.

At the proper moment Mannering took Nina's hand—it was limp and yielding to his touch—and placed the ring on her finger.

The solemn words of exhortation were gasped by the young priest, the prayer book dropped from his weak fingers, and he extended his hands above their heads and panted out the benediction. With a great effort he wrote some words on a sheet of paper and put it in Nina's hands, then, with a low cry, he fell back.

Mannering sprang to his feet and bent over him.

"He is—dead!" he cried hoarsely, to Nina, as she knelt, with her face covered by her trembling hands. "He is dead—and we are married!" he added inaudibly.

CHAPTER V
A WEDDING SUPPER

Mannering had read the burial service over Fleming, and Nina, who had stood beside the grave until the last spadeful of earth had fallen, went slowly, and with bent head and tear-blinded eyes, to her hut.

When his task was finished, Mannering leaned on his spade and gazed after her, with a moody and perplexed brow. The girl and he were married; they were alone on this desolate island; but they were man and wife in name only: they were as far asunder as the poles.

What a situation! And how were they going to take it? Would she trust him, rely on his word, or would she be—afraid of him? The thought made his hands clinch tightly on the spade, and the blood rush to his face. Already a feeling of embarrassment, a tragic shyness and discomfort, had assailed him, and he knew that she must be feeling in exactly the same way, but worse. It was for him to help her; it was his duty to make life possible under the circumstances. He knew that it would be better to leave her alone for a while, and he got his fishing lines and went down to the rocks to catch fish and think over the situation.

Meanwhile, Nina closed the door of the hut, and put in its place the thick bolt of wood that Mannering had fixed for her. Then she sank into the chair, and covered her face with her hands. Grief for the loss of the young clergyman, whom she had loved as a brother, mingled with the dismay and embarrassment of her own condition. Presently she took from her pocket the piece of paper which Fleming had pressed into her hand.

It was a certificate of marriage, and, as she read the feebly written lines, a burning blush rose to her cheeks, and her lips quivered. She was married to a man of whom she knew nothing but his name. She was in his power—the power which a husband holds over his wife. He had said that the marriage should be one in name only. And, ah, yes, she could trust him! He had proved himself so brave, so unselfish, so self-sacrificing; he had even risked his life for hers. Yes, she told herself, striving to gain confidence from the reiteration of the assurance, she could trust to his honor.

She sat for some time, the certificate in her hand, her brain half dazed with thought; then she remembered that she had work to do, and—blessed be drudgery—she sprang to her feet with the sense of relief which comes at the mere thought of action, of something definite, something, however trifling, that must be accomplished.

And—and after all it was the duty of a wife—the name stung her—to feed her husband.

She opened the door and looked out with shy embarrassment, but Mannering was out of sight on the rocks, and she went to the spring, and filled the can, and trussed the wild duck she was going to cook for dinner. She smiled as she performed the task. It was an extraordinary wedding, a singular honeymoon. Where were the bridesmaids, the breakfast, the wedding guests in frock coats and gorgeous costumes, the monstrous and always hideous cake, to all of which she had looked forward, like all other properly brought up girls, as the fitting and only accompaniments of her marriage day!

Every now and then, as she moved about, keeping as near the hut as possible, she glanced round, expecting to see Mannering; but he did not make his appearance, and at the usual hour she carried the meal to the men's hut and waited.

Half an hour, three-quarters, passed, and he did not come. A grim suggestion flashed across her mind, and sent the blood to her face: had he, in terror at what he had done, taken the raft and left her—fled from the woman he had been forced to marry?

The idea was a wild and foolish one, and she was suffering from the shame of it when she heard his step. She rose from her seat beside the fire, then dropped down again, and bent over her pot.

Mannering had schooled himself—had, indeed, rehearsed his part—and he came in with a cheerful countenance, as if no marriage had taken place—as if their position toward each other had suffered no alteration. Nothing—no word of his, no sign—he had sworn to himself, should remind her of the fact that she was tied to him.

"Dinner ready? I've had good luck to-day," he said, holding up the fish he had caught. "I mean to catch a lot of these fellows presently, and salt them down for the winter."

She paused as she was lifting the pot from the fire, paused with dismay at the prospect, but he thought it was because the thing was too heavy, and he went to her and took it from her hand.

"Let me. It smells delicious! And I'm fearfully and wonderfully hungry."

He forced himself—he had been rehearsing his facial expressions as well as his words—to look steadily and frankly at her as he sat opposite her at the table, and she contrived to meet his gaze as openly and as unreservedly.

"You have proved yourself a remarkably good cook," he said, as he tasted the stewed duck. "You would be worth at least thirty pounds a year in England."

She winced at the word which meant home. Oh, how dear, how sacred, was the word to the girl cast on this desolate island! And full of remorse, he murmured: "Forgive me! I beg your pardon!"

But she ignored the slip, and responded with a cheerfulness equal to his own.

"Should I, really? That's strange; for I know nothing whatever about cooking. My father"—she kept her voice steady—"and I lived alone. He had given up practice for some years, and amused himself with scientific research. He used to write articles and things for the magazines and reviews, and I acted as his amanuensis; so that I had no time for what is called domestic duties. If I had only known that I should have needed a knowledge of cooking and, oh, so many other things that other women can do!"

"You have soon picked them up," he said promptly. "It is wonderful how quickly you have learned to do things; by a kind of instinct. It's the intelligence of the cultured mind. It's always easy for an educated person to learn the duties of a servant. That's why lady helps should be such a success."

"But are they usually?" she asked, as she took her plate, and cut him a slice of bread. "I've always been given to understand that the lady help does everything *but* help. She presides at the table, over an underdone or overdone joint and a watery pudding, and is much aggrieved if she is asked to do anything in the shape of work."

Mannering nodded and kept the ball rolling.

"Yes; something like the ordinary landlady. I used to live in lodgings, and the landlady—she was too liberal with her h's, and said she was the daughter of a clergyman—left the cooking to an infant of sixteen, whose notions of a meal would make a red Indian quail. Until I was landed here I scarcely knew, away from home or at a restaurant, what a decent dinner meant. You make coffee splendidly. It is quite a surprise to find that it doesn't taste like baked horse beans."

"I am sorry to say that the coffee is giving out," she said gravely.

"Oh, well," he responded cheerfully, "we can manage without it—though I'm sorry, for your sake. It's supposed to be bad for the nerves."

Nina smiled.

"I've almost forgotten that I had any," she said.

"You have gone through so much," he commented sagely. "There is nothing half so good for nerves as real trouble and danger, and right down hard work."

As he spoke he drew his chair to the fire and took out his old brier pipe; then remembered that he had nothing with which to fill it, and, after a loving look at it and a sigh, replaced it in his pocket. But Nina, upon whom no action or word of his was lost, took a packet from her pocket, and held it out to him.

"You've no tobacco. I wonder—of course, it won't—but I wonder whether this would do? I found some leaves on the edge of the plantation, and they looked so like tobacco leaves that I dried them in the sun, just on the chance——"

He took the packet, smelled it, filled his pipe, and lit it, and, after a draw or two, looked at her gratefully.

"It's first rate!" he said, with a profound sigh. "It was splendid of you to think of it. Intellect again."

She laughed, but as she cleared the things away her eyes went to him, where he sat smoking enjoyably, and there was a strangely happy glance in them.

There was silence for a time; both were thinking of the dead; but Mannering would not refer to them—would not say a word to voice their sense of solitude.

"To-morrow I intend exploring the island, as far as I can," he said, with an assumed casualness. "I shall be away all day. You won't mind?"

"No," she said. "Why should I? There is no one here but ourselves."

It was out—had slipped out at last—and she went pale, then red; but she turned away swiftly, and he did not notice her embarrassment.

"I thought you might get lonely," he said simply. "I have not been so far away before. Perhaps I ought to have made the exploration before this. I shall set up another signal on the north, though I am convinced that no ships pass that way. I remember—it's wonderful how things come into your memory, when you think they have gone forever!—seeing these islands—or what I think were them—in a map at home."

"Yes," she said mechanically; for she was wondering where his "home" was. Should she ask him? It was haunting and burdensome: This complete ignorance of his past history, his very identity. But, before she could find courage to put her question, he went on:

"I believe the mainland of Australia is behind us, so to speak, but I'm not sure." He sighed as if impatient of his ignorance. "It is just possible some traders may drop in on us; on the other hand, we may be left——"

He had been communing with himself, as much as talking to her; and, as he suddenly realized that he was talking aloud, he glanced at her penitently. But there was no sign of grief or pain on the beautiful face, and she said quite calmly:

"There is nothing for it but patience."

"Yes," he sighed.

She moved about in the quiet, soothing way some women possess naturally, then, presently, she looked round as if everything were done, and said quietly:

"Is there anything else I can do—anything else you want? If not, I will go."

"No, thank you!" he replied as quietly. He rose and opened the door for her, as if they were parting for the night in a house in Mayfair, and, drawing her cloak round her, she passed him.

"Good night," she said, and "good night," he responded.

He waited by the open door until he had seen her enter the hut, then he closed the door, and lay down by the fire. He could not sleep that night, in the hut he and Fleming had occupied; it was too full of memories of his fellow castaway and friend.

When he rose next morning and went to the door he saw Nina running toward the men's hut. She stopped short at sight of him, and seemed to hesitate; then, after a pause, she came on.

She was panting a little and the color was coming and going on her face, fresh as the morning itself, and as beautiful.

"You gave me a fright!" she said, as if explaining. "I went to the hut to call you and could not make you hear——"

"I slept here," he said. "Why, where did you think I had gone?"

She dropped her eyes.

"I didn't know. I thought you might be ill," she said rather coldly. "Breakfast is ready, I'll bring it."

He had his morning swim in the sunlit bay, and returned, to find the breakfast laid. But she did not sit down with him.

"I have had mine," she said, as she gave him some really well-cooked fish and the remains of the duck. "There is some lunch to take with you. Dinner at seven, I suppose?"

"Yes; I'll be back by then. You always remember to wind up your watch? That's right."

"I shall want some more birds to-day," she said.

"I'll get them before I go," he responded. "Is there anything else?"

"No, thanks. I'll leave you now. I am very busy turning out my hut."

After he had finished his breakfast—it was not so pleasant a meal as that of last night; he missed her—he took his gun and went down to the piece of marsh, where he usually found the ducks. It went to his heart to shoot them, for, being unacquainted with the tender mercies of man, they were friendly and unafraid, and, being a sportsman, he had to frighten them on to the wing before he fired.

He got a couple of brace, and went up to her hut with them. It was the first time he had approached her quarters since Fleming's death. She was standing outside in the midst of a fairly good imitation of a "spring clean," and she paused in her task and regarded his approach with a touch of color in her cheeks and a certain coldness in her eyes.

"Sorry to interrupt you," he said, in a matter-of-fact way. "Here are the ducks."

"Thank you," she said. "Will you put them on the ground, please? Oh"—as he obeyed her and was walking away—"what shall I do with these?" pointing to a small heap of stones. "They are the stones father found."

Mannering nodded.

"Yes; they are gold," he said, regarding them with indifference. Then he smiled. "Gold! It's strange to think that, if we were within reach of the world and civilization, you would be rich—rich beyond the dreams of avarice."

"We, you mean," she corrected him, with a smile.

Then the blood burned in her veins, for it flashed upon her that he would think she had remembered, and referred to the fact that they were man and wife, and held things in common.

But Mannering, with a man's dullness, took her literally.

"No," he said. "You forget that your father found it, and that you are his daughter and heiress."

"Oh—yes," she said casually. "Well, what shall I do with them? They are in the way, and make my room untidy."

"Pitch them anywhere," he replied. "They are of no use, unless we should be found and rescued. Put them in a heap—oh, better bury them! I'll get the spade."

"Oh, don't trouble!" she said; "I'll put them somewhere."

"I wish they were coal," said Mannering, eying them thoughtfully and complainingly.

"Or potatoes, or pots of marmalade, or—oh, fifty other things I want!" she sighed.

"Never mind," he said soothingly. "Perhaps I shall find some coal; the marmalade is hopeless, I'm afraid. Good morning. Can I help you move the heavy things?"

"Oh, no, no, thanks!" she returned quickly—it seemed to him nervously, as if she did not wish him to enter her hut—and, with another nod, he shouldered his gun and went off.

CHAPTER VI
THE PORTRAIT OF A WOMAN

Nina finished her own "spring clean," and, the strain being relaxed, began to feel lonely.

It was perhaps for the best, in some respects, that he should go off for the day; it lessened the embarrassment of the situation; but she thought rather wistfully of the hours she must spend in solitude.

And to pass them she resolved to rearrange his own hut. Sleeping in the men's was not nearly so comfortable for him, and—and besides he was farther away from her than in the cabin he and Fleming had occupied; and, though she was not nervous, she was conscious that she liked to have him within call.

She went down to the hut after a while, and entered it shyly and hesitatingly. Her woman's sense of neatness and order was shocked by the untidiness of the place, and she set to work to clear and rearrange it. While she was folding and packing Fleming's few belongings, and putting them in a box, she came across the kind of diary "log" he had kept on board the *Alpina*. She sat down and turned its pages, and found several references to herself and Mannering. One of them caught her attention, and she pondered over it. It ran thus:

"The fellow passengers I like best are a Miss Vernon—her Christian name may be Christina; she is called Nina by her father. She is a very lovely and lovable girl. Her father, a doctor, has come out for change and rest. He is a savant of the old school, a learned and an absent-minded man. She is, I am sure, as good as she is beautiful, and her light-heartedness and amiability have done much to make the voyage so far a delightful one. I walk and talk with her frequently. How happy will be the man who is fortunate enough to win her love!"

Nina blushed at this assertion, and looked up from the diary with a sigh. Then she read on:

"The other is a man named Vane Mannering. I have 'made friends' with him, though it was rather difficult to do so at first, for though he is by no means morose, he is somewhat taciturn and reserved. He is a gentleman and distinguished-looking—which some gentlemen are not. In addition to great physical advantages, he has a remarkably pleasant voice, deep and musical. He does not 'mix' with the other passengers, and is given to walking and sitting by himself. I consider myself favored by his liking, if the word is not too strong; at any rate, he does not shun me, and is even willing to stroll about the deck and chat. If I were a novelist I would construct a romance round him; it seems to me that he is just the kind of man who may have had what the lady writers call 'a past.' I don't mean a guilty past; no, there is something about him which impresses me with a sense of his worthiness. I fancy—how one indulges idle fancies on board o' ship—that he has had a recent trouble; may have lost the woman he loved—really, I must take to fiction—or, perhaps, lost a fortune. From a word or two he let slip, I gathered that he was poor, and was going out to earn his living. The more I see of him the more I like Mannering. I have—I hope in an inoffensive way—endeavored to make him and Miss Nina friends, but he is shy, in his grave way, and he is disinclined for the society of ladies—anyway, he avoids all of them, which makes me think that his trouble may be connected with one of the gentler sex. Notwithstanding all the efforts of the women on board to 'draw him out of his shell,' he resists their blandishments."

Nina frowned thoughtfully over this. Yes, she remembered, Mannering had seemed to avoid her and the other ladies.

The journal was continued to the day of Fleming's death, and his anxiety on her account, his plan of a marriage with Mannering, even the reasons for it, were set down.

"I had hard work to induce him to take the course I myself pressed on him," Nina read; "and even after he had agreed to the marriage, and I had gained Miss Nina's consent, he partly executed an idea of escape for her and me in order to avoid the ceremony. I respect his scruples. Alas! they will have to yield to inexorable fate! I am dying! I must make them man and wife before I go. It must be so, for her sake, for the sake of her future. Heaven will, I feel, give me strength to perform the ceremony, though it may not vouchsafe me sufficient to set it down here. I hope I am acting for the best for both of them. If not, as Mannering said, may God forgive me!"

It was the last entry; he did not live to make another; and Nina's eyes, as she bent over the book, filled with tears. And her heart, too, was filled with bitterness. It tortured her pride to read, in black and white, Mannering's objection to, dislike of, the marriage.

But she put the book at the bottom of the box in which she had placed Fleming's things, and set to work vigorously. There were very few articles belonging to Mannering. He, who had thought of so many necessary things for the rest, had, apparently, ignored his own comfort. There were a few spare clothes, which, quickly, timidly, and, of course, without examination, she folded and laid aside, with a strange sense of shyness. It seemed to her as if he might resent her interference; but surely it was her duty to "tidy" the place and make it comfortable. It was the least she could do for him, who did so much for her.

She did away with Fleming's "bed," and altered the arrangement of the rough furniture, so as to give the room as different an aspect as possible, and she completed her work by putting on the table a bunch of gloriously colored flowers in an empty bottle. While she was making up the posy her eyes caught the signet ring which Mannering had placed on her finger for a wedding ring. Be sure it was not the first time she had looked at it; indeed, it seemed to her that, even in her sleep, she had been conscious of its presence. But now, after reading the paragraph in Fleming's diary, she viewed it with a feeling of revolt against the fate that had placed it there; and, obeying a sudden impulse, she took it off and slipped it in her pocket.

The moment she had done so she was vaguely sorry; she missed the thing; her finger looked bare and "unclad" without it. But she was too proud to put it on again. No, it should not remind him every time that he glanced at her hand of the unwelcome tie which bound him to her.

It was late before Mannering came slowly over the hill and toward the saloon—as Nina had decided to call the men's hut—and, as she looked at him, she saw that he was very tired. Now she had on her best skirt—the one she had been mending when Fleming came to propose the marriage to her. She had tacked a bit of dark-blue ribbon under her collar, and had done her wonderful hair with more care than she had taken since the wreck.

Her freshness and the general effect of these attempts at adornment—he was too much of a mere man to take in the details—struck Mannering, and he said apologetically:

"If you'll wait a moment, I'll go to the stream and have a wash and tidy up."

"Well, don't be long, please," she said. "I have been experimenting with a soup, and I'm anxious and nervous about it; and nothing sooner puts a cook into a bad temper than keeping the dinner waiting."

He came back very quickly, and sank into his chair with the sigh of a man who has a great deal on his mind.

"I've been to the north end," he said. "It is, as I expected, more barren than this. The trees don't grow so thickly and vegetation generally is sparser——"

"Oh, speaking of vegetation, do you think you could find me some more vegetables? This soup wants carrots and onions——"

"It's a first-rate soup," he said.

"Oh, thank you!" she retorted dryly. "I was afraid you didn't like it. You didn't say so."

"I beg your pardon," he said meekly. "I was pondering over——"

"More important things. I'm sorry," she caught him up in a quick little way that was so rare as to be charming. "Please go on."

"I'm confirmed in my opinion that the largest of the group of islands lies to the southwest; and I propose building a boat—it will be safer than a raft—in which I—we—can make a cruise of discovery."

She listened earnestly, and forgot to serve him; then she remembered it, and with a start begged his pardon, and took his plate.

"I also found more evidence of gold. Some of the quartz, or whatever they call it, show quite plainly on the big stones or rocks, in the dry river beds."

"Yes. Do you like the ducks best this way or stewed? I put it in an empty tin among the ashes of the fire. Is it all right—done enough?"

"It is very good," he said. "It is a delightful dinner, and I am enjoying it. Where was I?—oh, the gold. And I think there is copper; in fact, the place seems to abound in valuable minerals."

She nodded carelessly, and sighed.

"We seem to find all the useless things," she said. "Now, if we'd been two persons in a book of adventure, cast on an uninhabited island, we should find all the useful things, or the materials out of which to make them."

"Ah," he said, rather resentfully. "I always had, even as a boy, a suspicion of fraud in those shipwreck stories; but I little thought that the thing was so tragic and uncomfortable as it is."

"I am sorry you are not comfortable," she said. Then she remembered the two she had lost, and the tears came into her eyes. He saw them, and tried to divert her mind.

"We haven't tried the old trick they always perform in the adventure books—sending empty bottles with 'We are shipwrecked on an unknown island. Help us! Rescue!' " he said, with a smile.

"I've only three empty bottles, and I couldn't spare them," she said. "One is a rolling pin, and worth its weight in gold."

"Yes, but your people. Their anxiety will be, must be, very great," he said gravely.

"I haven't any people," she replied. "My father and I were alone in the world. I suppose we must have relatives, but I never heard of them. We lived for one another." After a pause she said, with her eyes on the table: "If you would like to try to communicate with *your* people I will sacrifice my bottle."

He shrugged his shoulders.

"It's of no consequence," he said.

She looked at him with almost startled surprise.

"Your sister, brother? Why, surely you have some one?"

"Why should I, any more than you?" he answered. "I haven't father or mother, or a sister or a brother; and as to the rest of my people—well," grimly, "they won't suffer any anxiety over my disappearance."

"Are you not going to smoke?" she asked, after a moment or two.

He thanked her, and sat down on the ground before the fire and lit his pipe. He was terribly tired, and presently, as she glanced toward him, she saw his head fall on his breast—he had fallen into a doze. His attitude was an uncomfortable one, and she longed to put something for him to lean against. The desire grew so intense—she told herself that it was only the sight of him sitting so "fidgeted" her—that she stole on tiptoe to him.

As she stood over him hesitatingly, her eyes wandered over his face and form. She noticed the short curls that clustered closely on the bend of the strong neck, the great shoulders, broad yet flat, the handsome face, the grace of the whole figure. The thought flashed across her that he was the best-looking man she had ever seen. And how tired he was! The maternal instinct, which lies dormant in all women, awoke in her, and her heart ached with pity for him.

She drew the box gently against his back. But the touch, gentle as it was, awoke him; in a moment he was on his feet and had seized her arm in a grasp of iron, his vacant eyes glaring at her sternly. She thought he was going to strike her, but suddenly he was awake fully and staring at her with dismay.

"I—I beg your pardon!" he stammered. "I must have fallen asleep; and I dreamed that the Lascar had come back. I must have thought you were he, and—oh, I beg your pardon!"

"If you'd let my arm go," she said, with a painful smile. "You are hurting it. I am glad I am *not* the Lascar!"

He released her arm, and in doing so saw that the ring was not on her finger. He did not frown or show surprise; but his face became thoughtful, and he avoided her eyes.

She noticed the subtle change in his manner, though she did not discern the cause.

"I will go now," she said; it almost seemed a formula. "Give me your coat, please."

"My coat?" he repeated vaguely.

"Yes. You have torn it; I will mend it for you."

"Oh, don't trouble," he said, rather coldly. Why had she taken off the ring? Was she afraid of him—afraid that he would forget his promise? His heart swelled with bitterness.

"Give it to me, please," she said, with her queenly air of command. "You have not too many coats, I know."

Obediently he took off his coat, and she flung it over her arm, wishing him "good night," and left him. He refilled his pipe with her tobacco—it was not half bad, but he sighed as he thought of his favorite brand—and sat over the fire smoking for a time, then swiftly he rose, resolved to conquer his reluctance to take repossession of the hut. As he passed hers he saw that the light was still burning.

He lit the pine torch at the door, and stood dead short at the threshold, astounded by the change she had wrought in the hut. Looking round, his eyes caught the flowers she had put on the table, and he took them up and smelled them, then put them down and frowned at them thoughtfully. Why had she taken the trouble to turn out the hut, to alter the arrangement so that he might not be haunted by the memory of his dead friend? Why had she put the flowers there for him? Something lit a fire in his eyes, then they grew dull. She had taken off his ring. It was just a woman's idea of pity that had impelled her to tidy up and arrange the hut. With a sigh, he set down the bottle of flowers and began to undress.

Nina carried the coat to her hut, and, finding her needle and thread, lit the ship's lamp. But she paused, with the coat in her lap, and, turning up her sleeve, looked at her arm. The marks of his fingers showed on the white flesh. She held her arm to the dim light and looked at it with a faint, pensive smile. How strong he was! His grasp had been like that of a vise. She had felt that if she had moved her arm it would break. How strong he was, how handsome, and yet how gentle to, and considerate of, her! He was treating her with the chivalry of a knight errant. Yes, he was good, good! If she had met him, say in London, under ordinary circumstances, and they had grown to know each other in the usual way, mid all the surroundings of civilization, perhaps he might—she might—they might——

The color rose to her face. Whither were her foolish thoughts leading her? With a gesture of self-rebuke she took up the coat, and mended the worst rent the bushes and undergrowth had made in it. She could not do much for him, but at any rate he should not go about in a ragged coat.

As she turned it over something fell from the breast pocket. She groped about on the ground and presently came upon a small, flat leather case. She turned it over and over curiously, then put it on the table. Whatever it was it did not concern her. It might contain banknotes, letters—no; it was not bulky enough for that: it was just simply a flat case. It haunted, mocked, fascinated her. She tried to keep her eyes from it, to concentrate her attention on the coat, but the thing seemed to exercise a power over her; and at last, with a gasp of shame, she snatched it up.

It was fastened by an ordinary spring clasp, and, pressing it, it flew open slowly and revealed the portrait of a woman. It was a colored miniature, and of so lovely a face, of such almost perfect beauty, that Nina's first emotion was one of unalloyed admiration. The eyes were blue, the complexion a delicate ivory—old ivory—the hair a rich auburn. The neck was bare, perfectly modeled and of snowy whiteness.

Admiration at first; but suddenly it gave place to—what? The blood rose to Nina's face, her eyes darkened and grew hard. Her bosom—as white, by the way, as that of the portrait—rose and fell with instinctive resentment, and her breath came thickly.

He carried a woman's portrait in his pocket—over his heart! Her own heart grew cold, then burned hotly. She put the miniature close to the lamp and studied it. There was some writing at the bottom of it:

"To my dear Vane. Judith."

The words struck her like so many strokes of a dagger. Her "dear Vane." Here!

Who was she, this beautiful, perfectly beautiful, woman?

With a sudden thrill of relief that seemed to set the blood running in her veins again she thought that it might be his sister. Then, cold as ice once more, she remembered that he had said he had no sister.

Her hand closed spasmodically over the portrait, and she rose in passionate indignation and resentment.

This portrait she had found in the pocket of her husband's coat. Her husband! Her husband! Ah, yes; but her husband in name only. He had married her under compulsion; he had fought, argued against the marriage. No wonder, with the portrait of this beautiful woman on his breast! Oh, what should she do, what should she do?

With a gesture of loathing and despair she flung the miniature from her and, sinking into the chair, buried her face—in his coat.

CHAPTER VII
NINA FLEES FROM LOVE

Nina lay awake all that night. Wedded to a man who married her against his will, and who carried the portrait of another woman—and how beautiful a woman—in his breast pocket.

But Mannering slept soundly, rose a little after the wondrous dawn, and, having got through his usual work, went to the saloon. Nina was not there, and he saw that breakfast was only laid for one. She came in as he was pondering over this fact, came in with a quick step, and said, in a matter-of-fact way:

"Good morning. I have had my breakfast." She had not been able to eat anything. "I had so many things to do. Have you got everything you want?"

"Yes, thanks," he said absently. Something in her tone, a coldness and aloofness, struck him; and, glancing at her, he saw that she was paler than usual, and that her eyes were dull.

"I hope you are not overworking yourself," he said earnestly. "There is really no need for it. We have plenty of time to do what is necessary; and I could help you in ever so many ways. For instance, for the future you must let me bring the water from the spring; the can is heavy. And I will light the fire."

She laughed, but mirthlessly.

"And do the cooking, and lay the table, and wash up the things; and I could sit by with some fancy work and watch you. Oh, no, I am not working too hard; if it were not for the work I should——" "Go mad," she was going to say; but she stopped short and made a gesture of impatience.

"I am going to set about that boat," he said; "but I shall be back to lunch."

"Oh, I've tied up your lunch for you," she said coldly, pointing to the package.

"Very well," he responded, almost meekly. "Perhaps it will be better; it will save time."

"There is your coat," she said, taking it up and holding it out to him.

"Thank you," he said simply, as he put it on. He did not know that her eyes were raised to his searchingly, almost accusingly. "I'm afraid you sat up late last night to mend it. I saw the light in your hut. I'm sorry. I'll be more careful in future. You look tired this morning."

"I'm not in the least tired," she retorted, with a little snap in her voice, usually so calm and low. "If you do not want anything else——"

She went out, and Mannering turned to his breakfast again; but her coldness, her strangeness had spoiled his appetite. What was the matter with her? She had removed his ring from her finger, was standoffish and sharp with him.

With a sigh he pushed his plate away from him, and, shouldering his gun, went off to the woods, Nina watching him from her partly opened door.

Mannering selected the biggest tree, felled it and, scooping out a length of the trunk, made a fairly good canoe.

It was a tremendous day's work and he regarded it with pardonable pride; but he was too tired to haul it down to the beach, and he left it reluctantly.

When he entered the saloon, she was standing by the table. He saw, with a sigh of relief, that it was laid for two. But she had on her old frock, and the bit of ribbon was absent from her neck; and she scarcely lifted her long lashes as he wished her "good evening."

"I hope you're better," he said, blundering like a man.

She bit her lip impatiently.

"I have not been ill," she said with ominous emphasis, as she passed him his plate.

"I've finished the boat," he said, trying to speak as if he did not notice her coldness.

She fixed her eyes on the plate.

"Why did the raft not do?" she asked.

"Oh, it is not nearly as safe as a boat. I could not steer it or sail it as well. I made the raft because"—he hesitated and stammered—"there is no immediate hurry now. Oh"—hastily—"this boat—it's only a canoe—is ever so much better! I'm hoping that we shall be able to reach one of the inhabited islands; perhaps, if we have luck, the mainland."

Her face grew set and her lips came together straightly, as if she were bracing herself to an effort.

"And—and—if we do, Mr. Mannering," she said in a low voice, which palpitated with her agitation, "what will you do? Will you tell the people we meet that—that we are married?"

Mannering gazed at her blankly, as if he were trying to see what was passing in her mind.

"I—I don't know; I haven't thought of it," he stammered, his face flushing. "What—what would you wish me to do?"

"I—I would rather you did not," she replied. "I—I want to make a—a—bargain with you."

"Yes?" he said interrogatively.

She raised her eyes and looked him steadily, bravely, in the face.

"I want to tell you that I know how great a sacrifice you made in mar—in doing what poor Mr. Fleming wished."

"As to that—the sacrifice was yours," he put in eagerly, earnestly; but she ignored his interruption and went on:

"If we escape to England—and, oh, I hope and trust we may!—I want you to understand that—that the marriage, what we have done—hasn't any meaning, significance; that we shall part as if—as if it had not been done. I will give you my word—I will swear it if you wish it—that I will never tell any one of—of the ceremony we went through, never, as long as I live; and I need not say that I will never—oh, never!—make any claim on you."

Her voice broke and the tears burned in her eyes; but she drove them back and continued:

"And I want you to promise that you will tell no one—that you will never make any claim on me."

He was silent for a moment or two, his eyes bent on his plate.

"I understand, and, of course, I promise," he said in a low voice, and rather grimly. "I know how you feel, at least I think I do, and I respect that feeling. It would be very strange if I didn't see the—the way in which you regard our marriage——"

"Was it a marriage?" she broke in abruptly. "There were no witnesses; we were not in church——"

"It doesn't matter," he said, almost gently. "What I have to do is to study your wishes—to follow them. All I ask is that—that while we are together——"

He stopped and gazed at her earnestly.

"Well?" she asked, as he paused.

"That you will not treat me as if I were an enemy—as if I had planned the shipwreck and the—the marriage from sheer malice. See, now, Miss Nina, you and I are the victims of fate. It was not my doing that you and I were left alone on this desolate place, but the will of Providence——"

"I know, I know!" she broke in. "I am not blaming you. But for you I should not be alive at this moment. Oh, I am grateful for all you have done for me; but, oh, don't you see how I am placed? I want you to promise that you will not—not claim me, if we escape, if we reach England; that you will not tell any one that—that we were married."

"I promise," he said gravely.

"And I promise on my side," she responded earnestly. "If Heaven should befriend us, and help us to get away from this dreadful island, I swear that I will not tell a living soul that—that poor Mr. Fleming persuaded us to be—married."

"Agreed!" said Mannering grimly.

She drew a long breath of relief, and rose from the table.

"What a wind is blowing!" she said, in a more cheerful voice.

"All the better for us; it is blowing from the right quarter," he said.

"But it is blowing very hard," she remarked. "See how it shakes the saloon! I—I am glad we have agreed so well, Mr. Mannering. I will go now. You say we shall be able to sail to-morrow?"

"Yes, to-morrow," he said, rising as he spoke.

She wished him good night and went out, and Mannering lit his pipe and sat pondering. The vein of reflection which he struck was not a flattering one. The girl he had married was so indifferent—disliked him so much, to put it plainly—that she had bargained with him to conceal their marriage. And he had consented. He drowsed over his pipe for half an hour or so, then he rose and made for his hut. But when he came in sight of the spot where Nina's hut had stood, he stopped short with his heart in his mouth. The hut was no longer there and only a litter of poles and undergrowth remained.

He ran, calling upon her name, and found her lying on the ground, with one of the heaviest poles across her slim form.

With a herculean effort he dragged the pole from off her, and, raising her in his arms, called upon her frantically:

"Nina, Nina! Are you killed—dead? Nina!"

Her eyes, upon which his frantic gaze was fixed, did not open, but he felt her shudder in his arms, and, unconsciously, he pressed her still more closely to his breast.

"Nina, Miss Nina, are you hurt?" he called, his lips close to her ears, for the storm had risen again. "Oh, speak to me! Try—try to speak to me!"

She opened her eyes, and, as a flash of lightning lit up their violet depths, a gasp of relief, of thanksgiving, escaped his trembling lips.

"Oh, thank God! I—I thought you had been killed. Are you—are you hurt?"

She clung to him—still unconsciously.

"I—I don't know!" she breathed with labored breath. "The—the hut fell in as I entered——Oh—I—am going! Hold me!"

He held her tightly to his breast, and, not knowing what he was doing, put his lips to hers.

It was a kiss—a kiss of infinite pity rather than passion—but, weak and distraught with fear as she was, Nina was conscious of it.

The blood burned in her face for a moment, then left it pale and wan.

"I—I am all right," she faltered, struggling feebly to free herself from his grasp. "I—I am more frightened and faint than hurt."

"Are you sure—are you sure?" he demanded hoarsely. "You do not know yet. The beam may have fallen on you. Don't try to stand. Lean on me. Oh, poor girl, poor girl! And it was my fault—mine! I heard the storm. I ought to have come with you to have seen that the hut was safe."

As he spoke he pressed her to him still more closely, and, so great was her weakness, that she yielded to his embrace—for it was nothing less—and, half unconscious as she was, found a subtle pleasure, comfort, in the yielding.

"I'll take you to the other hut," he said. "No, you can't walk. I must carry you. Ah, let me!"

She struggled faintly, feebly, but he lifted her in his strong arms, and carried her into his hut, and laid her on his bed.

"Now rest there. Try and sleep!" he exhorted her, in a low and gentle voice. "Let me see if you are hurt. Where did the beam fall on you—your arms, your chest?"

She shook her head, and feebly strove to put his hands from her.

"I don't think you are badly hurt. It must have been the shock, the fright. Tell me, do you feel any pain?"

"No, no!" she gasped. The gentle, commiserating touch of his strong hands was like an anodyne and hypnotized her. "I am in no pain; I am not hurt. If—if you will go now——"

He rose at last, but still bent over her, his face lined with anxiety.

"All my fault!" he muttered. "Let me put the pillow higher for you. Oh, God, if there were only a doctor to see you! I don't know whether you are hurt or not!"

"No, no, I'm not hurt!" she gasped once more, but in so low, so feeble a voice that he bent low on his knees to catch it. "Go—now."

He went at last, slowly, reluctantly, and with a backward glance that held pity—and was it something warmer?—in it.

The storm fell as suddenly as it had risen; and Mannering, slowly and with immense calm and patience, rebuilt Nina's hut. His heart was full of pity for her—of something warmer, of which he was only partly and dimly conscious. He did not know that he had kissed her, that his words, his actions had been full of love, of a man's love, for the woman.

And Nina! She lay awake, tossing from side to side—on his bed. The memory of the kiss burned in her consciousness. She had lain in his arms; she had yielded herself to him; she had, though he did not know it, been glad of his embrace, the touch of his lips.

Maiden shame burned like a fire within her bosom—a fierce, merciless fire. Had he known, guessed at, the thrill of surrender that had run through her at his embrace? Had he known what his kiss meant to her? Like a flash of lightning from the rent skies, she knew that she loved him. This man who had saved her life at least twice—first from the sea, and secondly from the Lascar—who had watched over her, guarded her, provided for her life's daily needs, was more to her than life itself—was the being one means when one whispers "lover." And he was her husband by the caprice of fate—her husband against his will.

Had he kissed her, or did she imagine it? If he did, it made matters ten thousand times worse, for he had kissed her in pity, not in love. Not in love, for did he not carry in his breast the portrait of another woman?

She rose, feverish and parched with thirst; but above her physical suffering towered her mental, spiritual agony. She loved him, and he? The fair face of that other woman rose before her mockingly, tauntingly, and embittered, poisoned the glorious, wonderful dawn which rose as a daily miracle upon the fairy island.

As if impelled by the spirit of her maidenly pride, which would not let her rest, she went down toward the beach. On her way she had to pass the saloon, and, after a moment's hesitation, she opened the door and looked in.

Mannering lay at full length before the fire, his head resting on his arm, on which was the blood of a wound caused by one of the falling beams. His face was troubled, his breath came short and painfully. Her own grew labored and painful as she bent over him, and her love for him welled up in her heart and ran over, so that it was hard for her not to touch him, if with her finger tips only. As it was, she bent so low that her lips nearly touched his, and her breath stirred his hair. But alas, and alas! at that moment he moved in his sleep, and she heard him murmur, "Judith, Judith!"

She rose as if something had stung her, and, in a conflict of emotions, went down to the beach. It was high tide and the raft tugged at its moorings. She gazed at it thoughtfully, then the color rose to her pale face and her eyes glowed with an idea.

She knew that if she remained on the island with him her love would betray her. Why should she not go? Here were the means—the providential means—of escape. The provisions which Mannering had prepared were close by the raft; it was as ready for use as on the day he had intended that she and poor Fleming should set sail. Why should she not go?

She might reach the group of islands of which Mannering had spoken; on the other hand she might not. At any rate she would have saved her self-respect—would save herself the shame of revealing her love for this man.

The idea, the thought, sent the blood to her face. She ran up to the hut and put her spare clothes in a bundle, and, wrapping the marriage certificate and Fleming's diary in a piece of oilcloth, put them in the bosom of her dress, then returned to the beach and the raft.

But she could not go without a word of farewell. She was fleeing as much from herself as from him, but she owed him a word of explanation—of good-by.

She tore a blank leaf from Fleming's journal, writing on it:

"I am going for both our sakes. Remember our promise.

Nina."

She fixed it with a stone to the rock nearest the spot where the raft floated. Then she took the box of provisions on board, set the raft loose from its moorings, ran up the sail to the mast, and pushed off into the rolling sea.

Mannering did not awake until some hours later. His phenomenally hard work of the previous day, and the stress and strain of the events of the night, had exhausted him. He waked with the guilty consciousness of being "late," and he went about the routine tasks of the morning.

He laid and lit the fire, and filled the can with water; and all the time he was performing the tasks he was doing so mechanically, with the memory of last night's experiences humming in his brain. He had held Nina in his arms. Had he—had he kissed her? Had he spoken a word of the love for her that welled up in his heart?

He would know when he saw her—when he looked into her eyes. Would she be angry, resentful? he asked himself. Poor girl, poor girl! Should he tell her that he had learned to love her, that he wanted her for a wife in more than name?

He went up to the hut, intending to call her—to get her outside, and have it out with her there and then. After all, she was his wife. His wife! He murmured the words to himself fondly, with a thrill of passionate longing. His wife! How much it meant to him!

But he would not call her. No doubt she was tired. He would wait, and at breakfast, as they sat opposite each other, like husband and wife, he would open his heart to her—would tell her that he loved her, would—yes, claim her!

He went back to the saloon. No breakfast was laid; but he made up the fire and sat down to wait patiently. Half an hour passed, then, thinking that he had better call her—that she would be angry if he did not do so—he went up to his hut and knocked at the door.

No answer came, and, after knocking again, he strolled down to the beach. He missed the raft in an instant, and stared with surprise at the place at which it had been moored. Then the piece of paper, fluttering under the stone on the rock, caught his attention. He went to it, took it from under the stone, and read it.

Read it not once or twice, but a dozen times; then stood gazing with unseeing eyes and torture-racked heart out to the sea on which the frail raft had ventured, bearing away from him the girl he had learned to love as only strong men can love.

CHAPTER VIII
"YOU ARE EARL OF LESBOROUGH"

Mannering sank on to the rock on which Nina had placed her farewell letter, and, covering his face with his hands, sat motionless as a statue of grief. He did not think of himself—of the awful solitude to which her flight had doomed him. Only one thought racked him, and that was that she had flown because she was afraid of him. She had preferred to trust the treacherous, murderous sea rather than him.

It was a hideous reflection, and it nearly drove him mad. She had not waited until the boat had been launched, but had taken the raft—had run all and every risk, rather than remain another day on the island with him, or confide herself to his care in a joint voyage.

Hours passed, and he still sat staring with vacant eyes at the sea. It did not occur to him to launch the boat and attempt to follow her. What good would it be if he came up with her? She would probably throw herself into the sea at his approach, she was so proud, so mistrustful of him. He got up at last, and wandered about with the air of a man distraught. Every now and then he plucked a flower or picked up a shell and gazed at it as if it were of the most intense interest to him, but he was scarcely conscious of what he held in his hand. He felt neither hunger nor thirst; but after a time a strange feeling of exhaustion, of craving for sleep, came over him, and he dropped down just outside his hut and fell into a deep sleep.

It probably saved his reason, and prepared him for the still heavier blow that fate was to deal him.

He slept right through the night and past the dawn; and it was the soughing of the wind and the harsh crash of the waves on the beach that awoke him. It had been raining heavily, and he was wet through, but he did not feel cold, for fever was warming his blood with a baleful heat. As he stretched himself, back came his misery with a sharp torture; and with a groan he dropped his arms to his side and looked round as if he were trying to persuade himself that it was a dream, and that he should see Nina coming swiftly toward him.

But, instead of the vision of her fair, fresh grace and beauty, his burning eyes fell upon something on the beach. Long before he had reached it he saw what it was.

It was the raft, or, rather, the remains of it. The sail had gone, the mast was broken, half the logs had been torn away; the thing had been wrecked in the storm which had raged while he slept, and the incoming tide had cast it at his feet.

And Nina! While he stared from the wrecked raft to the sea and back again, from the sea to the raft, a small object, floating on the water, caught his eye.

He fixed his gaze on it, then, beginning to tremble and shake, flung himself into the water and swam for the thing. When he came back with it clutched in his hand, his face was white and his eyes starting.

It was the little woolen cap Nina had worn.

Panting with his exertions and the agony that the assurance of her death caused him, he lay full length on the sand, his face upturned to the sun which broke out suddenly and mocked him pitilessly.

It was three days after this that in a dogged, sullen fashion he hauled the canoe down to the beach, and, putting in some provisions, made ready to sail. He was going, not because he had any desire for life, or to go back to civilization, but because the island had become intolerable to him. You see, it was impossible to forget her in a place of which every feature kept her vividly, agonizingly in his memory; and he knew that if he remained any longer brooding over his loss and the tragic circumstances attending it, that he must inevitably go mad. Once or twice, in his terrible solitude, a devil in his brain called "Suicide" had whispered alluringly to him. He was going, because there was just enough of the spirit of a man left in him to make him shrink from insanity and self-destruction.

For the last time he wandered over the familiar scene, the exquisitely beautiful place which his dawning love had been rapidly transforming into home; but it was a hell now. His lack-lustre eyes fell upon the heap of gold quartz which lay outside Nina's hut, but it did not keep his attention for a moment, and it never occurred to him to take even a specimen. Of what use was wealth to a man who had lost all hope in life, and only craved a natural and painless death?

Instinct, rather than any desire to choose a favorable time, made him wait until the turn of the tide; then he got into his canoe and, keeping his gaze fixed seaward, set sail. The weather was more favorable to him than it had been to poor Nina, and carried him due south. Once or twice he thought how full of joy and hope he would have been if she had been with him in the boat, and he sighed with callous indifference to his good fortune. Why had fate not spared her instead of him—her so full of life and the joy of living? Why had it struck down so rare and beautiful a creature, and left him to drag on an existence of anguish and futile remorse?

For a couple of days the weather remained fine, then the wind changed and grew rough. His cramped position, the solitude of the sea, and the glare of its sun-flecked surface, which produced an almost intolerable burning of the eyes, began to tell upon him. His small supply of water was rapidly diminishing, and he had to put himself on short rations.

On the fourth day he caught himself holding snatches of conversation with Nina, but shook himself, and tried to pull himself together; but again and again he relapsed into this form of delirium, and, when the trading schooner *Eliza Anne*, bound for the port of London, almost ran down the canoe, it picked up a half-crazy man who laughed and cried in a breath and implored the captain, with frantic gestures and broken, accents, to put the ship about and search for "Nina."

The captain was a good-hearted fellow, and, thinking that there might be a basis of reason in the castaway's ravings, hove about for some time in the latitude in which the canoe had been found, but he came across nothing to reward his humanity, and while Mannering was prostrated in his bunk with brain fever, the *Eliza Anne* got on her course again and made for London.

* * * *

Three months later Mannering was one night wandering along the Strand. It was just after eleven, and the theatres were pouring out their crowds into the already congested thoroughfare. Mannering had not reached London destitute, for, all unconsciously, he had brought with him the small amount of money he had with him on the *Alpina*; but he had, since his disembarkation, lived with little regard for comfort or appearances; and as he moved slowly with the crowd he looked, in his old serge suit and weather-stained cap, so much like a tramp that now and again the policemen eyed him with something like suspicion and one had actually bidden him "move on."

Mannering obeyed mechanically, looking neither to the right nor the left, but drifting aimlessly with the crowd which surged along the wet pavement. The crush, the noise of the cabs and carriages, the shouts of the 'bus conductors, and the talk and laughter of the people acted as a narcotic and soothed him after a fashion. But in the midst of the turmoil he could hear the boom of the sea on the sands of the island, and hear Nina's voice calling to him "Dinner is ready!" or "Will you bring me some wood for the fire?" and the commonplace phrases took to themselves a mystic, sacred significance.

Presently he found himself brought up against the Gaiety Theatre. The people were just streaming out, and Mannering was standing by a lamp-post waiting for an opportunity to go on, and, looking absently at the beautifully dressed women and the "smart" men emerging from the illuminated doorway when one of the gentlemen said:

"Hi, my man, will you get a cab for us?"

Mannering looked round, and saw that the request was addressed to him by a gentleman by whom a lady, richly dressed, was standing. A grim sense of humor seized Mannering, for he knew them both, and he forced his way down the street and got a cab.

"Thanks!" said the gentleman, and he held out a shilling; then, as Mannering laughed mirthlessly, the gentleman threw up his head, and looked at the supposed cab-runner, and broke into a low exclamation of amazement.

"Mannering! Good Heaven!" he cried; and before Mannering could reply or step away, the gentleman caught him by the arm and, turning to the lady, said in eager consternation:

"Blanche, it is Mannering! Get into the cab; I'll follow."

He still kept his grip of Mannering's arm, and when the lady, too startled to do anything but stare at the pair, had gone, he called another cab and almost pushed Mannering toward it.

"Get in, get in, for Heaven's sake!" he said. "Why, Mannering, you, and here in London, and in this—this state! Why, we all thought you'd gone to Australia. We've been searching for you. What's happened? You're ill, aren't you? Where have you been? What——But you shan't answer any questions till I get you home."

Mannering gazed before him at the crowd, with its canopy of umbrellas, the flashing, ever-moving lights of the cabs and carriages. This man's voice was like a voice from the life of the past—the past he had left behind—lost.

"I was wrecked, Letchford," he said hoarsely, as if he had only just been picked up in the canoe.

Sir Charles Letchford looked at him keenly, curiously, and not a little pityingly.

"Wrecked! But, no, you shan't tell me till we get home. Have a cigar, old chap!"

It was a subtly wise and kind suggestion. Mannering's hand closed on the cigar, and, lighting it, he leaned back and smoked himself into calmness; he had not been able to afford a cigar for the last fortnight.

The cab drew up at one of the handsome houses in Sloane Court, and Sir Charles led Mannering into the dining room. It was as exquisite as modern taste and lavish expenditure could make it. Sir Charles looked round.

"Blanche——You remember her? We were married two months ago." Mannering nodded in an absent way, and Sir Charles scanned him, aghast. "She has gone to her room. Come to my dressing room and have a wash. Supper is laid. The servants have gone to bed."

He took Mannering to his dressing room, then went into the bedroom to Lady Letchford.

"Great Heaven, Blanche!" he exclaimed, "I scarcely knew him! I took him for a tramp. The man has aged, is broken down—looks as if he were drugged! You remember what he was!"

"Poor fellow! Oh, yes, I remember! Of course I remember. Did—did you tell him, Charles?" she asked in a low voice.

"No! There hasn't been time! He's washing his hands. You must help me, Blanche. I'll go to him!"

He found Mannering seated at the dressing table absently fingering the silver-backed brushes, and took him down to the dining room. Lady Blanche, in the splendor of her evening dress, came to meet him cordially but half fearfully, for there was a strange, hunted, strained look in his eyes.

"I am so glad to see you back, Mr. Mannering. And of course you remember me—Blanche Favasom"—she blushed as she gave her maiden name—"Judith Orme's great friend, you know."

Mannering's eyelids flickered as he bent over her hand.

"I remember," he said in the deep, hollow voice with which he had spoken since the day of his great loss.

"Sit down," said Letchford, with a warning glance at his wife, a glance that said: "Let him alone for a time; leave him to me."

Mannering did not look down at his unsuitable attire, did not appear conscious of himself or his surroundings, but sank into the chair, and accepted a plate of the soup, which had been kept warm at the fireplace.

"Rattling good piece at the Gaiety," said Letchford; and he went on to speak of it, addressing his wife rather than Mannering, and studiously avoiding looking at him.

Mannering got through his soup and some cutlets in silence, glancing in the same absent-minded, preoccupied way at his host and beautiful hostess. Presently Lady Blanche rose, but her husband signed to her to remain.

"Don't go, Blanche," he said with the nervousness of the man who relies on his wife in difficult moments. "We want to have a chat with Vane. Now, old chap"—he leaned forward and laid his hand on Mannering's arm—"tell us your adventures!"

Mannering looked from one to the other, first with a kind of suspicion, then blankly, and he sighed, the sigh of a man who has been living in himself for months.

"Adventures? I haven't had any. Ah, yes; I was wrecked. The *Alpina* lost her course, struck, and went down."

"Good Lord! And you—you were picked up?" exclaimed Letchford.

Mannering was silent for a moment, then he said, as if mechanically, "Yes; I was picked up!"

"But you suffered a great deal? I can see that you did. You—you look the shadow of your former self, Vane! You must have had a bad time!"

"Yes—I suffered," assented Mannering, staring at the tablecloth and fingering his fruit knife. "Oh, yes—I suffered!"

"And was no one else saved?" asked Letchford.

"No—no one else was saved. She——" His voice died away, and his head sank on his bosom.

Lady Letchford leaned forward, all tender pity and anxiety; but Letchford rose and got some cigars.

"Smoke, old man," he said. "Blanche doesn't mind; in fact, she likes it."

Mannering took the cigar as eagerly as he had taken the one offered him in the cab; and, as he smoked, his face cleared of some of its gloom.

"And—and so you came to London?" said Letchford, with seeming casualness. "And have you seen any one, any of your people, the Lesborough lawyer, any one?"

"No, no one," said Mannering.

"That's—that's strange, and—and it's a pity!" murmured Letchford.

Mannering raised his eyes.

"Why? Why should I see them? I didn't want money. I have some still left." He put his hand in his pocket and took out a few, a very few, shillings.

Letchford stifled an exclamation.

"My dear fellow, my dear Vane! Do you mean to say that you have been wandering about London in poverty, in—in this condition; and that you didn't know—oh, good Lord, help me, Blanche!"

Her face flushed as she leaned forward, and put her white hand on Mannering's hard but shapely one.

"Mr. Mannering, Charlie is trying to tell you something, to break something to you; and he wants me to help him. And I don't know how!"—piteously—"but I must try, I must try, and you—you must be patient with me."

Mannering looked at her with scant interest, and with a sigh she went on: "You have not been down to Lesborough?"

Mannering shook his head.

"No; why should I?"

"I know that you and your uncle, Lord Lesborough, were not—good friends," she said, "but I thought you might have gone down, might have heard——"

Mannering shook his head again.

"No. I've not heard anything. What is it?"

Letchford rose and went to Mannering's side and laid a hand, at once soothing and warning, upon his shoulder.

"It's—it's bad news, Vane," he said gravely. "Pull yourself together. The earl's dead!"

Mannering nodded and his lips twitched.

"I'm sorry," he said in his deep, hollow voice. "I—I—liked the old man, though we never got on together. He thought me too independent—I wouldn't accept his money. Poor old fellow! He was a good sort! Dead! And so Augustus is the Earl of Lesborough!"

Letchford drew a long breath, shrugged his shoulders, and looked helplessly toward his wife, and of course she came to his relief.

"There is still—worse news, Mr. Mannering," she said in her sweet, gentle voice. "Lord Augustus and his boy—you remember him, he was at Eton? You were fond of him."

Mannering nodded.

"Yes; nice boy, Harry. The only one of the family I cared for," he said thoughtfully.

"They were going down to the funeral. There—there——"

"There was an accident to the train," Letchford took up the burden of the story, as her voice faltered and broke. "A bad accident. Fifteen killed. Among 'em was—was Augustus and his boy——"

Mannering looked up, and from one to the other.

"Killed! The boy killed! I'm—I'm sorry!" His voice grew hoarse. "A nice boy; we were great friends! Killed!"

The husband and wife exchanged glances, and Letchford's hand closed more firmly on Mannering's shoulder.

"Yes, it's bad, shocking bad!" he said slowly and impressively. "And—and it alters things for you, old man, doesn't it!"

Mannering looked round at him.

"Alters things? How?"

"Good heavens, don't you see, don't you understand!" said Letchford. "The old earl is dead, and Augustus, and the poor boy, and so—and so——"

"Mr. Mannering, you are the Earl of Lesborough," said Lady Blanche, in a low voice.

Mannering looked from one to the other dully, then he began to tremble, and presently his head was bowed in his hands, and his great, gaunt frame was shaken by tearless sobs.

CHAPTER IX
ALONE IN LONDON

The storm did not break upon Nina upon her raft until the favoring wind had carried her far out to sea; and it may safely be said that she did not realize the rash nature of her enterprise until the first flash of lightning and the first clap of thunder; for, like most of her sex, she had acted on the impulse of the moment, and without counting the cost.

But as the sky grew inky black, and broken only by the weird streaks of lightning, terror and remorse assailed her in equal proportions; terror on her own account, remorse on Mannering's; for here she was on the raging sea, and she had left him to the awful solitude of the island.

She had picked up enough of seamanship to lower her sail, and she lay, or, rather, crouched, on the raft, drawing the sail over her to afford her partial protection from the rain and the wind. Presently she felt rather than saw that the raft was becoming disintegrated, and, rising to her knees, she reached for the sheet, the rope attached to the sail, and, winding it round her, fastened it to a couple of the poles of which the raft was composed. She did this mechanically, and after, half unconsciously, asking herself what Mannering would do if he were in her plight. It was singular how, even in this moment of her solitude and extremity, she relied upon him.

It was well that she had taken this precaution, for, the storm growing more furious, the raft soon after broke up, and she found herself floating on the smaller portion. The howling of the wind, the dull roar of the sea deafened, and the salt and spume of the waves blinded her, and she closed her eyes and prepared for death; but instead of the death which she would have welcomed there fell upon her a kind of, the stupor of exhaustion and terror.

The storm fell as suddenly as it had arisen, and she opened her eyes to see the sun shining through a thick mist. The sea was quite calm now, and the logs to which she was tied floated almost motionlessly. She was parched with a thirst which made hunger of no account, and she knew, in a subtle fashion, that her brain was giving way. Just as Mannering had done, she found herself talking and holding conversations with him; she went through the whole of the marriage ceremony with him, reënacted the scenes in the saloon, lived over again the life in the island. Then she fell into profound unconsciousness, but after a time she came to again, and found that she was still floating in this dreamlike mist. Her whole past life seemed like a dream. Was this wide sea, the island, her marriage, only a dream?

How long she floated on the calm millpond of a sea she did not know, but presently the mist was penetrated by the sound of music. With closed eyes she listened. Was she dead, and was this the music of the heavenly choir? If so, she was at rest in the bourne from whence no traveler returns. But Mannering, her husband—he was still on his desolate island. Oh, how could she have left him!

The music grew louder and more distinct, and it seemed to her more earthly; she heard a voice, a deep, stentorian voice, call: "Man overboard! Stop her!" Then her senses slipped from her slowly, easily, and when they returned, and she opened her eyes again, they met the pitying ones of a young girl who bent over her with anxiety eloquent in every curve of her body.

"Are you better? Can you understand? Oh, I hope you have come to!" said the voice belonging to the body.

"I—I am better," said Nina; and, as if it were a formula, she asked: "Where am I?"

"On board the *Island Queen*—one of the Weldon Line, you know," replied the voice.

Nina did not know, but she sighed and turned her head away.

"We found you tied to a part of a raft," said the voice, which sounded nearer now, "and we are all so anxious about you! But you mustn't try to talk. The doctor said that if you came to I was to keep you quite quiet."

"Who—who are you?" asked Nina, but without any great display of interest.

"Polly Bainford," replied the voice. "It was I who first saw you. I was leaning over the taffrail, or whatever they call it. But there! I shall have the doctor on me if I talk to you. Try to go to sleep."

Nina turned over and endeavored to obey, and presently fell into a deep sleep.

When she woke Polly Bainford was still sitting by her side, and she nodded approvingly and encouragingly.

"That's right! Why, what a sleep you've had! Eighteen hours by the clock. And you look so much better! Hush! Here comes the doctor!"

The ship's doctor, a young man, came in rather shyly, and felt her pulse.

"You are much better," he said; then he started as Nina thrust his hand aside, and, sitting up, exclaimed:

"The island! Where is it? I want to go back! You must find it! He is there! You must rescue him, take him away. I—I left him—alone, all alone!"

"Hush!" murmured the doctor; but, as she still continued to rave, he went off for the captain. The captain had five daughters of his own, and he stood beside Nina's berth and looked down at her fever-flushed face with paternal pity and tenderness.

"What is it, my dear young lady?" he asked soothingly.

"The island!" panted Nina. "It is close by; you can find it! He is there alone—in solitude—quite alone! In pity, I implore you, I beg of you to go back and bring him away! I—I—left him. I was foolish—mad——"

The captain patted her hand and glanced at the doctor.

"What island?" he asked gently.

"I don't know! How should I know?" she murmured. "It has no name. We were wrecked——"

"My poor girl, we picked you up on the open sea," said the captain pityingly. "And that's days and days ago. We can't put back——"

"Leave her to me," broke in the doctor. "She's raving. Very probably there is nothing in it—no island whatever. Leave her to me."

Nina relapsed into delirium, and Polly Bainford and he nursed and attended her. It was a week before she recovered full consciousness, and by that time the vessel was nearing England.

Nina, when she came back to her senses, lay with closed eyes and aching heart, listening to the wash of the waves against the ship, mingled with the sounds of music and singing. They reminded her of the sounds she had heard as she tossed on a portion of the raft.

"What are they singing? What is the music?" were almost her first words.

Polly smoothed the bedclothes.

"It's the company—Mr. Harcourt's company," she replied. "They're singing one of the songs of our last success, 'My Lady Pride.' Does it disturb you? I'll get them to stop. I'm sure they will, for they are most anxious about you; and they're all a good sort."

"No, no," said Nina. "Don't stop them. And are you one of them?"

"Yes," said Polly, "I'm one of the company. But I'm not a principal. I've only got a small part—what's called a 'singing chambermaid.'"

Nina looked at her uncomprehendingly, and Polly laughed.

"Oh, it means that I'm only small potatoes. You see, I haven't much of a voice, and so I take a back seat. We've been touring in Australia, and we're going to do the provinces—and London—if we've luck."

"I see," said Nina, with a sigh that was a little envious; for this girl with the bright eyes and the mobile lips had her future marked out for her, while she, Nina, was adrift on the world, homeless and friendless. She closed her eyes, Polly stole away, and Nina pondered deeply. In her delirium she had implored the captain to turn from his course and search for the island. It had been a hopeless prayer then; it was still more hopeless now. Besides, even if she could achieve the impossible, and persuade them to turn back, they might not be able to find this particular island among the group, and if they did, Mannering would probably have left. He had the canoe, and she knew him too well to think he would remain there in solitude. Then, again, there was their mutual promise. She had pledged herself to keep their marriage secret, and how could she do so, if she told them about the island?

The captain and the doctor visited her a little later, and when the captain rallied her on "her island" she colored, bit her lip, and turned her head aside, and she heard him say to the doctor as they left the cabin:

"I told you so! Just a fancy on her part. People talk like that when they're in her state. She must have been wrecked from the *Alpina* that's missing."

The doctor nodded assentingly.

"Better let her alone, and say no more about it—unless she does," he said sagely; and, meeting Polly, on deck, he cautioned her to refrain from questioning the patient.

"As if I should!" retorted Polly, with a toss of her pretty head.

But she had to ask one question, and she asked it the next time she went to the cabin.

"Don't think I want to bother you with questions, or that I'm a bit curious, dear," she said, "but I—I don't know what to call you."

Nina hesitated a moment and a blush rose to her face, which Polly, looking straight before her, affected not to see. Nina thought: "If I give my real name it must be Nina Mannering—but I don't know whether I am properly married, and there is my promise." She was almost as reluctant to give her maiden name, and, on the spur of the moment, she replied:

"My name is Decima Wood." It was one belonging to an ancestor on her mother's side.

"It's a very pretty name, almost as pretty as its owner," remarked Polly, with a brisk nod. "And now, Miss Wood, you've got to get well and strong, and come up on deck as soon as ever you can. I can see you have had a bad time——"

Nina looked at her a little piteously.

"Ah, if you knew!" she breathed.

"But I don't know, and I don't want to know, unless you want to tell me"—Nina drew a long sigh—"and I see you don't. I've undertaken to ask no questions, dear, and I'm sure you won't be bothered by any one else; so you needn't look so anxious and unhappy."

In a few days Nina was strong enough to leave the cabin, and the doctor and Polly helped her on deck, and ensconced her in one of the long deck chairs, in a corner warmed by the sun and sheltered from the wind. The vessel was crowded, and her appearance created a great deal of interest and curiosity; but the passengers, with the consideration which is one of the few good things for which we have to bless the modern civilization, did not intrude upon her, but left her alone in her nook, to look on dreamily at the life on board a ship.

Every now and then, as she watched the promenaders, the gay and noisy groups playing at deck quoits and similar games, her hand stole to her bosom, in which still lay hidden the oilskin pocket containing Fleming's diary and her marriage "lines," as if she were trying to realize by actual touch the reality of the past.

All day the theatrical company made the ship gay by laughter and snatches of song, and in the evening there were informal concerts in the vast saloon, to a corner of which Nina sometimes stole, to listen and look on unobserved, as she listened and looked on from the nook on deck which had tacitly been reserved for her.

Sometimes the captain approached and spoke to her, or one of the passengers offered the stereotyped courtesies, but Nina seemed to shrink from them all, save Polly, and, recognizing her reticence and reserve, they gradually ceased to address her.

But they were nearing England, the voyage was drawing to a close, and, on the last evening the captain pulled up beside her, and in his gruff voice, which his kindly smile fully discounted, he said:

"We shall be in port to-morrow, Miss Wood. Can I wire to your people to meet you? You are in my charge, you know."

Nina colored and looked down for a moment; then she raised her eyes bravely.

"No, thank you," she said; "I—I will not trouble you."

The captain tried not to look surprised, and Nina hurried on:

"My passage—I must pay for that. I—I ought to have spoken of it before."

The captain laughed and shook his head.

"Never mind the passage money, my dear young lady. The Weldon Line hasn't dropped down to asking fare from a castaway. Why, we're only too proud to have picked you up and carried you with us!"

Nina drew a sigh of gratitude and relief, for she knew that her slender purse—the small stock of money which she had brought with her from the island—would have been exhausted by the heavy fare.

The captain hung about for a moment or two, shuffling from one leg to the other awkwardly; then he said, as gruffly and with as tender a smile as before.

"If—if there's any difficulty about your people meeting you, Miss Wood, I'm sure my wife would be glad if you'd come home to us. I've got five girls of my own, and you wouldn't feel lonely."

But Nina pictured those five girls plying her with friendly, sympathetic questions, and, with moist eyes, thanked him and declined the offer.

"My plans are all made out," she said. "But, oh, I am very grateful!"

The next morning Polly came and sat down beside her.

"I suppose the captain will wire to your people to meet you," she said; "but if anything happens, if they don't turn up in time, how would you like to come home with me? I've got diggings in Chelsea. They're quite the 'humble cot' kind of thing, far too small and modest for a swell like you, Miss Wood——"

Nina smiled at her and laid her hand—the fever had left it thin and white, very different to the brown "paw" of the island—on Polly's arm affectionately and gratefully.

"I'm not by any means a swell, Polly," she said. "I am very poor——"

"A great many swells are," interrupted Polly, with a worldly-wise nod of her curly head.

"And I shall have to work for my living; but"—repeating the words with which she had declined the captain's offer—"my plans are all made out, and——"

"All right!" broke in Polly, with a nod of comprehension. "I didn't mean to intrude. Anyway, here's my address, and if you can you'll look me up, won't you? I rather think Harcourt intends taking a London theatre; if so, I shall be settled there"—she put a card in Nina's hand—"for some time; and if I go into the country with the company, the landlady will give you my address."

Nina glanced at the card, and, trying to express her thanks, put it in her pocket.

"And now can I help you to pack——" She stopped awkwardly, as Nina, with a laugh and a blush, shook her head.

"You forget that I haven't anything—why, even this dress and other things are yours! I will send them to you when—when I get some others."

"That's all right," said Polly. "But I'd rather you come yourself than send the things, for—well, I've got fond of you, you see, if you don't mind my saying so."

The last day of the voyage was one of bustle and confusion, lightened by the electric gayety of the company of actors, who sang from morn to night, and got up another charity concert, in which they performed with an enthusiasm far and away beyond that which they would have displayed on the ordinary and professional stage.

When the vessel glided slowly into port, Nina said her grateful good-by to the captain and Polly, and shook hands with some of the people who had been kind to her, and in the confusion slipped away.

With the clothes she stood up in—and they were mostly Polly's—and a small handbag, also Polly's, she found herself in the whirl of the crowded thoroughfare. She had remembered a cheap and quiet hotel in one of the streets in the Strand—Durham Street—at which she and her father had stayed many years ago, and she went there in a cab, and was fortunate enough to obtain a room. It was a small one, near the roof, and she sat down on the bed and looked around, and, through the window, at the opposite roof, with a sense of loneliness which she had never experienced, even in her worst moments on the island, for Mannering had been there to rely on, to cheer and encourage her.

She tried to drive all thoughts of the past from her mind, and to fix it on the future, and, when she had washed and rested, she took out her money and counted it.

There were only a few pounds, and for a moment the reflection flashed across her that there, on the island, she had left wealth which, as Mannering had declared half cynically, was beyond the dreams of avarice.

But the island was far away, so far as to be the island of a dream, and her present needs were very near and pressing.

She remained in her room until the morning; then she rose early and, with every regard to economy, purchased some clothes. After breakfast she made a parcel of the things Polly had lent her, and, with a few lines of gratitude, sent them to the address on the card: "26 Percy Street, Chelsea."

Then she set out to begin that most difficult of quests, the search for a livelihood. It need scarcely be stated that she looked through the advertisements in the daily papers. There were several that seemed to her suitable to her case, and she selected one which set forth the desire of "X. Y. Address Messrs. Sloper & Slyne, 249 Rutland Street, Regent Street," for a young lady secretary.

Nina, in the simple black dress she had bought, and with her veil down, found, not without some difficulty, the Rutland Street mentioned in the advertisement, and was somewhat surprised to find that, instead of a private house, which she had expected it to be, it was an office over a rather seedy-looking bonnet shop.

Knocking at the door, which bore in black paint the name of Sloper & Slyne, she was bidden by a shrill voice to enter, and, obeying, found herself in a small room furnished, as far as a desk and two chairs went, as an office.

The first thing that struck Nina was the strong perfume of hair oil, with which she rightly credited the sleek, black head of a young man who was seated at the desk surveying himself in a small, crooked mirror which hung conveniently above it. Seeing that he was an extremely commonplace youth, one would have thought that the glass could have afforded him little satisfaction. Nevertheless he did not withdraw his eyes from it as he drawled in a rich cockney accent:

"Well, what is it?"

"I wish to see Messrs. Sloper & Slyne," said Nina.

At the sound of the musical voice the youth swung round, opened his mouth—it was like a gash across his ill-favored face—and stared at her with watery eyes.

"Oh," he said at last, as if he were slowly recovering from the shock of her beautiful face and low, sweet voice, "you want to see the guv'nors? Sorry; they're both away. Gone on special business to the Marquis of Quisby.

Wired for this morning. Awfully sorry. P'r'aps I'll do. I'm their confidential clerk, you know."

"I came in answer to this advertisement," said Nina, taking it from her purse and laying it on the desk.

The youth looked at it curiously, critically, as if it were a curiosity of the rarest kind.

"Oh!" he said at last. "Ah, yes. Quite so! So you want a situation as secretary?"

Nina expressed assent.

"Yes; will you take a chair?" He dragged one forward. Nina sat down and waited, and the youth stared at her and stroked the place where, if the gods are good to him, a mustache will some time grow. "Well," he said, when the silence and the stare had become almost intolerable to Nina, "this place has gone."

Nina promptly rose, saying: "I'm sorry. Good day."

"Oh, here, stop a moment, you know!" exclaimed the youth in an aggrieved tone. "Don't go like that! There's no hurry, is there? This thing's gone, but there may be something else to suit you. Lemme see."

He turned—his eyes left Nina's face slowly and reluctantly—to the desk, and opening a ledger ran through the pages, muttering in a sing-song voice to himself, but glancing the while out of the corner of his watery, vulgar little eyes at Nina.

" 'Nursery governess, fifty pounds a year.' Ah, that's gone. 'Lady help in a nobleman's family.' That's gone. 'Companion to a clergyman's widow.' Filled up last week. 'Secretary to a member of Parliament.' And that's gone. Don't seem to be anything left to suit you at present. You'd better let me put you on the books, Miss—Miss—er——"

"Wood," said Nina.

"Wood. Right. And address?"

"Hickley's Hotel, Durham Street," said Nina.

"Right. One guinea booking fee, please," he remarked in a business-like tone.

"Is this a registry office for situations?" asked Nina, with pardonable surprise.

"Of course it is!" he responded briskly. "What did you think it was, a cheesemonger's? Sloper & Slyne—sorry they're not in; they'd be glad to see you—employment agents. See? I'll enter your name and let you know if anything turns up likely to suit you. Though, by the way," he added, with a glance at her, "it would be better if you looked in now and again."

Nina was foolish enough to take a sovereign and a shilling from her purse and place them on the desk. The youth caught them up, as if he feared they might fly away if he lacked promptitude, and put them inside the desk.

"That's all right," he said, as it assuredly was from Messrs. Sloper & Slyne's point of view. "You look in again; early and often, you know. Come in to-morrow—in the afternoon. I get back from lunch about four. See? Good morning."

He got off his seat, and opened the door, and stood gazing, with his gash of a mouth stretched in an admiring grin, as Nina went down the stairs.

"My, she's green!" he ejaculated as he tore himself away from the door and returned to the desk. "But she's prime, prime! Wonder if she'll come back, or whether she'll spot the game!"

Nina was not without her suspicions; but she did not spot the game, and the next afternoon—oh, the desolation and the solitude of that day in London, in a place which owned to a population of four millions, and not one friend for the solitary girl!—she again presented herself at Messrs. Sloper & Slyne's.

The youth was in his accustomed seat, and carried a pungent cigarette— it mingled affably with the scent of hair oil—in his loose and bibulous lips.

"Ah, how are you?" he said, with a mixture of impudence and deference, for the refined, beautiful face, with its grave, violet, eyes awed even him.

"Glad to see you. Guv'nors still away. The marquis can't part with 'em. Important business. Sorry to say nothing has turned up." He referred to the ledger and mumbled over it as before. "Rather a slack time just now. Dessay you find time hang 'eavy on your hands. Do myself sometimes. Now, what do you say"—he had sufficient grace to stammer and look uneasy— "what do you say to doing one of the halls this evenin'? I'm not particularly flush—Sloper & Slyne don't pay me a princely salary, oh, by no means—but I can run to a couple of dress circles for the Frivolity. Know the Frivolity, I s'pose?" with a leer; "I dessay we can manage a bit o' supper afterward, eh?"

Nina regarded him with an amazement which evidently disconcerted him, for he turned away and eyed the glass and fingered the incipient mustache with some embarrassment.

Nina leaned forward in her chair, her heart beating fast with a sensation of disappointment tempered by disgusted amusement.

"Are you asking me to go with you—with you—somewhere?"

"That's so," he said uneasily. "You'd better."

Nina laughed bitterly, for her eyes were suddenly opened.

"Tell me—though it isn't necessary—is this pretense of business, of getting me a situation, only a pretense? Tell me the truth, please."

Something in the musical voice, so low and yet so clear and commanding, compelled the youth to an unaccustomed veracity which afterward astonished him.

"Well, you know," he said grudgingly, "if you drive me into a corner— and that's where you are driving me, don't you know—it's something like what you call it. We're a registry office. We take the fees, don't you know. As to the situations"—he shrugged his narrow shoulders—"we might get 'em or we mightn't; most often and generally we mightn't."

Nina rose pale and statuesque in her anger.

"But don't you cut up rough! Look here, you're no good for any of this 'secretary' or 'companion' business. You're a lady; anybody can see that with 'alf an eye. What you want, with that face of yours, is the theatre or the 'alls. You come with me to the Frivolity and we'll talk it over——"

Nina rose, pale to the lips, but smiling.

"My good boy!" she said. "Haven't you a mother, a sister? Is there no one to teach you—no, I will not go with you to this place. Will you give me back my guinea?"

The youth's face fell.

"Can't!" he ejaculated. "Entered it in the books. More than my place is worth. Sure you won't come with me? Pleasant evenin'."

As Nina moved toward the door he followed her.

"Hi!" he said. "Look here. You're new at this game. Take my advice and cut it. There's no good in it. They'll—Sloper & Slyne or any one else, it don't matter—pocket your coin and do nothing for you. Cut the secretaryship business. Better go on the stage. Why, lor', you're made for it! And I say, won't you be nice and friendly, miss? Won't you join me in a regular beno of an evenin'?"

Nina left him pleading and expostulating, and made her way out into Regent Street.

Early in the afternoon as it was, the well-known thoroughfare was crowded, and she was jostled and elbowed as she made her way to the Strand. She went back to the hotel, discouraged and dismayed. She had spent a guinea at the sham registry office, and saw no prospect of employment. She was too tired, too heartsick to eat, and she spent the rest of the evening in the attic near the sky. At nightfall, weary of her solitude and the thoughts that weighed upon her like a physical burden, she went out. The streets were crowded and her solitude in the midst of the multitude was almost intolerable. She made her way to the Embankment and, leaning against the stonework which keeps the slow but mighty Thames in bounds, looked listlessly, yet longingly, at the brown water sweeping placidly toward the sea.

There, across the ocean, to which the tide was tending, was the island where she had known a happiness beyond the power of words to express. Was Vane Mannering, her husband—her husband!—still there? Was he mourning for her? No; for there was the unknown woman, Judith! All his thoughts would be of her, of the woman he loved, and of whom he murmured when he slept.

She leaned her head on the cold stone and gave way to the despair which is so fitting an emotion to "the finest thoroughfare in Europe," and the most desolate, the most heartbreaking in its magnitude and solitude to one in Nina's situation.

A footfall roused her from her absorption. A woman in most unwomanly rags crept up to her, and in weak and abject tones begged of her.

"Just enough for a night's lodging, my dear!" she moaned. "I 'aven't slept in a Christian bed for the last three nights!"

Nina raised her head and looked at the woman. A wave of pity swept over her. How long, or, rather, how soon would it be before she herself was in a similar plight? She took out her purse, and, in the light streaming from the Savoy Hotel—the strains of the supper band floated toward her on the night air—she was hunting for half a crown, when a man—the woman's accomplice—hustled against her, snatched her purse, and, with the woman, disappeared as suddenly as if they were as unsubstantial as the mist that was rising over the river. Nina uttered a cry of dismay and started after them, but a policeman who had witnessed the latter part of the familiar act stopped her with a friendly hand on her shoulder.

"No use, no use! They've got clear off into the Strand. You should never think of taking your purse out on the Embankment and, begging your pardon"—as he looked suddenly at her face with its pure, distraught eyes—"this is no place for you. Shall I call a cab, miss?"

"No, no!" said Nina, bethinking herself that she had no money left. "It—it does not matter. Thank you—and good night."

The theft of her purse had left her penniless. She tried to face the situation bravely, to laugh, but the laugh would not come. Unconsciously she turned and walked up the Embankment. It was, at any rate, quiet and solitary, and she craved solitude and quiet. She had to think, to decide where she would go. She was penniless, friendless, in this great city; and already she had found how heartless it could be to the friendless and penniless.

She made her way slowly, mechanically to the Chelsea end of the Embankment. She had no thought of Polly in her mind, and it was with a gasp of surprise rather than relief that, in the garish gaslight, she saw the name of Polly's street staring at her from the end house.

Still mechanically, and half unconsciously, she walked up the street, and, as if in a dream, stood before the house with the number Polly had given her.

By this time she was weak and faint with fatigue and excitement, and she stood, swaying to and fro, and gazing at the house. At this moment a hansom cab drove up and a girl alighted, paid the cabman—after the usual dispute—and was entering the house, when her eyes fell upon the figure clinging to the railings.

Polly—for it was she—hesitated a moment, then she went up to Nina.

"Now, then," she said in a matter-of-fact voice, "what are you doing here; what is the matter?"

Nina turned her white face, and Polly uttered an exclamation of surprise and dismay.

"Miss Wood! Not really! You, and here! No, cabby, not a sixpence more! I know your fare! Off you go! Miss Wood! Oh, my dear, what has happened? Here, come in with me! Dear, dear! to think that I should find you here! And like this! Oh, come in; come in!"

CHAPTER X
THE DISAPPOINTED HEIR

The Earl of Lesborough!

The title rang in Mannering's ears mockingly. He fought with his emotion, and, with a gesture of shame and apology, raised his face from his hands.

Lady Letchford had slipped away—with the tears in her own eyes—but Sir Charles still stood beside his friend.

"I beg your pardon," said poor Vane; "it—it is so sudden, and the boy—great Heaven, to think that he—and Augustus—are dead, and that I—I, who never dreamed of it, should stand in their shoes!"

"Yes, it's awfully bad," said Sir Charles, shaking his head, but feeling mean because he could not mourn as keenly the loss which had made his friend a peer. "But you have got to pull yourself together, Vane. There's no end to do, to see to. You'll make a first-rate earl, old man! You'll go to Tressider"—Mr. Tressider was the Lesborough family lawyer—"first thing to-morrow morning. I'll go with you if you like—no, better go alone. Oh, yes; I'm as sorry almost as you can be for the catastrophe, but—well, after all, you're my pal, you know, and for the life of me I can't help a sneaking feeling of satisfaction that the succession falls on you. Here, have a drink!"

He poured out a glass of champagne and Vane took it mechanically, but sat with drooping head and moody brow, twisting the glass round and round by its slender stem; and Letchford watched his friend anxiously and curiously.

"Better get to bed, old man," he said after nearly half an hour, "you look played out, and as if you, wanted a good night's rest. In the morning——"

Mannering nodded and rose, and Letchford took him to his room.

"Is he better?" asked Lady Letchford when Sir Charles entered their room. "My heart aches for him. I have never before seen a man break down; and it makes it all the worse when he is such a great, strong fellow as Mr. Mannering—Lord Lesborough, I mean."

Sir Charles shook his head reflectively as he brushed his hair.

"I can't make him out, Blanche. You saw how he looked when we found him—wandering about the streets like a—like a man half out of his mind——"

"The wreck, perhaps?" suggested Lady Letchford.

Sir Charles rejected the idea promptly.

"Not much! Vane could stand half a dozen wrecks."

"Judith? Oh, Charlie, how could I have been so *gauche* as to mention her!" she wailed.

Sir Charles shook his head.

"Rather unlike your usual tact, old girl," he admitted. "Yes, I'm afraid he was hard hit there. I'm sorry Judith is a pal of yours, Blanche——"

"Was, Charlie. Be just! You know I have not spoken to her since she jilted Mr. Mannering. Of course, he must have felt it, for no doubt he loved her. She is not only the most beautiful woman in the world——"

"Present company excepted," said Sir Charles, with a fond glance over his shoulder at the figure sitting up in bed.

"Nonsense," retorted Lady Letchford. "Don't be foolish! I was never in the same street—oh, I wish I did not pick up your slang so easily—I never could be compared with Judith. She was, and is, and always will be, simply incomparable. But I hate her for treating Mr. Mannering so cruelly."

"Well, she was punished, anyhow," said Sir Charles. "Fancy chucking over a man like Vane for old Marlingford——"

"He was a marquis, you see," murmured Lady Letchford.

"A man old enough to be her grandfather! That he should die two days before the wedding is—er—what do you call it——"

"Poetical justice, do you mean? It served her right. But, Charlie, if it isn't the wreck and the privations he suffered—did you notice how he shirked speaking of them?—and it isn't Judith, what is it that has changed him so?"

Sir Charles shook his head.

"I don't know. Anyway, whatever it is, it has hit him hard, deuced hard. I don't suppose we shall ever find out. Vane can be as close as an oyster when he likes."

"Well, you've got to help him all you can," concluded Lady Letchford, with a sigh. "And do put those brushes down—you'll brush all the hair off your head—and come to bed! The look in that poor man's face will keep me awake all night—if I don't go off at once."

Mannering paced his room for some hours, feeling that bed was impossible for him.

He was the Earl of Lesborough, owner of an historic title and a vast estate, and wealth which had been accumulating steadily during the reign of the late earl, who had lived a penurious existence, devoted to amassing money and finding good investments for it.

And of what use to him—Vane—were the title and the money? His heart was buried on the sands of an unknown island in the Pacific. It had died within his bosom in the hour he had seen the wreck of the raft at his feet, had swum out to the little woolen cap which was all that remained to him of Nina, his wife, the woman he loved.

He threw himself on the bed at last and slept; but it was only to dream of the island, only to go over the scene of the marriage and the too few days that followed it.

Letchford, going to him in the morning, found him asleep, but tossing restlessly, and returned to Lady Letchford with a doleful shake of the head.

But when Mannering appeared at breakfast he was, outwardly at least, calmer and more like a man in a normal condition.

"I'm afraid I upset and distressed you last night, Lady Letchford," he said, with grave apology. "The—the shock——"

"That's all right. Blanche understood," said Letchford cheerily. "Have some more bacon—it's of no use offering you anything else, because no one eats anything at breakfast but bacon. Shall I go with you to Mr. Tressider, Vane? I will, if you like."

"We will do anything and everything you like, Lord Lesborough," murmured Lady Letchford.

Mannering started at the "Lord Lesborough," and abruptly set down his coffee cup which was on its way to his lips.

"No, I think I'll go alone," he said; and soon after breakfast he set off.

Mr. Tressider was one of the old-fashioned lawyers who stick to the Inns. His office was in Grey's, and Mannering, as he mounted the steep and not too clean stairs, paused and looked absently at the trees in which the rooks had nested and brought out their young; he did not seem in any hurry to put in his formal claim to the title.

A confidential clerk, of as old a fashion as his master, received Mannering, and with a grave earnestness ushered him into the presence of the lawyer.

Mr. Tressider came to meet him with outstretched hand, and exclaimed with intense satisfaction and pleasure:

"Lord Lesborough! At last! How do you do? I need scarcely say that I am glad to see you! My advertisement will be sufficient proof of that."

"I've seen none," said Mannering. "I've been abroad—been wrecked. I heard the—the bad news for the first time last night, from my friend, Sir Charles Letchford——"

Mr. Tressider nodded; he had a nod which Lord Butleigh would not have been ashamed to own.

"Quite so; quite so! I have the honor of Sir Charles Letchford's acquaintance. So, of course, you know the—er—sad circumstances which have placed you in possession of the title. Very sad; very sad! But I am very glad to see you, my lord."

The title was still strange to Mannering, and he moved uneasily.

"All the more glad," continued the old lawyer, "because, at one time, we almost feared that you had completely disappeared, in fact, were lost. Of course, we heard of the wreck of the *Alpina*. I am so rejoiced you were saved!

I have done the best I could during your absence, and I think the business of the estate has been carried on as you would have wished it to be."

Mannering nodded. It all seemed so unreal, so impossible. Why, a few months ago he had been a mere nobody, of no consequence, a kind of adventurer, free to do and go as he willed, in whose affairs no one was interested. And now——He looked round the snugly furnished office, at the white-haired, smiling, deferential old lawyer, as if the whole thing were a dream from which he should presently awake.

"Of course you will go down to Lesborough at once," continued Mr. Tressider. "Do you propose living there, or will you go into the town house? It has been closed for some time; you know that the late earl was—er—economical? He amassed a large fortune; you will benefit by his economy and prudence, my lord!"

Vane gazed absently at the window, through the grimy panes of which he could see the rooks which had attracted his attention as he entered; and they still seemed to have more interest for him than the lawyer's remarks.

"I think I'll go to Lesborough," he said, at last, but with an indifference which disappointed Mr. Tressider, who had expected the new earl to display some eagerness if not excitement. "I haven't made any plans."

"Quite so; quite so! Too early yet; you have scarcely realized your sudden accession to the title, the change in your life. I will write to the steward, Mr. Holland—you remember him? He will want to make some preparations. Dear, dear, how glad I am to find you are alive! None of your friends can be more rejoiced, I assure you, my lord. Strange"—he smiled and paused—"I was just writing to the next heir. I am afraid you can scarcely expect him to share in my satisfaction."

Vane looked interested for the first time.

"The next heir?" he said inquiringly.

"Yes; your cousin, Mr. Julian Shore. He wrote to me, and called on me when poor Lord Augustus and his boy died, and we feared you were lost in the *Alpina*. He was, very naturally—er—interested in the question of the succession."

"How can he, with the name of Shore, be the next heir?" asked Vane.

"Oh, don't you know? Weren't you aware that there was a feud between his father and the late earl? So great and bitter that he discarded the name of Mannering and took the name of Shore, which Mr. Julian now bears."

"I never heard of him," said Mannering. "I'm afraid he will be very disappointed at my turning up," he added grimly.

"No doubt; no doubt," asserted Mr. Tressider dryly.

"What kind of man is he?" asked Mannering.

Mr. Tressider hesitated. It was the sort of question which a cautious old lawyer would not be disposed to answer very readily.

"He is a young man about five-and-twenty, I should say—a remarkably good-looking young fellow; not like the Mannerings, by the way; but dark, very dark. His mother was a Spaniard. He has very nice manners—nothing could be more tactful and—er—proper than his way of regarding his claim to the title and estates."

"Is he poor or rich?" asked Vane.

"Well, he is not particularly well off. He has a small income, left him by his father, and he makes a little in some way on the Stock Exchange, I fancy; but I am not quite sure. Of course, I knew his father, but I had not seen Mr. Julian since he was a lad until the other day."

"Is he married?" asked Vane.

"No; oh, no! I asked him that question. By the way, Lord Lesborough, it is one I should like to ask you. I am under the impression that you are a bachelor."

Vane looked away to the window again.

"I have no wife," he said gravely.

Mr. Tressider nodded with almost obvious relief. For the moment, as Vane hesitated, he had dreaded that he should hear that the young earl had married—and probably beneath his present rank.

"Ah, yes, yes!" he murmured. "Plenty of time; though I trust I may have the pleasure of seeing a Countess of Lesborough before long."

Vane rose, but Mr. Tressider extended his hand appealingly.

"Oh, pray, don't go yet, my lord," he said; "there are so many things I want to speak to you about, to arrange. And—er—perhaps the first subject is the important and inevitable one of—er—money. I do not know whether you need any at the present moment—you will excuse me?"

Vane smiled.

"I have a few shillings," he said.

Mr. Tressider nodded as if this were not the least satisfactory moment of the interview.

"Quite so; quite so! I will make arrangements—will pay a sum, as large as you please, into the bank this afternoon. Meanwhile, you will permit me to be your banker. Let me see. I have some notes and will not trouble you to cash a check."

He went to the safe and from his cash box took out a little pile of notes, counted them, and laid them on the table before Vane.

"There is a hundred and twenty pounds there, I think you will find. It is fortunate that I had just received a payment this morning. If that is not sufficient I will send a clerk to the bank——"

Vane smiled gravely.

"I shan't spend more than a hundred and twenty before to-morrow," he said.

As he spoke the door opened and the clerk brought in the usual piece of paper with a visitor's name written on it.

Mr. Tressider looked rather embarrassed.

"Strange coincidence!" he said. "It is Mr. Julian Shore. Ask Mr. Shore to kindly wait——"

Vane looked up quickly.

"No, no. Will you let him come in? I should like to see him," he said.

Mr. Tressider nodded, and the clerk went out and ushered in a tall, thin young man with a remarkably handsome face and a graceful bearing. He was almost as dark as a typical Spaniard, with eyes that were well-nigh black, and screened by long silky lashes.

As he entered, he looked from the lawyer—still rather embarrassed—to Vane; then his eyes fell on the sheaf of notes, and the black orbs seemed to deepen suddenly, swiftly, but in an instant the fleeting expression had vanished and given place to one of courteous curiosity.

"I beg your pardon, Mr. Tressider," he said, in a singularly soft and low voice. "I did not know you were engaged——"

"Pray take a seat, Mr. Shore," said Mr. Tressider, "you have called at a most auspicious——" The word seemed rather inappropriate, not to say heartless, and he paused and stumbled in search of a better, but failed to find one, and so gave up the idea of "breaking" the news to the next heir, and blurted out the introduction:

"I must make you two gentlemen known to each other. Mr. Shore, this is Mr. Mannering—tut, tut! I mean Lord Lesborough."

Vane, with a feeling of pity and sympathy, was watching the man whose hopes he was destroying, and he saw the polite look of inquiry, doubt, and dismay and pain which passed over the dark, handsome face. The lids fell over the dark eyes, as if their owner desired to hide them.

"Lord—Lesborough!" fell from his lips, which had grown almost white. "Lord Lesborough! Then—then——"

"Exactly!" put in Mr. Tressider, as the soft voice broke and fell away. "Mr. Mannering was not lost in the *Alpina*. He was rescued, and has only just returned to London; has indeed only been here with me a few minutes. Of course, I should have let you know——"

It was an awkward, a trying moment for both the young men. Vane felt as if he had been guilty of inexcusable meanness in not getting drowned; and with a flush and a frown he rose and held out his hand.

"I'm sorry——" he began, then he shrugged his shoulders. What could he say?

But Julian Shore had recovered from the shock, and, rising instantly, he took Vane's strong, firm hand in his soft, white one; a smile glittered in his eyes and curved his rather thin lips, and the low, musical voice said:

"And you are the new earl! Well"—he drew a quick, short breath, then he shrugged his shoulders—"we can't both have the title, and, Lord Lesborough, I assure you that I am heartily glad that you are alive!"

Nothing could have been better done; and Vane, feeling if anything still more guilty and ashamed of his existence, gripped gratefully the white hand of the disappointed man.

"Thanks," he said. "Thanks! I'm almost sorry that I didn't go down with the ship. You'd have made a better earl than I shall, Mr. Shore."

"Oh, come, come!" murmured Mr. Shore, laughing softly. "Don't say that—and—we are cousins, aren't we? I hope you'll call me Julian!"

CHAPTER XI
VANE MAKES AN OFFER

Would he call him "Julian"? Of course Vane was pleased by such good nature and magnanimity displayed by the man between whom and the prospect of an earldom he had stepped.

"Certainly—Julian," he said, with so much lighter a tone in his voice that Mr. Tressider was surprised. "And of course you'll call me 'Vane'; we are cousins, as you say, and, though we haven't met before, I hope we shall be friends. I only heard of my good fortune last night, and I am a bit confused. I see it is lunch time. Mr. Tressider, will you let us off for an hour or two? I should like to go out and get something to eat with—Julian."

The old lawyer smiled, but rather ruefully, as he thought that the new earl was likely to be rather an erratic client.

"Oh, well!" he said, with a shrug of his shoulders. "I'll wire to Holland to say you may come to Lesborough at any moment, and I hope you will pay me a visit before long. There is much to be done, to be seen to."

"That's all right," responded Vane serenely. "I'll leave everything in your hands, Mr. Tressider, and it will be sure to pan out perfectly." He pocketed the notes, and Julian watched him with lowered lids.

The two young men went down the stairs and into the courtyard, where the pigeons fluttered and strode at their feet with the fearlessness of the London bird.

"Where shall we go?" asked Vane. "I used to have a club, but my subscription ran out, and I couldn't afford to renew it. Restaurant?"

Julian laughed—his laugh was as soft as his voice, and his smile soft and caressing.

"How strange to hear that from the Earl of Lesborough!" he said.

"Yes; but I wasn't earl then, and I was poor," said Vane.

Julian slowed up for a moment.

"I was going to lunch at my place," he said, with a hesitation that was only momentary. "Perhaps you won't mind coming home with me? It's rather out of the way, though it isn't far from here. We shall be free to talk——"

"Right," said Vane. "I shall be very pleased."

Julian called a cab and gave the address—Vane did not catch it—to the cabman; and they drove across the Strand and alongside the House of Parliament, to an old-fashioned row of houses facing the river.

Vane, as they alighted, looked round him curiously. It was a bit of old London hemmed in and flanked by newly built flats and modern residences.

"Quaint place," he said. "I've never been here before."

"No? I live here because it's quiet and out of the way; and I own the house. It was my father's. It's rather a nice view, especially at night, with the lights on the water. The house is old, very old, and it wants repairing, modernizing, and all that, and I mean to do it—when I can afford it."

He pulled at an old-fashioned bell, and the door was opened presently, and with an air of caution, by an old woman, with so strange an expression on so pallid a face that Vane could not help staring at her; and he stared the harder when, instead of speaking, Julian Shore made signs to her in the deaf-and-dumb alphabet on his fingers.

The old woman took her eyes for a moment from her master's face to glance at Vane, then nodded assentingly, and, closing the door, disappeared through another which led to the basement.

"Come upstairs, will you?" said Julian. "I live on the upper floor for the sake of the view."

He led the way into a sitting room, which was as old-fashioned as the exterior of the house. The walls were of oak, blackened by age—not Tottenham Court Road varnish—there was a massive mantel-piece as black as the paneling, and the furniture, old and heavy, was in perfect harmony with the room. There was a piano, also of oak. It was a very quaint room, and imposing, but it struck Vane as sombre, not to say weird.

He went to the window and looked out.

"You've a fine view of the river," he said, "and this is a grand old room."

As he spoke, he noticed a faint smell, like that emitted by pungent chemicals. It came from a door leading out of the room, and Julian stepped to it and closed it softly.

The old woman appeared with a tray, and presently set out a nice little lunch. The claret was in a Venetian flask, and a small bottle of yellow Chartreuse stood beside it. Having laid out the table, the woman, after a fixed look at her master—the kind of look one sees in the eyes of a well-trained and devoted spaniel—left the room, and Julian drew a chair to the table for Vane, and invited him to be seated.

"You seem to have very comfortable quarters," said Vane. "Your servant is deaf and dumb, isn't she?"

"Yes," said Julian. "She was an old servant of my father's. I'm afraid to say how old she is. But she is very faithful and attentive, and serves my purpose."

"And you don't mind her—affliction?" said Vane, as he helped himself to sweetbread.

Julian smiled.

"No," he replied. "I suppose it's because I'm used to her. She is very—intelligent, and, as I say, she is devoted to me."

"She looks it," remarked Vane. "This is splendid claret."

Julian smiled, the smile of a man whose wine is praised.

"It is some my father left me. By the way, I fancy it came originally from Lesborough Court."

"Then I hope there is some left there," said Vane. "You know the place?"

"No," replied Julian. "I have never been there. My father and the earl quarreled—but, no doubt, you know all about that. No, I have never been there. But you know it; you have stayed there?"

Vane nodded as he looked round the room. It seemed strange, improbable that he should be sitting here so cozily with this newly discovered cousin.

"Yes; I used to go there as a boy; and until recently I was asked to pay a kind of regulation visit. But the earl quarreled with me as he quarreled with your father. He—expected too much."

"As how?" asked Julian, filling his glass.

"Oh, well, he wanted to plan out, direct my life. Wanted me to go into politics and stand for the borough, in the Conservative interest."

"And you are Liberal?" suggested Julian.

"No, I'm not. I'm nothing. But I declined to take my politics from his lordship, and also declined to become a—a dependent. So we parted, and I went abroad——" His voice died away.

"And were wrecked?" said Julian interrogatively.

Vane seemed to dry up, to freeze, on the moment.

"Yes," he said absently. "But let us talk of something else, of yourself. I could almost have found it possible to be sorry that I was alive when you came into Mr. Tressider's just now."

Julian's dark face flushed for a moment, and his lids drooped—his face looked like a mask when his eyes were closed, so expressive were they—then he raised them, smiled, and shrugged his shoulders, and waved his hands with a gesture that reminded Vane of his cousin's Spanish blood.

"That's very kind and generous of you—Vane," he said, with a little pause before the "Vane." "Of course I should have liked to have been the Earl of Lesborough; but—ah, well, perhaps I shall be as happy as if I were."

"I dare say," said Vane, in his blunt way. "I don't suppose"—he stifled a sigh—"that it will make me any the happier."

Julian looked at him with veiled curiosity.

"Oh, you!" he said. "I can imagine that you will make quite a typical English nobleman. You are cut out for the position, and will fill it well. While I"—he waved his white hands again—"I'm scarcely so suitable a subject. I'm only half English. My mother was a Spaniard, and I have nothing—what do you call it?—feudal about me. You will marry—but perhaps you are already married; yes?" he broke off, his almost almond eyes on Vane's, with an apparently frank and disinterested interrogation.

Vane filled his glass and replied, as he had replied to Mr. Tressider: "No, I have no wife."

"Ah, but you soon will have one," said Julian, smilingly. "You will be a great catch. The parti of the season. You know that you are tremendously rich, as well as noble?"

Vane nodded.

"So I'm given to understand," he said. "But I shall never marry."

"Never is a long time," commented Julian, with a smile. "Try this Chartreuse, will you? It also came from the Lesborough cellars, I believe. You will go down there at once, will you not?"

Vane filled his liqueur glass.

"I suppose so," he answered slowly. Then, with his characteristic abruptness, he said: "See here, Julian. My turning up in this fashion must have been—inconvenient to you. I—I want to make it up to you, in some way; but upon my life I don't quite know how to. Do you mind telling me something about yourself, your—your means?" He faltered and looked at the table and round the well-furnished, though weird and rather sombre, room. "I don't want to play the inquisitive business, you know, but———"

Julian laughed at his cousin's embarrassment.

"You have a particularly transparent mind, my dear Vane," he said, in his soft voice. "I know exactly what you are going to do. You are going to offer to—make it up to me for the loss of my—expectations. Is it not so?"

"That's about hit it," assented Vane, in his direct fashion.

"I thought so!" said Julian, with his charmingly candid smile. "You would offer me an allowance, an income———"

"That's so," assented Vane. "Why shouldn't I? I'm immensely, beastly rich, I believe, and if I hadn't turned up you would have been the Earl of Lesborough."

As he pronounced the title Julian Shore's lids quivered, but the smile was still hovering about his lips.

"As it is," went on Vane, "you are the next in succession, the heir. I shan't marry—you shake your head, but I know what I am saying—and you will come into it all. Why shouldn't you accept an income, allowance, from me? If you were my brother or son you would have to do so."

Julian shook his shapely head again.

"But I'm not your brother or your son; I'm only your cousin. And—we are speaking candidly, are we not?—I do not like the rôle of a dependent. No! I will not take a penny from you."

"You are an awful fool," put in Vane, in his blunt way.

"Perhaps; but I have a small but sufficient income, enough for a bachelor, and I value my independence. No! I refuse your money; but—but if you offer your friendship, your affection, may I say——"

Vane extended his hand.

"Put it that way," he said gravely. "Blood is thicker than water. See here, we will go down to Lesborough to-morrow. I as the earl and master, you as the heir apparent—I think that's the way they describe it. We'll be friends. Julian——What on earth is that peculiar scent, odor, which hangs about this room?" he broke off to inquire.

Julian looked round absently, then smiled and shrugged his shoulders.

"I am rather fond of dabbling in chemistry. My father had a like taste; it was one of the reasons for his rupture with the late earl. His lordship could not understand how a Mannering could interest himself in such a commonplace subject. I use the room next this as a kind of laboratory. Come and see."

He arose, and, going to the door, opened it and stood aside for Vane to enter.

Vane looked in. It was a small room lighted by a window with a screen of yellow silk. There was a strange-looking fireplace, with crucibles and retorts, and there were tables and shelves, on which were books and chemical *apparati*.

Vane glanced round, with faint interest; he was not scientific by any means.

"Rum fancy," he remarked. "What's the good of it?"

Julian shrugged his shoulders.

"Oh, I don't know. Not much, I suppose. But it amuses me. Now, you, I imagine, go in for sport?"

Vane nodded.

"Yes; sport of any and every kind. If I remember rightly, there was not much hunting or shooting at Lesborough."

"The late earl starved it—so Mr. Tressider said."

"Quite so. Well, I'll alter that, at any rate," said Vane. "What's that thing on the fire? I fancy it's that that smells so?"

Julian Shore lifted a steel pot or kettle from the slowly burning fire.

"Oh, only an experiment," he said.

He led the way back to the sitting room.

"Are you fond of music?" he asked, in a casual way. "I'm no performer, but I'm a splendid listener. You play, or sing? Let's hear you!"

Julian pushed a cigar cabinet to Vane, then, with a gesture of apology and self-depreciation, went to the piano and struck a prelude of chords, and sang.

Vane listened with rapt attention and admiration.

"My dear fellow, you're almost good enough for grand opera!" he said. "You've got a devil of a voice!"

"My mother sang well, I believe," said Julian modestly.

Vane, who was as sensitive to music as a cobra, heaved a sigh; for the soft, dulcet strain had brought back the island to him.

"I must be going," he said. "My friends, the Letchfords—I'm staying with them—will wonder what the devil has become of me. Well, it's fixed; you and I go down to Lesborough to-morrow. What's the train, do you know?"

Julian knew. Had he not looked it up in Bradshaw when he thought that he should be the next earl?

"Ten-fifty," he said, "from Waterloo."

Vane held out his hand and gripped the soft, white one warmly.

"Right. We'll go down together."

Julian accompanied him to the door and stood there, watching the stalwart figure as it strode away. Then he mounted to the sitting room. The old woman was clearing away the luncheon things, and she stopped and looked at her master questioningly.

But he motioned to her to go, and, sinking into a chair, leaned his handsome head on his hand. Presently his thin, crimson lips moved, and he murmured:

"Only him between me and an earldom, between me and wealth— wealth! And he is not married. A young man, like myself. Only him! If anything were to happen to him——But it won't! He'll live to be ninety. It's just like my luck, to be within an ace of a peerage and miss it. I feel like cursing him for all his good-natured offer of friendship. But cursing wouldn't kill him. If it would——"

There came a hissing sound from the laboratory, as if something were boiling over, and he sprang to his feet and ran eagerly into the next room, as if he had forgotten Vane and the lost earldom.

CHAPTER XII
VANE MEETS JUDITH

Vane, as he walked away from Julian's house, was in a peculiar state of mind. He felt drawn toward his cousin; blood is thicker than water; and Vane had been touched by the way in which Julian had accepted his disappointment, and had proffered his friendship to the man who had crushed his hopes of a peerage. But there was something about Julian—his weird place of abode, his taste for chemistry, and indifference to the awful odor arising from his experiments—which jarred upon Vane, something in the expression of his dark eyes, the sudden drooping of the lids, which militated against the favorable impression created by the handsome face and graceful form.

Vane shrugged his shoulders.

"I'm a fanciful beast, and my nerves are rags," he said to himself. "Anyway, I've got to make the best of him. He's the only relative I know, and he'll be the next earl; I shall never marry. I'll make a friend of him, treat him as the heir."

The reflection sent him off on the old track, and, as he strode along, he thought of Nina. Though he was convinced that she had been lost, he had, for weeks, after his arrival in London, sought among the shipping companies for tidings of a castaway, but, chancing to miss the owners of the *Island Queen*, he did not hear of the picking up of the girl tied to a portion of a raft. Yes, she was dead, and he had been spared that he might spend the remainder of his life in futile remorse and regret.

Quite heedless of the direction in which he was going, he sauntered on, and presently, awaking from his reverie, he found himself in Piccadilly, at the entrance to Hyde Park. He turned in absently, and strolled toward the Row. It was the fashionable hour of the day, and the place was crowded, and Vane lit another of Julian's cigars, and, leaning on the rail, surveyed the riders as they passed him. The walk was thronged with promenaders; and little groups of friends and acquaintances were chatting and laughing together, making a pleasant little hum and buzz which, pleasant as it was, made Vane feel very lonely.

Some of the voices were so distinct that they reached his ear. He listened mechanically and heard a man who was talking with some ladies say:

"Yes, she's just gone past. Looks wonderfully well and fit, doesn't she?"

"It's the first time she has put in an appearance since his death, isn't it? What a terrible blow and—disappointment it must have been to her! Think of missing being a marchioness! And so narrowly! Most girls would have been utterly crushed."

"But not she," drawled the man. "She's a good-plucked one. Yes, she's missed the marquis, but I shouldn't wonder if she goes for a duke next time. There she is again."

"Yes, there she is," said the lady. "I suppose that black habit is for mourning?"

Vane was turning away, when his eye fell on a lady who was riding slowly toward him. It would have been difficult for him not to have noticed her, for she was an extremely beautiful woman, and she was riding a superb horse, which she sat with a perfect ease that the restless movements of the high-spirited animal did not in the least appear to disturb. By her side were riding two or three men; and, as she pulled up close to the railing, just above where Vane was standing, other men pressed up to the spot, snatching off their hats, and evidently eager to attract her attention and exchange a word or two with her, while every one who rode or walked past her, whether they knew her or not, regarded her intently and with evident interest.

After all, and with a due regard to the claims of other nationalities, is there anything in the wide world more moving and heart-stirring than a beautiful young English girl? And this was one of the loveliest of the type. She sat erect on her thoroughbred, with her face full in the sunlight, that lit up the exquisite color of her thick hair of bronze and gold, which the gentle breeze had blown in soft rings over her forehead. Her eyes shone like sapphires in the clear ivory of her face, and her lips, as perfectly formed as those of a Grecian statue, were curved with a pensive smile. When she was alone, the sapphire eyes were apt to grow cold and a trifle hard—one hates to write "calculating"—and the lips, without their smile, narrowed and lost their exquisite curve—but in public both the well-trained eyes and lips were on duty, so to speak, and took upon them any and every expression which their owner willed.

As Vane looked at her his heart gave one bound, then seemed to fall into an almost unnatural calm, a calm which made him marvel at himself; for, not so long since, the sight of this face, the sound of this girl's voice had set his heart beating for more than a moment, and had never failed to send the blood racing through his veins.

Quite unreflectingly, he remained where he was, leaning on the rail, and watching her with moody eyes, which expressed the dead calm and indifference which had fallen on him; and when, after a moment or two, she nodded her adieus to the group—the members of which had all the attitude and manners of courtiers—and, touching her horse, moved toward him, he still leaned over the rails and waited for her. She was almost abreast of him before she saw him, for she was bowing, with the pensive smile, to some friends on the other side of the ride, but it would have been well-nigh impossible for any one to have passed his stalwart figure and handsome face, with their indefinable air of distinction, without noticing him, and presently her glance fell on him.

The sapphire eyes contracted and closed for a moment, the ivory of her face went a dead white, the smile fled from her lips, and her hand involuntarily closed so tightly on the rein that the horse stopped and tossed his head impatiently.

She was so close to Vane that he could see the quiver of the lips, the flicker of the lids, which had dropped over the brilliant eyes. He stood upright, and, regarding her with the calmness which still vaguely surprised himself, raised his hat.

She bent her head and her lips moved, but at first with no sound, then she said in a low, still voice:

"Vane!"

"How do you do, Lady Marlingford?" he said, in just the ordinary tone of polite greeting.

Her white teeth closed on her lip for a moment, then she bent her head. The "Lady Marlingford" was like a blow to her from the man who had been wont to breathe "Judith" as if it were a psalm of life, a sonnet of love.

"I—I did not know you were—back," she said. "And why do you call me Lady Marlingford?" she added, her brows drawn, as if with pain.

He ought to have been startled by the question, but it would have taken very little less than an earthquake to startle poor Vane at this period of his existence.

"How do I err?" he asked, not bitterly, but with a placidity which cut her more deeply than any bitterness would have done. "You were just on the point of marrying Lord Marlingford when I left England—if you remember."

She raised her head and looked at him. The group to which he had been absently listening was quite close, and within hearing, and she made a slight gesture with her hand.

"Will you come a little farther up the ride?" she said, in a very low voice.

Vane hesitated for an instant. He had loved this girl with a love which he had thought eternal, had well-nigh lost his reason when she had betrayed and deserted him; but now he had not the least desire to talk with her. His love for Nina—how in its purity and truth it shamed his old passion for Judith Orme—had wiped out all thought of and desire for any other woman, even for this exquisitely beautiful one. But he could scarcely refuse her request, and, with a nod, he moved beside her to a vacant space. She took her horse close to the rail and bent down, so that she could whisper to him; he was still sensible of the grace of her movements, but only sensible of it as one is conscious of the grace of a particularly beautiful statue or a singularly charming picture.

"Don't you know? Have you not heard?" she said, with the faintest tremor in her voice, the voice which used to thrill him.

"Heard what?" he said, almost bluntly.

"Poor Lord Marlingford died just—just before our—our wedding day," she said brokenly.

Vane's eyelids did not even flicker, and he looked at her steadily.

"Poor beggar!" he said. "I'm sorry for him." And he was genuinely sorry, for he remembered what the loss of her had been to himself. "I hadn't heard——"

She drew a long breath. "No? When did you come back to England? We heard that you were lost. And I—I was—sorry. I felt—when did you come back?"

"Some time since," he replied. "And so Lord Marlingford died! Accept my most sincere condolence, Miss Orme."

The sapphire eyes rested on him with sweet reproach.

"Miss Orme! Oh, Vane, you cannot forgive! You did not understand. You do not understand, even now——"

Vane's lips began to curl.

"I beg your pardon," he said, with polite interest, nothing more.

She sighed again, as she curbed the impatience and restlessness of the Arab.

"I want to tell you—but this is no place. But I must congratulate you, Vane."

"On my succession to the title?" he said. "Thanks!"

Her eyes swept over his seedy serge suit, and, as if in response, he said:

"I only heard it last night. I came back from—I was in London, hard up, and, well, I suppose looking for something to do, when I heard the news. Sir Charles Letchford happened to spot me——"

She tossed her beautiful head slightly.

"The Letchfords? Yes. They used to be friends of mine, but Blanche has cut me lately, since—— She did not understand, as you do not understand, that I was a victim of circumstances. You know what my father is—what my life has been——"

Vane regarded her calmly. There was a note of appeal in her musical voice which would have reached his heart and elicited a quick response some months ago; but it did not move him now.

"I—I can't tell you all now, here," she said. "Will you not come to see me?"

Vane hesitated a moment. If the woman who hesitates is lost, how much more so is the man!

"Thanks, I shall be very pleased," he said.

Her lips parted with a smile, a smile that was almost one of humble gratitude.

"You will? Ah, that is good of you! And I want to hear all that has happened to you. You will tell me, won't you?"

Vane, thinking that he certainly would not, replied, as in duty bound:

"Certainly."

"You—you are not looking well," she murmured, the sapphire eyes sweeping over his face and the seedy serge suit.

"I've been down on my luck," said Vane, in response to the glance, "and I heard of the change in my fortunes so recently that I haven't had time to pull myself together."

"And I am changed, also; don't you notice it?" she said sadly.

"Can't say I do," replied Vane. "You seem to me as—as charming as ever, Judith." He had intended to say "Miss Orme"; but the familiar name escaped him.

Her eyes lit up for a moment, but she veiled them instantly.

"Do you think so? Oh, I am changed; very much so. And you will come? The old address."

"Thanks," he said. "Yes; certainly, I will come."

"Thank you; it is good of you!" she murmured. "When? To-morrow?"

"Not to-morrow," he said mechanically. "I am engaged. I am going to Lesborough. When I come back."

She drooped over her saddle, and held out her long, thin hand, so perfectly gloved that the kid seemed an outer skin. Vane took it—how often had his lips kissed the white hand that glove covered—pressed it with the proper amount of pressure.

"When you come back—directly you come back," she said, and turned her horse.

Judith Orme rode toward Queen Anne's Gate, with her beautiful eyes fixed on her horse's ears, and, though she bowed and smiled, in response to the many greetings she received, she was scarcely conscious of them.

She pulled up at one of the small houses in St. Margaret's Place, which are as fashionable as they are small and inconvenient, and, having alighted, with the aid of her discreet and well-mounted groom, entered the house and went up to the drawing-room.

The tea table was set by the window overlooking the park, and Judith, after ringing the bell for the urn, sank into an easy-chair, and let her beautiful face fall into the warm, white hands from which she had stripped her gloves with a restless, feverish haste.

As the maid was placing the urn on the table a step, light but unsteady, was heard on the stairs, and presently there entered a seemingly middle-aged, if not quite young, man. He was small and slightly built, with features almost as delicately moulded as a woman's. His hair—it was a really admirable wig, a perfect work of art—sat, with a fine imitation of nature, over a face painted and enameled so artfully that it might have belonged to a young man of five-and-twenty. The figure, slight and debonair, was clothed with a sartorial skill and cunning to which Saville Row alone could aspire; and it was only the eyes, a little bleared and prominent, which aroused the suspicion of the keen observer—a very keen observer—and let out the secret of Sir Chandos Orme's age.

Judith's hands fell from her eyes as her father entered the room, with his jaunty, would-be juvenile air, and the expression of her lovely face grew hard and matter-of-fact.

"You're home early, father," she said curtly.

"Yes; yes, I am," he said. He had lunched at his club, lunched unwisely and too well, and the natural flush on his face strove, with praiseworthy but futile energy, to pierce the coat of enamel and paint. "But I came home because I have some news for you. Vane Mannering is here—here in London!"

He sank into a chair and smiled at her, with a significance which was somewhat drowned by the effects of the bottle and a half of champagne he had taken with his lunch.

"He's back," he continued. "Old Fanworthy saw him—trust old Fanworthy for spotting a man—and, as you know, Mannering is now the Earl of Lesborough."

"I know," said Judith quietly. "And but for you I should be engaged to Vane Mannering, should be his wife."

"No, no, my dear Judith!" broke in Sir Chandos. "It was your own doing."

"My own doing!" said Judith bitterly. "It was you, you, who stepped in between us, who persuaded me to throw Vane over and accept Lord Marlingford. You know it, father."

Sir Chandos waved his white hands—they were still famous, though they had been waving for considerably more than half a century.

"My dear Judith, do me justice! Vane Mannering was, at that time, ever so far removed from the peerage."

"And so you sacrificed me," she said bitterly. "Persuaded, compelled me to throw him over and accept Lord Marlingford——"

"Who most—most inconsiderately died," put in Sir Chandos. "But when you say I compelled, I suggest, I merely suggest, that you were easily persuaded—compelled; and rightly."

"And now—now Vane has come back to England?" said Judith. "And is——"

Sir Chandos shuffled in his chair, and toyed with the cup of tea which he did not want.

"The Earl of Lesborough," he said. "You will, of course, my dear Judith——"

She rose, almost upsetting the fragile table with its dainty Worcester china.

"You expect me, you want me to—to——Ah, it is too shameful, too base!"

Sir Chandos eyed her rather nervously.

"My dear Judith, my dear child!" he murmured. "Circumstances alter cases."

She turned her face from him, and it may be hoped that the recording angel will give her credit for the tears that shone in the sapphire eyes.

"You knew that—that I cared for him; yes, loved him. I love him now. Yes, I love him now."

Her voice faltered and broke suddenly.

Sir Chandos eyed her with a faint and murky surprise.

"Really? Is that so? 'Pon my word, my dear Judith. Well, well! Tut, tut! But this windfall is lucky for us!"

She dried her eyes and regarded him with a bitter, defiant expression.

"What do you mean?" she demanded. "Why is it lucky?"

Sir Chandos at last put down the cup that cheers, but which he abhorred, and blinked his bleared eyes at her.

"Oh, I only meant to say that if you still care for him, if you want to be the Countess of Lesborough; well—well, we are all right. My dear Judith"—he leaned forward, and pointed a forefinger at her—"you know as well as I do that no man can resist you; and that if you mean going for Vane Mannering—I beg his pardon, I mean Lesborough!—there is no escape for him."

She bit her lip, and stared thoughtfully, moodily, at the carpet, and the flush of shame, humiliation, came and went in her face.

"You haven't seen him since he came back. He is much changed. He—he was quite cool, cold to-day. Not angry—worse, indifferent."

Sir Chandos laughed softly, the kind of chuckle which is born of a knowledge of the world and an incapacity for shame.

"I have every confidence in you, my dear Judith," he said. "Every confidence. I—I think I will just drop in at the club on the chance of a rubber. Every confidence!"

CHAPTER XIII
AT LESBOROUGH COURT.

When he left the park, Vane—remembering the state of his attire—went to Shadbolt's, the Lesboroughs' tailor, in a quiet street off Bond Street.

The worthy tradesman received him with outspoken joy, but was shocked by the sight of the seedy serge suit, and still more shocked when he learned that it was Vane's best. For the first time in his life Mr. Shadbolt procured a ready-made suit—which Vane indifferently donned there and then—and measured his noble client for a variety of others: shooting suits, frock suits, dress suits, riding coats, and so on.

It was a trifling incident, but it had its effect on Vane. Mr. Shadbolt's obsequiousness and the presence of the roll of notes in Vane's pocket were indicative of the change that had come over his fortunes. It was nearly dinner time when he returned to the Letchfords'; and they received him with open arms and an obvious air of relief.

"Thought you'd disappeared again, did, indeed, old man!" said Letchford, while Lady Letchford smiled in sympathy with her husband.

"And you saw Tressider?"

"Yes; and I am going down to Lesborough to-morrow," said Vane. "I am going down with a cousin of mine—Julian Shore."

Letchford shook his head. "Never heard of him."

"Nor I till this morning," said Vane. "Seems a very decent fellow; very good-looking chap. He would have been the heir, if I hadn't, unluckily for him, turned up. I've taken rather a fancy to him—though he's rather peculiar."

"As how?" asked Letchford.

Vane shrugged his shoulders.

"Oh—I don't know. Goes in for chemistry and—and looks half a Spaniard: mother belongs that way."

"I'm so glad you are going to the Court, Lord Lesborough," said Lady Letchford. "You will feel so—so sure, you will realize the change; and there will be so much to do to occupy your mind."

"Yes, old fellow, you'll have to wake up and fill the bill, you know," cut in Letchford cheerfully.

Vane suppressed a sigh.

"Yes, I suppose so," he said, rather wearily. "Will you lend me a dress suit, Letchford? I'd like to sit down to dinner with Lady Letchford looking rather more like an ordinary human being than I did last night."

The husband and wife exchanged glances—they were still anxious ones—behind Vane's back. What was the nature of the cloud that rested upon the spirit of the new earl?

The next morning Vane called in a hansom for his cousin, and Julian himself came down to the door as if he had been waiting. The deaf-and-dumb woman stood at the door, and looked at Vane fixedly. Julian wore a dark tweed suit, and looked extremely well, almost too graceful, in it.

"Ready?" asked Vane, without alighting. "Come on, then."

They got into a smoking carriage of the express, and chatted in a friendly way or read their papers. A well-appointed carriage was waiting for them at Lesborough Station, and a footman came forward, and, touching his hat, addressed Julian.

"The carriage is outside, my lord. Mr. Holland sent it on the chance of your coming by this train."

Julian colored slightly.

"This is Lord Lesborough," he said, indicating Vane.

"Oh, all right; thanks," said Vane quickly. "Get in, Julian; thoughtful of Mr. Holland; though for my part I'd rather have walked; it's no great distance."

Julian leaned back, but looked out of the window with veiled keenness and eagerness. The road from the station to the Court goes through some beautiful scenery, and the road is trim and neat, as befits the road to so great a place. The people they passed in the road stopped at sight of the carriage and touched their hats or curtsied, and women and children ran out to the gates in front of the cottages, and stared, with a mixture of awe and curiosity, after the Court landau and the servants with their powdered heads and expensive mourning liveries.

Presently the carriage turned in at the south lodge gates, and into the avenue of magnificent trees, which wound in graceful curves to the front entrance.

As the Court came in sight, an exclamation escaped Julian; and Vane, who had been gazing vacantly at nothing, awoke and looked up.

"Fine place, isn't it?" he said, in a matter-of-fact way, as he let his gaze wander along the wide-stretching front of time-stained stone, half covered by ivy.

"It is magnificent," said Julian. "I had no idea that——"

"I ought to inflict the history of it on you; I've heard it often enough," said Vane. "It's one of the oldest houses in England. It used to be a show place, but my uncle—our uncle, pardon—shut it up and kept visitors at bay.

He was not one of the best-tempered of men—but we mustn't speak ill of the dead, poor old chap!"

"Oh, I can understand," said Julian, under his breath. "If this were mine I should not like to have Tom, Dick, and Harry, to say nothing of their belongings, tramping about it. The place is a poem! You'll throw it open again, I suppose?"

"I suppose so," assented Vane indifferently. "Why not? It's too big for one man—or a dozen, for that matter; and there are all sorts of collections in it. One of the Lesboroughs, our great-grandfather, I fancy, was a collector. I believe the pictures are particularly fine, they run all over the hall and the galleries, and the rooms generally; and there's a famous library, and a collection of armor and gems, and that kind of thing. Oh, yes, I suppose it ought to be open to the public, as it used to be. Why not?"

"What magnificent trees!" remarked Julian; "and this is the terrace—I can picture it crowded with ladies and gallants in silks and satins——"

"Like a fancy-dress ball," said Vane listlessly. "Yes, a shooting suit and a brier pipe, to say nothing of swallow-tails and tailor-made gowns, don't seem very appropriate, do they? Good lord, we're evidently going to have a reception," he broke off, with dismay, as he caught a glimpse of a row of servants standing in the hall.

A short, wiry little man came hurrying down the steps, his bowler hat in his hand, his face red with excitement.

"That's Holland," said Vane. "Seems a bit fussy."

Mr. Holland put the footman aside and opened the carriage door.

"Good morning, my lord! Welcome—er—welcome to the Court, welcome home! I got Mr. Tressider's telegram yesterday, and—er—have done the best I could on such short notice——"

Vane shook the steward's hand, and introduced Julian.

"Mr. Shore, my cousin, Mr. Holland," he said. "He's been good enough to come down with me."

The steward was rather taken aback—he had expected the earl would be alone—but he shook hands with Julian, and extended the welcome to him.

"Glad to see you, Mr. Shore; of course, I know who you are, though I have not had the pleasure——"

He escorted the two up the broad stone steps, flanked by the heraldic monsters which figured on the Mannering arms, and cast a swift and critical glance at the row of servants, who drew themselves up and, as Vane and Julian passed between them, murmured:

"Welcome home, my lord; welcome home."

Vane, who detested fuss, nodded and grunted an inarticulate response, but Julian, his eyes brilliant with the appreciation of the scenic effect, smiled on either side of him in a fashion that went straight home to the hearts of the female servants, who, in their neat dresses of black merino, with white collars and cuffs, looked like the servants in one of the modern musical farces whereof we all wot so well.

Prance, the stately butler—"Mr." Prance, as he was called in the servants' hall—came forward with a bow that would have done credit to a bishop.

"Luncheon is ready, my lord, and shall be served in——"

"Ah, how d'y do, Prance," said Vane, holding out his hand. "I'm glad to see you here."

"And I'm glad to be here to receive your lordship," responded Prance, with a mixture of deference and dignity which was almost awe-inspiring.

"And is that Mrs. Field?" said Vane, as the housekeeper moved from the line. "Glad to see you, too, Mrs. Field." ("His lordship's a true Mannering," Mrs. Field remarked to an appreciative audience in the servants' hall after "the reception." "He shook hands with me and Mr. Prance; not merely bowed, you noticed, but shook hands. And any one could see that he was a nobleman by the way he did it; not haughty and coldlike, but as if we were real friends. His lordship, being a lord, knows what's due to his servants.") "Lunch ready? Right. We'll just wash our hands."

"Your lordship's man?" asked Prance, looking toward the carriage.

"Eh, oh, a man. No, haven't got one. Forgot all about it."

"Just so, my lord; your lordship's been busy, much engaged. I thought perhaps you wouldn't bring one; so I made so bold as to ask Fenton, his late lordship's valet, to stay till——"

Fenton came forward.

"Thanks, Prance; very thoughtful," said Vane.

He thrust his arm through that of Julian, who had been looking round the fine old hall in silence, and led him up the stairs. Fenton followed, and opened the door of the late earl's room.

"Here? Oh, all right," said Vane. "Where are you going to put Mr. Julian? The best room is ready, I hope? Here, I'll come and see."

The best guest room was ready; it was not far from Vane's, and Vane gave Julian a friendly little push into it.

"Don't be long; you must be famishing; I am. Fenton, you look after Mr. Julian. I can manage for myself."

Fenton, with the expressionless face of the perfectly trained servant, went with Julian, who protested faintly, and Vane walked across the room, in which so many Lesboroughs had slept—and died—and stared out of the window. He looked toward the south, and upon a view which was perfect of its kind. The admirably kept gardens lay at the foot of the terrace, with its marble vases and statuary; beyond were lawns, with magnificent specimen trees, and still beyond was the home park. Over this he could get a glimpse of the uplands, dotted with the farms and homesteads; a faint line of blue on the horizon stood for the sea.

It was a lovely view; but, alas, alas! Vane saw it not. His eyes were looking at the exquisite form, and coloring of a fairy isle, beside which the view from the Court paled to insignificance.

If only Nina had—had married him of her own free will, if she had loved him instead of detesting, fearing him, so much that she had preferred to risk her life rather than live alone with him—ah, well, with what different eye he would have looked at these possessions of his, how happy he would have been sharing them with her!

A footman, bringing in Vane's portmanteau, aroused him, and with a sigh he turned from the window, had his wash, and went down.

Julian was waiting for him in the hall; and Vane, throwing off his gloom, led him to the dining room, a stately apartment large enough to be called a banqueting hall.

Vane motioned Julian to the bottom of the table and Mr. Holland to the side, and Prance and a couple of footmen served the lunch. Mr. Holland was still all a-quiver with pleasant excitement.

"I hope your lordship—and Mr. Julian—are intending a long stay?" he said. "I noticed that you did not bring much luggage——"

Vane shrugged his shoulders. "Oh, thank you, Mr. Holland!" he said. "I don't think we know; a few days, perhaps——"

Mr. Holland's face fell.

"Oh, I hope longer than that, Lord Lesborough!" he said earnestly. "Everybody is expecting—hoping that you are going to settle down at the Court; in fact, I happen to know that some—er—preparations, something in the way of welcoming your lordship, are——"

Vane turned off his dismay with a laugh.

"Ought to settle down, eh, Mr. Holland?" he said. "Well, we'll see."

"You have been traveling so much, been abroad so long," suggested Mr. Holland, as if eager to make excuses for him, "you find it rather hard to settle down. Of course, we've all heard of the wreck——"

Vane looked down.

"Yes, yes; bad business being wrecked. Prance, is this the wonderful claret? It's like yours, not a bit better, anyway, Julian."

"It's the same," said Julian, nodding across his glass.

"Lord Fanworthy desired me to let him know when you arrived, Lord Lesborough," said Mr. Holland.

Vane nodded.

"Lord Fanworthy, of the Grange," he explained to Julian. "Our nearest neighbor. He used to be kind to me; I liked him. We'll go over and see him, eh? In fact, there'll be a lot of visiting both ways, won't there, Mr. Holland?"

Mr. Holland nodded cheerfully.

"Yes, yes; certainly, my lord. Everybody is delighted to hear that you are—er—home; the Lisles are——"

"Place called the Moat," said Vane to Julian.

"And the Denningtons——"

"Forget the name of their house," remarked Vane.

"Limmington," supplied Mr. Holland.

"Ah, yes, Limmington. And there are the Chases, and the Protheroes. Plenty of society for you, Julian."

Mr. Holland looked slightly puzzled. It was as if his lordship and his cousin had things in common; but he rambled on with local names and local gossip, and Vane listened—or looked and nodded as if he did—and Julian smiled his soft, pleasant smile; he was certainly listening.

The lunch was over at last, and Mr. Holland, looking beseechingly at Vane, said:

"If your lordship would kindly give me half an hour, say an hour, in the library——"

"Not if I know it," retorted Vane, with a laugh and a shake of the head. "No, no! I remember those half hours in the library you and my uncle used to go in for. Not to-day, Mr. Holland. Have mercy on us. I want to show Mr. Julian over the place. It's his first visit, you know. Come on, Julian! Got one of those cigars of yours to spare? Ought to have brought them down——"

"Cigars, my lord?" said Prance, promptly appearing at his elbow with a box; but Vane declined them, pleasantly enough.

"Thanks; rather have one of Mr. Julian's, Prance; I've tried 'em. Though these are all right, no doubt. Come, Julian."

Prance held a light for their cigars, and the two young men went out, with Vane's arm linked in his cousin's.

Mr. Holland filled his glass and sighed, and, as if emboldened by the sigh, Prance remarked gravely:

"It's good to have his lordship at the Court, Mr. Holland. His lordship's looking well, sir?"

Mr. Holland frowned and fidgeted in his nervous way with his claret glass.

"Well? Did you think so? Well, yes, perhaps; but—but he's much changed, Prance. Can't say exactly how, but he looks—looks as if he'd got something on his mind. Fancy I saw a speck or two of gray at his temples—my fancy, perhaps."

"No, Mr. Holland, sir, I noticed it myself," said Prance solemnly. "But from all accounts his lordship's been through a great deal since we had the honor of seeing him last; and that may account for the change in him. He certainly *is* different—more grave and absent-minded than I remember him. No doubt it's that wreck, Mr. Holland."

"Yes, yes; I dessay," assented Holland, slightly encouraged. "In one thing he isn't changed: he's just as restless and disinclined for business. I do hope that he'll pay some attention to the estate. It's a tremendous responsibility for me, and if I can't get him to give me——" Then, suddenly remembering that he was perhaps a trifle too confidential with the butler, he said, with an abrupt change of tone: "Cigar, if you please, Prance. Thanks. I shall go into the library when I've finished it, and shall be there if his lordship should want me."

Vane and Julian paused in the hall, and Julian looked round at the figures in armor, the trophies, the tattered flags depending from the vaulted roof, the cabinets full of curios, the pictures, most of them family portraits, on the oak-paneled walls.

"Fine hall, eh?" said Vane.

Julian nodded.

"A bit—stagy, theatrical, isn't it? But I suppose it's because they put this thing on the stage so well. Portrait of our uncle. Poor chap! He led a devilish solitary life, I'm afraid. I wish he'd married——"

Julian glanced sideways at him, at first incredulously and with suspicion, then with genuine surprise.

"There's a fellow who's awfully like you, Julian," Vane went on. "Wonderful how features perpetuate themselves. That gentleman in the armor and a helmet, which appears to be two sizes too large for him, was our great fighting ancestor, Sir Rupert—the peerage didn't come until after his time: we got it, I fancy, for political services; crossed from one side of the House to the other: ratted, in other words. Or was it because the monarch of that period took a fancy to a then Lady Mannering? I forget; but you'll find it in the County History in the library. We'll go there presently. Come into the drawing-room. Prance and Mrs. Field like to call it 'the state apartments.' We used to entertain royalty, you know."

Julian's face flushed, in fact, he was in a glow all over, as he surveyed the magnificent suite of rooms which terminated in a conservatory large enough to be called a palm house.

"It is superb," he said, and he stole a glance at Vane's calm and rather indifferent countenance. "You ought to be a proud man, Vane."

"Eh?" said Vane. "Oh, ah, yes! Yes; it's a fine place; but—but—it's rather inconveniently large, isn't it? Fancy sitting here after dinner! In solitary grandeur, with one hundred—two hundred—how many are there?—wax candles blinking at you! We only burn candles here; no gas allowed. Shall we put on the electric light, Julian? Lord, I think our poor uncle would turn in his grave! Come on! Music room. Uncle hated music. But it's all there, piano—there's an organ in the gallery upstairs—harp, guitar, sackbut, and psaltery. Oh, by George, this will be in your way, won't it? You can pipe and sing to your heart's content—and mine. What a voice that is of yours! Yes; this shall be your special department."

Julian glanced at him curiously, but said nothing.

"Here we are in the library. There's the chair the poor old man used to sit in when he lectured me. 'Duties and responsibilities of property.' 'Parliament the proper place for a Mannering, not wandering like a tramp over the face of the civilized and uncivilized world.' 'Extravagance the curse of the age.' 'Country gradually but surely hastening to ruin and decay,' et cetera, et cetera. Poor old fellow, as if we're the kind of men to stop it. Fine lot of books! They're in your line, too, Julian. By the way"—he stopped and looked at Julian with a grim smile—" 'pears to me that most of it, up to the present, is more in your line than mine. Ah, but this suits me a little better."

They had entered the gun room, and, for the first time, Vane looked about him with appreciation and satisfaction.

"They've kept it up very well. By George, there's the gun I used to shoot with when I was a boy!" He handled it lovingly. "And there are my foils and boxing gloves. Can you box, Julian?" He held out a pair, but Julian shook his head and smiled a negative. "Fence?"

"A little," admitted Julian.

"Catch hold!" said Vane, tossing him a foil and a mask.

Julian hesitated a moment, then slipped on the mask.

"Ready? Right!" cried Vane, putting himself into the first position. They fenced for a few minutes in a perfunctory way, then Vane, warming, began to press. Julian paused, parried skillfully, and presently slipped under Vane's guard and touched him.

Vane flushed, but laughed—laughed more lightly than Julian had hitherto heard him.

"Bravo! that was smart! Yes; you fence 'a little,' as you play and sing 'a little'! My dear fellow, you handle 'em like—like a Frenchman. Let's have another turn."

"Oh—shall we?" said Julian.

They fell to again, but this time, though Julian could have touched Vane more than once, it was Vane's button that dabbed against Julian's waistcoat.

"Mine, that bout," said Vane. "But two out of three, eh?"

But Julian shrugged his shoulders and took off his mask. "Too hot," he said carelessly. "My dear Vane, you would pink me seven times out of nine."

"That's your modesty," said Vane. "Get rid of it; it will be your ruin, as it has been mine."

The exercise, the trial of skill, had warmed his heart for a moment—because for that moment he had been able to forget.

"Come on, or are you bored?"

"No, no!" said Julian.

"Let me see," said Vane, looking round; they were in a small passage. "There's a way out here——Oh, to the old part of the place, to old castle. Is it open? Hi!" to a passing footman. "Bring me the key, will you, please?"

While the man went for the key, Vane and Julian lit their cigars.

"Phew! rather musty, isn't it?" said Vane, as the door opened stiffly.

They passed into a narrow passage and under an arched way into a room with closed shutters. Vane went to them, stumbling over a chair, and drew them open.

"Years since I was here," he said. "This is one of the old rooms. Notice the thickness of the walls! Dampness, isn't it? Smells like a vault. Don't suppose it's been opened for—oh, goodness knows how long! Nice old furniture, isn't it? Pity to leave it here to spoil. Look at that picture over the fireplace; it's spotted with mould."

Julian looked round with an interested air.

"It's a grand old room," he said. He went to the window. It looked out upon a small paved courtyard, deserted, neglected, and weed-grown, with walls so high that they shut out all view from the windows. A door, green with moss and lichen, was the only outlet from the court.

"Quaint, isn't it?" said Vane. "This is called the Wizard's Room. Portrait of the wizard over fireplace, I should say. Looks forbidding enough for a wizard, at any rate," he added, and Julian, with his back to the window, looked up at the mould-spotted face scowling down at them.

"I like it," he said. "The room, I mean. It's so quaint, and old-fashioned, and remote. Ah!" his face lit up as if an idea had suddenly struck him.

"What is it?" inquired Vane.

Julian turned away.

"Oh, I was only thinking that it would make a good laboratory," he said carelessly.

"By George! So it would!" assented Vane, with a laugh. "Right away from the rest of the house—I suppose that even the awful smells I noticed at your place wouldn't get through that passage and that thick old door? We could put another door, a baize affair, warranted smell-proof, couldn't we? See here, Julian; why not have this room for your—what do you call it?— laboratory?"

Julian's face flushed and his lids drooped.

"My dear Vane, you speak as if—as if I were the owner, as if I had the right to dispose of, to choose, any room in Lesborough Court——"

Vane regarded him with a grave smile.

"So you are, so you can," he said. "You will be the owner——"

Julian's face grew pale, and he smiled a polite contradiction.

"As I told you, I shall never marry. You are the heir, the next earl. See here, Julian: let us understand each other. I want you to make the Court your home—that is, if you care to do so, and while you wish to do so. You don't imagine that I intend living here alone? No, thanks! I know what loneliness, solitude, means——" He broke off suddenly. "I want you to understand that the Court will be yours, and that you have as much right to live here as, well, as I have. Make the room your laboratory, by all means."

"But——"

"But me no buts," interrupted Vane. "I mean it. I've got a trick of saying what I mean. I—well, I'm not the sort of man to settle down anywhere. I'm a restless, Wandering Jew kind of fellow, and I shall probably be off on the tramp again presently. Now, you—well, I fancy you are quite a different sort of man; you are a 'home bird,' as the song says. Fond of music and science and all that sort of thing. Good! this is evidently the place for you."

"But——" began Julian again; but Vane made a slight gesture.

"Oh, don't think that I want to interfere with your independence, or to be a bore and a drag on you. Not a bit of it. You can keep up that old place of yours by the Thames, if you like. I should; it's a queer, quaint old diggings; but make the Court your home. Now, don't argue. I'm a poor hand at arguing, and invariably lose my temper. You can send for that old servant of yours—what's her name, by the way?"

"Deborah," said Julian. His brows were knit, and he stood with drooped lids and tightened lips; he seemed to be reflecting so intensely as scarcely to be breathing.

"Deborah; name seems to fit her. Well, send for her, if you like. In fact—there! do just as you like, and we shall get on very well together. Let's get out of this, shall we? If you decide to turn the room into a laboratory, it will want thoroughly doing up——"

"Oh, no," said Julian, glancing round almost lovingly. "Just clearing out and cleaning. The fireplace would need some little alteration. An intelligent mason——"

Vane laughed.

"First, find your mason," he said, "then sound him for intelligence; result——" he shrugged his shoulders. "We can get out through that door into the stable courtyard. Why, where is the door leading from this room?" he broke off to remark.

Julian looked round. "There does not appear to be a door. Perhaps it has been bricked up or paneled over."

"Ah, p'r'aps so," said Vane indifferently, and he led the way out by the door at which they had entered.

"My department again," he said, with a laugh, as they entered the stables. "But perhaps you ride as well as you fence, Julian."

Julian shook his head.

"I'm not much of a horseman," he said.

"Modesty again!" retorted Vane. "Well, you must pick your mount. There used to be a fairish lot of animals——Ah, Dodson," as the coachman came hurrying across the yard from his cottage to receive his new master, "how are you? We are just looking round, but in a hurried kind of way only. Got anything worth looking at?"

Mr. Dodson hastened to display his animals.

"Hem, the carriage horses are all right; and that's a decent mare, Dodson; so's the chestnut; and the cob in the end stall looks a nice little lad. The hunters—well, well—hem!"

"Just so, my lord," said Mr. Dodson, with respectful eagerness. "There's nothing here fit to carry your lordship. The late earl gave up hunting long ago, as your lordship knows——"

"Well, keep your eyes open, and I'll do the same, and we may pick up two or three likely ones. Meanwhile—chestnut quiet?"

"Quite, my lord. I bred him myself, and broke him."

"Good; then he'll do for Mr. Julian, here—my cousin, Mr. Julian Shore, Dodson."

Mr. Dodson touched his cap to Julian, who remonstrated with Vane. "Oh, but—my dear Vane! You will surely keep the chestnut for yourself——"

"Oh, the mare will do for me!" said Vane carelessly. "She's a good sort, though not so handsome as the chestnut——"

"Nor so quiet, my lord; a little bit of temper," put in Dodson.

"So I see," said Vane. "I noticed her eyes and ears when I went up to her just now. But I like a bit of temper. Anyhow, I'll give her a trial. We'll just glance at the coachhouse——"

"Ah, we want a new carriage or two, my lord," said Mr. Dodson.

"Just so, just so. Ah, well, plenty of time," said Vane, as he cast a comprehensive eye round. "Glad to see you looking so well, Dodson."

"Thank you, my lord, and the same to your lordship, if I may make so bold," said the gratified Dodson, with a touch of his cap.

"We'll go under the arch and round to the front," said Vane, as they walked away. "Nice fellow—Dodson; remember him putting me on my first pony. Hello, who's this—Fanworthy, by George!"

They had passed under the tall archway and entered upon the drive along which an open landau was coming toward the house. An elderly man, with the air of a sportsman and an aristocrat, was the sole occupant, and as he caught sight of the two young men he leaned forward and waved his hand.

"Ah, Vane!" he exclaimed. "What luck to just catch you! I heard the news of your arrival, and drove over on the chance of seeing you."

"The luck's mine, Lord Fanworthy," said Vane. "It's very kind of you, very! Let me introduce my cousin—Mr. Julian Shore."

Lord Fanworthy raised his hat with old-world courtesy.

"Come into the house," said Vane; but Lord Fanworthy shook his head.

"No, no. Can't! Against positive orders. Her ladyship emphatically bade me not leave the carriage. 'If he is there, just tell him that he is to come back with you: that I say so.' Her very words, Vane, I assure you."

"In that case, there's only one thing to do: obey," said Vane.

"That's right, my boy!" said Lord Fanworthy approvingly. "Pray get in, Mr. Shore; my wife will be delighted to see you. It's not far. What a beautiful day for your return, Vane! By Jove, you must have a rare budget to tell us! Not a word till you get home! You're looking—yes, well! Been knocked about a bit, eh! Thought so." Then he turned to Julian. "I remember your father, of course, Mr. Shore. He may have spoken of me?"

Julian colored slightly. "I am sorry to say that he did not, Lord Fanworthy. My father never spoke of—old times."

"Ah, yes, yes, quite so!" assented Lord Fanworthy quickly. "Great nuisance, family feuds! You have a look of the Mannerings, Mr. Shore. I think I should have known you as one of them, even if I had met you elsewhere."

The three men chatted as the horses spun along the well-kept road, and, after a short drive, they reached the Grange. Lord Fanworthy led them into the drawing-room, calling "Em'ly!" as he went. Lady Fanworthy was seated in a low chair by the window, knitting. She had been a reigning beauty; she was beautiful still, with her silvery hair, wonderful complexion, and the gray eyes which were almost as brilliant—and far keener—than those of most girls. She held out her snow-white and exquisitely shaped hand to Vane; and nodded and smiled, her eyes flashing over him as if they were taking in every feature of his face; then they passed from him to Julian, inquiringly, and as keenly.

"It's good to see you, Vane," she said; and there was almost a maternal note in the low, clear voice; for Vane, as a lad, had been a favorite of hers, and, with the tact for which she was famous, she had often slipped in between his uncle and him, and prevented a quarrel. "And it was good of you to come so quickly. And this is——" Vane introduced Julian, and she bowed and smiled graciously. "And so you have come into your own, Vane? And it feels strange—at first?"

"It does, Lady Fanworthy," said Vane, as he took the seat beside her, to which she had motioned him.

"And you are going to settle down, to be a model landlord and a pattern peer?"

"No," said Vane. "Part's already filled," and he looked toward Lord Fanworthy, who had gone to the next room to show Julian the view.

"Godfrey will be glad to have you at the Court," said her ladyship. "He was always fond of you. And I——So that is Julian Shore?" Her voice scarcely dropped, but it was so soft as to be inaudible to the others. "A handsome young man; darker than the Mannerings usually are."

"Yes; he's quite an Adonis," said Vane. "And an extremely good fellow. I hope you'll like him. We are great friends already, though we only met a day or two ago."

"I will see," she said, with a swift, searching glance at Julian. "But I want to talk about you. Where have you been? No! are you well, happy, Vane?"

His eyes fell before her brilliant ones, which seemed to reach his sadly tried heart.

"Fit as a fiddle, my dear lady; almost as fit as Lord Fanworthy, there. And I am so glad to see you looking so well. Not a day older."

She raised her level brows. "Why should I be? My dear Vane, at my age, women grow younger nowadays. Where have you been not to know that! And you are well and—happy?"

Vane's eyes dropped, then he raised them, but with an effort, for this old lady was a difficult one to deceive.

"As happy as I deserve," he said smilingly.

"And you have been traveling a great deal, and, if rumor speaks the truth, have had some adventures."

Vane nodded, his lips tightening. "Yes," he said, "all sorts of adventures. You still stick to your knitting, I see, Lady Fanworthy."

It was enough for her; and she asked no more questions.

"Here's the tea," she said, as the butler brought it in. "But, of course, you'll stay to dinner. Godfrey shall send for your things——"

But Vane declined.

"I've ordered dinner at the Court," he said, "and Prance would break his heart if we didn't turn up on this, the first night."

She nodded approvingly. "Quite right, Vane."

"But, see," he said, "it will be rather lonely for us two bachelors. Now, if you want to be as kind as you always used to be, you bring Lord Fanworthy to dine with us!"

She did not hesitate a moment.

"Yes," she said smoothly.

The other two men came to the tea table and her ladyship conversed with Julian. She asked no questions, but almost unconsciously he found himself telling her that he was unmarried, that he lived alone, that he had no profession, and was content with a small income; indeed, nearly all the details which another person would only have extracted by a series of categorical questions; and he did not make the discovery until the two young men were going home in the landau.

"A wonderful woman!" Vane remarked. "You admired her, of course? She used to be a great beauty; and she is as clever as she is beautiful."

"Yes; she's clever," said Julian absently, as he reflected on the way in which her ladyship had "pumped" him.

"Yes; she used to play an important part in the political world," Vane went on. "Kept what used to be called a 'salon'; entertained the people of her husband's party: Fanworthy was in the Cabinet. They say that she kept the party in power for six months longer than it ought to have been. Don't understand politics myself. She was very good to me when I was a lad—they both were—and I like her, naturally. I don't know any one to whom I'd sooner go, if I were in trouble, or in a mess. I think you'll like her, Julian."

"I am sure I shall," said Julian, with an admirably feigned tone of conviction.

"Oh, Prance," said Vane, as the butler came to meet them, "Lord and Lady Fanworthy dine here to-night. And light up the music room, will you? Right!"

It was more than a pleasant dinner, for Lady Fanworthy made it a charming one. In spite of himself Julian was drawn within the circle of the spell of her brilliant eyes, and the clear, low voice in which she said the wittiest things, with the air of an innocent girl.

"We won't let you go all alone to that Madam Tussaud of a drawing-room, Lady Fanworthy," Vane said, when the dessert was over. "We'll go into the music room. Julian, here, is a tiptop performer. Send the coffee in there, please, will you, Prance! You won't mind our cigarettes, I know, Lady Fanworthy?"

"Not if you give me one for myself," she said.

Vane led her, with a certain courtesy which he did not usually display, to the easiest of the chairs, and, when the cigarettes were smoked, took Julian by the arms and gently pushed him toward the piano.

"Sing us that thing you sang to me at your rooms, will you?" he said; and he went and seated himself in a low chair beside Lady Fanworthy's, and, with his arms folded behind his head, listened, with half-closed eyes; he was back on the island again, to be sure.

Julian sang three songs in response to Lord Fanworthy's eager murmur of admiration and delight, and Vane's almost proprietorial "Go on, Julian!"

The light from the shaded candles fell full on the performer's dark face, and Lady Fanworthy watched it steadily.

"Julian's a regular nightingale, isn't he?" said Vane, in a low voice. "Isn't it a fine voice?"

The old lady withdrew her eyes slowly.

"Yes," she said. "He is very good-looking, and has a fine voice, and quite pretty manners. Did you ever see the black panther at the Zoo, Vane?"

Vane stared at her, then laughed.

"The black panther when it is asleep, or has just been fed, and is purring and licking itself."

Vane colored with momentary annoyance; then he laughed again.

"This is the first time I have ever known you to be—unjust and hard," he said, in a low voice.

The brilliant eyes regarded him steadily, gravely.

"How do you know that I am—unjust and hard now?" she asked, with a slight imitation of his voice.

Vane moved, with a gesture of impatience and deprecation.

"He's too good a fellow, is Julian, to be compared to a tiger," he said.

"Panther, I said," retorted Lady Fanworthy sweetly. "And a black one. Thank you so very much, Mr. Shore. You have a charming voice, charming. Godfrey, we must not rob these young people of their beauty sleep: it is late."

Lord Fanworthy was glowing all over with satisfaction as they drove home.

"Splendid thing for the county, Vane's succession. I'll get him to take the hounds! And, I say, Em'ly, what a delightful young fellow, this Julian Shore is, eh?"

"Delightful," responded Lady Fanworthy; but as she spoke she looked at her radiant husband with the tender pity with which the clever wife tolerates the spouse whom she loves, notwithstanding his duller intelligence.

"There go the happiest pair I ever met," remarked Vane, as the two men sat in their smoking jackets in the billiard room.

"They seem devoted to each other," said Julian. "I suppose the man who said that marriages were made in heaven must have had such a couple in his mind."

"Marriages are made in heaven, but they smuggle a very fair counterfeit from quite another place," observed Vane absently. "How is it you never married, Julian?" As the question left his lips he would have liked to have checked it, for the subject was a sore one for him; but the question was asked, and he waited for the answer.

Julian knocked the ash from his cigarette, and looked before him, under his drooping lids.

"I don't know," he replied, as if he himself were wondering. "I suppose it is because I have never seen the woman I wanted to make my wife."

"You have never been in—love?" asked Vane, though he could have kicked himself for the banality of the thing.

"No," said Julian, after another pause. "No, I suppose not!"

Vane laughed grimly.

"You suppose not," he said. "You certainly have not, or you'd have known it. Bed? Right!"

Julian went to his room, but it was some time before he went to bed. It was a moonlight night, and he leaned against the window, and looked at the park, and the hills beyond, the land that represented to some small extent the vast wealth into which his cousin had come; looked at it with an expression in his eyes which, if she could have seen it, would have justified Lady Fanworthy's comparison.

But it was not the black panther asleep, or placidly satisfied and purring. There was a hungry, restless look in the dark eyes, and the white, even teeth gleamed, as the lips closed and unclosed with a nervous movement.

They stayed three days at the Court, and during the whole of that time Vane treated Julian as the heir, and "did him honor," as the significant old phrase has it; so that the servants, even Mr. Holland, came to regard Mr. Julian Shore as almost of equal importance to the earl himself.

Before they started to return to London, Julian gave orders for the cleaning and doing up of the Wizard's Room, and, at Vane's suggestion, even instructed a mason to alter the fireplace.

They reached London just before tea time, and Vane, suddenly remembering his promise to Judith Orme, said:

"Engaged this afternoon, Julian?"

Julian replied in the negative.

"Well, then, come with me to call on a lady, will you?"

It would be as well, if he were going to call on Judith, that he should make the visit as conventional and void of significance as possible, by taking a friend with him. A year ago the proposal of a tête-à-tête with Judith Orme would have set his heart beating; but now——There is safety in numbers, though it be only two.

"Who is it?" asked Julian.

"Miss Orme," replied Vane.

"*The* Miss Orme?"

Vane nodded.

"The very Miss Orme," he assented. "You know her?"

"No; I have not even seen her," said Julian; "but, of course, I have heard of her; who hasn't?"

"Who, indeed?" said Vane dryly.

A neat maidservant admitted them and took them upstairs. Judith was seated at the piano, but at the sound of Vane's name—he had not given Julian's—she rose quickly. But at sight of Julian she paused in her advance, and the color of resentment rose to her beautiful face. It was there only for an instant; the next she came forward with outstretched hand, her sapphire eyes smiling, her lips half parted.

"How do you do, Lord Lesborough? Did you meet my father? He has only just gone out. I'm so sorry!"

"I've brought my cousin, Mr. Julian Shore," said Vane.

The smile shone on him, and her hand went out to him, and, as Julian took it, he drew a long breath and raised his lids slowly, as a man does who is trying to hide some deep, intense emotion.

What had happened to him? A moment or two ago, before he had entered the room, he had been master of himself, sole possessor of his soul. And now? His dark eyes sought the lovely face, and all the world seemed to stand still, as if it were gazing with him, and listening with him to the exquisite voice, so low and sweet, so full of music, so sad, and yet with a subtle suggestion of tenderness and passion.

He threw his head up, as if he were trying to throw off the impression, the spell, under which he had fallen as suddenly, as helplessly, as if he had been mesmerized.

"We've just come from the Court," Vane was saying in cool, conventional tones. "Mr. Shore and I have been playing bachelor hall there."

She turned her eyes to Julian, and smiled, and he felt a thrill, the thrill of a sudden passion which sways a man, as a reed is swayed by the wind, the passion against whose tyranny the strongest man is as weak as the veriest babe. Unconsciously he moistened his lips with his tongue, for the power of speech seemed to have deserted him.

"My first visit," he said, scarcely knowing what he said.

"Yes?"

That was all, just the one word; but in Julian Shore's ears it was like a note of heavenly music.

CHAPTER XIV
NINA'S GOOD SAMARITAN

Nina had, at last, found her good Samaritan.

"To think of your finding the way to the very street, and me just driving up at the very moment!" Polly exclaimed, the next morning, with infinite satisfaction. "That's what they call the long arm of coincidence, isn't it? Anyhow, whatever it was, I'm jolly glad. You look better after your night's rest, dear, and as beautiful as ever. What luck for me that I haven't gone to the Provinces! Mr. Harcourt's taken a London theatre. The Momus, you know, and 'My Lady Pride' is going strong. Now, do try to eat some breakfast, there's a dear, good girl! And don't sigh so! You're safe, and with a friend—if you don't mind having me for one."

Nina tried to express her gratitude, but Polly waved it aside with the hand in which she held her needle; she was hard at work trimming a hat.

"Don't you talk like that, Miss Wood; and you wouldn't if you knew how proud I was to have you here. Why, too, didn't you see that I'd taken a fancy to you on board the ship? I've thought of you ever so many times since, and wondered what had become of you, and whether we should ever meet again. Bother this feather; it won't go right! And now; you're actually sitting there—and going to sit there, leastways stop here with me, for a long time—for always, if you like. But, Lor' bless me, I know that's nonsense! You'll be off to your friends directly and forget all about Polly Bainford—no, I don't mean that! You're not the sort to forget."

"No, I shall not forget you and your great kindness, Polly," said Nina. "Won't you call me Decima, please?"

Polly jumped up, to the infinite peril of the hat, and kissed her.

"Of course I will! I've been dying to do so, but I thought you wouldn't like it. You see you're a swell, a lady, and I'm only a poor girl."

Nina sighed woefully.

"You cannot be so poor as I, or so friendless," she said. "I haven't a penny in the world, or a friend——"

Polly jumped up again, and taking an old tobacco jar from the mantelshelf emptied its contents on the table.

"You've half of that, anyhow," she said emphatically, "and you've got one friend, at any rate. There, don't cry"—for Nina's eyes had filled with tears. "There's nothing to cry about in being poor. If I haven't been quite without a penny, I've been pretty near it. Something always turns up just when things are at their worst. There's a kind of luck, chance, in it. It's always just when you think you're going under that a friendly wave carries you on shore. I'm your friendly wave."

"Yes, indeed!" said Nina. "But, Polly, dear, I could not be a burden to you. I cannot stay and be a drag on you. I must find some work——" she sighed bitterly. "How easy it is to say that, but how difficult it is to find the work!"

She gave Polly an account of her experiences with the agents, and Polly snorted wrathfully.

"I should like to punch that young bounder's head!" she said. "The colossal impudence he must have had! To think that you'd be seen out with him! But there are plenty of things you can do. Let me see. You wouldn't, for instance, like *the* profession, I suppose?"

"What is *the* profession?" asked Nina eagerly.

"Why, the theatrical—mine—ours!" replied Polly with surprise. "Don't you know that it's the only profession worth speaking about?"

Nina shook her head and smiled.

"I'm afraid I've no talent for the stage," she said. "And—and I don't think I should like it."

"Really?" said Polly, with a surprise that was flattering to the dramatic profession. "That's a pity, for you're cut out for it. Such a face and figure! Oh, you may smile; but in my opinion you're one of the prettiest girls I've met; and Mr. Harcourt would agree with me if he saw you. Well, of all the stupid hats! And yet I thought I'd got the one I saw in the window quite fixed in my mind. I went in and bought the materials; you see you get the hat so much cheaper if you trim it yourself. But I suppose I've forgotten just how the trimming went." She put the hat on her head, and, surveying herself in the glass, uttered an exclamation of impatient disgust, and made a grimace at herself in the mirror. "I wouldn't be seen dead in a ditch with it!"

"Let me look at it. Give it to me. May I try?" said Nina.

Polly tossed it to her, and, leaning back in her chair, watched her as she twisted the feather this way and that, and arranged and rearranged the ribbon. At last Nina held it out deprecatingly, and Polly tried it on.

"Oh, you dear!" she exclaimed joyfully. "That's splendid! It isn't quite like the one in the shop, but it's twenty times more pretty and stylish. I've never had such a hat; it's a duck and a darling! And how quickly you did it! Why, I've been hours and hours fumbling at it!"

"I'm glad you like it," said Nina. "I used to trim my own hats and make my own dresses——"

"And no wonder, if they were as good as this!" said Polly. "Why"—she stopped suddenly and pursed her lips—"I'm going to rehearsal in that hat, and if I don't knock the rest of the girls with it, well—I'm afraid I must go now, dear. You won't feel lonely while I'm away? And you won't fret? Promise!"

"I shan't feel so lonely if you will leave me something to do," said Nina. "Isn't there another hat, for instance, or a blouse or a dress that wants mending?"

Polly dragged a blouse from a box under the bed and slipped it on.

"That was made for me, if you please!" she cried with infinite scorn. "Observe the fit! You can't tell the back from the front, can you? And I paid twenty-two and six for it; I did, indeed!"

"It wants taking in here," said Nina.

"It wants burning!" retorted Polly indignantly. "You don't mean to say you can alter it?"

"I can try. Let me, while you are away, Polly."

She set to work at it, immediately Polly had gone, and in her pleasure and satisfaction in doing even a little for the girl, who had not only befriended her but bestowed her affection upon her, she found some relief of mind and spirit. She tried to think only of the present and her terribly vague future, but every now and then, in the quietude of the room, the picture of the past rose before her, and one man's figure stood out prominently in it.

Polly was away about three hours, and when she returned she carried a hat box in her hand. Her face was flushed, her eyes were sparkling.

"Not done the blouse, really?" she cried.

"Oh, yes, some time ago. Slip off your jacket and let me try it on. Is that better? Oh, I hope so!"

"It fits like a miracle!" said Polly solemnly. "I tell you what it is, Decima, you are a born genius. And look here! What do you think I've got here?"

She whipped out a hat and some materials.

"See that! I told you I should knock 'em! Why, the girls were like a flock of bees round me the moment I stepped on the stage. 'Oh, what a pretty hat, Polly! Where did you get it?' and that sort of thing. They were positively green with envy. Then I worked the idea that struck me just before I went out, and I told 'em I'd get as pretty a one for 'em for twelve-and-six. They wouldn't believe me at first; but Jessie Green said she'd trust me and fished out the money there and then. I told 'em my terms were cash, you know. So I bought the things as I came home—the same shop; it's a cheap but stylish one—and here you are. Hat and materials cost eight-and-nine; profit, three-and-three. But perhaps you don't think it's enough——" doubtfully.

Nina actually laughed up at her.

"Give it to me!" she said. "Why, it will take no time. And how pretty it is! Oh, I do hope I shall trim it to please her!"

Polly snorted. "Trust you for that! Jessie's bound to like it; and, if she does, the other girls will want to have their hats trimmed, for she's one of the best-dressed of our lot. I told her I'd got a swell milliner who'd do the things for us on the cheap."

"What a clever girl you are—notwithstanding the fib," said Nina, laughing again. "I think this ribbon ought to go like this."

"It won't go any way until you've had some lunch," said Polly, taking the hat from her. "Oh, I know your sort at sight; you're one of those girls who'd work themselves to death if they weren't stopped at it. You've done a hat and a blouse to-day, and that's—oh, don't color up and look at me like that; I'm not going to offer to pay you for them!"

"I should think not!" said Nina indignantly.

Polly allowed her to go to work soon after lunch, but, though the hat was finished, Polly refused to take it with her to the theatre that evening.

"Not much!" she said knowingly. "What! Give the show away! No, no! Friend so full up with work that she couldn't think of even looking at the hat to-day. Oh, no. If you want to get on in any business, you mustn't make yourself too cheap; you must give yourself airs and put on frills. Why, don't you know that real swells, ladies and duchesses, have gone into the millinery business? Some of 'em run afternoon tea shops. Last would suit me better; more change and society, don't you know. But perhaps you wouldn't like that so well?"

"No, I think not," assented Nina.

"So I thought. I know your sort. You're the 'humble violet shrinking in the shade.' There ain't many of 'em about nowadays," added the shrewd Polly, "more's the pity!"

She brought home another order—a toque this time—and Nina worked at it—for some reason inexplicable to the male mind a toque is a more elaborate performance than a hat—all the next day. Polly approved of it, but looked at Decima with stern scrutiny.

"You're working yourself to death. And you're thinking all the time." Nina colored quickly. "Look here, you want a change. Come to the theatre to-night. I'll pass you in."

Nina shrank from the offer for a while, but finally gave in. Polly got her a seat in the upper circle—a back seat with a pillar to dodge—and went off behind.

Nina felt strange at first. She had never been to a theatre alone before, and the troublous times she had passed through made her nervous and self-conscious. But presently she grew calmer.

Mr. Harcourt was a liberal manager and had "presented" a first piece to his audience. "Presented" is not altogether inappropriate; for certainly the one-act "comedy" was not worth paying for. It was supposed to be sentimental, with a touch of comic humor and pathos. Unfortunately the comic and the pathetic changed places now and again, and the sentiment either irritated Nina or made her want to laugh. The rest of the audience stared at it with an

Arctic indifference or guyed it under their breath; and when, the curtain fell upon the forced situations, the forced dialogue, and the wooden acting—for not the best actor or actress alive could talk the stuff set down for them and remain flesh and blood—the people yawned and the male part promptly went to the bars for the refreshment they sorely needed. But it was very different when the band struck up the overture to the musical farce. The thing was well done, and Nina enjoyed it. She recognized Polly among the chorus, and once or twice caught a scarcely perceptible nod from her in the direction of the upper circle.

"Well, what did you think of it?" asked Polly, when they got home. "All alive, isn't it, and it goes with a bang, eh?"

Nina expressed her admiration for the big piece, but was silent about the first; and Polly nodded, as if Nina had criticised it.

"Yes, the first piece, 'For a Sister's Sake,' is feeble, isn't it?"

"Yes," said Nina, with deference. "The idea is a very pretty and effective one, but they talk——"

"Like people in a book, one of the old frumpish books, I know."

"And they're never surprised at the most extraordinary coincidences," continued Nina, warming to her subject. "Nothing astonishes them. When the man comes back from America with a million of money nobody asks him how he made it in four months; when the heroine gives up her sister to the hero they all take it as a matter of course, as if it didn't matter——"

"And it doesn't—to the audience," said Polly.

"And the little girl——"

" 'Shall I be a hangel when I die, mother?' " quoted Polly. "Yes; if any sensible mother had a child like that she'd put its head in a bucket."

"How is it that Mr. Harcourt, who must be a clever man, puts on such a silly first piece?" asked Nina.

Polly shrugged her shoulders. "Oh, they don't think of anything but 'My Lady Pride.' Anything's good enough to play the people in. It's only the pit and gallery and a sprinkle in the upper circle."

"Poor people! What have they done that they should be bored to death?" said Nina.

"Oh, well," responded Polly, "perhaps it makes 'em all the keener to see the big piece. See? But, all the same, I'm sorry for the people who play in it. Miss Tracey, for instance—who plays the idiotic sister—can act awfully well if she has a part to suit her."

The toque was as great a success as the preceding "confections" Nina had turned out, and nearly every day Polly brought home a fresh order. She put the price up, of course, and the joint earnings of the two girls enabled them not only to live better, but to go for little outings in the daytime; so that Nina's face began to lose its sharpness and something of the old light began to creep back to her eyes. Polly made her promise not to work at the millinery at night, and Nina passed the time while Polly was at the theatre in reading—and dreaming of the past.

One night Polly asked her to go to the theatre to see Miss Tracey, who wanted a new hat, and insisted upon giving the instructions herself. "We can't have her here; they'd all want to come." Nina hesitated, but at last consented. "Behind the scenes" is always somewhat awe-inspiring to the novice, and Nina made a nervous grab at Polly's hand as they passed among the forest of wings and "back cloths" to Miss Tracey's dressing room.

That young lady was making up for the idiotic first piece; but, after a stare of something like surprise, she received Nina in the friendly "hail-fellow-well-met" fashion of *the* profession, and explained what it was she wanted. The call boy summoned her in the midst of her elaborate description.

"Don't go yet; wait till I come off again, Miss Wood," she said. "P'r'aps you'd like to go to the wings and see the play. I'll put it right with the stage manager."

She got the permission, and Nina went up and stood out of sight. She'd seen the play once too often; and instead of listening to the vapid dialogue she let her mind wander. It wandered in so strange a direction that she roused herself with a start.

"Well, silly thing, isn't it?" said Miss Tracey, with a *moue* of disgust. "I wonder they stand it. But it's wonderful what the Great B. P. will stand."

Nina could not sleep that night. The idea that had come to her as she stood at the wings haunted her; and the next evening she almost mechanically got a pen and some paper and began to write. She was so absorbed in her task that she lost count of the hours, and had only just time to snatch up the many sheets she had covered and thrust them into a drawer as Polly came in.

The next night she took them out and fell to work again, read what she had written, and was going to tear it up; but something held her hand, and, with a grimace, she put them away in the drawer again.

She had a headache the following evening, and Polly insisted upon her staying in bed to breakfast.

"You'll take a holiday to-day, Miss Wood," she said sternly. "In fact, if you're not better when I come home, I shan't let you touch a hat for a fortnight. You're looking almost as pale as when I fou—when you came to 'cheer my solitary lot.' You'll just sit up with a shawl over you, like the regulation invalid. Wonder why we always put on a shawl when we're queer? A man doesn't put on a greatcoat."

She went to the drawer for the shawl and found the sheets of paper. On the front page was written:

"Betrothed: A Play in One Act."

Now, a play has no sacredness for an actress, and Polly, after she had put the shawl round Nina, went back to the sitting room they now shared and read "Betrothed" without a scruple.

When she had finished it she jumped up, slipped on her hat and jacket, and stole stealthily downstairs to the girl typewriter who lodged on the first floor back.

"How soon can you copy that?" she asked.

"This day week," said the girl wearily.

Polly laughed.

"Get it done in three hours—oh, I know how long it will take: lodged with a typewriter once—and I'll give you an extra two shillings."

"Make it half a crown," said the girl wistfully; and Polly made it half a crown.

Nina got up in the evening—she felt strangely exhausted all day—and, going to the drawer, took out the manuscript and burned it carefully and slowly, sheet by sheet. Then she sighed heavily, and, shaking herself, as one shakes off an illusion and a weakness, got a book and read; but every now and then she looked at the fire which had consumed her "Betrothed," and checked a sigh larger even than the first.

Polly carried the typewritten copy to the theatre. But she did not fly to the manager and exclaim that she had a masterpiece in her possession; she was too clever for such folly. She knew too well that Mr. Harcourt would recoil, as if the word "play" were synonymous with "snake."

It is true that managers live by plays, but—ah, well, it is easier for a millionaire to dispose of his millions than for a new author to persuade a manager to look at the first effort.

She went to Miss Tracey—to talk about the hat—and dropped the play just by the door, where Miss Tracey found it, glanced at it with surprise, pitched it behind the looking-glass, and promptly forgot it. Her maid, hunting for some grease paint, found it, and laid it on the top of the pincushion. Miss Tracey picked it up resentfully and attacked the manager with it when he came into the room a little later.

"I wish you wouldn't leave your silly plays about, Mr. Harcourt," she said pettishly.

"No play of mine," he said, with listless indignation.

"Then where did it come from?"

"Don't know, don't want to know. Want to speak to you about this first thing. Have to come off. People won't stand it."

"I'm not surprised. It's worse than bad. What will you put in its place?"

Mr. Harcourt mentioned an "old favorite."

Miss Tracey shrieked, "Not for me, thanks!"

" 'Pon my soul, there's no pleasing you!" he grumbled, as he left the room.

Miss Tracey threw the play aside, then picked it up, saw that it was typewritten, and began to read it. In less than five minutes her attitude changed from peevish disquietude to one of absorbed attention, and presently she sprang to her feet and called impatiently for her maid.

"Jenny, this play—who brought it here—who's been in my room? Yesterday it was. Now, keep your eyes in your head, though so far as their usefulness goes you might drop them. Quick!"

Jenny assured her that no one had been in the room—excepting Miss Bainford.

"Then fetch Miss Bainford."

Jenny had not far to go; Polly was hovering In the corridor.

"Oh, Miss Tracey, I left it here, then!" she exclaimed. "I'm so glad I found it! I thought I must have dropped it in the street. Oh, thank you!" She held out her hand, with an innocent expression.

Miss Tracey whipped hers behind her back.

"Who wrote it? It's—it's not bad," she said. No actor will admit that a play is good, unless he has the leading part actually in his possession. No manager will admit, under any circumstances, that a play is good. It would hurt him too much.

The belief that no woman can write a successful play still exists, notwithstanding some notable instances to the contrary; and Polly, who was quite aware of the prejudice, which is as hard to kill as an annuitant, said, with the same innocent expression:

"Oh, it's my friend Miss Wood's brother. He's an invalid—a cripple. His name's Herbert. He lent it me to read, but I haven't had time. Oh, Polly, Polly! He'd be mad if I hadn't found it!"

Miss Tracey still held on to the play.

"It's not at all bad," she said guardedly, "and there's a part in it that I rather fancy. I'll speak to Mr. Harcourt about it, if you like."

Polly went home in a state of suppressed excitement, which she concealed beneath a show of extreme weariness.

"Don't you ever have anything to do with the theatre, Decima," she adjured. "It's a poor game at the best, and at the worst——" She shrugged her shoulders.

"I'm not at all likely to," said Nina, with a smile and a sigh, which, quiet as it was, Polly heard.

Mr. Harcourt sent for her two days afterward. Oh, the suspense of those two days! If the "Betrothed" had been Polly's own betrothed she could not have suffered more keenly.

"Oh, Miss Bainford," he said, with touching listlessness, "Miss Tracey showed me that little play. It's not good, of course, but we might knock it into shape. Miss Tracey says the principal part will suit her. I'm inclined to try it. Of course, your friend, Mr.—Mr.——"

"Wood," suggested Polly.

"Ah, yes, Wood, wouldn't expect anything for it?"

"Oh, but he would!" said Polly. "He's not poor—not what you'd call poor. His father left him an independent income——"

Mr. Harcourt took up a bundle of letters and kept his eye on them in an absorption so long and profound that any one less sophisticated than Polly would have been convinced that he had forgotten the play and her. But Polly waited in bland security. She knew she had her fish on the hook; the thing was to land him.

"Eh?" he said, looking up at last and pretending to be aware of her presence. "Oh, ah, yes; the play. Oh, well, usual terms. He'd better come and see me."

"He can't, poor fellow; he's a cripple. But I'll tell him what you say, and get him to sign the agreement."

Mr. Harcourt looked at her sharply.

"You weren't born yesterday?" he said, with a smile.

"No, the day before, sir," said Polly demurely.

"I should have said last week, now," he retorted. "Here, Mr. Thompson, fill in an agreement for this thing, will you?"

Polly took a cab home, held her hand to still the beating of her good little heart, and entered the room with a yawn which stretched her expressive mouth to cavernous proportions.

"Been reading all the time, dear?"

Nina put down her book.

"No. I've got the supper. Is there any news?" For, actress as she was, Polly could not quite conceal her excitement.

"N—o, nothing. Oh, yes! They're going to put on a new curtain raiser."

Nina bent over the saucepan she had taken off the fire.

"It was time," she said quietly. "What's the title of it? Who is it by?"

"The title is"—Polly got close to her, took the saucepan from her, and set it on the table, regardless of the cloth—"the title is 'The Betrothed,' and it's by a new man named—Herbert Wood!" she said, as she flung her arms around Nina's neck and hugged and swayed her.

CHAPTER XV
A GREAT SUCCESS

The play was put in rehearsal at once, and, of course, the troubles which always beset a play, from its birth to its production, and not seldom afterward, at once set in. There was a part in it for which Mr. Harcourt cast the low comedy lady—she used to be called a soubrette—but the lady didn't like it—said it wasn't "strong" enough.

"Not strong enough, if you please!" exclaimed Polly to Nina, with a snort. "Why, it's as strong as Sandow, only it's in a new and quiet way. She likes a part that lets her tear about the stage and knock the men's hats off; and, of course, this doesn't suit her. Not strong! Why, listen to this!"

She did a bit of the part, and Nina's eyes sparkled. But she said nothing; she could be as secretive as Polly—it is a gift which most women possess—but the next evening she gave Polly a letter for Mr. Harcourt.

He read it, stared fixedly at Polly, frowned doubtfully, then said with acute misery in his voice and countenance:

"Well, you can try it—only try it, mind! We'll see how you get on at the next rehearsal. Now, what are you staring at?"

"I don't know what you mean," said Polly.

"Oh, don't you? Well, your friend, Mr. Wood, wants you to have the part of *Sally Brown*."

Polly uttered a cry, and the tears sprang into her eyes.

"Oh, Mr. Harcourt!" she gasped. But Mr. Harcourt sniffed and hurried off; perhaps he was unaccustomed to gratitude.

Polly, when she got home that night, kissed Nina very quietly.

"You know you are giving me the chance of my life, dear?" she said gravely. "But, oh, if I miss it I shall spoil your play!"

"You won't miss it, and you couldn't spoil my play if you tried," said Nina tenderly. "I mean that you will play the part splendidly."

"If you'll only help me I'll—I'll do my best," faltered Polly.

They went over it there and then, and kept at it until the dawn peeped in at the window at two pale-faced, excited girls; so that at the next rehearsal Polly was not only perfect in her words, but in her business. The stage manager did not throw up his arms in delighted satisfaction—they only do this in novels—but he grunted and nodded at her, and Polly thrilled with pride and hope.

Nina suffered a great deal during the rehearsals because she could not be present. ("You couldn't cut off that beautiful hair of yours and come down to the theatre in a blue serge suit and a limp?" suggested Polly.) But the little play was well cast, and the stage manager knew his business.

Polly reported every day, reported fully, and Nina gave a hint or two which Polly—Heaven knows how—managed to convey to the other actors.

Presently Polly brought her an advertisement announcing the play, and Nina, when she was alone, bent over it with a strange mixture of ecstasy and sadness; for even the production of this, her first effort, could not bring her perfect happiness. The fly is still in every piece of amber which we mortals carve for ourselves.

But at the last rehearsal Polly got permission for "Mr. Wood's" sister to be present; and Nina, hot and cold by turns, watched it from the stage. It sent her down to the lowest depths of despair; because even a last rehearsal is a hopeless and appalling thing.

"I didn't think it could be quite so stupid," she said, meaning the play. "The poor people won't be able to sit it out. Oh, Polly, I'm so sorry for all the trouble I've given you and everybody else concerned! Do you think Mr. Harcourt would let me withdraw it?"

"I don't know; but I'll ask him, if you like. You silly, it's splendid, and they all know it. Miss Tracey was tired, and I don't mean to give myself away till the night. It will go with a rush, you see. And, oh, Decima, we'll—we'll have a supper at the Cri—and a bottle of champagne—a big one!"

The night arrived. Polly wanted Decima to have a box, but Nina said she preferred her old seat behind the pillar in the upper circle.

"No one will see me, and if it's a failure—as it will be—I can slip out and drown myself quietly and without any fuss."

"Better hang yourself—round my neck," said Polly.

Nina crept to her place. One or two persons were already seated, and they glanced curiously at the lovely girl, with the white face and anxious eyes; but she drew well behind her pillar, and tried to possess her soul in patience.

A first night is a bad time for the manager and the actors—to say nothing of the audience—but it is worse for the author, because he, poor wretch, can only look on and endure in inaction. Nina thought the overture would never end, the curtain never go up; but it ascended at last, and the play began to a crammed pit and gallery, an upper circle fairly well filled, and a sprinkling in the dress circle and stalls.

For a moment or two the scene swam before Nina's eyes, and she could not see the actors, nor hear their voices; but presently sight and hearing came back to her, and, incredible as it may seem, she almost forgot her authorship in her interest in the play. Were these sparkling words hers? Was it she who wrote the lines that, spoken by Miss Tracey, brought the tears very near Nina's eyes? Did she invent the business, which, in Polly's clever hands, caused the theatre to ring with laughter? Oh, how sweet, how sweet was the sound of that laughter in Nina's ears! The color stole to her face, her eyes grew bright. Was her poor play going to be a success—really a success?

She began to glance round the theatre—only glance—for she could scarcely take her eyes from the play. What did these gentlemen in the stalls, the critics, think of it? She saw one, whom she supposed belonged to the awful tribe, laugh and nod to a fellow member. Was he really satisfied?

The people were laughing, the play was going smoothly and "strong." Her heart beat with almost painful rapidity, but still fearfully, for your author is a modest and a timid cony. How splendidly Miss Tracey played! And Polly—oh, you dear, sweet girl, to make them laugh every time you open your lips! How, *how* do you do it?

Her eyes wandered from the stalls to the boxes and scanned the faces of the few occupants, with eager, anxious inquiry. Then suddenly she forgot her anxiety, the players, the play itself, and her face grew pale and her eyes fixed as she gazed, spellbound, at the box nearest the stage on the first tier.

A lady and gentleman had entered. A lovely woman, with auburn hair, with golden lights in it, with sapphire eyes of wondrous hue, with a face of clear ivory, and lips on which men might swear away their lives, their honor, their souls. The man was young-old, beautifully dressed, with an orchid in the silk facing of his irreproachable coat, and a fixed smile on his painted lips. But Nina had no eyes for him. She knew the woman in a moment—at the first glance.

It was the original of the portrait in Vane Mannering's coat; it was the woman he loved, the woman whose name he had breathed, as Nina had leaned over him that night in the men's hut. It was Judith!

As Judith Orme sank into her chair, and, dropping the opera cloak from her white shoulders, looked round the house with a languid and yet serene gaze, Nina felt as if the sapphire eyes were fixed on her, and her heart seemed to cease beating. Her breath came in painful gasps. She tried to look at the stage again, but her eyes, as if magnetized, wandered back to the exquisite face, the exquisite grace of the woman.

The young-old man went out of the box, and presently another, a younger man, entered. He was dark, almost sallow, with brilliant black eyes and thin lips. Both eyes and lips seemed restless as he bent over Judith's chair, and Nina fancied that she could almost see his hand tremble as it rested on the chair back.

"Oh, are you here?" said Judith, with a slight uplifting of the beautiful brows, a curve on the perfect lips.

"Yes," he said, in a low voice, with the thrill in it which passion alone can give—the passion that burns like the smouldering fire of a volcano, the fire that, though it seems so still, so innocent, may burst into a death-dealing flame at any moment. "Yes; you said you were coming, and—I am here."

She smiled with the woman's tolerance for the love she does not desire.

"You may stay," she said. "My father—well, he may look in for a moment before the musical farce is over. Are you alone? Is"—she paused an imperceptible instant—"is Lord Mannering here?"

The question was put in the most casual way, but a cloud descended on the sallow face, and the lids drooped over the brilliant eyes.

"Vane is here, or will be here, I think," he replied. "I came early. I wanted to see—this new piece."

"Yes?" she said. "It is rather good, is it not? The people are laughing a great deal."

"But not the piece alone," he went on, in a lower voice. "You said you were coming early, you remember."

"Did I?" with a smile. "I forget."

"Ah, yes, but I do not!" he said, not in the tone with which such compliments are paid, but a little hoarsely, with a twitch of the thin lips, a restless movement of the white hands so near her gleaming shoulder. "I never forget, never lose the chance of being near you, you know."

"Hush!" she whispered, with her voice of subtle music. "You must listen to the play—and let me do so."

There was a pause, during which he looked, not at the stage, but at her—looked with the passion smouldering in his eyes, beating in the sallow cheeks, which had grown somewhat sunken, breathing from the set lips—and she, leaning back and feeling his gaze, seemed so serenely, exquisitely calm and emotionless that one would have said that no passion could have power to touch her, even with the ends of its burning fingers.

But suddenly, though her eyes did not move, her bosom rose and fell quickly. She had heard a step in the corridor—Vane entered the box.

She did not turn her head, but despite herself, her marvelous power of self-control, the color dyed her face and her eyes shone.

Julian saw the momentary change, the flash of emotion that betrayed her, and his face went pallid, his lips grew straight, and there flashed into his now sombre eyes a gleam of hate—the hate which, joined with jealousy, is of all kinds the most malignant, the most merciless.

Vane did not come forward, but, with a bow and a smile, dropped into a chair behind the curtain, so that he was unseen by Nina, whose eyes were still turned to the beautiful woman, now languidly fanning herself, with a new touch of color in her face, a new light in her eyes.

So they sat, in silence now, for Vane was one of those persons who, oddly enough, in these days, when most well-bred people appear to regard the theatre as a place for conversation, did not talk while the curtain was up. He leaned back and looked on at the play, with at first an absent air, but presently an interest awakened in spite of himself. She listened—to Vane's regular breathing; and Julian sat with his arms folded, his lids lowered, his eyes fixed on the hem of the dress of the woman he had grown to love with a passion that absorbed, devoured him, and left him no rest for body or soul. And nothing about him moved but the tick, tick of the nerve in his hollow cheek.

As the play drew to an end, the interest, the laughter of the audience increased, and when the curtain fell there was one of those outbursts of applause which managers, actors, authors, love to hear.

"The Betrothed" was a genuine, unmistakable success.

The applause seemed to deafen Nina. She watched the actors and actresses cross before the curtain, and she longed to clap her hands—for, oh, how grateful she was to them!—but she felt incapable of movement. Her heart beat so wildly that she did not at first hear the cries of "Author! Author! Author!" but as they grew louder and more insistent she began to tremble, and, clutching her opera cloak round her, she rose and fled; so that when Mr. Harcourt came forward, with his hand on his heart, and announced that the author was not in the theatre, he, marvelous to relate, spoke the truth.

Vane moved forward and stood by Judith's chair.

"A pretty play," he said, "and a clever one. I am sorry I did not see it all."

She swept her magnificent dress from the chair beside her, but he did not accept the invitation. He glanced wearily, listlessly, round the house, then, as if he remembered why he had come to the box, he said:

"Julian and I go down to Lesborough to-morrow. There is to be a house party in a week, as you know. May I ask Sir Chandos to bring you? Lady Fanworthy plays chaperon. I hope you will come."

Her heart beat swiftly, but she looked straight before her, so that Julian, who was watching her from behind with a feverish eagerness, grew sick with suspense.

"Thanks, very much," she said at last, with an instant lifting of her eyes to Vane's face. "You know"—in a lower voice, one scarcely above a whisper—"that I should come!"

"I am glad," he said gravely. Then he looked at his watch.

"Are you going?" she asked, in the same tone.

"Yes, presently," he said, "Good night. I will find Sir Chandos."

After he had gone, she sat and looked straight before her. Julian moved, and she turned to him, her eyes cold as ice, and glittering like the diamonds on her breast.

"Will you find my father and tell him I am going on to the Vandaleurs' after the first act, Mr. Shore?"

Julian rose and left the box. But in the corridor he paused and pressed one burning white hand to his lips as if to still the quiver of hate and jealousy; then, with drooped lids and face set like a mask, he went on his errand.

Nina could not go back to the theatre, and she paced up and down the Strand, seeing nothing, hearing nothing, with the applause still deafening her, the lights of the theatre still blinding her.

Her play was a success. Oh, how happy, how glad she must be! A success! She had found her true work at last—no, so soon, so soon! The gods had been good to her beyond all measurement. A success——

Then suddenly she stopped and an inarticulate cry rose from her lips.

Judith! The woman he loved!

Back it all swooped on her, and her joy turned to misery.

She found her way to the stage door. Polly came rushing out and caught her by the arm.

"Decima!" she gasped. "Decima! What a success! Oh, oh, oh! But what is the matter?" she broke off, aghast at the white face, the misery-haunted eyes. "You look as if you'd seen a ghost. You're not—ill?"

"No, no!" said poor Nina. "It is—is the suspense, the excitement."

Polly drew a breath of relief.

"I know. Here—a cab! Get in! Oh, let us get home! Never mind the supper! Let us get home!"

CHAPTER XVI
A PROPOSAL BY PROXY

It was not a large party at Lesborough, but it was a very pleasant one, and all were agreed that Vane made a splendid host. He did not make the mistake of attempting to amuse his guests. Nowadays we refuse to be amused and are best left to ourselves; and what we like is a large house, run on the lines of a first-class hotel, where we can do as we please—and have no bills to pay at the finish.

Breakfast at Lesborough was a movable feast, so also was lunch, and not seldom the guests met together, for the first time in the day, at the eight-o'clock dinner, which was a meal that met with the approval even of Sir Chandos Orme, who was somewhat exacting in the matter of his food—and drink.

Most of the men were out all day with their guns or their rods—there are sea trout in the Lesway, that runs through the estate—and some of the women joined them at lunch, or rode out with the tea baskets. Vane had his gun and his fishing rod standing each morning against the terrace ready for either sport, and did not seem to care which it was; indeed, he usually sat on the coping with his pipe in his mouth while the programme was being settled, and took up either weapon with equal cheerfulness—and, alas! indifference.

The Letchfords, who were, of course, of the party, discussed him in the privacy of their own room.

"He seems very little better than he was on the night we found him," Sir Charles remarked regretfully. "Whatever he had got on his mind is there still. He's behaving like—like a brick and keeping everything going here splendidly, but——"

"But he is not happy," finished Lady Letchford. "He tries to hide the trouble, whatever it is, and I dare say most of the people here think him the happiest and most fortunate of men; but you and I know better, don't we, Charlie? And there is some one else who knows it—Lady Fanworthy."

"Ah, she always was a clever one!" remarked Letchford.

"Yes; and she's fond of him," said his wife. "I see her looking at him every now and then, with a curious and pained glance, as if she wondered what was the matter, and wishing she could help him."

"So do I," said Letchford, with a sigh. "I'm deuced fond of him, Blanche."

"It is not difficult—to be fond of him, I mean," responded Lady Blanche comprehensively.

"Jolly good thing he's taken a fancy to his cousin, Julian Shore. Good-looking chap, isn't he, and agreeable, too!"

Lady Letchford was silent for a moment.

"Yes," she said. "He is good-looking enough; but——"

Sir Charles laughed and yawned; he had been shooting all day.

"But you don't care for him, eh? What fancies you women get! I should have thought he would have been just the sort of man you would have admired and liked; a fellow who sings like an opera chap and looks like—like an Adonis, and always says and does the right thing."

"Perfection, in short," said Lady Letchford. "But, then, we don't care for perfection in a man—that's why I like you, Charlie, I suppose—it's poaching on our preserves, you see. Do make haste or we shall be late for dinner, and it's the one thing dear old Lady Fanworthy sticks at. She almost frowned at Judith Orme when she came in late last night."

"Ah, yes; I see you and Judith have made it up, Blanche."

"You see nothing of the kind," retorted Lady Letchford, from her dressing room. "Perhaps you mean that we are civil to each other—we couldn't quarrel or cut each other in another man's house."

"Oh, that's it, is it?" said Sir Charles. "By the way, do you notice how smitten Julian Shore is?"

"Of course I do," said Lady Letchford. "I am not blind. But I won't talk any more, or you'll never be ready. I cannot understand why it should take a man so long to tie that ridiculous white tie. I'd do it in half a minute——"

"Better come and do it now."

"I shall do nothing of the kind. You're quite old—and ugly—enough to dress yourself. Oh, go away, Charlie! Here comes Louise! And shut the door or you will go on talking. I am sure we shall be late!"

They were in time for dinner, after all. It was, as usual, a merry meal, for the men had had a good day, and the women were rejoiced to have them back. Vane, alone, was rather silent, as usual, but from his place at the bottom of the table, facing Lady Fanworthy, he smiled, whenever the conversation required a smile from him, and he spoke now and again to Lady Lisle, who, with her husband, was dining at the Hall that night, and who sat at his right. A little farther down the table was Judith Orme, the most beautiful and the best-dressed woman present. Lord Lisle was next her, and she seemed to be listening with interest to his detailed account of the day's sport; but every now and then her eyes wandered to the grave face at the bottom of the table; and every time they so wandered, Julian, who sat opposite her, noted the glance, though his soft voice never hesitated and his pleasant smile never faltered. He seemed scarcely to look at her, but not a movement, not a word of hers escaped him, though he appeared engrossed with the young girl whom he had taken in, and who was chatting with the volubility of nineteen.

The talk ran its course in the light, desultory manner of table talk, and Lady Fanworthy, in her black silk and priceless lace, leaned back with the serenity of the hostess when her dinner is going well, and looked thoughtfully at Vane, with the expression in her keen eyes which Lady Letchford had noticed.

Presently Sir Chandos Orme's thin falsetto voice was heard in a moment of silence.

"Dropped in at the Momus last night," he said—he had run up to town to interview his beauty doctor the day before—"they're going well and strong. Was in time for that first piece: deuced clever! Harcourt—I went behind to—er—see a man I know—told me that he's commissioned the author to write a comedy; and Harcourt expects a big success with it."

"Quite a new man, and very young, isn't he?" said Julian.

"Quite a boy. His name's Herbert Wood," replied Sir Chandos, signing to Prance to fill his glass—for the fourth time—"and a cripple. Harcourt hasn't seen him yet. He's a friend of the Polly Bainford who's made such a hit in the first piece; and Harcourt communicates with him through her."

"Quite mysterious and—stagy," murmured Judith Orme. "You remember the piece, Lord Lesborough?"

"Yes, quite well, what I saw of it," said Vane. "I should think the author would write a very good comedy. We must all go and see it."

"I say, Shore," said Sir Chandos, with the flickering of the eyelids and the twitching of the lips which always followed his fourth glass of champagne, "I had a regular fright just now."

Julian raised his eyes.

"Metaphorically speaking, of course," he said. "You were in the Seventy-second, Sir Chandos?"

Sir Chandos showed his perfectly constructed teeth.

"By gad, yes; we weren't easily frightened! But I give you my word I was—well, rather startled. I was coming down from my room the short way—a little late"—he smiled and bowed to Lady Fanworthy—"and I ran up against the most extraordinary-looking person. She didn't seem to hear me, when I came behind her, and when she turned—well, outside Madame Tussaud's, I've never seen anything like her. A walking corpse, by George! And I fancy she must be deaf and dumb, for when I apologized for running against her, she just turned and looked at me like—like a statue, touched her lips and ears, and glided into that den of yours. Who is she, eh?"

Julian watched Prance fill his glass, and stopped him when it was half full, before he replied, quite casually:

"She is an old servant of mine. Her name is Deborah. I'm sorry she startled you."

"Oh, that's all right," said Sir Chandos, but grudgingly. "But you must have a queer fancy."

"The fact is," said Vane, with a nod and smile at Julian, "no one but an old and faithful servant would stand the awful smells of Julian's den."

"You go in for chemistry, I understand, Shore?" said Lord Lisle. "A most interesting study. I used to dabble in it, but quite unprofessionally. What branch have you taken up?"

Julian shrugged his shoulders, the slight shrug which hinted at his Spanish blood. "Oh, well," he replied modestly, "I am trying to find a new color."

"Really! How interesting! How clever you must be!" exclaimed a young girl. "I hope it will be a nice color, one that will suit us ladies."

"Any color I am fortunate enough to discover will possess that virtue," he retorted, with a slight bow.

"One of these days Julian will awake to find himself famous," said Vane; "and in quite a new line for the Mannerings. I don't think any of them has come out strong as a scientist."

"I should so like to see your—laboratory; is that the right name?" said the young girl.

Julian smiled at her indulgently. "So you shall; whenever you please; though there is very little to see."

"Take my advice, Miss Limmington, and—don't," said Vane. "You'll see nothing but pots and pans, in a variety of glass and iron; and you will be assailed by a smell that will haunt you more than any ghost you have at the Grange."

"Lord Lesborough's advice is good, I assure you," said Julian, with a charming frankness and modesty.

Lady Fanworthy, who had been listening to the conversation, with a noncommittal smile and drooped lids, looked up and around the table, gave the sign which every woman at once sees and no man ever notices, and the ladies rose and followed her to the drawing-room.

Vane gathered the men round him and sent about the claret jug and the port, and set an example by lighting his old brier—the brier which he had smoked on the fairy isle. The conversation promptly took a sporting direction, and Vane bore his share of it; but every now and then he became preoccupied and absent-minded, and presently he said:

"Won't any one take any more wine? Orme?"

Sir Chandos filled his glass, tossed it off, and rose, a trifle shaky, with the others.

When they entered the drawing-room, Judith was at the piano, playing in the soft, indolent fashion in which women play while they are waiting for the men; and she stopped and looked mechanically at Julian, for, as usual, everybody wanted to hear him sing.

"Is it too soon after dinner, Julian?" said Vane, with his hand on Julian's shoulder.

"No," he said, "if Miss Orme will play the accompaniment."

She looked at him, beyond him. "You usually play your own," she said.

"This is a new one," he said, "and I can't play at sight."

With the faintest suggestion of resignation, she played the prelude, and he sang.

It was Pinsuti's " 'Tis I," and he sang it—well, his rendering of the famous song would have satisfied even the composer. The conversation faltered and died out, and every one listened in a profound, an emotional silence.

"Oh, it is beautiful, beautiful!" murmured the young Miss Limmington. "What a lovely, lovely voice Mr. Shore has; and how exquisitely he sings!"

Vane, who happened to be near her, nodded perfect agreement.

"Yes; my cousin has a wonderful voice, hasn't he?" he said warmly. "Ask him to sing 'Kathleen Mavourneen.' I shouldn't be surprised if he makes you cry."

Julian sang "Kathleen Mavourneen," and succeeded in bringing tears to the eyes of more than Miss Limmington.

"First rate; splendid!" said Sir Charles, with a half-defiant glance at his wife. "Sing us something else, Shore?"

But Julian courteously declined. With the Spanish shrug of the shoulders he left the piano, and sauntered to the French windows, which had been left open, for the night was warm, and passed out on to the terrace. He lit a cigarette and leaned against the stone railing, his eyelids drooping, his long lashes sweeping his sallow cheek. Music excites the performer as well as the listener, and his heart was beating quickly.

While he had been singing his eyes had rested upon Judith Orme's profile. From her beauty he had drawn the inspiration which had enabled him to move his hearers as they had been moved. And now his heart was aching for her, as it always ached the moment he was out of her sight. At first he had fought against the passion which had taken possession of him, had tried to argue himself out of it; but he had long ceased to struggle, and now surrendered himself, as the demoniac surrenders to the spirit that enthralls it. And jealousy was adding another torture to that of unrequited love, for he had seen, almost on the first day, the day he had called on her with Vane, that she was in love with his cousin.

Love makes the dullest man quick-witted and sharp-eyed where the woman he loves is concerned, and Julian had discovered that Judith was not heartless, as the world considered her, but that her heart had been given to Vane. Fate had willed that his cousin should not only step in between him and the Lesborough peerage, but that he should stand between him and the woman whom he loved with an absorbing passion which was nearly akin to madness.

With a gesture of despair he flung the end of his cigarette away and went toward the end of the terrace. As he was descending the steps he saw Sir Chandos Orme coming out of the smoking room, where he had been for the brandy-and-soda which pulled him together after his dinner. At the same moment there was the frou-frou of a woman's dress, and one of the ladies stepped on to the terrace from the drawing-room, and Julian heard Sir Chandos say cautiously:

"Is that you, Judith?"

Julian went softly down the steps and stood under the terrace, listening.

"Yes, father: do you want me?" replied Judith, coming toward him. They stopped almost immediately above Julian, so that he could hear every word, though both father and daughter spoke in a low voice.

"Yes," said Sir Chandos, with a slight hiccough. "Look here, Judith, I want to talk to you. I'm getting anxious, uneasy. You don't seem to be making much of this game—now, don't be offended and turn away like that. I won't have it! I've been a good father to you——"

She laughed with a kind of weary scorn.

"I am listening," she said coldly.

"Well, then, I'll go further and say you seem to me to be making a mess of it. We've been down here—how long is it?—and you are no 'forrader' than you were in London. I've got eyes in my head, of course, and I can see, any one could see, that Lesborough isn't in the least smitten. The man seems to be like a block of ice, confound him! 'Pears to me you've completely lost your old power over him——"

She leaned against the stone coping, her hands clasped tightly, her eyes fixed on the darkness.

"Now, don't go over the old ground and tell me it's my fault; that's all past and gone."

"I was not going to do so," she said, in a low voice. "It would be useless."

"Quite so," he asserted. "Nothing is more painful than that kind of—of bickering between father and daughter, especially when they understand each other as you and I do. What I wanted to say was that, in my opinion, Lesborough isn't a marrying man, that he doesn't intend to marry; and that he intends this Julian Shore to succeed him here. You can't help observing the—the fuss Vane makes over the fellow."

"Well?" she said, after a pause.

Sir Chandos got out a cigar, but, after a glance along the terrace, refrained from lighting it.

"Well," he said, shifting his small, tightly shod feet uneasily. "Well, you can't be blind—no one could be—to the fact that Julian Shore is—er—very much in love with you, my dear Judith."

"Well?" she said again, and in exactly the same tone.

"Well! Bless my soul, you don't want me to point out that you ought to shift your objective? If you can't get the present king o' the castle, why not—not make for the next?"

She laughed wearily.

"You talk as if Vane were an old man, on the brink of the grave."

"No, he's not an old man, but—well, accidents are always occurring," retorted Sir Chandos. "Look at the way Providence shot him into the title, and—and—well, I've a fancy Vane won't make old bones. He looks to me like a man who has ceased to take an interest in life, and by gad, when that's the case, life soon ceases to take an interest in the man! Then—then he is a reckless devil; you saw him riding that horse of his yesterday? It was a marvel he wasn't thrown. Mark my words, he'll break his neck some day!"

Her face went white in the darkness and her hands clinched each other.

"Until he does——" she began, then stopped.

"So, what I say is," resumed Sir Chandos, with the redundance and emphasis of a half-tipsy man, "keep the two strings to your bow, my dear girl. For instance, there's no need to treat Shore so cavalierly. He's a decent chap, he's fond of you, and it's my opinion that he'll come into this sooner or later——" He swept his hand across the view comprehensively. "At any rate, I'm dead certain that you're making no headway with Vane. Of course, with your beauty—by gad, I'm as proud of it as you are!—you might marry anybody; but, well, you've got into the pace here and—— Now, take my advice, and think the matter over."

She laughed again.

"If I do not marry Vane, if I have lost him," she said, almost to herself, "it does not matter——"

"That's what I say," her precious father caught her up, with an eager hiccough. "It's been my motto all my life—and a very prosperous life it's been—that, if you can't get the moon, good cream cheese is an admirable substitute. Now, do be a sensible girl, my dear Judith!"

He stretched out a wavering hand to lay it upon her shoulder, but she shrank slightly but perceptibly, and Sir Chandos, carrying his hand to his mustache, murmured: "I'll just go and get a drink. Too much salt in that last savory." He shuffled jauntily back to the smoking room.

Julian, with a pale face and a throbbing heart, was stealing away, when he heard another step on the terrace, and he waited. It was Vane's. Judith also heard it, and with a smothered sigh turned toward him.

"Who is it?" said Vane. "Ah, it's you!" as she moved into the light from the window. "Have you seen Julian? They want him for bridge."

"No," she said, in the soft, low, and deliciously musical note which always came into her voice when she spoke to him. "He left the drawing-room some time ago."

"Gone into that den of his, I suppose. If so, it's useless to attempt to draw him. What a good fellow he is, isn't he?"

"Yes?" she said half interrogatively, as if she knew he had a purpose in his praise.

"Such a—a likable chap," said Vane, with the awkwardness with which a man approaches a delicate subject. "And he's clever, too. The sort of man who would make his mark in the world if—if he had an object."

He lit a cigarette, tossing the match almost on to Julian, and smoked furiously for a moment or two.

"You—take a great interest in him," she said, in so low a voice that Julian had to strain his ears.

"Rather!" assented Vane, "and naturally, seeing that he will follow me here."

"Will—follow you?" she repeated mechanically.

Vane nodded.

"Yes. I shall never marry." She moved out of the light and leaned against the railing in her old attitude. "I'm one of those fellows who are better single."

"Ah, I understand!" she breathed, with a long-drawn breath.

Vane frowned and set his teeth.

"See here, Judith," he said, in the tone of a man has resolved to speak his mind, and to spare neither himself nor his hearer, "I don't think you do. Of course I know you are thinking of the past and—and our old engagement. You don't mind my speaking of it? Why should you?"

"Why should I?" she said, in a still voice.

"Quite so. That's all past, and I don't want you to think you have anything to reproach yourself with. We—well, we made a mistake, that's all; and it was precious lucky for you that you discovered it before it was too late!"

"Was it I only who discovered it?" she asked.

Vane hesitated for a moment. It is never easy to tell a woman that you have ceased to love her.

"Let us say that you were the first to make the discovery," he said gently. "We won't discuss it."

"No; it isn't necessary," she said, in a strange voice, as if she were holding herself under control. "You have told me enough. I—jilted you, Vane; but—you found consolation. There is another woman!"

Vane did not start, but he set his teeth and his brows as if she had struck him. For a moment he was silent, then, looking straight before him, he said grimly:

"You are right, there is—there was another woman."

Her hand stole to her bosom and clutched the lace there. She had hoped against hope for a swift denial; the confirmation of her dread was almost more than she could bear. Scarcely breathing, she stole a little closer to him.

"Tell—tell me about her," she whispered.

He shrank again; but, after a pause, during which she thought he must hear the wild beating of her heart, he said:

"I don't think I can. There are some things——No, no, just let it rest at that."

"Is she—is she any one I know?"

"No," he replied almost curtly.

"She is, of course, very beautiful? I—I can't imagine your caring for a plain woman."

He drew his hand across his brow.

"She——Let it rest," he said hoarsely. "I did not want to speak of myself, but—Julian."

She stood motionless, as if she had not heard him, then, as if she had suddenly become conscious of his words, she said, in a voice absolutely emotionless:

"Mr. Julian Shore?"

"Yes. Judith, he—has fallen in love with you."

"And *you*—you have come to plead his cause!" she said swiftly through her closed teeth.

"I have come to plead his cause," he assented resolutely. "It's like my impudence, you think? But, consider, Judith! He is of my kith and kin; I like him, I am fond of him; and I don't like to see him suffer. The poor fellow has got thin and worn—oh, but you know, you must know! I know what you are going to say; that he might speak for himself. But Julian is the last man to do that in such a case. He is poor; I stand between him and the title, the estate. He thinks, and rightly, that you are far above him. And he is just that sensitive, high-minded kind of fellow who would suffer in silence—and you treat him, well, not too gently."

Her breath was coming fast, and she moved a little away from him, that he might not see the passionate heaving of her bosom.

"So let me plead his cause," Vane went on, warming to his advocacy, and deaf and blind to the passion which was rending her. "I'm convinced that he would make you——"

"A good husband," she finished quite calmly.

"Well, it sounds pretty banal; but that's what I was going to say," he admitted. "And that he loves you with all his heart and soul, I've seen—and you must have seen—for some time past. I know the signs," in a low voice, but without bitterness. "And, mind, I am not altogether disinterested."

"No?" she said, keeping the surging mockery from her voice.

"No. I want to see the man who will come after me make a better thing of his life than I have done. I want him to be—happy. And, by George, Julian will never be happy until he has won you!"

"Or you have won me for him?" she said.

He looked at her quickly.

"You are offended, indignant?" he said. "I'm sorry. I beg your pardon, Judith, beg it most humbly! And I'm afraid I've done Julian more harm with you than good. But I—well, I presumed on our old—friendship——"

She moved suddenly, as if she were losing the control over herself which she had maintained by an almost superhuman effort. If Vane Mannering had sought for a mode of avenging himself for her treatment of him, he could not have found a more deadly, a more cruel one. For a moment or two her lips trembled with the rage—and, yes, hate—which possessed her; but she pressed her hand to her lips and forced the hot words back.

"You—mean well," she said at last. "Your cousin should be very grateful to you——"

"Then—then you are not offended? You'll think it over, and—and be a little kinder to Julian?" he said gravely, earnestly.

"I will think it over, and Mr. Shore shall have no cause to complain of my unkindness," she said. Then suddenly she laughed, not loudly, but so strangely that Vane started and looked at her with questioning surprise; for, as he had ceased to love her, as his heart was buried there on the fairy isle, he had no suspicion that she still cared for him. Had she not left him of her own free will?

"What—what is the matter?" he asked, with all the denseness of the straightforward man.

"Nothing," she replied, the laugh dying suddenly, and her voice once more impassive and emotionless. "I was only thinking how well you had performed your task; that—that if I had known the truth I might have spared myself some, as it proves, quite unnecessary remorse. But the past, *our* past, is past, as you say——"

"Quite, quite," he said gently. "Shall we go in now? The air is chilly."

"Thanks, no; I should like to remain out a little longer, should, naturally, like to be alone to think of—Mr. Julian Shore."

Vane regarded her with a vague uneasiness, then, having nothing to say, said nothing, but, with a slight nod of acquiescence, went into the house.

She stood for a moment or two as he had left her, then, supporting herself by the rail, moved slowly to the end of the terrace; there, out from the light of the windows, she flung up her hands to her face, and choked back the moan of wounded pride, of outraged love, of the worst humiliation which a woman can suffer; the avowed indifference of the man she loves. Loves! There was not one ember of love left in the fire which smouldered in her heart, but in its place a hate as savage as death!

Half unconscious of what she was doing, where she was going, she paced back as far as the steps, and, drawn by the stillness and darkness, went down to the garden—and saw the figure standing against the terrace wall.

She held her breath for a moment, then glided forward and laid her hand on Julian's arm. He turned and she saw his face.

"You have been listening!" she panted. "Coward! I will call to them—tell them!"

She swung round toward the house, but he caught her arm. His face was white, his eyes glowing; but, just as he had restrained himself when he found that he was dispossessed, so now he mastered his self-command.

"Wait," he said quietly. "Do not move, do not speak! Wait!"

She stood still, stood motionless, rendered speechless by his unnatural calmness, and peered at him breathlessly.

"Yes, I have listened," he said as quietly as before. "And it is true. I love you—ah, do not speak—yet! I love you. Is it a crime to do so? Then I am the greatest of criminals, and I throw myself at your mercy. But you know I love you, you have known it since the day we first met. Do you suppose I am going to ask you if you care for me? I am not so great a fool! I know that Vane stands between us——No, not yet! Wait, I beg you to wait until I have said what I have to say. It is him you care for. I am—well, just the dirt beneath your feet. But he—ah, well, I have listened; there is no need to remind you. Vane does not count. You are less than nothing to him."

She put up her hands as if, indeed, she were about to strike him, but he did not move, and his dark eyes did not quail before the lightning in hers.

"While I—God, how I love you! You are just my whole life and soul!"

"You love me?" she said, gliding closer to him. "Prove it! Prove it!"

"Tell me how——"

"Thrash him! Thrash him within an inch of his life!" she hissed.

He smiled.

"No," he said, as if in response to quite an ordinary, everyday proposition. "That would be a cheap kind of melodrama; and I should be the one who would be thrashed; Vane is a stronger man——" He shrugged his shoulders.

"You are a coward!" she said, her bosom heaving, her lips twitching. "You prate of love, like—like an actor, and a bad one; but you stand by and see the woman you say you love insulted. But you want my answer to your kind proposal—your cousin's kind proposal, coward! Take it, then! I will marry you the day you reign here as master, instead of dependent, the hanger-on you are."

He caught her by both wrists and leaned forward, his breath coming as fast as hers, his eyes sinking into her own.

"I accept your conditions," he said hoarsely. She shrank back, but he still held her. "You made it in jest, in mockery——"

She watched him closely, hungrily.

"No!" she panted. "I—I am serious. It—it is you who jest, who trifle——"

He smiled, and, for a moment, his self-possession left him.

"Coward! The word stings! You shall see! I accept the conditions. Give me—give an earnest of your promise."

She shrank from him as he drew her closer to him; but suddenly she lifted her face, white and set.

"Take it!" she whispered.

He bent his head slowly and kissed her on the lips. With a low cry she broke from him and sped up the steps; but on the terrace she turned and looked down on him with a strange expression in her eyes, an expression in which fear, and hate, and the longing for revenge fought for predominance.

Julian stood looking up at her, at the spot on which she had stood, with glowing eyes, while one could count twenty; then he went softly round the house, unlocked a door in a wall on which the laboratory looked, and, passing through the small yard—it had once been a ladies' garden, but was now moss and weed-grown—unlocked the laboratory door with his chub-key and entered the room.

There was an air of comfort about the apartment. The walls were colored a dark maroon, the woodwork was of walnut, beautifully polished, there were pictures on the walls, and a baby grand piano; but its scientific purpose had not been forgotten. Vane, with the generosity which characterized him at all times, but never more than in his dealings with Julian, had given him carte blanche, and Julian had transformed the Wizard's Room into a model laboratory.

The room was sound and air-proof, and ventilated by a casement in the roof, which could be opened a quarter of an inch or thrown wide, so that the fumes from the crucibles and chemical retorts could escape in a few moments. The walls were covered with a composition which resisted the corrosive effects of the noxious fumes on which Vane so often animadverted. A draught, even a breath of air, is often fatal to a chemical experiment, so Julian had contrived that the room should be rendered absolutely hermetically sealed by the closing of the ventilator, which was worked, on the simplest principle, by a couple of ropes, passing over a pulley, which he could control by a lever fixed under his writing table.

As he entered he saw, by the light from the furnace, the bent figure of Deborah. She was moving about the room in her noiseless way, a tortoise-shell cat, which had attached itself to her, following her as noiselessly and rubbing against her. A silver tea equipage stood on a small table near the furnace, and, as Julian entered, she pointed to it.

Julian nodded and sank into the easy-chair near the table, and Deborah stood quite motionless and as if waiting for his commands, her full gray eyes fixed on his as a dog's are fixed upon his master.

Julian wiped the sweat from his brow, and poured himself out a cup of tea, as if unconscious of her presence, then he looked at her and said, on his fingers:

"Deborah, keep away from the front of the house. Sir Chandos Orme has seen you—and spoken to me."

"Yes, Mr. Julian," she replied, with a swift movement of her thin fingers. "Is there anything else?"

"Nothing," he signed. "You can go now."

She turned, then paused and looked at him.

"Are you sure there is nothing else? You are not looking well; you are looking as if you were ill. Is there nothing Deborah can do? You would trust me, sir?"

"Yes," he said impatiently. "What should there be? I am quite well. Have you made up the fire?"

"Yes, Mr. Julian."

"Well, then, you may go. Here—take this cat with you."

She went for the cat, but it eluded her and crept close to Julian.

"Oh, never mind, then," he said impatiently. "Let it be. How hot the room is! It is the fire, I suppose. Open the ventilator, please."

She went to the lever, and opened with difficulty the window in the top of the wall.

"It wants a new rope," she signed.

Julian nodded irritably. "Yes, I'll see to it."

She glanced at him, with the devotion of the spaniel, waited a moment to see if there were any other orders, then left the room, carefully closing the hermetically sealed door after her.

Julian leaned back and sipped his tea. His heart was beating fiercely, his brain was in a whirl. The melodramatic scene in which he had played a principal part danced before him. His lips had touched hers, Judith's! She had promised to be his wife! His wife! He closed his eyes, and a smile curved his lips.

But the condition! That he should reign as master at Lesborough. He had accepted it in the moment of excitement, of passionate ecstasy, as he would have accepted it if it had been the advent of the millennium. Was there any condition, any stipulation, which he would not have accepted?

His! That beautiful woman he loved with a passion that absorbed his whole being. Her kiss, cold and fierce as it had been, burned on his lips, and still thrilled him. His! Judith, the loveliest woman on earth, the one woman to be desired of all others. His passion left no room for thought of Vane, who had pleaded his, Julian's, cause. Some natures are incapable of gratitude, and Julian's was one of them. He put Vane's advocacy aside as if it had not occurred. All his thoughts, his heart, were bent on Judith.

And he would call her his, when he reigned as master at Lesborough! It did not occur to him to doubt her promise, for that promise had been dictated by jealousy and hate, and they are stronger and more binding than love.

When he was master! That meant when Vane was dead and he, Julian, reigned in his stead.

But Vane was alive, was but a little the elder of Julian. No matter. He had her promise; there was hope for him. All sorts of accidents might happen, as Sir Chandos, with his worldly wisdom, had said. Vane might be killed in the hunting field; a careless shot in the——

He wiped the sweat from his forehead again and looked round the room. His eye fell upon the crucible on the spirit furnace, and the lover gave place, for the moment, to the scientist. He rose and went to the furnace. The liquid in the pot was emitting a bluish flame, a strange and pungent odor, so dense and penetrating that, as he bent over it, it caught his breath and made it difficult.

He looked round the room. The ventilator was half closed; his hand went to the lever which admitted or closed the air; but he shut the ventilator, and stood for a moment as if considering deeply. Then he went to a cupboard, took out a length of muslin, and, after soaking it in a liquid which he prepared in a bowl, wrapped it round his mouth and nostrils.

With deliberate movements he locked the door, saw that the ventilator was tightly closed, then lifted the iron cover from the pot on the furnace. A subtle, penetrating fume arose and filled the sombre room; the air became thick and palpable.

Protected as he was by the muslin soaked in the antidoting solution, he was conscious of a heavy pressure on the lungs, and heart, a pressure that seemed almost intolerable. But he displayed no fear or dismay; indeed, a smile of triumph shone in his eyes.

"It is the Borgia fume!" he mumbled behind his muslin mask, as the atmosphere grew thicker, more dense; a cry pierced the silence. It was a moan, a piteous moan, from the cat which had sprung upon the table and was crouching there, looking at Julian entreatingly.

"Puss, poor puss!" he murmured, a cruel, pitiless light in his eyes. "You don't feel well, eh? No wonder! You can't breathe in this atmosphere? I'm not surprised. But it is going to be worse!"

Protected by the muslin bandage, he went to her and stroked her, and the wretched animal dropped on its side and wailed to him imploringly.

"Nearly gone, eh?" he said. "Let us see what a stronger dose will do."

He glided to the furnace and stirred the compound; the fumes grew thicker, denser, and the cat, with a spasmodic jerk of all her limbs, fell prone on the table, her claws extended, her mouth wide open.

Julian went to her and turned her over.

"Dead!" he said. "Dead, quite dead. It was a pity you stayed, pussy! But it would have killed a man, to say nothing of a cat——" He stopped suddenly, with his eyes fixed on the unfortunate cat. "It would have killed a man, unless he were protected as I am. Killed a man!"

He took up the cat and examined it closely.

"No one could withstand it," he muttered. "A cat has nine lives, so they say, a man only one. Poor puss!"

Suddenly he started. There had come a knock at the door. He stood staring above his bandage from the cat to the door. Then he caught up the dead animal, tossed it unceremoniously into a cupboard, opened the ventilator to its widest, removed the protective muslin from his face, and, after watching the fumes disappear through the ventilator, opened the door.

"Oh, it's you, Vane," he said casually. "Come in."

"Phew!" said Vane. "What an infernal smell! What on earth have you been doing?"

"Only an experiment, quite an ordinary experiment," answered Julian. "Come in."

CHAPTER XVII
NINA HAS AN "ADVENTURE"

Success is sweet, we are told, but the sweet was embittered to Nina by the sight of Judith at the theatre, though she tried to be grateful to the Providence which had rescued her from poverty, given her so good a friend as Polly, and, ah! best of all, provided work for her.

Blessed work! The curse which we have changed into a blessing; and not more blessed to any man than the artist, whose one prayer, after he has finished one task, is, "Give me strength for the next!"

Nina sprang at Mr. Harcourt's suggestion that she should write a long play, and she set to work at it at once with feverish energy; for she knew that only by brain toil—the toil the artist delights in—could she escape from brooding over the past and the fate that had linked her to a man who was in love with the beautiful creature she had seen in the box at the theatre.

But if Nina's joy was dimmed, Polly's shone brightly.

"I can see your future as plainly as one of those fortune-telling people in Bond Street," she declared solemnly to Nina. "You are going to be a famous authoress and play writer like——" She mentioned two or three of the women who have scored success as dramatists, and so broken the spell which has so long rested upon women writers for the stage. "You are going to be famous, Decima. Why, you *are* famous, already! Haven't you had most wonderful notices; and aren't the stalls almost full when the first piece begins? A thing unheard of till 'The Betrothed.' And wouldn't you like to have better rooms, and have a maid of your own, like Miss Tracey?"

But Nina shook her head and laughed.

"No, no, Polly. Let us go on as we are. Who knows? This next play may be a failure, and then—then we should have to go back to the millinery business."

"Not you! You've seen the last of bonnet building!" retorted Polly confidently. "But, oh, I do hope you won't be so silly and wicked as to overwork yourself. You are looking pale and thin—no, it's no use your denying it; I can see quite plainly. You don't take enough exercise; and I'm sure you want it. I've read somewhere that literary people ought to spend nearly all their time in the open air."

"You're thinking of consumptives, I fancy, Polly," said Nina; but she knew there was sound sense in the suggestion, and she went out more frequently.

There are worse places in the early autumn than the London parks—one sometimes wonders whether Londoners are as intimate with those parks as they ought to be—and Nina found, in this, the dead season, that they were almost as lonely as a country lane. There is one part of Hyde Park—which wild horses shall not induce me to indicate—where one could wander to and fro for hours without meeting a fellow human being; and it was here she found the plot of her new play, and worked out its characters and scenes, coming home in the afternoon to put the thing on paper. During these hours she was almost happy; it was at night, as she tried to sleep, and in the early hours of the morning, when she lay awake counting them as they were boomed by Big Ben, who hath no pity upon the sick and the sleepless who lie within hearing of his loud and insistent tongue, that her unsatisfied heart cried: "I am ahungered; give me food!"

Now and again she stole to her seat at the back of the upper circle at the Momus, and looked at her little play, and, of course, she saw its many faults more plainly at each visit, and learned the lesson which can only be learned by these faults of ours.

Sometimes she stayed to the end of the musical piece, and went round to the stage door to wait for Polly; and one night she had what Polly would have called an adventure.

She was standing in the passage, near the doorkeeper's den, the piece just over, and some of the men and women already leaving the theatre. As a rule they were all too tired or too much engaged in talking and laughing among themselves to notice her, as she stood in a corner, but to-night a super, who had been drinking, caught sight of her, and, stopping, eyed her with a tipsy smile.

"Waiting for me, miss?" he asked.

Nina glanced toward the glass box, but the man had gone away for a moment. She turned her head away as if she had not heard, but the fatuous young fellow approached her with what he considered an ingratiating smile, and offered his arm.

"Come along with me," he said. "Come outside where we can talk, miss."

Before he could say another word or touch her, there came a light, firm step along the passage, and a gentleman hurried down it. He was a young man, with a handsome and pleasant face, in which a pair of frank and boyish blue eyes were the most noticeable feature. They were quick, as well as good-looking, eyes, and he saw, in a moment, what was going on. Without a word his hand fell on the man's shoulder, and he swung him round toward the doorway as if he were a skittle, and not a heavy one, at that. The man looked round with an angry oath, but it died on his lips, and with a sullen "All right, my lord!" he went unsteadily on his way.

The young fellow was about to follow, when, hesitatingly, he stopped and raised his hat.

"I'm afraid the man was making himself a nuisance," he said, and his voice was as frank and pleasant as his eyes. "You—you have not been frightened, I hope."

"Not in the very least," Nina replied. "He had only spoken a few words before you came up. But I am very much obliged to you for sending him away."

She did not color or seem a whit embarrassed, but met his gaze of frank but quite respectful interest with the conventional ease which is the lady's birthright.

"I am very glad," he said, in the tone in which one addresses an equal. "Are you waiting for any one? Shall I go back and bring them up?"

"No, thanks," said Nina. "I am waiting for—ah, here she comes!"

He looked round and saw Polly hurrying down the passage.

"Oh, Miss Bainford!" he said, and he raised his hat. Then he added, after a pause: "This lady might wait in the greenroom, Miss Bainford."

"Oh, thank you, my lord!" said Polly gratefully.

"Thank you," Nina also said, "but I shall not come again."

He raised his hat once more and left them.

"Well?" said Polly, as they got into the cab. "Aren't you going to ask who that was?"

"I wasn't, but I will," said Nina, with a smile. "Whoever he is, he was very kind. A stupid man spoke to me and——"

"Lord Sutcombe knocked him down! It's just what he would do!"

"It's just what he didn't do, I'm glad to say," said Nina, smiling. "That would have been too severe a punishment for a piece of unconscious impertinence."

Polly stared at her. "Lor'! I should have thought you'd have been glad if he'd done it! What a strange girl you are! But I see! Of course, you wouldn't like the fuss. Yes; that was Lord Sutcombe. He's the son of an earl, or a duke, or something."

"And what may a son of a duke be doing behind the scenes at the Momus?" asked Nina, but without any great interest.

"Oh, they say he's backing Mr. Harcourt—got a share in the theatre. And he's fond of the stage; there's a good many swells like him; they're never happy unless they're behind. But he's not a stage-struck idiot like some of them. He's a gentleman, and all right, and doesn't spend his time flirting with every girl about the place. Didn't 'The Betrothed' go well to-night, dear? Did you hear the hand I got in that last speech of mine? And the 'House Full' boards were up quite early. Oh, how glad I shall be when the new play's finished! If you'd tell me what that man was like, I'd get Mr. Harcourt to discharge him."

"Then I certainly shan't tell you," said Nina. "Don't think any more of it. It won't happen again."

Lord Sutcombe walked away from the theatre briskly, but suddenly he stopped, and, with a gesture of impatience, he strode back.

"Who was the young lady who was waiting for Miss Bainford?" he asked of the doorkeeper.

"That was Miss Wood, sister of the author of the first piece, my lord," he replied. "I've heard that one of the supers has been annoying her. I'd only turned my back for a moment. I'll find out who it was, my lord——"

"No matter," said his lordship. "For the future take Miss Wood to the little room adjoining the greenroom."

"Yes, my lord," said the man. "I'm sorry it should have happened——"

Lord Sutcombe nodded and went out again. His rooms were at Eversleigh Court, on the Embankment, and all the way he thought of Miss Wood with a persistence which annoyed him.

"A beautiful girl—and a lady. She ought not to be hanging about a stage door. Miss Wood—then the brother must be a gentleman. But that's not in any way remarkable. That first piece is full of refinement and the touches of a cultured brain. Should like to see him. I wonder whether Harcourt knows more about them—him—than he pretends."

He was still thinking of Nina as he went up the stairs to his flat and entered a handsome and delightfully furnished drawing-room. On a settee by the fire a young girl was lying, with a book in her hand. She was his sister, Lady Vivienne, and an invalid. A fall from a horse, when she was a child, had injured her spine, and consigned her for the greater part of her time to a couch. She could walk only a few yards with assistance, and that assistance she preferred from her brother. Between the two existed an extraordinary affection which dated from their childhood, and deepened every day. Vivienne regarded her brother as the handsomest and the best man in the world, and Sutcombe was sure in his own mind that Vivienne was the sweetest and noblest of her sex. They had lived together in a London flat, in a hotel on the Riviera, at a cottage up the river, since the death of their parents, and, strange to say, Sutcombe had no secrets from her, from which fact the reader will gather that he deserved Polly's description of him; for the man who can lay his life open before his sister must possess a pretty clear record.

"Home early, Sutcombe. I'm glad!" she said, smiling at him through eyes that were a reflection of his own. "I thought you were going to a dinner at the Savage?"

"I was, but I changed my mind," he said, standing before the fire and looking at it absently. Her soft eyes rested on his face with gentle scrutiny for a moment or two, then she said, in a low voice:

"What is it, Sutcombe?"

He started slightly, and smiled at her rather shamefacedly. It did not occur to him to evade the question, to conceal the cause of his preoccupation.

"Something that happened to me to-night," he said; and he told her of the little adventure.

"Such a beautiful girl, Viv! Coming along I tried to describe her to you; but I can't. For the life of me I couldn't tell you the color of her eyes; gray, I think, or violet. And her voice—somehow it reminded me of yours; you don't mind?"

"Not in the least, for I can gather that it was a nice one. And a lady, Sutcombe?"

"Emphatically so!" he returned promptly. " 'I knows a lady when I sees her.' "

"Did she look—poor? I mean, was she shabbily dressed?" asked Lady Vivienne, going to the feminine point.

"No; certainly not. She was very plainly dressed, but in perfect taste, and like a lady. What I mean is, that she was as quietly dressed as any other lady, and that there was nothing suggestive of the theatre about her."

"She may be poor, and yet dress with refinement and taste," said Lady Vivienne shrewdly. "And her brother is the author of the first piece, and is going to write the new play. And a cripple—poor fellow!"

She did not sigh with self-pity, but Sutcombe drew a little nearer, and laid a hand gently on her head.

"I should like to see him—and her, of course," she said, acknowledging the caress of his hand, by a touch of hers.

He shook his head. "So should I. But I don't see how it could be managed. Viv, you know that I—and you, too—hate intruding on other people. I mean that because this lady is connected with the theatre there is no reason why one should force one's self on her—them. And, to tell you the truth, I don't think it would be easy, any easier, indeed, than it would be for them to intrude upon us. By George, not so easy, for she was, in a way, more dignified and—and aloof than you are, Viv!"

"You are very interested in—them, Sutcombe," she said very softly.

He colored and bit his lip, but he did not turn away from her.

"I'm so interested in—let's be candid, Viv!—*her* that I can't get her out of my mind. I'd give a great deal to see her again."

Lady Vivienne was silent for a moment. She knew her brother, as few sisters know their brothers, and was aware that Sutcombe was not a susceptible man; indeed, that he was rather unimpressionable. There had been a fleeting "fancy" or two in his life, but it had been a fancy only, and had been as transient as it had been superficial. He had never displayed an interest in any woman like the interest he was confessing to-night. Had he really fallen in love at last; had he at last met the "one woman in the world"? she asked herself; and, if so, how would it be with him? A girl he had met at the theatre! With a sister's loving anxiety she had always been "afraid" of Sutcombe's connection with the stage; plenty of good women are to be found there, but there, also, are Sirens who have wrecked many a fair bark, and devoured the crew body and bones. She leaned on her arm and gazed at the fire musingly.

"You will see her again, Sutcombe?" she said at last, almost prophetically.

"I shall try," he said. "I must. Don't laugh at me; but you won't, Viv——"

"No," she said, in a still voice, and with a smile that was pathetic. "I am more likely to—cry. Forgive me, dear! It is only jealousy, the jealousy of the poor girl who has had you to herself for so many years."

"And who will have me to herself for very many more," he said, in a low voice. "What nonsense we are talking, Viv! I shall forget her before the morning."

"I hope so!" she responded fervently; "for—for, Sutcombe, dear—a girl at the theatre——"

"No!" he said quickly. "She has nothing to do with the business——By George, you're right. Viv! She is connected with it, is—is—out of our set! Oh, I know all you're thinking, and—of course you're right. We'll say no more about her."

And, of course, five minutes afterward he came to the door from the adjoining room, where he had been smoking, and returned to the subject.

"See here, Viv. It's not at all unlikely, as you say, that they are badly off. I might help her brother in the matter of this play, might see that he gets fair terms from Harcourt——"

"And so earn the sister's gratitude," she said, with a smile. "Come in here and sit down, and let us talk about her. It's better than your brooding by yourself in there, dear!"

CHAPTER XVIII
NINA'S NEW FRIENDS

Sutcombe said no more about Nina, but, like the famous parrot, he thought a great deal; and he found it imperatively necessary to go down to the theatre very often—one knows that business must be attended to. But, though he hovered about the stage entrance and doorways at the beginning and close of the play, he did not again see the girl whose face and voice haunted him; and it is probable—though not very likely, for Nina's face was not one to be easily torn from one's memory—that he might have forgotten her if the long arm of coincidence had not been stretched out in grim irony to draw closer the links of the chain.

It chanced, a week later, that Nina was standing on the edge of the curb, in the middle of Bond Street, waiting to cross. She was not in any hurry, for she was thinking of the last act of the play; and she was looking absently before her, when she felt something brush past her skirt, and saw a child attempt to run between the carriages. It was a London urchin of the usual type, and there is no doubt that he would have threaded his way safely among the horses if an old lady, who was standing beside Nina, had not uttered an exclamation of terror and apprehension. The child heard it, turned to look, having not the faintest suspicion that he was the cause, and in another moment he would have been under a carriage if Nina had not sprung forward and hauled him out of the way.

The coachman had pulled up his horse almost on its haunches, and, very red in the face, was trying not to swear; and Nina heard a very soft and sweet, and at that moment a very anxious, voice exclaim:

"Oh—the child! Have you run over it?"

By this time Nina had got the urchin on the pavement, and she looked up and saw that the inquiry had come from a very pretty, delicate-looking lady in the carriage. The usual crowd and policeman almost shut Nina and the rescued one from Vivienne's view, but at last she caught Nina's eye, and beckoned to her anxiously. Nina went to the carriage, still half unconsciously grabbing the boy.

"Oh, is he hurt? How brave of you! How very brave!" said Vivienne fervently. "Is he hurt?"

"No, I don't think so," said Nina. "If he would only leave off crying——"

"Will you—would you mind—bringing him in here?" asked Vivienne timidly. "I—I am an invalid and cannot get out, or I wouldn't trouble you."

Before Nina could reply the boy seized so good a chance of escaping an interview with his natural foe, the policeman, and of his own accord slipped into the carriage.

"There is nothing the matter with him," said Nina, and with a slight bow she was turning away, when Vivienne said eagerly, almost imploringly:

"Oh, won't you come in, too? Do, do please! I—I am not at all sure *you* are not hurt. I live quite near here—if you would come."

Nina hesitated a moment, then got in; the policeman took Lady Vivienne's address from the coachman, and he drove off.

The boy was still rubbing his eyes with his dirty fists, but he was eying the two ladies with monkey-like cunning, and, shrewdly concluding that he had landed in clover, kept up an assumption of much grief and tribulation.

"Poor little fellow!" said Vivienne, leaning forward and stroking his arm rather gingerly. "If he would only tell us whether he is hurt or not!" Then she turned her attention to Nina. "How quick you were! It was like—like a cat springing for a kitten—but that sounds rude!" as Nina's eyes twinkled. "And how strong, as well as brave, you must be to be able to lift so big a boy! And the horse did not touch you?"

"Not in the least," said Nina. "And now, if you will kindly stop the carriage I will get out—and take this young gentleman with me."

But at this Vivienne looked very hurt and injured.

"Oh, please don't! Please come home with me. I live at Eversleigh Court. Why, we are nearly there! Your dress is muddied—you can't walk home like that! My maid will clean it—besides, we don't really know that the child is all right. Oh, please come!"

It was hard to resist the pleading voice and wistful eyes, so Nina yielded, though she anxious to avoid making new acquaintances.

A footman helped Lady Vivienne to alight, and the two ladies and the boy went up to the flat, where they were immediately surrounded by the curious and rather amazed servants.

"Hurt! Oh, poor, dear little boy! Where!" exclaimed Vivienne's maid, kneeling before the urchin, who responded to her anxious inquiries with a low howl indicating excruciating pain. There was a chorus of "Oh's" from the maids; and, in the confusion, Lord Sutcombe's step was heard to pass into the other room. Vivienne knew the step, and, helping herself by the chairs and the wall, limped out.

"Oh, Sutcombe!" she exclaimed. "We've had an accident—well, scarcely an accident. The carriage nearly ran over a boy—and we've got him in the next room. Wait a moment! I'm sure we should have killed him if a young girl had not sprung forward and saved him. Such a lovely creature, Sutcombe!"

"The boy?"

"No, no! Don't be silly! The girl. The most charming, lovable girl I've ever seen. And so brave! The horse was nearly touching her, indeed, I thought she must be knocked down. And so calm, and—and serene, amid all the fuss."

"You seem to have discovered a paragon," he said, with a smile. "Where is she, gone?"

"No, in the next room. I had the greatest difficulty in keeping her. The boy's there—we're seeing if he's hurt!"

"A street arab, I suppose? Don't alarm yourself; you can't hurt 'em. And the young lady—have you put her in the glass case? Let us go and look at this rare specimen."

He drew her arm within his, and led her into the next room; that is, as far as the door; there he stopped short and stared—his face very red—at Nina, who was standing, with loosely clasped hands, looking, with very little alarm, at the child.

Vivienne looked up at him with surprise.

"Why—what is the matter, Sutcombe?" she inquired, in a low voice; then she stopped short and looked from Nina to him, for Nina had turned and was regarding him with a blush, and a surprise almost as marked as his own.

Sutcombe recovered his presence of mind almost immediately, and, coming forward, said quietly, but with a smile of pleasure in his frank eyes:

"How do you do, Miss Wood! What a strange coincidence! I mean——"

"Then you know——This is your Miss Wood!" The exclamation broke from Vivienne involuntarily.

Sutcombe colored at the "your."

"I have told my sister of our meeting the other night, Miss Wood," he said. "I hope you are not hurt. No? And the boy? Let me see."

After a moment's examination and a question or two, which the boy answered promptly enough—he was dealing with a man now—Sutcombe looked up with a smile. "I think a good meal and——" he slipped something into the grimy hand, which closed over it instantly—"will be all the surgery needed. Take him away, cook."

The boy, grinning like a chimpanzee, was led away, and Sutcombe, quite casually, though his heart was beating fast, besought Nina to sit down, for Vivienne was still half dazed by the surprise.

"Yes; yes, oh, yes!" she said eagerly. "The tea is coming, and you must want a cup so badly! And your dress—we have thought of nothing but the boy! How indifferent you must think us! Sutcombe, if you had seen Miss Wood——"

"I can imagine the scene," said Sutcombe, in a low voice. "I know how calm and self-possessed Miss Wood can be in moments of difficulty. I'll be back in a moment, Vivienne."

He went into the next room and stood quite still, looking at nothing, for a few moments. He wanted to realize that she was here, in the next room, to obtain full control over himself, to be able to move and speak as if his heart were beating with its normal pulse. When he returned the tea was on, and the two girls were chatting pleasantly. It was evident that the discovery that her girl hero was "the Miss Wood of the theatre" had not changed Vivienne's admiration of, and liking for, Nina.

"We've got over the coincidence, Sutcombe," she said, as she gave him his tea, "and we are talking about the new play—Miss Wood's brother's, you know."

He nodded.

"May I, too, hear about it?" he said. "You know I am—well, interested."

At this Nina became rather shy—for talking to him about the play was a very different thing to talking to the gentle girl, whose pale face and blue eyes were all aglow with sympathy and interest, and the eager desire to admire and approve; but love maketh a man cunning, and, after a while, Sutcombe led her on to the subject.

"Your brother must be very clever," he said. "It is a wonderfully good plot, I should say. There's only one thing——"

"Oh, what is that?" Nina inquired earnestly. "Pray tell me—it is so full of faults—he would like to know——"

"Well, it's the card-playing scene. It's very 'strong,' as they call it; but it's just a little wrong in one detail. Baccarat isn't played as the characters play it——"

Nina smiled and blushed.

"Oh, thank you so much!" she said. "How can one help making mistakes when one is writing about things one knows nothing about! Of course, I've never played baccarat."

The silence, the breathless silence with which Vivienne regarded her told her what she had done. Her face flamed, then went pale, and her brows came together.

"What does it matter?" said Sutcombe, in a low voice that quivered with sympathy. "Besides, I guessed your secret while you were describing the play. But why should you be ashamed of it; why should you wish to hide yourself behind a man's name? Oh, I see! But that prejudice is dead! Strange as it may seem, the world is beginning to have a suspicion that women are as clever as, more clever than, men."

"And—you—wrote 'The Betrothed,' and *this* play!" exclaimed Vivienne. "Oh, you dear, clever girl! But how did you guess it, Sutcombe?"

Sutcombe smiled only.

Nina made the best of the matter.

"I think I should like to keep my secret, so far as the public is concerned, Lord Sutcombe," she said quietly.

He inclined his head.

"Your wishes shall be respected, of course," he said. "Perhaps—perhaps I can be of some use? I mean there may be some other little detail which, as a man of the world, one who plays other games than baccarat, I might help you in——"

"Oh, yes!" put in Vivienne eagerly. "Do make use of him, Miss Wood!"

"What I would suggest, if I may, is that Miss Wood should bring the play and read it to me," said Sutcombe, in the most business-like tone he could assume.

Nina, the unsuspecting Nina, gave him a grateful look from her lovely eyes.

"Oh, will you?" she said. "How good you are to me! It is just what I want! But—the trouble!"

"Oh, don't mind that!" said the unselfish Sutcombe. "I've always got time to spare. How would it be if you came to-morrow?"

"Yes, yes!" Vivienne cut in again. "And I'll call for Miss Wood and drive her here. She lives with that bright girl—you remember how she made me laugh, Sutcombe?—Miss Bainford."

Sutcombe glanced at Nina, wondering how she would take this suggestion; but Nina, having no false pride, and, consequently, not being ashamed of her and Polly's humble diggings, accepted at once.

"That's all right," said Sutcombe. The phrase—it was Vane Mannering's—made Nina's heart leap. "Then I'll be off. I've to be at the theatre on business."

With love's cunning, he left the two girls together, and went out into the streets to ask himself whether he was awake or dreaming.

When he returned Vivienne received him almost shamefacedly.

"Oh, Sutcombe! And I meant to help you, to help you to forget her! But I know now that it would have been impossible! I don't wonder at your——"

"Infatuation," he said quietly; "don't hesitate."

"She is too beautiful and lovable for words," she said. "If I were a man, I could not help falling in love with her. But——"

"But me no buts."

"But there is something about her. There is—an aloofness; I don't know how to describe it. Sutcombe, that girl has a history."

"Most of us have," he said, with a smile.

"I know. But hers is not a common or garden one. She has passed through some great trouble. I'm sure of it. We women are quick at reading other women——"

"Too quick," he said half impatiently. "What trouble, beyond that which falls to the common lot, can she have had? She may have lost her father, mother, some near relation——"

"No, it is not that," she said thoughtfully. "That would not cause the air of reserve and——"

He put the idea from him with the lover's impatience.

"You're making mountains of molehills, Viv," he said. "You were always romantic. What 'secret sorrow' should she have?"

When Nina got home she gave Polly an account of the adventure and the coincidence, and Polly nodded in open-eyed acquiescence and approval.

"The very thing, dear!" she said. "Lor'! What luck you have! Lord Sutcombe can do what he likes at the Momus. Oh, we're in luck! And isn't he handsome?"

"Is he? I didn't notice," said Nina absently. She was at that moment thinking of her last act, and when your playwright is thinking of that, all the rest of the world doesn't count.

Vivienne called for her, as arranged, and they drove to Eversleigh Court. Sutcombe did not come in till tea was nearly over, and—he had schooled himself—greeted Nina in quite a casual way. She read the play, as far as it had gone; read it at first in a faltering, apologetic manner, but, presently, warming to her work, and forgetting herself, read it with spirit and expression. Sutcombe, with his eyes upon her profile, listened intently, and now and again suggested some alteration in the details. Nina listened with the eager humility of the author, and jotted them down in her notebook. Then Sutcombe disappeared, and left the two girls to talk over the dresses, a subject which kept them so fully employed that Nina was persuaded to stay to dinner.

Nina was one of those women who possess the power of influencing the members of her own sex as well as men, and Vivienne, already predisposed, fell a victim to this unconscious influence. In a word, Lady Vivienne was not happy unless Nina spent some portion of the twenty-four hours at the flat. And if Sutcombe was not there all the time, he spent many hours in Nina's society. They were the hours of his life.

At last the play was finished and handed to Mr. Harcourt. "My Lady Pride" had nearly run its course, and he was eager to try the new comedy, and, if it went well in London, he intended running two, or even more, companies in the provinces. He was so satisfied with the play that he mounted it with more than the usual sumptuousness.

But, before the eventful night had arrived, Lady Vivienne had shown signs of the wear and tear of the London air. The doctor, on whose skill she and Sutcombe depended, had said that she should winter abroad.

"You used to have a yacht," he said. "Take her for a cruise, a long cruise. Anywhere out of the English east winds. I fear them more than anything else for her."

Sutcombe nodded; then frowned.

"Give me to the sixth of next month," he said.

It was the date of the production of the new play, about which he was anxious, probably more anxious than Nina herself. When he told Vivienne that they would have to go abroad, she at once said:

"Let us persuade Miss Wood to go with us."

Nina received the suggestion as if it were a jest.

"Perhaps my poor play will be a failure," she said, "and I shall have to work for my living in some other way. Oh, it is quite impossible for me to go!"

The eventful night arrived, and Nina, in her old place in the corner of the upper circle, went through the usual agony; but there was really no cause for apprehension, for the end of the first act caught the audience, and they were tightly held during the remainder of the play. It was an unqualified success, the kind of success about which there can be no possibility of doubt. The house was charged with enthusiasm, and it was for some time in vain that Mr. Harcourt, coming forward, with his hand upon his heart and a smile from ear to ear, to inform the house that Herbert Wood was not present, could make himself heard. The house seemed very disappointed, but it was the only disappointment of the evening.

It is nice to be able to record the fact that "the promising young actress," Miss Polly Bainford, scored very heavily in a part peculiarly well suited to her by no means limited capacity. Sutcombe, flushed with excitement, went round to the upper circle in search of Nina, who, her identity little suspected by the audience, was leaning back with her hands tightly clasped in her lap, and a look of relief and thanksgiving on her rather pale face.

"I congratulate you!" he whispered. "Let me take you round to our box. If you would help Vivienne down, I will go round and bring Miss Bainford. Yes," he added, with a smile, in response to Nina's look of surprise, "Vivienne admires Miss Bainford very much, and is anxious to know her. It is quite a concession on her part, isn't it? But prejudice always melts away, in the sunshine of common sense."

It was a very delightful little party at the flat, and Sutcombe proposed Nina's health, and insisted upon, them filling their glasses as if they were at a city public dinner, and all Nina could say in response was, "Thank you very much!" But her eyes, not undimmed with tears, were more eloquent.

Sutcombe lit his cigar after supper, and, on his way to the cigar cabinet, took up some letters which were lying on the table. He opened them quite mechanically and absent-mindedly; for he was all aglow with love and admiration for Nina, and he was asking himself whether he dared venture to tell her that she held the happiness of his life in her hands. He had been so careful to conceal his love, he had set so stern a watch on lips and eyes, that he knew Nina had no suspicion that he had lost his heart to her. Should he tell her to-night? He asked himself the question with an anxious dread, for he knew that she would not give herself to any man unless she really loved him, and the fact that he was of higher rank than herself would not influence her.

His thoughts were running in this and similar directions, when something in the letter he was mechanically reading caught his attention. The blood rose to his face, then left it very pale, and he stood, with his back turned to the others, staring at the letter as if he could not grasp its sense. Then he put it in his pocket, went back to his place at the table, and tried to appear as if nothing were the matter.

But Vivienne's eyes were quick to notice his affectation of ease and gayety, and when he had come back from seeing the girls home, she said to him quite quietly:

"What is it, Sutcombe?"

"We are nearly ruined," he said, as quietly as she herself had spoken. "Partridge, the trustee, has broken and bolted. He has made away with everything, or nearly everything, you and I possess."

"What will you do, Sutcombe?" she asked, after a pause.

"God knows!" he said, with a note of despair in his voice; for how could he now speak to Decima?

They sat up for hours; but all the talking in the world could not lessen the disaster. They had not been rich, in the present acceptation of the word, but their joint income had been just sufficient for them, and they knew how much the "little less" meant. Fortunately, some of Vivienne's money was invested in her own name, and had therefore escaped the clutches of Mr. Partridge.

"There is that land in Australia, Sutcombe," she said. "Why not go out there, and see if we could do anything? We were going somewhere, you know."

"That is not a bad idea," he said. "At any rate, it will be action. Anything would be better than sitting still."

Nina had promised to go round next morning; and she saw at once that something was the matter, though both brother and sister put a brave face on it.

"Let us tell her, Sutcombe," said Vivienne.

He did so in a few words, and as cheerfully as possible, but his eyes were full of a wistful pleading, an unspoken prayer, which Nina, absorbed in the grave news, did not notice. She seemed to be thinking deeply, but not feeling very keenly, and Vivienne watched her with faint surprise.

Suddenly Nina looked up. Her brows were drawn straight, her eyes were grave and thoughtful, and there was a touch of unwonted color in her cheeks.

"Shall you have to give up your cruise?" she asked.

"Well—no," said Sutcombe; "as it happens, Vivienne has some land out in Australia, and we thought of taking the *Ariel* there to see—well, if any money could be made out of it—the land, I mean."

Nina looked down for a minute, then up at his face with grave earnestness.

"You asked me to go with you the other day. Will you take me now?" she said, in a low voice.

CHAPTER XIX
BACK TO THE FAIRY ISLE

The *Ariel* was skimming over an opal sea, her white sails filled with the light breeze, her bow rising and falling proudly as she sent the foam along her sleek sides; but Nina was not looking at the beauty of sea and sky. On her lap, as she sat in her deck chair, which was always placed as far for'ard as the weather would permit, was spread out the chart over which she had spent so many hours of the voyage, brooding, questioning, sometimes with a glow of hope, but oftener with a dull despair.

At a little distance Sutcombe stood beside Vivienne, reclining at full length and covered with her shawls, and both of them were silently regarding the slim, girlish figure bent over the chart. Sutcombe broke the silence at last.

"If one could only do something, something to help her!"

"Or persuade her to give it up!" put in Vivienne wistfully.

He shook his head.

"She would give it up if we insisted," he said, in a low voice, "but we shall not do that, Viv!"

Vivienne sighed. "How pale and worn she looks! While I have been gaining health and strength, she has been losing them. See how thin she is! Sometimes"—her voice grew almost inaudible—"I am half tempted to believe that—that—she is mistaken, that she is the victim of delusion. Have there not been such cases, Sutcombe?"

He smiled and shook his head.

"Decima is the last person to suffer from a delusion," he said. "There was never a more acute, intellectual—but you know, Viv! I shall go and speak to her. I must! I feel as if I could not stand by helpless and see her growing more anxious, more despairing each day. Wait a minute; she is talking to the skipper."

Barnes, the skipper, a young man with a shy smile, behind which lay a profound seamanship, was consulting the chart with Nina. They saw him reluctantly shake his head, smiling still, then pass on. Sutcombe went up to her. Her head had sunk on her hand, and when she raised her face at his approach he saw so wistful, so eager an expression in her eyes that it went to his heart.

"Will you not come into the saloon and rest?" he said gently.

She shook her head.

"I cannot," she said humbly enough. "We have been examining the chart again——Oh, Lord Sutcombe, how patient you are! It—it is that that hurts me! If you would only laugh at me, if you would only tell me that your patience is exhausted, that you will bear with me—my whim—no longer, I think I should be less heartbroken."

"Why should I tell you that which is not true?" he responded, his eyes resting on her bent head with unspeakable sympathy and tenderness.

"And yet it would be so—so natural, so well deserved!" she retorted bitterly. "Sometimes I wonder why you did not think that I am stark, staring mad, that I am the victim of a wild delusion——"

It was Vivienne's word, but he still smiled.

"For what is it that I have asked you to do, and you, so generously, so trustingly, have consented to do?" she went on, with a deep sigh.

"Not a very great thing, surely!" he said, trying to answer and reassure her in a breath. "You have asked us to leave the direct course, to turn aside that we may help you to find a certain island, of which you know, and which you want us to visit."

"An island not marked on the chart, a nameless place, as nameless and intangible as that of a dream. Sometimes," sighingly, despairingly, "I wonder whether it exists only in a dream; whether I shall wake to find that its only place is in my imagination. And yet—no! If you only knew! Why do you not insist upon my telling you all, everything? Why do you not refuse to continue in this mad search unless I give you better reasons for doing so?"

"Because I love you so dearly that if this island ever existed, and the search were as futile as that for the philosopher's stone, I would not turn from it until my heart told me you wished to do so," he might have replied; but instead he said:

"Why grieve so about the matter, Decima? No harm has been done. We have had, are having, fine weather; it does not matter whether we reach port this week or the next. And Vivienne is of the same mind as I. If you would only be less anxious! Do you think we cannot see that the strain is telling on you, and that we do not—suffer? Ah, do not be so unhappy! Nothing—*nothing* is worth that!"

She pushed the hair from her forehead and looked up at him gratefully.

"How good you are to me!" she said, in a low voice. "Well, bear with me a little longer. Listen, Lord Sutcombe: If—if we do not discover this island to-morrow, I will tell you why I have persuaded you to turn out of your course in search of it; I will tell you—all. It is only fair. But give me until to-morrow. Barnes tells me that he will try a new course, that he himself feels certain land, islands, perhaps, are nearer than the chart indicates. Give me till to-morrow at noon!"

"I will give you twelve months of to-morrows if you like," he said fervently; "we will run in at the next port and provision the yacht for a year's cruise——"

She turned from him half impatiently.

"Only till to-morrow!" she said, and she bent over the chart again.

But her eyes were dim with the pangs of disappointment and failure, for the *Ariel* had been beating about for weeks in search of the nameless island, and the dream, the bright dream which she had dreamed the night Sutcombe had told her of their loss, and she had been compelled to ask them to let her go with them, was growing faint and pale with the sickness of hope deferred.

After a time she folded the chart, rose resolutely, and, with a gesture, as of one throwing off a heavy weight, went to the other two.

"From this moment," she said, "I will say no more, no, not a word. If—if we fail, then you shall think it was just a dream, a delusion—ah, do you think I do not know what is in your minds!" as Vivienne colored and lowered her eyes.

"Let us go and have some music, dear," said Vivienne, laying her hand on Nina's arm tenderly, for she knew that, while they remained on deck, Nina's aching eyes would scan the sea, that seemed to mock her with its emptiness.

They went below, and Nina, acting up to her resolve, played, and sang, and talked, as if her heart were not racked with suspense; but as she lay in her berth that night the bitterness welled up in her. And it was not altogether unselfish. For as the *Ariel* had approached the spot where she imagined the fairy isle to be, there had arisen and grown an aching longing to see once more the place where she had suffered—and, ah, yes, for a short time, enjoyed—so much. Vane Mannering was lost to her—she did not know whether he was alive or dead—but for a few fleeting hours she had basked in the knowledge of her own love for him, and the hope that his love might turn to her.

She slept at last, a fitful sleep, but was up on deck soon after dawn, and Barnes, at his wheel, touched the peak of his cap and smiled his shy greeting.

"Nothing, Barnes?" she asked, with repressed eagerness.

"Nothing, miss," he admitted reluctantly. "I've changed her course for west due west, and—we shall see, miss. We may sight land before noon——"

"To find another group of islands—but not those we want," she said, with a sigh, as she turned away. Barnes shook his head at the sails. She who had been so ready with the sweet smile, the gentle word which had won the hearts of the men, as they had won the heart of their master, had grown almost irritable and impatient, and Barnes, as he watched her, standing at the bow with her hand shading her eyes, hopeless and incredulous of "Miss Decima's island," shook his head again.

But he held on his course, and about noon, Nina, who had been leaning against the taffrail, her eyes fixed on the sea, uttered an exclamation and pointed at some object floating on the waves.

"Seaweed!" said Sutcombe, coming quickly to her side, and he turned toward her with an eagerness almost as keen as her own, then shouted the word to Vivienne. In silence, almost breathlessly, they watched and waited. But "Miss Decima's luck," as the men had grown to call it, pursued her even now; for, as they gazed, a slight mist rose above the horizon, gradually crept upward and enveloped the yacht, shutting out sea and sky. Down came the sails, and the vessel floated like a bird through the white fog. They should have anchored, but Barnes withheld the order, and, taking some soundings, let the vessel drift.

Nina turned away; her eyes were dim and on her lips flickered a smile that was worse than tears.

"Fate is against me!" she said. "The time is up—and I am beaten! Lord Sutcombe, I—I—give it up!"

"Wait!" he said. "Look!" and he waved his hand toward the mist.

It was lifting as swiftly as it had fallen; before it had quite cleared, out spread the sails, and the *Ariel* drove through it. Clearer and yet clearer grew the air, and then, so suddenly that they had scarcely time to exclaim, there lay before them the vision of an island, green as an emerald, and set in a golden line of sand, with the shrill cry of the sea birds circling round it, the waving of the fir trees on its crest.

It was Vivienne who first cried out. Nina stood, her hands clinched on her bosom, her eyes like those of one in a trance. Sutcombe turned to her with an instinctive gesture of sympathy, for her lips were white and her breath came painfully.

"It is the island at last!" she said.

The skipper's word of command rang out, the "Ay, ay, sir!" of the men followed sharp upon it, the sails fell as if by magic, and the *Ariel* was anchored within, as it seemed in the clear air, half a mile of the island, which, even yet, Nina could scarcely help regarding as a vision.

Sutcombe took her hand and pressed it, and she turned to him as if awaking from a dream; but with surprise he saw that there was no joy in her eyes, only an expression of satisfaction that was not untinged with sadness.

"We will land at once," he said. "You wish it?"

"Yes," she said, "let us go. When—when we are there I will tell you, I will explain. Your patience—ah, how great it has been, how sorely tried!— shall not be tried any longer. Yes, let us land. But wait!" She put her hand to her head, as if trying to think, as if some difficulty had occurred to her. "Lord Sutcombe, I want that only you, and Lady Vivienne, and I should land—at first, at any rate. Can you manage it so?"

"Why, of course!" he responded, with an encouraging smile, as he looked into the lovely eyes whose every expression he knew by heart. "I will take just sufficient men to land us, and they shall remain in the boat until, well, as long as you wish them to do so."

She nodded, and stood watching the launching and manning of the boat. The crew of the *Ariel* were disciplined like a man-o'-war's men, and they rowed with stolid faces and incurious eyes, whatever they may have felt, to the nameless island which they had been chasing so long.

As the boat approached the sand-fringed shore, Nina's face grew paler, and she turned it away from the others, though there was no need, for Sutcombe and Vivienne studiously avoided glancing at her. He helped her out of the boat, almost as gently and carefully as he helped Vivienne; and, as if absorbed in her own thoughts, Nina silently led the way up the beach.

The huts were still standing as they had been left, but Nina's eyes were fixed on a spot where a mound rose on the shingly strand. She stood there for a moment, her head bent, her lips moving; then she walked on to one of the huts.

"Go in," she said, motioning them to enter her own hut. "Yes, I—I—am at home! Did you not guess?" as they entered and stood and looked round them, at last regarding her with astonishment. "I once lived on this island. I was wrecked here, with some of the passengers and the crew of the *Alpina*. Sit down, Lady Vivienne, I want to tell you."

Leaning against the rough hut, she told them the story of the wreck, that is, a part of the story, for she made no mention of Vane Mannering, who had been the prominent figure. "My father died—and a friend, a friend who was like a brother to me——It was at their grave I—stopped just now."

Sutcombe's eyes were fixed on her with the tenderest sympathy.

"I—I am not surprised at your wanting to find the island, at your anxiety to revisit it," he said, in a low voice.

But Nina shook her head.

"I had another reason," she said. She might well have said reasons, for assuredly the longing to see once again the place in which she had tasted such misery and such happiness had drawn her there. "It is the reason that I asked you to let us come alone. Lord Sutcombe, this island was discovered, so to speak, by the unfortunate castaways who dragged themselves to land here that night," she shuddered; "but my father made another discovery, and it is that which led me to ask you to let me come with you on your cruise, and gave me courage to persuade you to alter the course of the *Ariel*. You remember the night you told me of your loss?"

Sutcombe nodded. Was there any one night, any one incident connected with her, which he was likely to forget?

"That night I remembered—I think for the first time, strange as it may seem—this discovery of my father's, and an idea in connection with it flashed into my mind. Tell me, Lord Sutcombe: I am his only daughter, child. That which belonged to him, when he died, now belongs to me, does it not?"

"Most certainly!" replied Sutcombe, all in the dark, but patiently waiting for the light. "You inherit everything of which he was possessed."

"I am glad," she said, as if relieved. "Wait for one minute!"

She went outside, but even at that moment she paused and looked round with an aching heart, a heart that throbbed painfully with the memories of those short days of vague, uncertain bliss. The whole island seemed to speak of Vane; seemed to be crying to her: "You have come back; but where is he, our master?" She drew her hand across her eyes, and roused herself from her reverie, and, going to the back of the hut, scraped away the soil from a small mound, took up two or three of the pieces of gold quartz, and, reentering the hut, laid them on the rough table, just as her father had done on the night of their discovery.

Sutcombe and Vivienne looked from them to her questioningly.

"Do you not understand?" she said, with a smile, almost of contentment; for it was sweet to be able to repay, even thus inadequately, some fraction of the goodness of these friends of hers.

"What is it?" said Sutcombe, taking up one of the pieces. "Why! It's not——"

"Yes, it is gold!" she said, her face flushing, her eyes glowing.

But Sutcombe's face grew pale, and, laying the quartz down, he drew back.

"I—I congratulate you, Miss Wood," he said—not "Decima," as he had of late slipped into calling her. "If—if there is much of this, you—you must be very rich!"

"I!" she said. "Ah, yes, I suppose so; but—but it was not for myself——"
She stopped, for his face had grown hot, and his eyes flashed almost resentfully. Vivienne laid her hand upon his arm imploringly.

"Wait, wait till she has finished, Sutcombe," she whispered.

Nina looked from one to the other, and, comprehending, colored almost as hotly as Sutcombe.

"No, no!" she said. "I—I was not going to offer you *these*; indeed, they are not mine"—she paused—"only half of it is mine. But there is plenty more; my father said the island was an Eldorado; and the gold is yours, any one's who comes and likes to dig for it. Indeed, one need not dig very much, for it lies in the beds of the streams, and in streaks in the rocks——"

Sutcombe gazed at her in amazement too great for words.

"And—and no one knows of this but you!" he exclaimed at last.

"No one but I—and one other, the—the person to whom half of the gold found belongs."

He wiped his brow, for to the least mercenary of men the presence of a vast quantity of gold, with prospective possession, is rather a discomposing fact, one not to be contemplated without a thrill.

"And he?" he asked breathlessly. "Where is he? Why is he not here?"

The color left her face, and her lids drooped.

"I do not know," she said, in a low voice. "He—he may be dead!"

"He did not escape with you?" asked Sutcombe.

She made a movement of her hand, as if the question, the subject, pained her.

"No—I left him here. I—ah, do not ask me any more!"

Vivienne leaned forward and touched her hand.

"No, no, dear, we will not! Oh, do you think we do not understand! To be wrecked here on this lonely place! To have suffered, as you must have suffered—no, not a word more shall be spoken, dear Decima!"

Sutcombe leaned against the log wall of the hut, his arms folded, his eyes fixed, not on the gold, but on the floor.

"And it was for us, for us that you have worn yourself to a shadow with anxiety and hope deferred," he said. "That we might have this gold——"

"Why not?" she broke in. "Would you not have done the same for me, for any friend? And what true friends you have been to me! And what is the use of it, if it cannot be put to such good service?"

"And you never thought of yourself?" he said, very quietly. "You were not rich——"

"Very poor indeed," she said, with a laugh.

"And you never thought of finding this island, this Eldorado, for your own benefit?"

"No," she said simply; "what should I have done with it? What is the use of money when——" She paused. "Besides, I was lucky so soon. I thought so much of my work, of my play, that if the gold had been lying on Hampstead Heath, instead of on a mysterious island in the wide ocean, I don't think I should have troubled to take the train for it." She sighed, then, with a winning smile, she went up to him and touched his sleeve. "Lord Sutcombe, you won't let scruples interfere, you won't—make difficulties?"

He longed to take the hand that touched him so pleadingly, to draw her outside and say: "I will take the gold you offer me so generously if you will be still more generous and give me that which I value beyond all the gold in the world—yourself!" But he knew, though he could not have told how he knew, that this was of all moments the worst for such a question; of all places, this the least favorable.

"No," he said, drawing a long breath. "I'm not so churlish—so foolish. I am still too amazed—it all seems like a story out of an adventure book—to quite realize it; but—I accept your generous offer. If the gold is here for the finding—well, Vivienne and you shall be rich."

"Yes!" said Vivienne, with womanly cunning. "I accept unreservedly. I have hated the thought of being poor! Why, think of it! We should have had to sell the *Ariel* at Melbourne, have been obliged to go in for farming, or something of that kind, or settled in some stuffy town on the Continent. And now we can keep the dear old yacht, and we can all go back to England—and you can buy back Southwood, Sutcombe—I told you how it passed from us, Decima? And I can get those pearls I wanted, and—oh, what will you do with all your money, you millionairess?" she broke off, drawing Nina to her and hugging her.

Nina tried to smile. What, indeed? The uselessness of the gold mocked her at that moment, as it had mocked her the day it had been found. There was only one thing she wanted, and it is the one thing no money can buy—forgetfulness! But she strove to dispel the black shadow from her mind.

"Oh, I'll found a National Theatre—for the performance of artistic dramas—by 'Herbert Wood!' " she said. "But now let us be practical, as Polly would say. This is a dangerous secret, Lord Sutcombe. You know now why I thought it better that we should land alone?"

He nodded.

"Let me think!" He took out his pipe. "May I? Thanks! Yes, the men mustn't land here, at any rate; they must not come farther into the island than necessary. We want water——"

"There is plenty near the beach!" said Nina, stifling a sigh. Back came the times when she walked from the stream with the can in her hand, and Vane coming to meet her to take it from her.

"Quite so. They shall get what they want, and Barnes shall take the *Ariel* on a cruise, leaving us here. There are enough provisions——"

"And there are fish, and duck, and turtles in plenty," said poor Nina, trying to smile.

Vivienne clapped her hands and nodded gleefully, though all the time she was watching Nina from the corner of her gentle eyes. "Why, it will be like a picnic, a real picnic! Even if there had not been all this wonderful gold, it would have been worth all the trouble—ah! but not your anxiety, dear—just to see so beautiful and romantic a place. It is like a fairy isle!"

Nina turned away swiftly; the name was like a stab.

They talked over Sutcombe's plan, and presently he went down to the beach, signaled the boat, and sent it off for rugs, bedding, and provisions; and when these were brought he went aboard, told Barnes they intended picnicking on the island, and ordered him to take the *Ariel* on a cruise and pick them up in a week's time.

When he came back he found that the two women had already started the picnic. Nina's hut had been transformed into quite a snug and comfortable bower, with the aid of the rugs and other things brought from the yacht, and Nina, Vivienne told him, was down at the old "saloon" getting tea.

"It's the most wonderful, the most bewitching, place, Sutcombe," Vivienne said, from the cozy nest in which Nina had bestowed her. "The 'saloon' is the large hut where the men lived. We have arranged that you are to sleep in a corner of it—for the other hut is not so comfortable, Decima says. She thinks of everything; indeed, she is as wonderful as the island! I tell her she is the fairy of the enchanted spot, and that presently she will wave her hand and we shall wake up, to find we are on board the *Ariel,* and that we have been asleep and dreaming. Have you looked at those lumps of gold again, Sutcombe? Are you sure that they won't turn into 'chunks' of just common rock? Can you realize yet this good fortune of ours?"

"No," he said. "I can only realize that she has made us rich again, that—
—I'll go and see if I can help her."

When he went down to the saloon, carrying some provisions with him, Nina was sitting over the fire she had made, her head resting on her hands, her eyes fixed dreamily and sadly on the blaze. Her whole pose reminded him of Millais' exquisite "Cinderella," and he stopped and looked down at her for a moment, with his heart's longing in his frank blue eyes; and the longing slid into a yearning to pierce the secret of the sad face that she turned to him, sad though she smiled and said brightly enough:

"It is nearly boiling. Have you brought the tea? It is past Lady Vivienne's time, you know."

"Yes, here's the tea," he said. "But I was not thinking of Vivienne, Decima, but of you. How could I think of any one else at such a moment? To speak of thanks"—he made a gesture of despair—"but if you knew how full my heart is——"

"Don't!" she said quickly and with a touch of reproach. "Have I even tried to thank you both for all your goodness to me? Be as generous!" She laughed up at him through the thin veil of sadness. "There! It is boiling at last. The teapot! Thanks. Now, if you'll carry the kettle——"

She gave him no time for more words, but talked quickly and brightly, as she led the way back to the ladies' hut. Her effort at cheerfulness did not end here, and proved successful, for, notwithstanding the shadow of the past which hung over her, the fact that she had been able to befriend these two who had been so good to her uplifted her.

"We shall have to work hard," she said, as she poured out the tea, "for a week is not a long time."

"We can send the *Ariel* away again, or we can come back, now that we know the way here," said Sutcombe eagerly, for the thought that they three were alone on this island, that he should see her nearly every hour of the day, was a secret joy to him; but Nina did not respond.

"You will soon tire of the solitude," she said, in a low voice. "To-morrow I will take you where we—I—saw some of the gold. There is a spade"—she winced, as the scene of the burial of her father and poor Fleming rose before her—"and some other tools we brought from the wreck; and while you are getting the gold, I will go and fish——"

"You fish! Why, how did you learn, who taught you?" cried Vivienne.

"I—I—have watched—people fishing," said Nina.

Vivienne looked round wonderingly.

"Oh, it's just a dream, as I say!" she laughed. "Think of it, Decima! Here are you and we two, sitting here on this remote island, just we three on this fairy isle, and far away in giddy London, with its electric lights and its ceaseless crowds, are our friends, the people we know, leading the same old dreary, monotonous lives, in the same old, smoky air. Why, Decima, do you realize that they are just at this moment—or is the time different?—thronging to the Momus to see the latest successful play? If they could only see the author!"

They busied themselves with the necessary work of this most realistic picnic until nearly nightfall, and at last Vivienne, suddenly growing tired with the excitement, was persuaded by Nina to go to bed.

Sutcombe had said good night and gone off to his quarters in the saloon; but he could not sleep, and after a while he got up and went down to the beach and looked at the moonlit sea, as Vane Mannering had looked on many such a night. Presently, half unconsciously, he went up toward the other huts. The one in which he had left the two girls was dark, all was still; but as he turned he saw a dim light in the other hut, the hut he had not yet entered. Surprised and curious, he approached it noiselessly and cautiously, and looked in through the now gaping logs. As he did so the sound of sobbing reached him. It came from Nina, who was kneeling beside the rough bed, her arms outstretched on it, her hands closed over a paper; a ring lay on the bed rug as if it had fallen from her hand. Her attitude, so full of the abandon of grief and despair, smote Sutcombe to the heart.

Why was she kneeling there, in that rough hut on that desolate island, her eyes streaming with tears, her lips quivering with grief? His face went white, and his own lips twitched with an unspoken dread, a vague presentiment. He remained there for a moment only, for the sacredness of her grief smote upon him like a reproach; and he moved away and stood, with folded arms and bent head, pondering gloomily.

He lost all sense of time, of the fact that she might find him there, and he started as the rough door opened and she came out. The tears were still shining in her eyes, which she lifted to his, and her hand—did it clasp the paper he had seen?—went to her heart.

He took a step toward her.

"Decima!" he breathed. "Decima! Ah, what is it? What is the matter? You—you are unhappy, troubled about something! Forgive me! I did not know it was you, did not know you were there. I saw the light and came to find out if there was anything wrong. What is it, Decima? You will tell me, will you not? I've no right to ask—and yet I have. For I love you, Decima! No sorrow, no trouble can touch you that does not reach me, also! All my thoughts, all my life, are bound up in you! I've no thought, no care, but for you! Ah, don't look at me so! What—what—have I said, what have I done? Have pity on me, Decima, dear——"

He had drawn nearer to her, half unconsciously, but she shrank back from him with something, as it seemed to him, like terror and horror in her eyes, and on her quivering lips.

"No! No!" she breathed, with a shudder, as if a cold wind had passed over her. "Don't—don't say it! I—I never knew, guessed——"

"Not even guessed! Oh, Decima!" he whispered reproachfully.

"No!" she responded passionately. "Never! I—did not know. You must not say another word! You will not? Oh, how unhappy, how wretched I am! And I thought to—to make you happy——"

"You have, you have, Decima!" he pleaded, for her grief, her self-reproach, were almost unendurable. "I had never known happiness until I had known you, until that night I saw you——"

"Hush!" she whispered, almost moaned. "You—you don't know what you are saying, what—what I am!"

As she spoke she thrust the paper and the ring she had held in her clinched hand into her bosom.

"Don't say another word. Let us—let us try and think you have not spoken. For Vivienne's sake I will forget it, I will, indeed! And you must, you must, you *must*!"

He put out his hand to stay her, and tried to stammer out a remonstrance, an appeal, but she shrank back, and murmuring:

"No, no! Let us forget it. You don't know—don't know!" passed him and glided toward the hut where she had left Vivienne sleeping.

* * * *

And on a similar night, some months earlier, Vane strode up and down the terrace at Lesborough and looked into the mist that hid his lawns and park. It hid the familiar view from him, but it opened and let him gaze, with longing despair, at the fairy isle that rarely left his memory.

One of the drawing-room windows was open, and Judith's voice floated out to him. In a pause the sound of voices and laughter followed. The scent of cigarettes came from the smoking room, the lights, from the windows of the great house, fell garishly athwart the terrace.

It all jarred and weighed upon him. The man was infinitely weary of it all; for fate had robbed him of the one woman who could have made life worth living, and the rank, the wealth, that were his tasted as bitter as Dead Sea fruit upon his lips.

"My God, who would have thought it would have been so difficult to forget!" he muttered to himself, as he bit at the unlit cigar between his teeth. "How much longer, I wonder, can I endure this life? And what a fool I am to bear it a moment longer. Why don't I go?"

He smiled in grim mockery at the question. He was the Earl of Lesborough, "lord of half a county," with all the "responsibilities and duties" of his lofty position. Rank, wealth, the power which belongs by right to men in his position, wound round him like the chains of a galley slave, and cut into his aching, unsatisfied heart.

"If by some means, anyway, anyhow, I could get away from it all forever!" he mused, with a gesture of utter weariness.

He need not have worried himself over the hopelessness of the idea, for at that moment Julian, as he sat brooding in the Wizard's Room, was evolving a simple little plan which would make the gratification of Vane's desire quite easy.

CHAPTER XX
JUDITH'S PROMISE

It was the last night of the house party at Lesborough. Some of the guests had already gone, but, among others, the Letchfords and the Ormes still remained, the Letchfords because Vane was fond of them and had pressed them to stay until the last minute, and the Ormes because he was anxious that Julian should have every chance of paying his suit to Judith.

"Take it by and large, Blanche, we have had a very good time," said Sir Charles, in that hour before dinner which he always claimed for a confidential chat with his wife. "But, of course, I should always be all right anywhere with Vane."

"Y-es," she said, as she lay back in her chair before the fire, warming herself in her dressing gown. "Y-es. It is to be wished that Lord Lesborough could reciprocate and be 'all right' in your company."

"You think he isn't happy, that there's still something on his mind, Blanche? How you stick to that idea of yours! Do you remember how it seized upon you the night we found him?"

She nodded thoughtfully.

"Yes, the trouble is still there, whatever it was and is," she said. "No one could have played the part of host better than he has done; but he has been playing, acting all the time. He has been bored—no, that's not the word, wearied—to death every day and every hour; and much as he likes some of us—you especially, Charlie—he will not be sorry, I think, when he sees the last of us. Where is he going; do you know?"

Sir Charles shook his head. "I don't know. I don't think he knows himself. I asked him this morning what his plans were, and he shrugged his shoulders and smiled—you know that smile of his—as if he did not care, and it did not matter."

There was silence for a moment or two, then Letchford said:

"Is Judith engaged to Julian Shore, Blanche?"

She did not reply for a while, then she replied:

"I don't know. Sometimes I think she is, at others I doubt it; but I fancy there is some kind of understanding between them. He has looked—well, as a man looks who at least has some reason for hope."

"He looks jolly bad at most times," grunted Letchford. "There's a pinched look about his face, his eyes shine too much, and he seems to be in a kind of dream half his time."

"I know. And Judith has the same look about her mouth and in her eyes. Charlie, there is something mysterious about those two. They seem to be—to be watching each other, as if they were waiting for something to happen."

Letchford burst into a laugh. " 'Pon my word, Blanche, you talk like a shilling novel! Why on earth should they watch each other, and what can happen? I say, would you mind if I asked Vane to come South with us?"

"Not in the least. I have grown to like him. But he won't come, Charlie. As I said, he will be glad to be rid of us, for he wants to be alone to brood over this unknown trouble of his. But ask him, by all means."

"I'll have to ask Julian Shore as well."

Lady Blanche raised her brows, and made a little grimace.

"I suppose so; well, I *don't* like Mr. Shore—but it does not matter. Lord Lesborough will not come, and Mr. Shore would not accept without him. I have no fear. You'd better begin to dress, Charlie. I can hear that most of them have gone to their rooms, and you always take such a frightful time. I'm sure I don't know why; you only put on the same things every night, and ought to be able to do so blindfolded."

As Lady Letchford had said, most of the people had gone to their rooms; but one or two still lingered in the half light in the drawing-room and conservatory; and Judith stood in the latter listening moodily to the steady tramp of some one pacing the terrace outside. It was Vane, and though she could not see him, her eyes, as they followed his movements, as he passed to and fro, dilated and contracted in unison with the beating of her heart. The love she had borne him, even when she had deserted him, had changed into hate; but through the circle of that hatred, the memory, the sting, of that old love penetrated; and the sight of him, the sound of his voice, his footsteps, still had power to move her.

She was turning away to go to her room, when she heard another step, a softer one than that outside, and, turning her head, saw Julian enter the conservatory. Now, strange as it may seem, these two had not been alone together since the night she had enacted with him the melodramatic scene below the terrace. It had not been necessary for her to shun him, for he had not sought a tête-à-tête. Not by word or sign had either of them referred to the incidents, the speech, of that night. But Judith had, when Vane was present, been more civil, indeed, sweetly pleasant, to the cousin for whom he had pleaded; so amiable, in fact, that Vane assured himself that his words had borne fruit, and that all would be well between Julian and her.

She took up the book which lay on the marble table before her, and, without a word, would have passed out, but Julian extended his hand slightly to stay her.

"This is the last night," he said, in a low voice and with a glance toward the terrace on which Vane's steps still sounded.

"Yes," she said, in a casual way. "It has been a pleasant time, and my father and I have enjoyed it very much. We are going South—to Nice first, I think."

"Do not," he said; that was all. "Wait until—a few days."

She opened her sapphire eyes upon him with haughty surprise, but they flickered and fell under the steady regard of his sombre ones.

"Why should we wait?" she asked. "I think we are going straight through London; in fact, I know we are."

His lips drew together, and his lids fell over his eyes for a moment.

"Can nothing I can say dissuade you?" he asked, in a still lower voice. "Do you think that I can bear to part with you for—how many months? Have you forgotten what passed between us—there?" He pointed to the terrace.

She laughed with an affectation of contemptuous amusement.

"I don't care for the best of melodramas, Mr. Shore; and I am not likely to remember them," she said.

"And yet you do remember," he said quietly. "There is no moment when you do not remember it, even as I do. And our compact dwells with me night and day, is burned into my very soul."

She moved her queenly head impatiently, and tried to laugh.

"Then I wish you would forget it, please," she said, "or cut it out of your 'very soul.' It was a piece of madness, the madness of a moment, the moment of a woman's weakness, of which you availed yourself most fully, Mr. Shore. It was never more than that, it could not possibly be more. If I were not able to laugh at it, I should be ashamed of it."

"We agreed," he said, as if she had not spoken, "that if I were master here you would be my wife. You taunted me with the impossibility of the pact, but you swore, with the kiss which is a woman's oath, that you would keep it."

"It was a safe promise—a promise in which there was as little danger of fulfillment as if I had promised to be Queen of England when you were King. *There* is the master of Lesborough"—she raised her hand toward the sound of Vane's steps on the terrace—"and you are still, and will be, but the dependent."

"And the heir," he said as quietly as before. "You forget that. If anything should happen to still those steps forever, I shall claim the fulfillment of your promise, your oath, Judith."

His face was no paler than usual; indeed, a spot of color had come into the sallow cheeks, but Judith Orme fought with the shudder that ran through her, and tried in vain to meet the steady regard of the black eyes with a contemptuous smile.

"You cling to melodrama," she said, with a shrug of her shoulders.

"Will you wait in England for a week?" he asked, as if her taunt had not touched him.

"No!" she replied.

"Three days—two?" he said slowly, patiently.

"Not one!" was the instant response. "Will you let me pass, please? I shall be late."

He stood aside, but as she was sweeping by him he caught her hand and pressed it to his lips.

"For all your gibes and mockery, I know your heart," he whispered. "I can trust you. Hate is stronger than love, and I am sure of my reward. You will keep your word!"

She looked strangely at him over her shoulder, paused as if she were listening to the footsteps outside, then, with a flash of the sapphire eyes, as if a latent fire had suddenly sprung up within them, said, in a voice, almost as low as his:

"Yes, though I do not know whether I hate him or you worse, I will keep my word."

When she had gone Julian stood for a moment looking before him, his tongue moistening his hot lips. She had spoken of madness, and he knew that it was the right word to describe the passion which consumed him, the compact he had made with her. But there is a grim method in some kinds of madness.

He went out by a door at the end of the conservatory, and, making his way through the ladies' garden, entered the laboratory and sank into a chair.

"She will go," he muttered. "And it is only the sight of her that gives me courage. When she has gone I shall be as weak as water. It is her presence, the sound of her voice, that drives the fear out of my heart, and fills my veins with fire. No, I can't wait! I can't wait! It must be to-night or never!"

As he spoke his face grew livid with some emotion, with the ecstasy of fear, battling with the frenzy of desire. The door opened slowly, and before he could drive the terrible expression from his face, Deborah entered with her noiseless step. He started to his feet, and went to the table, while a thought flashed through his brain. The woman watched him too closely, knew too much of him; she was better out of his way. He turned again slowly, and, with a smile, signed to her.

"Is your box packed, Deborah?"

"No," she replied, with downcast eyes.

"Then pack it," he said. "I want you to go up to-night instead of to-morrow. It will be more convenient. You don't mind the short notice? A carriage shall take you to the station. There is a train at eight-thirty. It will give you time?"

She raised her eyes and looked at him with a keen but veiled anxiety, an anxiety bordering on dread.

"Don't send me, Mr. Julian!" she said, her thin fingers moving swiftly. "Let me stay to-night, till you go!"

He looked at her with a frown of surprise that was not altogether assumed.

"What do you mean? What is the matter with you, Deborah?" he asked. "Why should you object to leave here a few hours earlier than you intended?"

Her speechless lips worked and her eyes sought the floor as if they were afraid to meet his.

"Let me stay, Mr. Julian!" she pleaded. "You are not well—you do not sleep. I watch—I can see the light under your door. There—there is something on your mind, something——" Her fingers ceased and her hands gripped each other as if she had said too much.

Julian laughed noiselessly.

"Really, I don't know what can be the matter with you, Deborah!" he said, with an impatient gesture; but her strange reluctance to leave him only made him more determined that she should go. "If you said that you were not well it would be more to the purpose; in fact, I've noticed that you've not been looking the thing lately. This place does not suit you. Now, don't argue any longer, my good Deborah. I want the London rooms put straight by the time I get up there to-morrow—for I leave here to-morrow—and I intend you shall go to-night."

She made a gesture of resignation—it was almost Oriental in its emphasis—and busied about the room, putting a thing here and there in its place. Presently she touched him on the shoulder nervously and pointed to the cords of the ventilator.

"They are nearly broken," she said.

Julian glanced up and then turned away.

"I know! I know!" he said impatiently. "It does not matter; they will last. Let them alone, please!"

She moved toward the door, but paused and looked at him with a mixture of affection, entreaty, and despair; then she raised her hands and said on them, slowly, as one reluctantly preferring a claim, recalling an obligation:

"Mr. Julian, I—I served your father faithfully. I have served you, for love of him and yourself. I—I nursed you. I'd have laid down my life for him, I'd lay it down for you, Mr. Julian——"

He nodded, as if he were schooling himself to be patient with her.

"I am not like other women. I am deaf and dumb, but when any trouble has threatened you or him I have known it, known it though no word has been spoken, no sign, that others could read, has been made. There—there is trouble threatening now." She shuddered. "I know—who should know better?—when there is something on your mind, and there is something dark and dreadful on it now! Mr. Julian—ah, for God's sake don't do it! She's not worth it! She's beautiful—oh, I know, I know; but she's not worth it!"

Julian's face went white, and into his eyes crept the reflection of the nameless terror and dread which shone glassily in hers; then he laughed, a laugh that sounded forced and ghastly in the face of the woman's terror, and, taking out his purse, he held out some money.

"Here's your fare, Deborah," he said gently enough, but his lips, though they smiled, declared his inflexible determination.

As she took the money she clung to his hand, and slid to her knees, her livid face turned up to him imploringly.

"Master, I see more than most, feel more than those who can speak and hear," she signed. "I am afraid! I know that look! Your mother's face used to wear it—I am afraid! Ah, let me stay!"

He raised her, and, with his hand on her shoulder, led her to the door.

"Foolish Deborah!" he signed, as he opened it. "You are nervous and out of sorts, full of wild fancies and presentiments. I'll send you to a doctor when I come home."

She protested, pleaded no longer, but, with a look at him, the look of a dog which, indifferent to all the world besides, is faithful and loving to its master, bent her head resignedly and went out.

Julian stood frowning for a moment or two, gnawing at his lips, as if he were asking himself how much she guessed, or whether it was only an exhibition of nerves; then, with a gesture, the Spanish gesture which wipes away a distasteful subject, went up to dress.

The dinner that night was a very bright one. Judith, in a wonderful dress which set off her marvelous beauty to perfection, talked almost unceasingly, her eyes shining like stars, her lips, usually so immobile, curved with the smile which women wear when they are happiest—or wish you to think them so. Vane, with his grave regard, looked from her to Julian, and wondered whether they had at last—on this last opportunity—become betrothed; but he could glean nothing from Julian's face. Serene and unclouded, it told nothing.

Lady Fanworthy, at the head of the table, watched and listened with the faint smile in her keen eyes. The Letchfords almost flirted openly with each other; Sir Chandos ate—and drank—steadily, showing his teeth when a witty remark was made, and stroking the carefully dyed mustache, as he glanced covertly at that vision of loveliness, his daughter, to Julian and Vane, who, as the dinner proceeded, leaned back and dropped out of the discussion of plans for the winter.

Even at the most public moments he had this habit of "dropping out," and away soared his thoughts, and his spirit, to a certain nameless isle, where moved the slim, graceful figure of the girl he had loved—and lost. The voice round the dinner table smote vaguely on his ear, for he was listening to that clear, girlish voice which haunted him, sleeping or waking.

"Oh, my lost love! I held you in my arms but once. And then lost you!"

He awakened with a sigh and passed the port to Sir Chandos. The ladies had gone to the drawing-room, and when Sir Chandos had drunk his usual too liberal allowance, Vane rose.

"Come and sing to us, Julian," he said; "no mournful ditty to-night, but something that will cheer us." And he put his hand on Julian's slight shoulder.

Julian smiled at him, as Jonathan might have smiled at David, and, when he had finished his coffee, went to the piano. He did not ask Judith to play for him that night, and he sang the "Yeoman's Wedding Song" with a verve and swing which seemed to set every piece of china on the Chippendale cabinets ringing.

"Bravo!" said Vane. "Splendid, isn't it?" he demanded of Lady Fanworthy.

"Splendid," she answered dully, with a glance at the handsome face of the singer, now thrown back with parted lips and flashing eyes. "Do you take him with you where you go? By the way, where do you go?"

"I don't know," he said. "I shall stay here for a few days; a week, perhaps. Oh, yes; Julian will go with me, I've no doubt."

"My poor Vane!" she murmured; but he did not hear her.

Bridge was started, but Vane did not play. The fairy isle was haunting him that night, and he could not settle down. He lit a cigar and paced up and down the terrace. Later on the bridge players ceased, and, after the usual wrangling review of the game, went up to bed. Vane, looking in at the drawing-room door, saw Julian and Judith standing by the fire. They were apparently engaged in the usual commonplaces which are uttered before parting for the night, and he did not see the sombre fire that glowed in Julian's eyes as he murmured:

"You will not wait?"

"No," she said.

"But you will keep your promise?"

"Yes," she answered, in the same tone.

Nothing more. So are most of the tragedies of life preluded. He opened the door for her, and she passed out, and he went on to the terrace, meeting Vane face to face.

"Julian!" said Vane. "Is—is it all right? Have you asked her? Oh, I know your secret, my dear fellow!"

Julian hesitated for a moment, then he said:

"Yes, I have asked her. And it is 'yes.'"

"I congratulate you with all my heart!" said Vane. "Love—well, love is the one thing Judith wanted. And she has got that, I know. Splendid! I'm glad! Where are you going?"

"To my den," said Julian. His lips were dry, and he thought his voice was hoarse; but it was not. Vane saw nothing but the lover's dreaminess and embarrassment.

"I'll come to you—let me finish this cigar in the open air. I want to talk over our plans," he said.

CHAPTER XXI
THE TRAGEDY IN THE LABORATORY

Julian nodded and went to the laboratory. He looked round the room that, notwithstanding its luxurious appointments, was still suggestive of mystery, and, gliding to the wall on which the ropes of the curious ventilator were hung, nearly severed the already frayed strands. Then he closed the door that led to the ladies' garden and drew the portière curtain over it. The spirit furnace was in its place, but unlit, and he lighted it and placed beside it, but not upon it, an iron pot containing a bluish liquid. Then he lit a cigarette, and, opening a book, sat at the table as if reading; but the printed lines danced before his eyes, and he did not turn a page.

Presently there came a knock at the door, Vane's quick, sharp knock, and he entered. He had exchanged his dress coat for an old smoking jacket, a thick, comfortable jacket, with heavy brass buttons.

"No smell on to-night, Julian," he said pleasantly. "Now, about our plans, old man." He took out his pipe and filled and lit it. "What do you say to Monte Carlo and then, when we are bored of it, Egypt? Or would you rather stay on here and go in for hunting and the rest of it? You have only to say. I don't care. It's all one to me. But I ought to mention that Judith is going South."

"I know. I want to tell you all about it, Vane," he said hesitatingly.

Vane laughed. "You need not. Man, do you think I haven't eyes! Of course I've seen how it is with you! And, by George, I'm not surprised! There isn't a more beautiful woman in the world, or one better worth the winning. Julian, did I ever tell you——" He paused and puffed at his pipe.

"That you were once in love with her yourself?" said Julian placidly enough; but his lips twitched as they smiled.

Vane nodded.

"I wondered whether she'd tell you," he said simply. "I'm glad if she has. It wasn't to be. No matter. I can still wish you luck, old chap. What are you going to do?"

Julian had got up and, as if mechanically, had put the iron pot on the spirit furnace.

"An experiment," he said, in a casual kind of way. "I'm trying for this new color. I've got it in my head. You don't mind, do you?"

"No; not if you don't make too much of a smell," said Vane. "Well, what do you say to my plans? We could join the Ormes at Monte Carlo——Phew, that stuff's beginning to smell already!"

"It will be over in a minute," said Julian. "You leave it to me, as usual! You don't seem to care, Vane!"

"That's just it," said Vane. "I don't care. It's all one to me where I am. Few places or things hold any charm for me."

Julian looked at him with a strange mixture of curiosity and aloofness, as if his mind were preoccupied. Then he turned to the furnace again.

"Bother!" he said. "I shall have to get more spirit. Do you mind?" He looked over his shoulder at Vane, and the bluish flame cast a ghastly light on his pale face—"do you mind stirring this stuff while I'm gone? I shan't be more than a minute or two. I keep it outside——"

Vane got up from his chair and shrugged his shoulders good-humoredly. "All right; but I hope I shan't spoil it; I'm not used to this game."

"Oh, no," responded Julian casually. "Just keep it stirred."

As he opened the door he glanced over his shoulder again at Vane; and surely if Vane had seen the expression in the black eyes shining forth from the dark shadows surrounding them he would have felt some presentiment of coming ill; but all his attention was fixed on the task he had undertaken.

Julian's glance lasted but a moment, and he went out and closed the door softly behind him. He did not turn the key, for the door locked by a spring, as did that which led to the ladies' garden, and to both doors only he and Deborah had keys. Outside the door he paused a moment, biting his lips and driving the telltale expression from his eyes, then he went slowly, and humming the air he had sung a little while ago, into the hall. Prance, the butler, was standing there, and Julian went up to him.

"Oh, Prance," he said, "I've run out of methylated spirits; do you think you could get me some?"

"Yes, Mr. Julian. I generally keep some by me in my pantry. Shall I bring it to your room?"

"Oh, don't trouble; I'll wait here, thanks," said Julian. He sang rather more loudly as Letchford came down the stairs.

"Seen Vane?" he asked. "If he hasn't gone to bed I want him to come and have a pipe. I can't sleep, somehow," he laughed shamefacedly. "Usually drop off as soon as my head's on the pillow."

"Vane's in my den—writing letters. We were making our plans for abroad. I'll tell him when I go back."

"Oh, don't bother him if he's writing," said Letchford, and he went on to the smoking room.

Prance came back with the spirit can in his hand.

"Very sorry, Mr. Julian," he said, "but I've run out. Some of the maids must have been at it for their curling tongs. I dare say I could get some from one of them."

Julian thought swiftly. "Ah, yes," he said. "I wish you would. I want it particularly. Send up to Miss Orme's maid and ask her."

"I'll go myself, sir," said Prance, and he went up the stairs.

Julian, still humming, went to the smoking room and looked in. Letchford was walking up and down, smoking vigorously and rumpling his short hair, a trick he had when he was worried or puzzled.

"Come in and sit down," he said to Julian. "I've got what my wife calls a fidgety fit on me to-night; kind of a—a—what do you call it, presentiment."

Julian smiled. "That ragout was very rich," he said. "I think that chef always overdoes the butter. I'll come and have a cigarette presently; but I must go back to the den first. I'll bring Vane with me."

"Do!" said Letchford, with undue earnestness.

Julian nodded, and sauntered back to the hall. As he did so a tall figure in a tea gown glided down the stairs. It was Judith. He stopped short and their eyes met. In hers was a covert fear, a dread questioning and doubt; in his the gleam of a deadly determination.

"You sent for some spirit?" she said, in a low voice.

The expression of his face changed to one of passionate admiration, and his eyes roamed over the beautiful face and tall, light figure.

"Yes," he said, in an ordinary tone. "But I am sorry if I disturbed you, your maid——"

"My maid is getting it," she said. "Where—where is Vane?"

His lids drooped. She, too, was asking for Vane. Did she suspect anything? No matter if she did. At that moment he felt that he would like her to have known, would wish that she should share his guilt.

"In my den," he replied steadily. He looked at his watch as he spoke, and his lips moved as if he were making a calculation.

"In your den—what is he doing there?" she asked.

Julian smiled with an affectation of surprise. "He is writing; we are talking over our programme, and have decided to join you either at Monte Carlo or Cairo."

She drew a breath of relief, but said nothing. Prance came down the stairs with the can in his hand, and, with a murmured "good night," she went up.

"I've been able to get a little for you, Mr. Julian," said Prance.

Julian thanked him, and, taking up his song again, went slowly toward the Wizard's Room.

Vane had drawn a chair up to the spirit furnace and he leaned over the pot, stirring it mechanically. Yes; he was decidedly de trop; if he were out of the way, Julian and Judith would reign at Lesborough now in the heyday of their youth, with their capacity for enjoyment still at its height; while he——

He sighed listlessly; then the sigh was followed by a cough, for the fumes were beginning to rise from the pot and had got into his lungs.

"Phew!" he muttered. "Hope nothing's gone wrong with the beastly stuff; Julian will be disappointed. Am I stirring it enough?" The fumes grew thicker, so that he felt some difficulty in breathing. Gradually the difficulty increased, and, half choking, he looked round the room.

"Ventilator closed, of course," he said to himself. "These scientific chaps seem to be able to breathe without air; it's use, I suppose. I must open that thing."

He rose, and, to his amazement, felt his legs weaken under him. His breath was coming in gasps, the room was filling with the fumes. Staggering and holding by the table and the chair, he made his way to the wall where the rope hung, and pulled it with a jerk. It broke, and the lower part fell over his arms. He was half blinded and nearly suffocated by this time, and he made for the door with his hands outstretched like a blind man. In the confusion of his mind, caused by the deathly sensation of asphyxiation, he missed the door and groped with his hands along the paneled wall. At last, as his sight and his breath were utterly failing, he touched the portière curtain; but he could only cling to it. It came down with his weight, and he fell to the ground, still gripping it.

There is a moment, the millionth part of a moment, before the hand of Death crushes out all power of thought, when the past moves like a flash before the mental vision; and in that moment Vane saw and heard Nina as plainly as if she had been in the room with him. His lips formed her name, and, half fighting, half resigning himself to the end, he closed his eyes. As he did so he heard in the intense, horrible silence the turning of a key. "It comes too late," he thought; "I shall be de trop no longer!" But the sound was followed by a draught of fresh, of heavenly air; but he was too faint to move, and he was only conscious of the figure of a woman dimly outlined in the dense fumes. She stood for a moment looking round, then, noiselessly, she sprang toward him. As she did so the garden door by which she had entered closed.

She sprang from him to the rope, saw that it was broken, and, staggering, made for the garden door. By the time she had opened it, Vane had recovered sufficiently to get to his feet and heavily, blunderingly, was moving toward her, when, as if she had suddenly thought of something, she ran to the furnace, and, taking off the iron pot, poured out its contents. There should be no evidence against her beloved master. But her hand was unsteady, her whole frame, indeed, shaking, and some of the liquid fell into the furnace. The flame arose, piercing even the dim fumes, and lighting the room with a livid glare in which Vane saw her face, and recognized Deborah.

He saw something else that roused his bewildered senses with a quick horror: the flame had caught her dress, and she was on fire. Struggling fiercely with his weakness, he tore off his coat, and, wrapping it round her, essayed to drag her to the door. As he did so the burning liquid ran like a snake from the furnace and along the floor, caught the curtain, and in another moment the whole room seemed ablaze.

Vane struggled to the garden door, still grasping the inert figure. The silence, hers caused by her terrible affliction, his from the fumes that filled his lungs, was weird and ghastly. They were like two demoniac figures struggling through a nightmare of hell. Swaying this way and that, Vane reached the door at last. It was ajar, and he forced it with his weak, uncertain fingers, but even as he stood on the threshold his strength failed him, and as he fell outward, his burden slipped from him, the door closed on its spring, and she was shut up in the burning room.

Vane fell down the steps heavily, and, rolling under one of the thick bushes, lay there senseless.

* * * *

Letchford, still waiting for Vane, was knocking the ashes from his pipe, when he saw a shaft of yellow light shoot across the opening between the curtains. He thought nothing of it for a moment or two, but as it grew more intense he drew the curtain aside, and saw that the light came from some part of the house. His impulse was to open the window, but he remembered that a draught was, in cases of fire, an added peril, and he sprang to the door, shouting for help. In an instant, as it seemed, the stairs were filled with people, the hall itself, while his shouts were joined by screams and cries of "Fire!"

Springing from the corridor leading to the Wizard's Room came the tall figure of Julian. "Where? Where?" he cried.

Letchford gasped his answer. "I saw it from the smoking room; it is on the west side!"

"It must be in your room, Mr. Julian," said Prance.

A cry, a sharp cry of horror, rose from the group of women. It came from Judith.

Julian's eyes went toward her and held hers for a moment, and she shrank and covered her face with her hands, as if to shut out his gaze.

"We shall soon see!" he said, as he ran down the corridor, so swiftly that before the rest could reach him he had unlocked the door and flung the key into the room.

Before the dense volume of smoke and the sheets of flame which, like a demon spirit rejoicing in the evil that it has done, poured out to meet them, the terrified throng fell back. It was Letchford who sprang forward, his arm across his face.

"Vane! Vane was in here! My God!" he cried. "Water! Water! No, no! Don't open the windows! The room is closed. Vane, oh, poor Vane!"

There was, of course, a "perfect system of appliances for meeting cases of fire" at Lesborough, and, equally, of course, the perfect system broke down. Before the elaborate hose could be uncoiled and the water turned on and directed upon the burning room, it had been reduced to ashes; the other part of the wing was in flames, and the remainder of the building threatened. But every man worked with the energy of madness, and the women, too, bore their part. With Lady Fanworthy at their head they filled the buckets, which the men passed from hand to hand.

It was over an hour before the flames were mastered and the house saved; then, though the smoke and steam were well-nigh blinding, Letchford, followed by Julian, sprang and stumbled amid the ruins and began their search.

Julian worked like a man possessed, tearing at the blocks of stone, the charred beams, the thick debris which hid the floor.

"He may have left the room!" he gasped, pausing for a moment, and wiping the sweat from his blackened face.

"God grant it!" gasped Letchford; then his voice broke with a groan and he staggered back with something gripped in his hand.

"What—what is it?" gasped Julian, and his question was echoed by the rest.

"Send—send the women away!" panted Letchford. "For God's sake send them away!"

They fell back, all but Lady Fanworthy and Lady Letchford. The men closed round her husband, then fell back also. In his hand he held the charred fragment of the thick smoking jacket from which gleamed through the smoke the big brass buttons.

"Oh, my God! Vane is dead!" cried Letchford.

Julian stood staring at it speechlessly for a moment; then he moved his head slowly. One of the women had come forward and was standing looking at him.

It was Judith Orme. Their eyes met for an instant, then she uttered a terrible cry and fell back in a swoon.

* * * *

One does not recover from the deadly fumes of aconite, ammonia, and other deadly chemicals very quickly. Vane lay unconscious beneath the sheltering bush until nearly the moment the flames were extinguished, and his senses came back so slowly that for some time he was incapable of any desire for life. At last he raised his head, gazed vaguely at the dense volume of smoke and steam in an uninterested fashion, and, still dazed, crawled weakly to a safer position. He lay there for some minutes, panting for breath and fighting for strength, then he rose to his feet with the intention of going to the assistance of the others; but suddenly he heard his name spoken. He stopped and put his hand to his head. What had happened? Why, yes, of course, he had been in that room, had been nearly burned. Nearly? At that moment Letchford's cry arose, "Vane is dead!" and pierced the thick air.

Vane stood quite still while one could count twenty; then, obeying an impulse that came as swiftly as a flash of lightning, he drew back into the shadow of the shrubbery.

He remained there for a moment, trying to think clearly, consecutively, then he passed through the other door of the ladies' garden and, keeping in the shadow of the wall, reached the common room of the stablemen.

It was empty—every one was gathered round the scene of the fire—and Vane, still striving for an effort at thought and resolution, took one of the jackets and caps which lay on the table, put them on, and, going through the yard, made his way toward the park.

CHAPTER XXII
SUTCOMBE MEETS VANE

After Nina had gone Sutcombe stood and stared at the sea and faced the music like a man—and a gentleman.

Decima had refused him. It was a bitter, hard blow. And yet, notwithstanding her entreaty that he would forget his proposal, was there no hope left for him? From her reiteration: "You don't know, you don't know!" he inferred a mystery, a secret; and yet not much of a mystery, a secret, for what else could she mean but that she loved and was pledged to another man?

Anyway, be the explanation of her words, her almost anguished manner, what it might, he, Sutcombe, had to accept her refusal. In common courtesy he must refrain from pressing his suit while they three, were alone on this desolate island and she was unable to keep out of his reach.

So he went back to his bed in the "saloon," unhappy and unsatisfied, but not altogether despairing; for, if she was pledged to another man, where was he, and why had he not put in an appearance all these months?

He rose in the morning, and, filling the rôle which Mannering had so ably played, got some fuel, lit the fire, and went out with the gun to shoot some wild fowl.

When he came back he found the breakfast ready, and the two girls awaiting him.

Nina glanced at him half timidly, but Sutcombe was not the man to whine or wear the willow, and he met her glance cheerfully and reassuringly; indeed, he was so cheerful that Vivienne, notwithstanding her acuteness, did not guess that he had asked his question, and been rejected. Immediately after breakfast he set off with pick and shovel, to the spot to which Nina directed him, the ladies promising to follow him directly they had "cleared away." Sutcombe walked by no means quickly, for what his heart desired was love and not gold; but after he had taken off his coat, and been at work for some minutes, he was seized by a mild attack of the "yellow fever," and began to work with that enthusiasm which the gold-seeker alone experiences; so that when the two girls came slowly toward him, Vivienne supported by Nina's strong arm, they found him hot but exultant.

"You are quite right!" he said, pointing to the specks of yellow which shone dully among the heap of dirt and rock. "I'm not much of an authority, but even I can see that there is a large quantity of gold here!"

Nina nodded and caught something of his enthusiasm.

"I'll help you!" she said brightly. "Oh, yes, give me the spade. I know how to handle it. I used——" She stopped suddenly, and Vivienne, who was seated in the shade of the rock, cut in eagerly:

"Why can't I help!"

"So you can!" said Sutcombe; "you shall sort out the pieces with the gold in them."

Having thus made a division of the labor, they worked almost in silence, until Sutcombe and Nina had made a large heap, and Vivienne a smaller, but more valuable and precious one. Every now and then Sutcombe paused to wipe the sweat from his face—and glance at Nina; and he saw plainly enough that, though she was working hard—far too hard for his taste—she was not thinking of the gold; and once he saw her look round toward the sea, and heard her sigh as if her mind were dwelling on the past; and, as he stole glances at her sad eyes, and heard the sigh she tried to repress, a wave of bitterness rose within him, and he felt, not for the first time since last night, a resentment against the unknown man, the memory of whom was disturbing her peace and causing her unhappiness. But he worked on and said nothing; there was nothing for him to do but possess his soul in patience.

Stopping only for meals, they had by dusk, when Sutcombe insisted upon a halt, collected a good quantity of the gold-bearing quartz; but, as he and the girls bent over it, a difficulty presented itself to his mind.

"How are we going to get this away?" he asked thoughtfully.

"Pack it in boxes!" replied Vivienne triumphantly; but Nina saw what was passing in his mind, and shook her head.

"There would not be boxes enough," she said.

"And we could not get it away without taking the men into our confidence," said Sutcombe; "and though they are good fellows, well——Is there any man who could resist the temptation to desert and make for this Golden Isle? Of course, what we want is a mill to stamp, crush the quartz——"

"But not having it, we must get the gold itself," said Nina. "My father spoke of finding some in layers—placers, I think he called it; and he said it was in the valley, south by southeast. He said"—her voice shook a little as she recalled the scene—"that it was quite easy to get."

"I'll go there to-morrow," said Sutcombe. "I will go alone, for it will be too far for Vivienne, and, besides, Decima—Miss Wood"—he faltered, and Vivienne looked from one to the other as he stumbled over the names, "I think you ought to rest. I don't like your working as you have done to-day."

Nina shook her head.

"It has not hurt me; it has helped me," she said quickly. "But we will stay at home and keep house to-morrow, if you wish it," she added meekly.

That night, when the two girls were undressing, Vivienne laid her hand on Nina's arm with gentle deprecation, and whispered:

"Has he spoken, Decima?"

Nina's silence was answer enough.

"And—and is it of no use, dear?"

Nina shook her head and fought with the tears that rose to her eyes.

"No," she said, almost inaudibly. "I am so sorry! Ah, how cold the words sound; and what would I not give if—if I could have said 'yes!' Lady Vivienne, your brother is the best, the most unselfish——"

She stopped suddenly, for the words recalled those Fleming had used when he was speaking of Vane Mannering. Her face went crimson, then paler than before.

"There is some one else, dear?" whispered Vivienne. "Oh, poor Sutcombe!"

"Oh, poor me!" sprang from Nina's lips with mingled sadness and bitterness.

Vivienne looked at her. "Was it—was it some one in the ship that was lost, some one who was here on the island? Oh, don't think me curious, dear. I am wondering if I can help you. Is it not possible?"

Nina shook her head. "No, no one can help me," she said. Then suddenly the craving for the sympathy of this sweet friend of hers melted her into partial confidence.

"We were thrown together—linked by fate—but—but he did not care for me. There—there was some one else——" She stopped and turned her face away, calling to her pride to burn up her tears.

The clasp of Vivienne's hand became a caress.

"And you, dear—you cannot forget! You love him still, though you are parted——"

Nina's head drooped and Vivienne was answered. She thought of her brother.

"May I tell Sutcombe?" she said, in a low voice.

"Yes," said Nina; "please tell him. I—I want him to understand that—that what he wishes can never be, that I am bound——"

"Bound?" echoed Vivienne in surprise; but Nina, remembering her promise, would say no more.

The next morning Vivienne gave Sutcombe Nina's message.

He nodded almost savagely.

"I understand," he said. "The man, whoever he is, has broken her heart. And it is my fate to have to stand by and look on—helpless! Some day"—he paused—"some day I may have the luck to meet him. If so——"

"You will remember that she—she loves him still!" Vivienne put in with gentle earnestness.

He went off moodily to the valley. At his return, at nightfall, he brought with him a bag full of small nuggets and dust, and reported that, as Doctor

Wood had said, large quantities of gold were there in placers in the rock and soil, and plenty of dust in the bed of the stream.

"We'll go with you to-morrow," said Nina; but he would not hear of it.

"It is too far," he said; "besides, one man can get all we shall be able to take on this trip without the knowledge of the men."

He was not altogether disinterested in his objection to their company, for the poor fellow was rather glad to be alone with his disappointment. The proximity of the woman one loves but cannot win is at times a torture well-nigh intolerable. So Sutcombe went up again to the valley, there to fight, as best he could, the great disappointment of his life.

It was a lovely valley, and as solitary as it was beautiful. There was no sound besides that of Sutcombe's pick and spade, and the rattle of the rock and stones as they fell beneath his strokes. Now and again a bird flew high up in the sky or whirled close above his head, its bright eyes scanning this intruder on its solitude with a curiosity in which fear had no share, and a lizard crawled out of its cranny to blink at him.

But for his thoughts and his work Sutcombe would have found the intense solitude and silence oppressive, but they soothed him with that balm which Nature holds out to those of her children who are wounded at heart.

He had been working for some hours, since he had stopped to eat the lunch Nina had packed up for him in the empty gold bag, and was resolving that he would work for another half hour before he stopped for the day, and he took out his watch to see the time.

While he was looking at it he was conscious of a strange feeling, the sensation which comes to us when we feel a presence that we have neither heard nor seen. Oppressed by this curious consciousness, he looked over his shoulder and saw the figure of a man seated on a rock just above him.

The man sat, with his chin resting on his hands, his elbows upon his knees, so calmly, so absolutely like a statue, that Sutcombe was half inclined to believe himself the victim of a delusion, so much so that he straightened himself and stared speechlessly at the figure.

He saw that the man was young, but thin and somewhat haggard. He was dressed in quite a rough sea suit, but his hands, though tanned, like his face, with the sun, and roughened by the water and the wind, were those of a gentleman. But it was the eyes and not the hands which held Sutcombe's regard, so full of half-cynical, half-bitter amusement were they.

Sutcombe found his voice at last.

"Hello, sir!" he said, lifting his cap.

The man raised his hat in response.

"How do you do?" he said gravely.

"Where—where did you come from?" asked Sutcombe. "I did not see you, know you were there!"

The man jerked his head slowly toward the coast behind him.

"I landed from a fishing yawl half an hour ago, from that side of the island."

There was silence while one could count twenty; then the newcomer said as quietly and as gravely as before:

"You are gold digging, I presume?"

"I am," replied Sutcombe.

"And you are fortunate, I see."

"I am—very," assented Sutcombe.

"I congratulate you," said the stranger, in a tone which had no trace of envy in it; indeed, it was indicative of an indifference that surprised Sutcombe. "But you would be still more fortunate if you worked farther up the valley."

Sutcombe stared at him.

"You—you know the island; have you been here before?"

The faintest and grimmest of smiles shone for a moment in the other man's eyes.

"Yes, I know the island; I have been here before," he said quietly. "Is this your first visit?"

Sutcombe nodded.

"Yes. Are you alone, sir?"

"Yes, I am quite alone." He smiled as if he read Sutcombe's fear. "You need not be afraid. I shall keep your secret. And I have no desire to share in your find. I've no use for gold."

Sutcombe looked at him with amazement.

"That's a strange statement," he said gravely. "Most men, every man, wants money!"

"Please regard me as the exception which proves the rule," was the courteous response. "Gold is only worth what it will buy; it can buy me nothing that I desire. May I ask to whom I have the pleasure of speaking?"

"My name's Sutcombe," said Sutcombe.

The stranger nodded. "Lord Sutcombe, of Southernwood?"

"Well, yes; Southernwood was mine—I sold it."

"You can now buy it back, Lord Sutcombe, if you desire to do so," said the stranger, looking at the bag of gold. "You are a millionaire—of the English variety. My name is—Richard Mortimer," he added. "I am on a fishing and shooting expedition—a solitary one—and happened to make this island in the course of my cruise. Have you a match upon you?"

Sutcombe handed his matchbox.

"May I take half a dozen? Thanks! I must be getting back to my boat." He rose and picked up the gun which had lain at his feet, and raised his wide-brimmed hat. But Sutcombe put out his hand arrestingly.

"One moment, Mr. Mortimer," he said. "You know this island, and the secret of the gold. May I ask if—if any others know of it? I just want to know what to expect."

"No other living person is aware of it—but one," said Richard Mortimer, "and I do not think you have anything to fear from that person. Certainly you have nothing to fear from me. So far as I am concerned you are welcome to the island and all it contains. Good day."

"Wait!" said Sutcombe sharply. His face had grown pale, his eyes keen and suspicious. "Do you mind telling me the name of that other person, sir?"

Mr. Richard Mortimer regarded the flushed face, the suspicious eyes, thoughtfully.

"Yes, I do mind," he replied. "I have an objection."

"It is a woman?" said Sutcombe.

Richard Mortimer's face reddened and his eyes grew darker.

"You are at liberty to guess," he said curtly.

Sutcombe dropped the spade upon which he had been leaning and advanced a step or two toward the other man.

"The only other person who knows of this island and its wealth is a lady," he said.

"To whom you are indebted for your information—and your fortune." The retort came like a flash.

Sutcombe reddened again.

"That is true," he said gravely. "Her name is Wood, Decima Wood. You know her?"

Richard Mortimer shook his head. "I know of no lady bearing that name," he said. Then, suddenly, his manner changed to one of suppressed eagerness. "She may have borne another. Perhaps you can describe her?"

"She has dark hair and gray eyes—they are sometimes violet. She was wrecked in the *Alpina*——"

A faint cry rose from Mortimer and he threw up his head as a man does when he has received a sudden shock. Sutcombe smiled bitterly.

"You appear to be startled," he said sternly. "Shall I go too far if I suggest you know the lady, and that she has reason to regret the day she met you?" He did not need any answer. Instinctively he felt that the man who was the cause of Decima's unhappiness, who held the key to her secret, stood before him. "You also were wrecked in the *Alpina*. Do you deny it?"

"I assent to, I deny, nothing," said Richard Mortimer. "If—if you can give me any information respecting that lady——"

"I can and will," cut in Sutcombe. "She is well, and happy"—oh, Sutcombe!—"and is guarded and watched over by friends who—who will protect her happiness by any and every means——"

The other man stood erect, his tanned face set and stern.

"I presume I may count you as the lady's chief friend, Lord Sutcombe?"

"You may," retorted Sutcombe promptly. "And, that being so, I avail myself of the privilege to tell you that, if you are the man I suspect you to be, you are a heartless scoundrel!"

Vane, otherwise Richard Mortimer, stood for a moment as if turned to stone; then he smiled.

"Lord Sutcombe, I have learned from you that the lady we both have in mind is alive. Compared with such knowledge, all else is trivial. Alive! And happy, you say? Thank God! Think me what you will. It is a matter of indifference to me. Stop! You say the—the lady is happy. Let her remain so! Do not tell her that you have met me! I am going down to my boat. In less than half an hour I shall have sailed from the island; and I give you my word that I shall never revisit it; that, in all probability, I shall never cross your, or her, path again. Good day, Lord Sutcombe!"

Sutcombe nodded acquiescingly; but he gnawed at his mustache as if in doubt.

He was an honorable man, and the falsehood he had told rankled in his bosom. He had said that Decima was well and happy, whereas she was fretting after this Richard Mortimer, who had turned up in such an extraordinary fashion. Was it not his duty to bring them together? The man had been startled when he had heard that she was alive, had seemed as if he cared. The struggle raged within Sutcombe's mind for a minute or two; then he said, hoarsely:

"Stop! I—I can't let you go like this. I wish to Heaven you had not come here, that we hadn't met; but we have, and—I told you an untruth just now when I said Miss Wood was happy. She is not."

Vane looked at him gravely, intently.

"She is fretting over something that has happened in the past, something in which you are concerned. I think it would be as well if you were to meet her. She is here on this island."

Vane started and went white. There was silence for a full minute, then he said hoarsely:

"It would do no good; a meeting with me would only cause the lady pain——"

"In a word," cut in Sutcombe hotly, "you are afraid to meet her. You have behaved so badly that you shrink from facing her. It is as I suspected. You are a coward, Mr. Mortimer."

Vane's face went white, but he bit his lip, and, breathing hard, restrained himself.

"Yes," he said quietly, "I am a coward—but not quite the same kind you think me, Lord Sutcombe."

"I'm not good at making nice distinctions of that sort," retorted Sutcombe fiercely. "A man who slinks off as you are doing is a common or garden coward, who deserves horsewhipping. I've no whip, but——"

Half mad with anger and the bitterness borne of the situation, he caught up a bit of a branch of a tree which he had been using, and made to strike Vane across the face, but Vane, dropping his gun, caught Sutcombe's arm and averted the blow. Sutcombe endeavored to wrench himself from the steellike grasp; and almost before they knew it the two men were struggling. They were equally matched in strength and skill, but the gun, which they had disregarded, played a third hand. One of the men must have stepped on the trigger, for there was a flash and report, and, half blinded, Sutcombe felt Vane's grip relax and saw him stagger back.

CHAPTER XXIII
THE MEETING

In an instant the madness of anger passed from Sutcombe's brain, and remorsefully he supported the man whom a moment or two before he had been endeavoring to throw.

"Are you hurt?" he asked anxiously.

Vane tried to smile and answer in the negative, but before he could do so he fainted. Sutcombe laid him down, and, getting out a brandy flask, managed to get some of the spirit through the clenched teeth; and presently, to his immense relief, the wounded man came to.

"I'm afraid you're badly hurt!" said Sutcombe. "I am very sorry! It was an accident. One of us trod on the gun——"

"I know, I know!" said Vane promptly, though faintly. "The bullet—fortunately it was a bullet and not shot!—struck me in the shoulder. There's—there's no great harm done. A little more brandy, please! Thank you! If you can help me to the boat—it's no great distance—a drink of water, and I shall be well enough to manage it—there is something with which we can get the bullet out, if it's there still."

Sutcombe got some water in his panikin, and Vane took a long pull and struggled to his feet.

"I can get some help if you could wait," suggested Sutcombe; but Vane frowned and shook his head.

"No need. If you will give me your arm—— Thanks! We are all right now!"

The distance from the scene of the tragi-comedy to the boat seemed interminable to Sutcombe, more so probably than it did to Vane, who was only weak and not in any pain; but they got there at last, and Vane, throwing himself down on the beach, told Sutcombe where to find in the boat the things he wanted.

The yawl was a trim little vessel with an apology for a cabin, roughly but ingeniously fitted up for its solitary skipper. And Sutcombe saw at a glance that it was the boat and the cabin of a gentleman. He found the small leather case of instruments and some bandages, and he quickly had Vane's shoulder bare.

"The bullet has gone through the flesh and out in an upward direction; it's a clean wound," he said.

"So I thought," said Vane. "If you can stop the bleeding——It's not the first time you have rendered 'first aid,' I see, Lord Sutcombe," he added, as Sutcombe deftly stanched the blood and bandaged the wound. "My only pang is one of hunger. There is a tin of soup in the galley for'ard—and——"

Sutcombe got it and heated it at the spirit stove, and brought it, with some bread, to his patient.

"Join me," said Vane. "If we break bread together we shan't be able to quarrel again. Don't look so cut up, my dear fellow! It was as much my fault as yours; more, in fact. I'd no business here——"

Sutcombe shook his head.

"I have an impression that you have more right to be here, to the whole of the island, than any one, excepting——"

"Miss—Wood, you called her," said Vane. He knew intuitively that this handsome young fellow was his rival, and yet he could not help liking him. "I wonder," he went on ruminatingly, "what, how much, she has told you, Lord Sutcombe? I wonder also whether you would mind telling me? You came here with her——"

"Miss Wood brought me and my sister. We came in my yacht, the *Ariel*. We had lost a large sum of money, nearly all we possess, and Miss Wood, knowing of the gold on the island, conceived the idea of 'repaying' us for some imaginary kindness on our part—quite imaginary."

"It was like her," murmured Vane.

"What did you say?"

"Nothing. I was speaking to myself; a bad habit I have acquired through having no one else to speak to."

"Miss Wood was cast ashore here from the wreck of the *Alpina*," resumed Sutcombe. "Her experiences must have been painful, so painful, indeed, that she has never spoken of them."

Vane's head drooped. He was disappointed. Painful, indeed, seeing that she had never mentioned his name, for if she had done so, Lord Sutcombe would have known that "Richard Mortimer" was a false one. It was evident that she still disliked him, still regarded her forced marriage with regret and resentment. He stifled a sigh.

"Thank you," he said. "I wish I could be as candid as you have been, Lord Sutcombe, but my lips are closed. I will go on board and set sail presently, and, as I told you, I shall not return to the island." He paused a moment, then he said: "We both rather played the giddy goat just now. Like a couple of schoolboys, eh, Lord Sutcombe? Just as well, perhaps, if we confined the knowledge of that absurd little scene to ourselves?" Sutcombe regarded him silently, and Vane went on: "If you think you got the better of the business you can equalize matters by promising that you will not tell—the ladies anything of the affair, or of my presence on the island."

Sutcombe considered for a moment or two.

"I will—on one condition," he said. "That you give me your word of honor that the lady I call Miss Wood has no cause of complaint against you."

Vane looked surprised. "I assent to your condition, Lord Sutcombe. She has none. I have not willingly injured the lady in word, or thought, or deed. There is my hand on it!"

Sutcombe took it and nodded gravely.

"There is some mystery which I cannot solve," he said in a low voice. "But I believe you, and trust you. But you cannot sail at once; you are not fit. The risk—oh, it is impossible! Remain here until to-morrow. I will come about noon, and, if I find that you are well enough—well!" he shrugged his shoulders.

After a while Vane reluctantly agreed to the arrangement.

"Now, I don't want to seem inhospitable," he said, "but isn't it time you got back to the ladies? They will be anxious about you."

When Sutcombe had gone, Vane sat with his chin on his hands, gazing before him, the bitterness that welled up in his heart reflected in his eyes.

He thought he saw it all so plainly. This man, with the frank blue eyes and pleasant manner, was evidently in love with Nina, and she—of course, she returned his love. Why not? Was he not the sort of young fellow any girl might love? And he, Vane, stood between them; in short, barred their happiness, and wrecked their lives. It was the irony of fate that he should be doomed to be the marplot, the obstacle to other persons' happiness. He had stood between Julian and the Lesborough peerage; he had stood between Julian and Judith. But he had, by the aid of chance, effaced himself in their case. Could he not efface himself in this one? Why not? He pondered, with an increasing bitterness, for hours, and at last he arrived at something like a decision. He still felt faint with the loss of blood, and very tired, and, lying down, with his arm for a pillow, he fell asleep.

Sutcombe had promised to return by five, but he did not arrive, and as the half hours dragged on with no sight of him, the girls, Vivienne especially, grew uneasy.

"Do you think anything could have happened to him?" she said anxiously. "He is usually so careful not to be late, knowing that we should be alarmed. Think of him all alone there, dear!"

"I don't think anything has happened to him," said Nina; "but I will soon find out."

"Decima! You wouldn't go out there alone!" exclaimed Vivienne fearfully and yet half wistfully.

"Why not?" said Nina, with a smile. "I have often been as far on the island alone, and I am not afraid; indeed, there is nothing to be afraid of. We three are alone here, and there are no animals more wild than the ducks and the poor turtles. Of course I shall go—no, you could not come, it would be too far. I shall probably meet Lord Sutcombe close at home. Don't let the stew burn while I am away!" she added with a laugh, as she left the saloon.

She walked quickly toward the valley, and would have met Sutcombe if he had been returning from the spot at which he had been working, but he was coming from the direction of the coast, and so she missed him. When she reached the working and found that he was not there, she felt rather alarmed. She stood looking round her anxiously, and saw the footmarks leading in the direction of the beach. Still more anxious, she followed them for some distance, and presently, to her amazement, caught sight of the yawl. She stopped dead short, her heart beating rapidly. What did it mean? Evidently some persons had discovered the island and had come upon Lord Sutcombe! Had they taken him away with them, or had he gone of his own accord? It would be of no use going back to alarm Vivienne; she, Nina, must learn what had become of Lord Sutcombe before she did anything else.

Keeping behind the bowlders as much as possible, she approached the yawl, and was amazed at finding no sign of life about it. After a time she plucked up courage and stole toward it, her eyes fixed upon it, so that she came quite suddenly and unprepared upon the figure lying full length upon the ground.

She uttered a cry and sprang back, her eyes distending with fear, her breath coming painfully. The man was asleep, his face half hidden in his arm; but there seemed to her something familiar in the figure, and, with her heart throbbing like a steam engine, she stole nearer and nearer. Then she saw him distinctly, and the throbbing seemed to cease suddenly, and a mist swam before her terrified eyes.

It was Vane Mannering!

For a moment or two she thought that her senses had played her false, that she was the victim of a delusion born of her constant dwelling upon him and some similarity in the sleeping man to the man she loved; but as she crept nearer still and bent over him, she saw that it was indeed Vane.

In an instant Time became a thing of naught and was destroyed, and she was back to that other night long ago, when she had bent over him in the saloon, and, waking, he had caught her by the arm and hurt her in his fierce grasp; but as swiftly the present returned to her, and all that had happened since that night yawned like a gulf between.

Then, as she looked, she saw the empty sleeve, the blood-stained bandage on the shoulder, and a thrill of alarm, of pity, ran through her. Vane here, and wounded! Why had he come? What fate had drifted him back to the island and thrown him, so to speak, at her feet? Why had he come? Why had he left the woman he loved, the beautiful woman she had seen in the box at the theatre, the "Judith" whose portrait he had carried next his heart? Had he come in search of her, Nina? Had he come because the memories of the island had haunted him as they had haunted her?

The blood ran warmly and swiftly through her veins and rose to her face. For a moment she hugged the thought to her bosom, and her heart beat with something that was like happiness. The desire to look into his eyes, to hear him speak, assailed her irresistibly. She bent still lower, and touched his forehead with her lips, then drew back, breathless and expectant, half fearful, half hopeful.

Light as the touch of her lips had been, the pressure of a thistledown only, it awoke him. He opened his eyes, with a vague and dazed expression in them at first; then, as full consciousness came back to him, he stared at her with a perplexed frown as if he could not believe that it was really her.

The next instant he was on his feet, her name on his lips.

"Nina!"

She stood, her hands clasped but ready to be thrown round his neck, her figure standing upright, but as ready to fall on his breast. And, indeed, he did extend his arms as if to take her to him, did take a step toward her; then, as if some thought, some remembrance, had thrust itself upon him, he stopped short, and his arms fell to his sides, and, instead of words of love, of endearment, which would have brought her to him, never to be put away from him again, came the hoarse, broken words, like the dropping of icicles on her expectant spirit, longing for a softer tone, a loving word:

"I—I am glad you are here. I wanted to see you—speak to you!"

CHAPTER XXIV
THEIR HONEYMOON

Nina stood with her hands clasped tightly, her eyes fixed on Vane waitingly, and under their regard his courage almost failed him, the longing to take her in his arms well-nigh mastered him. But he thought of Sutcombe, the man who loved her, the man whom she doubtless loved, and he found his voice at last. It sounded harsh and hard in his own ears; how much more so, then, in hers!

"This—this is a strange meeting," he said. "The gentleman who came with you has just left me——"

She shot a quick glance of alarm at his shoulder; a glance which, of course, Vane misinterpreted.

"An accident," he said. "A mere trifle. Lord Sutcombe is not hurt."

The color flooded her face, and she drew a long breath of relief—of relief on Sutcombe's account, Vane thought, bitterly.

"He has told me how you happened to come here. I am glad you have done so, glad he should have the gold. Indeed, it is yours to do what you like with. But that's nothing! To me the all-important fact is, of course, that you should be alive. I have sought for you——" He checked himself, for he felt he should melt and his resolution break down if he dwelt on the past, the days that had passed since they had parted. "Will you tell me how you were saved? How fate has dealt with you? I'm—I'm naturally curious," he added, with a smile from which he tried hard to keep the bitterness.

Nina obeyed, speaking almost mechanically. The dream, the hope, which had illumined her spirit as she bent over him had vanished, and left her heart an aching void.

He listened, with his eyes on the ground, keeping from his face every sign of the emotions that thrilled him at her story. She had been struggling with poverty, while he had been burdened by the wealth that was useless to him without her! When she had finished she stood and waited. She did not ask him for an account of his life since they had parted. He noticed this, and again misunderstood.

"Thank God, hard times are over for you!" he said fervently. "You are well? But—but—not happy, Nina?"

She looked at him, an eloquent glance, but his eyes were fixed on the ground and he did not see it.

"Perhaps—perhaps I can guess the cause—and remove it," he said grimly. "May I speak quite candidly? Oh, what is the use of our beating about the bush! We are both thinking of what happened on this island. You were the victim of a cruel fate, Nina, a fate I appreciated, I—I strove to avert. You will do me the justice to acknowledge that, won't you? But I have kept my promise, the promise you asked of me. No one knows of our—marriage."

She turned her face from him and looked straight before her.

"I, too, have kept my promise," she said, in a low voice.

He nodded. "I knew you would—for your own sake," he said, not at all gratefully. "It was poor Fleming's doing entirely. Mind! I bear him no ill will. He acted according to his lights. And—and, after all, there is no harm done—I mean that it can be undone."

She looked at him for a second and waited.

"Since Lord Sutcombe left me," he went on, "I have been thinking of the—the tie that binds us two, and I've come to the conclusion that it—the marriage—was invalid; anyhow, that it would not stand good unless we were married again."

The blood threatened to rise to her pale face, but she kept it down.

"If you remember, poor Fleming said that we might go through the ceremony again if we escaped from the island, when we got to a port——"

She made the faintest gesture of assent with her hand.

"Therefore, in Heaven's name, why should you be bound to me by so frail and intangible a bond!" he broke out sharply. "I know how you must long for your freedom; you would do so in any case; but now——"

Her brows knit as if she were trying to understand this.

"And—and I admit that you have the right to be free; that, indeed, it would be a shameful thing to hold you by a chain which fettered you against your will."

She made no sign of assent or dissent, and, stringing himself up to the necessary pitch of self-sacrifice, he went on huskily:

"Fleming gave you a kind of certificate? You have got it still?"

She made a movement of her hand in the affirmative.

"Well, then," he said, almost savagely, "destroy it."

Her eyes flashed on him for an instant, with surprise and relief, as he thought.

"And the ring. Give it back to me, and—and so cancel our"—he laughed slowly and bitterly—"our agreement. There can be nothing then between you and—your freedom, except the—the ceremony. If that seems to you an obstacle, you can get it removed by a court of law. I—of course, I should not oppose. Lord Sutcombe would be able to help you in that part of the business. He—he is a good fellow; I am sure of that, and he—you——" The words stuck in his throat; he could not go any further.

Nina stood with bent head, her eyes flashing, the blood running fiercely through her veins. He had spoken as if it were her freedom he desired, but was he not craving for his own, that he might be free to marry—Judith? At that moment she saw the portrait as plainly as she had seen it when it had been actually in her hand; and, her heart racked with jealousy and wounded, outraged love, she could utter no word. Suddenly she turned from him and took from her bosom the certificate and the ring that was wrapped in it, and held them out to him.

"There they are," she said, with an unnatural calm.

Vane took them from her outstretched hand and looked at them for a moment as if he saw nothing. Then, without a word, he lit one of the matches Sutcombe had given to him, and held it to a corner of the paper. But, as he did so, something seemed to catch his breath, and, half choking, he flung the match from him, crushed the certificate and ring in his hand, and springing toward her caught her in his arms.

Through a mist of tears she saw his face, white to the lips and stern, almost savage, in its passion. Amazed, she struggled faintly in his grasp, but he held her so tightly as almost to crush her.

"No!" he cried hoarsely. "I won't do it! I can't! You are my wife; do you hear? I don't care whether the ceremony was valid or not, I hold you to it! You are my wife! My *wife*! Do you understand? You married me for better or for worse; I refuse to release you. I hold you to your vow. I refuse to give you up to any man. Do you understand?"

Her eyes closed, the languor of surrender stole over her; but she fought against it, though the pressure of his arms, the fierce, passionate words were sending the blood surging through her veins in a happy flood. But, though she loved him with a love that threatened to sweep away every barrier, she was a woman and not a child, and she remembered Judith. So she held her face from the pillow—his heart—which it craved, and retained possession of her soul.

"Why did you fly from me—risk your life rather than stay with me?" he demanded masterfully. "Did you dislike me so much? Were you so afraid of me? Could you not trust me? No matter! I don't care to know! You are my wife! I hold you to your vow, your promise, Nina! I love you! I loved you then; I've loved you all the time we've been parted. I love you now, and, by God, I'll hold you! Nothing shall part us!"

Then she spoke the word; reluctantly enough, for love's voice was clamoring to her, "Be satisfied! He loves you."

"Judith!"

He started slightly and stared down into her eyes with amazement and a dawning recollection.

"Judith?" he echoed.

"Yes," she breathed. "I—I found her portrait in your coat pocket. A beautiful, a lovely woman. I saw her in a box at the theatre in London. Yes; Judith!"

He gazed, questioningly, anxiously into her eyes, half dazed for a moment; then he laughed. And the laugh was almost sweeter in her ears than his words of passionate love and longing.

"Judith! Judith Orme! You found her portrait! I had forgotten it; forgotten *her*!"

The warm blood flooded Nina's face and she drew a long sigh of relief.

"Judith? I thought I was in love with her! In love! I did not know what it meant till I met you, Nina, my dearest, my—wife!" His arms closed round her again. "I had forgotten her! Judith!" he laughed again. "She is going to be married—is married by this time to—to another man! Judith! And you thought——"

Nina's eyes overflowed with the glad tears. Oh, it is well for women that they can weep, even in their joy!

"What else could I think? And—and—you don't care for her now?" she faltered, like any girl in her teens, woman as she was.

He threw back his head and laughed again, the laugh that was such sweet music to her.

"You only, dearest," he said. "And you never guessed it! Ah, well, if you could have seen me when I found you had gone on that infernal raft; if you could have seen me when its remains floated ashore with your cap! The dear little cap! Oh, Nina! I was mad with grief; I have been more than half mad since. All the world could not console me for the loss of you! And all the time you were thinking I was in love with—Judith!"

She nestled closer to him.

"Forgive me!" she murmured. "But what else could I think—her portrait, there in your coat, over your heart!—and knowing that you had been forced into the marriage——"

"I loved you then, before then!" he said earnestly. "It was on your account that I hesitated, pleaded with Fleming, made the raft. I thought you disliked me, and I loved you too well to get you against your will."

"How blind we were!" she murmured regretfully; for how much their blindness had cost them.

"Blind as young puppies! But our eyes are opened now, dearest! It is all right!"

"Your shoulder, your wound——Do you remember the fight with the Lascar?" she whispered, with a shudder.

"Yes, and how gently you dressed the wound; you little guessed how the touch of your dear fingers thrilled through me!" he responded. "My beautiful!" He gazed into her eyes, raised shyly but lovingly to his. "To think of your being a literary swell! A dramatic author! And to think of my looking on the play, and not knowing that my dear, clever *wife* had written it. My wife! Nina, you haven't kissed me yet! Kiss me now! Just that I may realize that you are actual flesh and blood, and not one of the visions of you that have come to me so often in my dreams."

She raised her head and kissed him, and did not tell him that she had already done so!

"And now, dearest, touching the future——"

He started at his own words. Future! Why, he had destroyed the future that belonged to her, had given away his birthright, the title, the wealth that should belong to her as his wife! It had been the act of a madman; but—the act had been accomplished, and could not be undone.

She nestled against him and laughed.

"I am too happy in our present to think of the future," she said in a low voice.

"You—you don't mind being the wife of—of a poor man, a man of no account?" he faltered.

She looked at him with surprise. "You forget the gold—Vane!" she said. The tone of her "Vane" thrilled him.

"Ah, yes, of course!" he responded, with relief. "Yes; yes! I'd forgotten the gold. No wonder, with such a treasure in my arms! We'll go to England, form a company——" He stopped and frowned. How could he go to England, he who had exiled himself from civilization, who was dead to the world, his world. "You—you wouldn't like to stay here?" he suggested, scarcely knowing what to say.

"Anywhere—with you!" she murmured.

Suddenly athwart this dream of happiness came a voice calling, "Decima—Miss Wood!"

Nina started. "Lord Sutcombe!" she whispered almost guiltily.

"Ah, poor Lord Sutcombe!" murmured Vane gravely. "Yes, I can pity him, Nina! To love you—and lose you! Don't I know what that means!"

Sutcombe came upon them hurriedly, and stopped short, looking from one to the other, the color coming and going in his face. Vane made a dash at the revelation.

"Lord Sutcombe—Nina—Miss Wood—we have met—she is my wife!"

Sutcombe started; then he remembered the paper and the ring he had seen Nina weeping over, and realized the truth—and his own absolute, irrevocable loss. He stood for a moment or two quite silent, then he came forward and held out his hand.

"I—I congratulate you," he said simply, and not even Vane could appreciate the effort the words, the tone cost him; but perhaps Nina could.

She laid her hand on his arm and looked up at him through a mist of tears.

"We—we—owe—our happiness to *you*," she whispered. "But for you I should not have come back to the island——"

Sutcombe patted her hand in silence for a moment, then he said:

"We must go back to my sister; she is anxious."

"Yes, let us go," said Vane.

Sutcombe would have preceded them, but Nina walked resolutely by his side; and so, all together, they came to Vivienne in the saloon. Nina flew to her and hid her face on her bosom, and Vivienne stared over her at the tall, rough-looking man, whose grave face had already the glow of his new-found happiness in it.

"Vivienne—oh, Vane, I can't tell her! You!" She broke down.

Vane came forward.

"It is soon told," he said gently. "This lady to whom you and your brother have been so good—God bless you for it—and I are husband and wife. We were married on this island a long time ago. My I name, *her* name, is Mannering. I am Vane Mannering——"

He stopped, aghast, at the slip of the tongue, and was more aghast still when he saw the brother and sister exchange glances. He was glad that Nina had—like a good housewife—turned to the fire to see after the supper.

"Vane Mannering!" exclaimed Sutcombe. "Are you related to the Lesborough family? There was a Vane Mannering—the last earl, who perished in a fire at Lesborough Court——"

Vane signed to him warningly, and Sutcombe, embarrassed and speechless, stopped and stared at him. Vivienne made a show of helping Nina, and presently Nina shyly invited them to supper. They sat down, and Vane told the Sutcombes of the wreck, and the story of the marriage, Nina sitting near him with bent head and face, that grew hot and pale by turns; and the Sutcombes listened with an amazement which grew still more intense when Vane abruptly said, as if he had suddenly arrived at a decision:

"And now for something else. Just now you asked me if I were connected with the Lesboroughs. I am. I am the man who was supposed to have been killed by the fire at the Court!"

"Supposed! Then—then you are Lord Lesborough!" exclaimed Sutcombe. Vane stretched out his hand and got Nina's, and held it tightly, and looked tenderly and reassuringly into her startled eyes.

"Yes," he admitted gravely. "It is a strange business. Listen!"

Amidst their breathless silence he told them the story of the accident, the sacrifice he had made for Julian.

"What was the use of the title, the estate, to me?" he said simply. "I had lost Nina, forever, as I thought; for even if she were alive, I thought she had risked death rather than remain alive here with me. Life was over for me; such a life as that which I should have had to lead was impossible. And Julian would make a ten thousand times better Lord of Lesborough—it was only pushing the clock on a little, I thought! I should never marry—even if I had been free to do so, for, you see, I loved my wife here, wife or no wife. And so

I disappeared that Julian Shore might reign in my stead! It wasn't much of a sacrifice; and it was lessened by the fact that the poor soul, the poor deaf and dumb woman, who was so devoted to him, had given her life to save mine. It was some kind of a return, acknowledgment of, her heroism. I could make the master she loved rich and happy. You see? You think I was mad; but—I hadn't found my wife again." And he colored and looked around. "She is my wife, Lord Sutcombe. Tell her so!"

Sutcombe nodded gravely.

"Yes," he said, "I am a barrister, though I've never practiced; and, strangely enough, while I was reading for the bar, I studied the marriage laws. The marriage was legal!"

"Thank you!" said Vane, with his eyes on Nina's face. She rose, and without a word, Vivienne and she left the saloon. At the door she paused for an instant and looked at Vane. He had started to his feet, but, before the look in her eyes, he sank down again.

"She is not satisfied," he said, almost inaudibly, as the door closed on them.

Sutcombe shook his head. "It is only natural. You must be married in due form. Though, mind, this one is legal and absolutely valid!

"But—but—there is another matter," continued Sutcombe. "Do you mind telling me again about the—accident, the fire? It is a painful subject—but I have a reason for asking."

Vane repeated the account of that awful scene in the Wizard's or Witch's Room, and Sutcombe stopped, him now and again to ask for some detail; then he said, very gravely:

"And you call it an accident?"

"Certainly!" responded Vane, with some surprise. "The poor woman upset the stove, furnace, whatever you call it, and the burning spirit ran over the floor and caught——" He shuddered.

"The fire? Yes, that was an accident," said Sutcombe, still more gravely, his face pale, his eyes fixed earnestly on Vane. "But the fumes which nearly suffocated you? The door was locked——"

"It locked with a spring."

"The ropes of the ventilator gave way in your hands. Your cousin, Mr. Julian Shore, did not return——"

"Good God! What is it you are suggesting?" cried Vane, white to the lips, not only at the suggestion, but at his own vague sense that it might be true.

"Murder," replied Sutcombe.

Vane fell back and regarded him with horror-stricken eyes.

"Murder! Julian—Julian plot, plan my death! Oh, you don't know him! He is incapable of——" The sweat stood thickly on his brow.

Sutcombe looked at him steadily.

"You had never met your cousin before that day at the lawyer's; knew nothing about him," he said. "I know more than you!"

"You!" said Vane.

"Yes; because I have not come under the spell of his presence, that peculiar charm of which you tell us. I, unbiased, untrammeled by the influence of his personality, can view his actions with a clear judgment. Wait! Think how much he had to gain by your death! A peerage, the estates, the woman he loved!"

"But—but," stammered Vane eagerly, "I was not in their way! She did not care—I did not care for her. She knew it!"

Sutcombe smiled grimly. "She had cared for you; I am not so sure, from all you tell me, that she did not still care. At any rate, he thought so. You were terribly in his way, Lesborough, and he—tried to remove you! Why did that poor woman come back to that infernal room, and by the other door? She suspected her master, as I suspect, and she came to save you from death and him from—murder!"

Vane sprang to his feet.

"My God!" he cried, "I can't, I won't believe it! I dare not! Julian—Julian, my own flesh and blood!"

"More kith than kind!" murmured Sutcombe. "Heaven grant that you may be right and I wrong. But your duty is clear. You must go to England and discover the truth for yourself. Go secretly, concealing your identity——"

"I will!" said Vane resolutely. "And I'll prove you're wrong! Yes, I'll prove it to your satisfaction. Julian try to—to murder me!" He laughed, but the laugh had a note of dread and doubt in it.

They sat and talked for some time; then Vane said he must go.

"I can't leave the boat; I'm not certain of the tide," he said. "I'll come around to-morrow, and we'll talk it over. Of course, not a word to the ladies!"

They shook hands and parted, but neither slept. Vane lay awake looking up at the stars and thinking of Nina, and Sutcombe paced the saloon and carried on the fight with his disappointment and loss.

Going to the spring quite early the next morning, he was surprised to find Vivienne seated on the beach a little way from the ladies' hut. She beckoned to him, and when he came within hearing held up her finger warningly.

"Hush!" she whispered. "She is asleep. She has been awake all the night, but has just fallen off. We have been talking; she has been telling me everything, and I have been thinking. Sutcombe"—she paused and bit her lip—"you are sure the—the marriage was quite legal?"

"Quite," he said gravely, and looking away from her.

"Then bend down; I—I want to whisper, Sutcombe."

With her face against his, she whispered something in his ear. He started and drew a long breath, then nodded assentingly.

"Yes!" he said, in a low voice. "We will do it. It—it is a clever idea of yours, Vivienne. How did you come to think of it?"

"I am a woman, dear!" she said. "But you will have to be quick—there is no time to lose."

"I will manage my part, if you will do yours," he said, and he laid his hand on her shoulder. "To see her happy—it is all I ask!"

The tears came to her eyes and she put up her hand and caressed him with the familiar gesture. It was not necessary for her to say anything.

It was late when Nina awoke—awoke to find that her dream that Vane was restored to her was true!—and Vivienne was standing beside the bed with a cup of tea in her hand.

"You lazybones!" she said. "We've all had breakfast, and Sutcombe has gone off to his work—how pretty you look when you blush, Decima, for it must be 'Decima' for me still! At any rate, until I can get used to the 'Nina.' I like the way he says it—Nina, Nina!"

Nina hung her head and blushed all the rosier.

"Mr. Mannering, or, rather, Lord Lesborough, has gone back to the boat to mend a sail, or something of the kind. And Sutcombe says, do you mind making some bags for him this morning? He particularly wants them at once."

"Why, of course!" said Nina eagerly. "Give me the stuff: I'll begin them this very moment. Are you sure everything is right in the saloon?" she asked, like a careful housekeeper. "What are you doing?"

"Quite sure!" replied Vivienne. "What am I doing? Oh, only tidying up a little. Shall we take the bags down to the clump of trees in the hollow? Oh, perhaps you'd rather stay here, in case *he* should come!"

Nina jumped up with suspicious promptness.

"Come along; it will be shady there," she said.

They went to the spot of which Vivienne had spoken. It was a little dip in the valley, from which the coast line could not be seen; and, as they worked, Vivienne enticed Nina into again telling her the strange story of the wreck, and all that had followed it; and they were so absorbed in the recital that, though Nina glanced round occasionally rather wistfully, the morning slipped away. Presently there sounded a step; but Nina's eyes did not brighten; for it was not the one for which she was waiting—and longing. It was Sutcombe.

"Done some of the bags? Thank you very much, Lady Lesborough," he said cheerfully.

Nina started and colored.

"I—I——Oh, you call me that!" she said, half proudly, half doubtfully.

"Yes; it is your name, your title," he said gravely. "But—but sometimes—often—I shall think of you as Decima."

She held out her hand, and he took it and pressed it.

"Lord Lesborough is busy with his boat," he said. "When you've finished the rest of the bags—if you're not tired of them already——"

"No, no!" she said, with unnecessary earnestness.

"Perhaps you'd bring them down to the saloon, if you don't mind. Vivienne, I want your help for a while."

They went off, but when they had gone a little distance, Vivienne paused, and, coming back, stooped and kissed Nina. There did not seem anything in the moment especially appropriate for the caress; but one woman is never surprised when another kisses her, and Nina took it gratefully, and returned it. After they had gone, she worked until the last of the remaining bags were finished, then she arose, and, with an unconscious sigh of relief, went toward the saloon. As she did so she looked round a little fearfully, and yet a little wistfully; but there was no one in sight. Nor was there any one in the saloon; and, putting the bags on the table, she went toward the beach. As she reached it she looked seaward, and to her surprise saw a vessel in the offing. It was the *Ariel*, and she remembered that it was the day appointed for its return. She was gazing at it when she was startled by discovering that it was going from the island, instead of making toward it. She ran down the beach to the cove where one of the *Ariel's* boats had been anchored, and was more than startled to find that it had disappeared. What could it mean? She gazed at the receding vessel for a moment or two, then ran up the beach, calling for Vivienne.

Vivienne did not appear, but a stalwart figure came swiftly from the saloon. It was Vane. She stopped short, and, panting, looked from him to the *Ariel*.

"What is the matter? You were calling, dearest?" he said.

"Yes!" she responded anxiously. "I was calling Lady Vivienne. I can't find her or Lord Sutcombe. And the *Ariel*—that is the *Ariel* sailing away from the island!"

He shaded his eyes with his hand and looked at it. Then he looked at her, a curious expression in his eyes, a dawning joy.

"I found this in the saloon," he said, holding out a note; "perhaps it will explain——"

She took the paper—it was folded in a lover's knot—and, opening it, read:

"Dear Nina:

Forgive me! It was my wicked plot! And mine alone. It occurred to me while we were talking last night. We have gone for a cruise—for a fortnight—when we will come back to see if you are still here. But Lord Lesborough has his boat, and you may both decide to spend the rest of your honeymoon elsewhere. If we do not find you, we will go to England and wait for you in the old rooms at Eversleigh Court. Till then, and as long as I live, dear, I am, yours,

VIVIENNE."

"They've—gone!" he said, in a low voice. "And—left us alone! Nina, my wife!" and the next moment his arms were round her and her face hidden on his breast.

* * * *

The wintry sun, stealing faintly through the blinds of the breakfast room at the Court, fell upon the black-garbed figure of Julian, as he sat at the table, looking distastefully at the good food set out for him. In his morning suit of black serge his thin figure looked thinner than of old, but just as graceful. His face was pale; indeed, looked almost as bloodless as the hands that broke the piece of toast on his plate. Beside it was the post bag, and every now and then he took up a letter, opened it and eyed it listlessly, then dropped it as listlessly on the table.

"Shall I give you some fresh tea, my lord?" asked Prance, in a subdued voice—all the voices at the Court had become subdued of late, since, in fact, the fatal accident which had killed the late earl.

"Eh? Ah, yes, thanks," replied Julian. "Is Mr. Holland here?"

"Yes, my lord. He is in the library with Mr. Tressider."

Julian nodded. "You can go. I don't want anything more, Prance. Tell Dodson to have a carriage ready—a close carriage—at eleven."

"Yes, my lord," said Prance, in the same low tone.

When he had left the room Julian turned to the letters again, and suddenly the gloom in his eyes gave place to eagerness. He had found a letter that interested him. He tore it open and read it with a red spot on his hollow cheek:

"Do not come to see me. I am not well enough to see any one. I will write when I am stronger.

"JUDITH."

He twisted the note in his nervous fingers, staring reflectingly at the opposite wall meanwhile; then he tore the note into small fragments, and threw them on the fire. For some minutes afterward he sat, his eyes fixed on vacancy; then, with a start, he rose and went into the library. The steward and the lawyer were seated at the table, with some account books and papers before them. Both men were in mourning. They had been talking about the new earl.

"Just the same, Mr. Tressider," Holland had said. "He seems like a man in a dream, and half dazed and bewildered, as if he could not get over the shock of—of that night."

"Well, it's not so very long ago," commented Mr. Tressider with a grunt.

"Quite so, quite so, Mr. Tressider! I am not saying that it's unreasonable; but, well, after all, he has the title and the estates; and, if I may say so, his lordship doesn't strike me as the kind of man to be so overwhelmed as to lose sight of the advantages which his late lordship's death have bestowed on him."

"No," said Mr. Tressider. "I should not have credited Mr. Julian—pardon! I can never remember to give him his title!—his lordship—the man to forget that he is now the possessor of the title and estates. He doesn't sleep, you say?"

"Fenton told me yesterday that very often his lordship's bed had not been slept in, and that he hears him pacing up and down his room the whole night through."

The old lawyer shrugged his shoulders. "Well! I shouldn't have credited Mr. Julian—tut, tut, I mean Lord Lesborough!—with so much sensibility. But, there, Mr. Holland, the longer I live the more I am convinced that there is one subject you can never learn—your fellow men!"

"Just so!" assented Holland. "Now I should have said that Mr. Julian—there! I've caught it from you, Mr. Tressider!—would have got over his poor cousin's death in less than a month; and yet, you see, it preys upon him and haunts him as if it happened only yesterday. And, talking of haunting, the whole house seems as if it were under a ban. Mrs. Field tells me that she can scarcely persuade a servant to stay, and that they who do consent to remain won't go near the ruins of the Wizard's Room——Hush! Here he is!"

They rose and bowed as Julian entered. He went to the table, and sinking into a chair, looked not at them, but between them.

"You wanted to see me?" he said to Mr. Tressider.

The old lawyer nodded.

"Yes, Mr. Julian—ahem—Lord Lesborough, I want you, please, to sign some papers."

"Is—is everything done—complete?" asked Julian, his white hands fidgeting with a paper knife.

"Er—well, not complete?" replied Mr. Tressider. "There have been difficulties in the way, of which the greatest is the difficulty in proving the death"—his voice dropped—"of the late earl."

Julian turned his dark, sombre eyes upon him.

"What difficulty can there be?" he asked, in a toneless voice. "He—my poor cousin was in the room; and though the—the remains were unrecognizable, his coat was identified."

"Quite so, quite so, Mr.—Lord Lesborough," said Mr. Tressider, "but the court needs rather more solid proof of death than that. At present, at any rate. Later, later they may accept it. Meanwhile, of course, as the next in succession, you will administer the estate. I shall make another application, which, if successful, will place your title beyond dispute. Will you sign this, and this, please?"

Julian drew the papers toward him and signed in his neat hand, "Lesborough," then he glanced at Mr. Holland.

"Do you want me? I am going for a drive."

"No, Mr.—Lord Lesborough. There is a lease or two, but they can wait; there is no hurry."

Julian rose slowly, with the heaviness, the slowness of a man of twice his weight.

"You are having the Wizard's Room bricked up, as I ordered?" he said, with his hand on the door.

"Yes, Lord Lesborough. The men are working steadily at it."

Julian nodded, held the door for a moment or two, then went out. The two men exchanged glances.

"Queer," said Mr. Tressider, pursing his lips.

"He is always like that—like a man in a dream!" said Mr. Holland, with a shake of the head.

Mr. Tressider shrugged his shoulders.

"It is to be hoped that he will wake up," he said resentfully, "or it will be a bad thing for Lesborough. Ah, poor Vane Mannering! He was the man!"

"And yet he didn't seem particularly happy, Mr. Tressider," remarked Holland.

The old lawyer grunted.

"Seems as if there was a curse on the place—and the race," he said.

Julian went into the hall, and a footman brought his hat and overcoat. But when he had got them on Julian stood looking round him vaguely. It was down those stairs Judith Orme had come with white face and horror-stricken eyes the night——

"The carriage, my lord," said Prance.

Attended by a couple of footmen, Julian got in; but, as the carriage turned the corner of the lawn, he pulled the cord; and as the horses came to a stop, got out and slowly, with bent head, went round to where the masons were at work bricking up the Wizard's Room. He stood and gazed at them for some minutes, then he reëntered the carriage, and it drove on.

Just as it was passing through the lodge gates, with the lodgekeeper's wife curtsying obsequiously, an open carriage entered. It pulled up, and Julian, looking from his window, saw Lord and Lady Fanworthy.

His thin face drew into a scowl for a moment, then he forced it into a smile, and, stopping the brougham, he alighted.

"How do you do?" he said suavely. "Were you going up to the Court? I'll turn back."

"No, no! Don't, Lesborough," said Lord Fanworthy. "I was only coming to ask you if you'd made up your mind about the hounds. Poor Vane, you know, was very interested in them——"

Julian stood beside the carriage, with his hat in his hands, "like a foreigner," as Lady Fanworthy would have said.

"I'm considering the matter," he said, "You are sure you won't let me turn back?"

He addressed Lord Fanworthy, but he was conscious of her ladyship's notoriously keen eyes. They seemed to pierce to his brain.

"No; no, thanks."

Julian waved his hat and backed toward his brougham, but Lady Fanworthy's voice arrested him.

"Oh, I wanted to ask you—you won't think me guilty of vulgar curiosity, Mr.—Lord Lesborough"—it was strange that she should share Mr. Tressider's difficulty in addressing his lordship by his title—"but have you heard anything of that strange servant of yours, Deborah? The woman who disappeared the night—the night——"

Julian lifted his pale face, his dark eyes veiled by their heavy lids.

"Deborah?" he said.

"Yes; you know she left the Court the day of the—the accident," said the terrible old lady.

"I know," replied Julian. "Oh, yes! She went to attend the sick bed of a sister. I expect her back every day. So good of you to ask for her! Are you sure you won't let me turn back with you?"

"Quite sure!" said her ladyship, as suavely.

As the Fanworthy carriage turned, Lord Fanworthy remonstrated with her ladyship.

" 'Pon my soul, don't you know! Rather unfeelin', eh, dear? What on earth made you drag up that awful business?"

Lady Fanworthy smiled for a moment, then became suddenly grave.

"My dear, I did it with an object. I want to find that deaf and dumb woman."

"Want to find her! Good heavens! What for?"

"Simple curiosity. I liked the woman," said Lady Fanworthy, after a pause.

CHAPTER XXV
THE RETURN

One evening Sutcombe came home—he had been down to the Momus—just in time to dress for dinner; and Vivienne, hearing his footsteps, called him into the dining room to look at the floral decorations.

"Aren't they pretty, Sutcombe?" she said, in the softened tones, which come so naturally to most women when they are speaking of flowers.

"Very," he assented. "Is it a special occasion?"

"Why, yes. The Letchfords are dining with us to-night. Had you forgotten?"

"Ah, yes!" he said apologetically. "I've been busy, and——Any news, Vivienne?"

It was the question he always asked when returning home, however short his absence.

Vivienne shook her head, and, as he sighed, she asked:

"Why are you so anxious, dear? Nothing can have happened to them."

He looked doubtful and troubled. "I don't know. Sometimes I'm afraid——It was an open boat; and—I should have thought one of them would have written."

Vivienne smiled reassuringly.

"I'd trust them in a cockleshell, Sutcombe!" she said. "There was something about Lord Lesborough, in his very voice, that inspired confidence. Oh, they are quite safe and sound—somewhere. Remember, dear, they are on their honeymoon. And whoever writes on their honeymoon? For them the world contains only two persons—Vane and Decima—I mean Nina. We shall hear presently, or they will walk in one evening. I am quite sure that they are well and—happy! Go and dress, dear; you have not too much time. Is everything going right at the theatre?"

He nodded. "Yes, the play is going better than ever. It will run for a twelvemonth. I'm glad the Letchfords are coming; the sight of their happiness makes one happy."

"And how much happier if one had helped them to their bliss!" she murmured. He understood her allusion to the other couple, and smiled at her appreciatively.

"That's so," he responded simply, as he left the room.

The Letchfords came up to time. They sat down to dinner. Strangely enough—and yet not so strangely, for the Letchfords often thought of their dead friend—the conversation strayed indirectly toward the subject of Vane's death and Julian's succession.

"I met Sir Chandos Orme to-day—you know him, I think, Sutcombe?" said Letchford.

Sutcombe nodded. "A little; who doesn't?"

"You'll be sorry to hear that he is breaking up—at last! I saw him in St. James Street, and scarcely knew him; and he did not know me at all. He was tottering along like an old man, his wig all askew, the enamel, or whatever it is, cracked and in blotches on his face, and his lips twisted into a fatuous, senile grin. A most dreadful wreck, poor old chap! What you call an awful warning and example. I crossed over and got hold of his hand—it shook with palsy—and contrived, after some minutes, to make him recognize me. I wanted to inquire after his daughter, Judith."

"And how is she?" asked Lady Letchford gravely.

Her husband shook his head.

"Very bad, I gathered. She has never got over the shock of"—his voice dropped—"of that terrible tragedy at Lesborough. I don't think you knew much of my poor friend, Vane Mannering, Sutcombe?"

Sutcombe colored and fidgeted. He had not been authorized to proclaim that Vane still lived.

"I—I have met him," he said.

"An awfully good fellow—one of the very best," said Letchford, with a deep sigh. "He had a very short innings; and they weren't particularly happy ones. There was some cloud. There's a kind of ban on the Lesborough family, and I'd hoped he'd broken it; but he didn't; and the present man doesn't look as if he would."

Sutcombe looked up quickly.

"You don't like him?" he said.

"Well, n-o," he replied reluctantly. "I never did, nor did Blanche. Awfully good-looking chap, and sang like a—like a blessed nightingale; but—— What was it Lady Fanworthy said to you, Blanche: That he reminded her of a black panther?"

"Mr. Julian Shore—Lord Lesborough—is very dark," said Lady Letchford, with a reproachful frown at her too candid husband.

"There was never any doubt of your Lord Lesborough's death, I suppose?" asked Sutcombe; and it was now Vivienne's turn to frown at him.

"Eh? What?" said Letchford, much startled. "Why, no; how could there be? We saw—or as good as saw—him die." There was a moment's pause, then he added: "By the way, now you ask the question, there is one person who refused to believe that he was burned—old Lady Fanworthy. But, then, as everybody knows, she is the most eccentric woman in the kingdom."

"Charlie!" murmured Lady Letchford rebukingly.

"Well, so she is, Blanche."

"I'm not sure that her incredulity in this case proves her eccentricity," said Sutcombe. He had been thinking during the conversation, and was rather inclined to prepare these good friends of Vane's for the shock that sooner or later awaited them.

"Eh? What?" repeated Letchford amazedly. "I was there, you know, when the terrible affair happened——"

"And saw Lord Lesborough's body?" put in Sutcombe.

"No; no one could see that," replied Letchford, in a low voice. "But there was enough to identify him. There was the coat, a fragment of it, and the buttons——"

"He might have left the coat there," suggested Sutcombe. "Or"—he paused impressively—"or he might have lent it to some one."

Letchford stared; then he shook his head and sighed.

"No good, Sutcombe! I wish it were! If my poor friend wasn't burned to death that night, what became of him; where is he?"

Sutcombe leaned forward, and, with all eyes, Vivienne's fearfully, fixed on him, he retorted:

"I'm lawyer enough to remind you that you have to prove that he is dead. See, now, Letchford: You say that there was a cloud over his life; that he had once before disappeared and been lost to his friends; that, although he had succeeded to the title and was well off—a rich man—he was still unhappy. How do you know that he didn't disappear again; that, for reasons you and I cannot guess, he did not yield to a desire to surrender the title and the money to his cousin, the heir, to whom he was, I believe, much attached——"

Letchford sprang to his feet, his face aglow.

"By Heaven, Sutcombe, you—you know, you have heard something!" he exclaimed.

Sutcombe crimsoned, then turned pale.

"I—I——" he stammered; but before he could say any more the servant came to the door.

"Would you step into the library, my lord?" he said very gravely.

Sutcombe, glad to escape, rose promptly.

"Excuse me a moment, will you?" he said. "Some business connected with the theatre, I suppose."

He went out covertly wiping the perspiration from his forehead. He had gone further than he intended, and the interruption came at a lucky moment, and would give him time to think over some way of explaining away the impression he had created. He entered the library, then started back with a low cry; for Vane and Nina stood there.

He closed the door sharply, then got hold of a hand of each, and all of them were talking at once, the two men laughing in the nervous way in which men try to conceal their emotion, and Nina standing silent, but with the happy tears in her eyes.

"When did you come back?" Sutcombe was at last able to inquire.

"To-day—this moment. We sent the luggage to the Carlton and came on here. All the dinner eaten?"

"No, no!" said Sutcombe, still wringing his hand. "Just at it. And Vivienne! Can't you guess how delighted she will be, De—Lady Lesborough! And we were just talking of you! But when aren't we! But, oh, by Jove!" He stopped aghast. "There's—there are some people here you know—the Letchfords!"

Vane's face lit up, and he nodded and turned to Nina. "She knows them, though she hasn't seen them. Don't you, Nina?"

"Yes," she murmured; for how often had she not listened to his story of the Letchfords' goodness to him?

"Come on," said Vane. "We're not in evening-dress, but——"

"But they think you're dead," said Sutcombe ruefully. Then his face cleared. "No, by Jove! for, as luck would have it, I've just been preparing them for the fact that you are still alive——"

"And kicking!" Vane finished. "Lead on, Macduff! Poor, dear old Letchford, how glad he'll be!"

"Give me a moment—just two moments. You stay outside the door till I give the word; you'll know when to show up!"

When he returned to the dining room Vivienne saw from his face that he had "heard news," and she uttered a low cry. But he addressed himself to Letchford.

"You asked me just now, Letchford, to tell you where Lesborough is, if he was not killed that night, as you concluded. I couldn't tell you a few minutes ago, but I've heard news, and I can now!"

Vivienne rose, supporting herself by the table.

"Sutcombe! You have seen them! Oh, where are they?"

"Here, Lady Vivienne!" came Vane's voice in response, as he and Nina entered; Nina with a cry, that was followed by one of amazement from the Letchfords, and delight from Vivienne, into whose arms Nina had glided.

For hours these good people talked, one against the other, in a state of excitement which threatened to exhaust the ladies, who, after a time, retired to the drawing-room and left the three men to more serious conversation.

"The question is," said Sutcombe gravely, "did Julian Shore know the truth?"

"I say 'no!' " responded Vane stoutly.

"And I——Dash it all, I wish I could!" said Letchford. "But don't be guided by me. I'm prejudiced. I never liked him."

"There is only one course to follow," said Sutcombe. "You must go down and confront him, Lesborough. You will see in a moment whether he is as guilty as I deem him. Take him by surprise, and you will find——"

"That you have wronged him!" broke in Vane. "I'll go down to-morrow. If I find that he is innocent, then I will share half the estate with him, with my wife's full and free consent. I can't give him the title; that"—he paused—"is not mine to give. But anything else——You will find I am right, Sutcombe."

But Sutcombe shook his head.

"And you are happy, dear?" Vivienne was saying to Nina, in the drawing-room, as they sat close together, hand in hand. "But what a foolish question! One has only to look at your face!"

Nina's eyes shone with her felicity.

"And I owe it all to you—and Lord Sutcombe!" she said. "There is scarcely an hour of the day that we do not talk of you; there is scarcely a moment that I do not think of you! And, oh! I am so glad to get back, though we have had such a lovely time. And my play?"

" 'Going strong!' That's Sutcombe's slang, dear! We will all go and see it the very first possible night!"

"And Polly?" inquired Nina eagerly.

"Polly is in the sixth heaven of bliss—and will be in the seventh itself when she knows that you have come back. We will bring her home to supper with us after the theatre; and——Oh, tell us all over again what you have been doing!"

CHAPTER XXVI
JULIAN'S CONFESSION

The following day Julian Shore was sitting in the library. Though the weather was warm, a fire had been lit, and he had pulled the armchair close to it, and was crouching over it, with his thin, white hands held to the blaze. If there were, indeed, a ban on the house of Lesborough, that ban was resting very heavily on the present bearer of the title; for Julian Shore looked the most wretched and unhappy of men. It was not remorse that brooded like a vulture upon his mind, but the sense that the prize for which he had sold his soul would probably evade his grasp. For, though Judith had not actually cast him off and disowned him, he was convinced that, in refusing to see him, she was only temporizing and preparing him for her final declaration—that she intended to break her part of the unholy pact. She had hated him from the first, he knew, and had only been impelled to make that pact by the stings of jealousy and the promptings of ambition. In a word, she had hounded him on to the crime, from which she now shrank, and for which she refused him the reward.

It was of Judith, and almost only of Judith, he thought, as he bent forward, his dark eyes fixed gloomily on the fire. Of Vane he thought not at all. Vane had been in the way both of his passion and his greed for rank, and wealth, and power, and—Vane was removed. Judith, only Judith, sat enthroned in the mind behind the sombre brow.

Even Lady Fanworthy's inquiry, almost anxious inquiry, for Deborah did not trouble him. Deborah had disappeared on the day of the—fire; but her disappearance had not moved him. It was probable, he thought, that the reason for her absence which he had given was not far from the truth; she had, in all likelihood, gone to a relative. The loss of her services was felt by him occasionally; he missed her now and again; but he was as indifferent to her fate as he had been to that of the cat he had suffocated, as he had been to the death of Vane.

Judith! How to force her to keep her pact. He was now the Earl of Lesborough; or, at least, would soon be the acknowledged master where once he had been the dependent. He had performed his part of the contract; how should he force her to fulfill hers? His mind was at work on the question all day and every day, and his thin, bloodless lips now formed her name inaudibly. He rose presently, his lips twitching, and, taking a spirit stand from the sideboard, he poured out some brandy, and drank it slowly, meditatingly. Then he went back to the chair, and fell into his old attitude, and fell to muttering, holding an imaginary conversation between the woman on whom his black soul was set and himself. After a while he looked round vaguely, then he rose, and, with a stealthy glance round him, paid another visit to the sideboard. He had drained the glass of, this time, neat spirit, and was going unsteadily back to the chair, when he heard a step in the hall outside.

He paused, and looked toward the door, and muttered in quite a matter-of-fact voice:

"That was like Vane's. Strange!"

He sank into the chair, and leaned back, with closed eyes, the white lids gleaming, in a ghastly fashion, from the dark shadows which encircled his eyes; but suddenly the lids flickered. The door had opened, and a step—so strangely like Vane's—was heard in the room. He raised his lids, heavy with insomnia, and, without moving his head, turned his eyes.

Vane stood looking down at him with an anxious, doubtful, troubled inquiry.

"Julian!" he said gravely, gently. "Don't be frightened. It is I!"

Julian regarded him with lack-lustre eyes.

"Too much brandy; no sleep," he muttered to himself. "I expected this. How like! It might be Vane himself."

"Don't you know me, Julian?" said Vane, still more anxiously, with a look of greater doubt and trouble in his face. "I have just returned to England. I came to tell you that I am alive. Get up, old fellow! Give me your hand, your congratulations! What is the matter? Julian, are you ill?"

"His voice, exactly!" muttered Julian, almost with admiration. "A perfect illusion, optical and aural. This is interesting; very!"

He rose, quite steadily, and went for some more brandy; and Vane approached, and would have laid his hand upon Julian's arm, but Julian drew back, not with fear, but with a laugh, and shook his head.

"No, no! You can't make your touch felt, you know. Ghosts can't materialize to that extent! No, no! So you are going to haunt me? I think not! I can lay you, my good cousin, as I raised you, with this!" He lifted the glass and drank a long draught. "It is only a question of quantity."

As Vane stood, regarding him with sad sternness, a foreboding of what was to follow, Julian went on:

"Not gone yet? What do you want? The orthodox, the regular thing—a confession? Take it, then, and be off, good ghost. And you *are* good, excellent! The very image of my dear, noble cousin. Won't that well-merited compliment send you back to hell—oh, no, good men like you go to heaven. I forgot! Pardon! Not gone? You will have that confession?"

His lips writhed into a mocking smile. "You insist? With all my heart. Well, then, my dear Vane, I laid the little plot which transported you to the good man's eternal reward. And you must admit that it was as neat and finished as any that even a Borgia could conceive. Come, now! confess that you had not the least glimmering of an idea that the laboratory was prepared for you; that the ropes of the ventilator had been neatly frayed, almost to parting point; that the combination of aconite and ammonia had been calculated to a nicety; that I had tried the fumes on a cat—poor, innocent cat; that I had the key of the door in my pocket, and kept it there while I lingered about the hall, until—well, until the fumes had done their work!"

Vane shrank back from the now glittering eyes, glittering with exultation over the fiendish work, the fluent words that left, gloatingly, the livid, working lips, shrank back with manly shame, as if he were the guilty one, and not the intended victim.

"Good God!" he gasped. "Are—are you mad, Julian?"

"Mad? Not a whit, thanks, ghost of my dear Vane!" retorted Julian, with a laugh, as he turned to the decanter of brandy. "I am the sanest of the sane; for I am one of those men who know what they want—and get it! I wanted your title, the Lesborough estates. I nearly had them, for you were supposed to be dead; but you were fool enough to come back to the land of the living, and robbed me. I could have killed you at that old idiot's—Tressider's—and, later that day, at my own rooms. But you didn't see it. Not you! You are one of those blind fools who are called honest, honorable men!"

The sweat stood thickly on Vane's forehead; the horror of the scene was almost intolerable. He tried to end it.

"Julian!" broke from him. "This is madness—stark, raving madness. You—you could not have done it!"

Julian took the glass from his lips to laugh derisively.

"Couldn't I? Not for the title and the estates, perhaps. I wanted them badly enough, but I—don't—think, I'm not *sure*, that I'd have murdered you for them. Murder's a serious thing, after all. But I wanted something more badly than I wanted the title and the estates. Can't you guess? You dull ghost, you obtuse phantom! I wanted the woman you once loved, and who still loved you—Judith!"

"Judith!" echoed Vane, in a horrified whisper.

Julian laughed.

"You echo her name pat enough. Clever ghost! Yes, I loved her. The day you took me to her—you remember?—well, it dated from that. Love at first sight. And you stood between her and me. 'When you are master where you are now dependent.' Those were her words. To win her I must be the Earl of Lesborough; for, you see, my dear Judith—oh, my love for her does not blind me to her faults!—is ambitious. She wants to be a countess—and, more than this, she wants to spite you, dear Cousin Vane! 'The woman scorned,' you know. You once loved her; she left you, and—you forgave her and forgot her.

No woman will forgive that! So she made her pact with me. I was to get rid of you, and then——"

His voice broke and paused a moment then went on:

"Judith! Why is she not here? I want her! She will not deceive me, will not rob me of my prize, herself, her love! No, no! The compact was too serious. Murder! Yes, it was murder. And did I shrink from it? And am I to be robbed—robbed—robbed——"

He staggered, and, making for the chair, fell into it, his head sunk on his breast, his long, thin hands extended, as if to clutch at something.

Vane strode to the decanter, but he would not touch it—it was contaminated by that other hand. He went to the half-conscious wretch and grasped him by the shoulder and shook him; and presently Julian opened his eyes, and, looking up, saw Vane—and knew him.

"Vane!" he cried.

"Murderer!" said Vane sternly.

Julian struggled to his feet and held out his hand, with a quavering laugh.

"Is it you? No ghost, but yourself!" he faltered thickly.

"Yes, it is I!" said Vane sternly, and yet with the pity one extends to the insane, criminals though they may be.

"Then—then you escaped?" said Julian. "How? I am glad, very glad! But—how?"

"Deborah, the deaf mute," said Vane huskily. "She saved me—I wrapped my coat round her——You hound! The woman who was devoted to you gave her life——"

Julian shrugged his shoulders, and drew his hand across his brow, as if to clear away the mist that enshrouded his brain.

"Deborah! I never thought of that. I thought she had fled—in horror! Deborah! Poor woman! Oh, poor woman!"

His voice broke, then he laughed the laugh of the insane.

"And I have shown your ghost—*you*, in fact—the whole bag of tricks. I have given myself away? Yes?"

Vane's stern eyes answered him.

"Well? What are you going to do? You can't accuse your own cousin, your own flesh and blood, of—murder! Think of the scandal! The indelible stain on the family name! You won't do that; what will you do?"

He had the best of it, as Vane felt.

"I ought to strangle you, kill you by any means, you—you traitor!" he said. "Get out of my sight! Get out of England—anywhere. I will see that you do not want. I will write to you; leave your address with Tressider. Get out of my sight. Wait!" as Julian walked with incredible steadiness to the door. "Tell me—tell me that Judith knew nothing of your hellish plot; that she is innocent of any complicity in your crime!"

Julian smiled. "My dear Vane, I wish I could set your mind at rest on that point; but I can't. I don't say that Judith was aware, fully aware, of the modus operandi; that she knew exactly how I was going to—remove you; but I'll swear that she knew you were to be removed! If you have listened attentively to my confession, you must have gathered that fact."

"Liar! Murderer!" said Vane.

"Murderer—well, yes, I admit; but a liar—I never lied yet. Lying is vulgar—and useless. But Judith. Oh, yes, 'when you are master,' et cetera. Oh, she knew! I saw it by her face that night, heard it in her shriek. And, mind you, Judith must abide by the compact. Judith is mine! Mine, by the right of the price I have paid for her! Not yours!" He advanced threateningly, his hand upraised, his fingers clutching at the empty air. "Not yours! You would not have sinned as I have done for her. You——"

His voice sank, and he laughed.

"Pardon! You will admit my claim to her. I am going. You will not see me again. When a man loses, as I have lost, after such a struggle, effort, he should efface himself. I admit that. I am going, and you will not see me or be troubled by me again."

He walked, quite steadily now, toward the table.

"Will you allow me to use a telegraph form? Thanks."

In horrified silence Vane drew back and watched him. He took a form from the stationery stand, and, after a moment's thought, wrote a message, very plainly and distinctly.

When he had finished he rose, looked at Vane with a calm, cool, indeed, critical, gaze, then with a smile said:

"Thanks! Good-by!"

Vane watched him as he went out of the room, then sank into a chair—not the chair in which Julian had sat—and buried his face in his hands. How long he sat he knew not, then or ever; but, suddenly remembering the unhappy wretch, he sprang to his feet and hurried into the hall.

He almost ran into the arms of Prance, who uttered a yell of amazement and fear, calling on his name:

"Lord Lesborough!"

"Mr. Julian!" cried Vane.

"Mr. Julian? Lord Lesborough! His lordship went out a quarter of an hour ago! But—but—oh, lord, who are you, sir? Oh, my lord, is it you, is it you?"

The whole household was in confusion. The clamor of tongues, the cries, and screams, and tears of relief and thanksgiving so confused Vane that he was thwarted in his intention of following the unhappy man. But, at last, he got a carriage and drove to the station, to find that Julian had departed by the train which had left a few minutes before Vane arrived.

CHAPTER XXVII
A TRAGEDY OF LOVE

"Decima!" screamed Polly when, with the merest apology for a knock, Nina entered the familiar rooms in Percy Street, the room in which she had found loving shelter in her time of need, the room in which she had trimmed hats and bonnets, and afterward—oh, great achievement—written plays for the members of Mr. Harcourt's company! "Decima!" and Polly, with the tears in her eyes, hugged her dear friend, never dearer than in this moment of her return. "How well you're looking, and how—how——Decima, something has happened to you! Something that's altered you in a way that I can't describe. You never looked so happy, and with such a light in your eyes, not even on the first night of the play! Sit down! Take your things off! Let me give you another kiss, you dear, sweet thing! And now tell me all about it! The voyage! The adventures you hinted at! Did you find that mysterious island—why didn't you tell me more about it? Did you find it, and is that what makes you look so heavenly radiant and running over with joy?"

"Yes, I found it, Polly," replied Nina, "but it was something else I found that makes me so happy. You'll never guess! Come closer and I'll—I'll whisper!"

Polly knelt beside her, and Nina, blushing like a schoolgirl, whispered one word, at which Polly shrieked:

"What! A husband! Decima! Who—who is he? Tell me quick, quick!"

And when Nina had told her that, and a great deal more—in fact, the history of the wreck and her strange marriage—Polly, all a-heap on the floor, could only stare at her, open-mouthed with wonder, delight, and awe.

"Married—married all the time! And to an earl! And you are a countess! Lady Lesborough! Oh, poor Lord Sutcombe!" Nina laid her hand on Polly's lips. "A countess! And been one all the time! And here was I treating you as if you were a mere nobody, just like myself! And yet, somehow, I always suspected——"

"That I was a princess in disguise! 'Changed at my birth with the rightful owner,' as the Irishman said. You dear, foolish Polly! As if it made any difference who and what I am! And—and I think you will like my husband, dear."

Polly emitted an "Oh! Like him. I—shall be afraid. An earl, a real English earl. De—I mean, Lady Lesborough!"

"You dare! 'Decima,' if you please. Oh, no, you won't be afraid of him. What nonsense! You are not afraid of Lord Sutcombe!"

"Oh, but he's only a viscount, or whatever it is, and yours is a real, belted earl!" explained Polly, with delicious naïveté. "What is he like, Decima?"

Nina laughed softly, and her eyes grew dreamy and fond.

"He is tall and very straight, with broad shoulders; and he is very strong and good-looking; quite bronzed and tanned, with eyes that——" She broke off with a laugh at herself. "Oh, he is a son of the gods—not our gallery gods, Polly, but the Olympian ones; 'a model of grace, and full of virtue'; but his chief one is that he condescends to love poor little me!"

Polly looked up at the radiant face, the graceful figure, and, laughing, tossed her head scornfully.

"As if he could help it! I'd like to see any man who could! Married!" Then she sighed. "You'll write no more plays, Decima; that's sure and certain! It's a pity."

"It's not at all sure and certain," said Nina. "Why shouldn't I? No one will know that 'Herbert Wood' is Lady Lesborough; and if they did! But you must talk it over with my husband when you meet him to-night."

"To-night!"

"Yes," said Nina, laughing at her tone of awe. "Here is a note from Lady Vivienne. She wants us all to go to the Momus to-night, and come back to supper with them. I am looking forward to it so much!"

* * * *

The play went splendidly that evening, and Nina, sitting well behind the curtain of the box, was all aglow with pleasure and honest pride in her work. It was sweet to see Vane applauding and looking over the delighted audience with glowing eyes, as if he were saying: "Clap away; shout your hardest, good folk; my wife wrote this play."

They went home to Eversleigh Court, where the Sutcombes had provided a supper, which, if it had not been so substantial, would have been suspiciously like a wedding breakfast; and, at Vane's warm greeting and the friendly look in his frank eyes, all Polly's awe and nervousness fled.

"I little thought, Miss Bainford, when I was watching you act, with the greatest admiration, that I was looking at my wife's dearest and best friend," he said, as he held her hand in his warm grasp. "I can't tell you how often she and I have spoken of you, or how much I have wanted to see you and—thank you! I hope you will share your friendship for her with me. Will you?"

It was a very happy little party, though every now and then a shadow stole over Vane's face. He could not altogether get rid of the memory of Julian—of the white, livid face, with its black eyes gleaming from their dark hollows.

"What do you think will become of him?" he had asked Letchford and Sutcombe earlier in the evening.

"He'll leave England," said Sutcombe. "Has gone already, no doubt."

"And will drink himself to death or get killed in a drunken row in the slums of Paris or Vienna," Letchford had suggested.

"He must be found," Vane had said quietly. "He must be found and—provided for."

"We'll put Tressider onto him," was Sutcombe's idea. "He will know better how to track him down than you can."

Vane tried to get his unhappy cousin out of his mind, and, as the supper progressed, had nearly, in some measure, succeeded, when Sutcombe's man came to his master's side and said something in a low voice. With a murmur of apology Sutcombe rose and left the room, and presently he returned, and quietly beckoned to Vane. Vane went out to him, and Sutcombe shut the door and drew him toward the library.

"I'm afraid something's amiss, Lesborough," he said. "Poor old Chandos Orme is in there. He tells a rambling, incoherent story. He wants to see you, and, hearing you were here, has come on after you."

They entered the library. Sir Chandos was seated at the table, a glass that had contained brandy, which Sutcombe had given him, already empty. He rose and held out a shaking hand to Vane.

"How d'ye do, Vane?" he stammered uncertainly. "Thought I should find you here. I say, you—you—know——" He paused to shuffle his false teeth into place. "What's the meanin' of all this? I—I don't understand it, don't you know!"

"All what, Sir Chandos?" said Vane gravely. "Is anything the matter?"

"Anything the matter? Dash it all, you ought to be able to answer that question! Sutcombe, for God's sake, give me another drink! I'm—I'm so upset and shaky that I can scarcely know what I'm sayin' or doin'! Thanks! a little more. I—I like it strong. No—no water. Water's no good; it's the brandy I want!"

They watched him as he drank the neat spirit—he reminded Vane of Julian—spilling some of it on his quivering chin and down his shirt front; then he turned to Vane and, in a somewhat firmer voice, repeated his question:

"What's it mean?" he demanded. "Must say it's a deuced queer kind of business; not at all the kind of conduct befittin' a gentleman, to say nothing of—personal friend, and a fellow one has trusted——"

"Tell me at once what you mean, Sir Chandos," said Vane.

"I'm talking about Judith; you know that well enough," retorted Sir Chandos.

"About Judith?" Vane's heart began to sink with a dark presentiment. "What about her?"

"Where is she? What have you done with her?" asked the old man, in a peevish tone.

"I!" Vane started. "I can't tell you. I've not seen Judith since—for many months."

"Oh, that's all tommy-rot, you know!" snapped Sir Chandos, with impatient irritability. "That dog won't fight. You sent for her——"

"I!" said Vane. "No, no; you're mistaken!"

"No, I'm not!" snarled the old man fiercely. "It's no good your standing there lying about it. I've—I've got the proof in my possession. You sent for her; you know where she is! And I shay itsh not the straight thing between gentlemen, between you and me, who ought to be father-in-law—son-in-law——"

He looked helplessly round and began to feel for the empty glass. Vane caught his arm.

"For God's sake, try to explain what you mean!" he said earnestly. "You say that Judith is—missing. When—where—how did she go?"

"Oh, drop it, Lesborough! You've got the gel, right enough. If you mean well by her, if you want to marry her, why not say so—why not do the whole thing in an open and proper manner? Is there any more brandy in that decanter, Sutcombe?"

Vane still held him by the arm.

"Presently, presently!" he said anxiously. "Sir Chandos, on my honor, I do not know where your daughter is——"

Sir Chandos drew himself up with the shadow of his old dignity.

"That's a lie!" he said. "And this proves it!"

As he spoke, he fumbled in the pocket of his dress coat, and drew out a telegram, and extended it with a shaking hand. Vane seized the telegram and read it, aloud:

> "I am alive and well," it ran. "Forget and forgive the past! I want you. Come to me at 24 Ponson Street, Chelsea, this afternoon, five o'clock.
>
> "VANE."

He stared at the words in silence, and uncomprehendingly, for a moment; then he uttered a cry and drew Sutcombe out of the room, closing the door after them.

"My God!" he said, in a whisper. "I did not send this! Don't you see who did? He asked for a telegram form, wrote this message, and must have sent it from the station. We must go at once—at once! Send Letchford in to keep the poor old man quiet till we return! Come! There's not a moment to lose! Five o'clock! Hours ago! Time for—for anything to happen! The worst!"

In five minutes, or less, they were in a cab and on their way. They reached the house—Vane recognized it at a glance—and found it apparently empty. The heavy door at which they knocked remained closed to them.

Vane hailed a policeman.

"There is nothing else for it!" he said. In a few words he explained his fears, and the policeman, climbing to the lower window, forced an entrance. He opened the door to Vane and Sutcombe, and, by the light of his lantern, they rushed up the stairs. As they did so, a strong odor of chemicals met them.

Vane groaned. He knew that odor!

"There's a fire somewhere, sir!" said the policeman. "Curious kind of a smell; quite suffocating! Seems to come from this room. Door's locked!"

"Force it, force it!" cried Vane hoarsely.

They set their hacks to it, and presently the lock gave, and they almost fell in. The lantern was raised, and its light flashed round the sombre room in which Vane had eaten his first meal with Julian Shore. The room was so full of the pungent smoke, the horrible mist, that for a time they could not discern anything; then, as some of the fumes escaped by the open door, they saw two figures. One was that of a woman lying back in one of the antique chairs. The form was motionless, the face white, the eyes wide open and staring. At her feet was stretched out the figure of a man, his face white as hers, his eyes staring upward at the face of the woman whom he had loved and—slain!

They bent over these two awful objects in silent horror, then the policeman shook his head.

"Lady's dead, gentlemen," he whispered.

The man lying at her feet was dead also, his fingers closed in a steellike grip on her skirt.

Vane staggered to the door of the laboratory. A small flame was still flickering in the spirit furnace, and the deadly fumes were still issuing feebly from the last dregs of the infernal compound in the iron crucible.

Sick and faint, half choking, as he had choked in the Wizard's Room, Vane knocked the pot from its place and, staggering to the window, broke some panes of glass. Then he sprang back to the two motionless figures in the vain hope that the policeman might be deceived.

But the policeman would not let him touch them.

"No use, sir," he said, with a shake of the head. "They're both dead—dead as they can be. Awful kind o' death, too! An accident, I suppose, in the other room."

"Yes, yes!" Vane got out hoarsely. "I—I know the man—the lady. It is an accident while experimenting with chemicals—you can see them there."

The policeman nodded, and, going to the window, blew his whistle.

"I must have some help, gentlemen. You'll stay here, please, till my mate comes, and we can send to Scotland Yard."

* * * *

The friends of Lady Lesborough—and how numerous they are—are never tired of dilating upon the romance of her life. And yet none of them, excepting the Letchfords and the Sutcombes, those friends of friends, whose lips are closed, know the whole of the story of her life. Few, for instance, are aware that Lord and Lady Lesborough, before they came to live at the Court, were remarried quietly in the quietest of country churches; few know the real story of Julian Shore's crime, and the tragedy at the gloomy house in Chelsea. And, though they know that the Lesboroughs and Sutcombes draw vast wealth from the Great Fairy Isle Gold Company, they do not know the real reason why the earl and countess, nearly every year, spend some weeks in the island from whence the gold comes, or that those weeks are perhaps the happiest of their happy lives.

It is good to be at the old Court, served by willing servants, and surrounded by the tenants, who regard the earl and countess with affection; it is good to be in London, where Nina reigns as a queen, by right of her beauty and her grace; it is good to be with the true and tried friends whose love and sympathy are so precious to Nina and Vane. But it is best of all to stand alone, side by side, husband and wife, upon the beach above the strip of golden sand, over which ripples the tide that washes the Fairy Isle. To know that, though all else were to vanish like the airy fabric of a dream, their love would still remain, and with it the memory of the days when, without their knowing it, their hearts were drawing together never to part while the life beat in them.

It was Lady Fanworthy who summed up the case of Vane and Nina so neatly.

"You see," she said to Vivienne one evening when they were seated on the terrace at Lesborough, and both the ladies' eyes were half absently watching the earl and countess as they strolled to and fro across the lawn, talking together like sweethearts, "you see, they; are so old-fashioned."

"Old-fashioned?" echoed Vivienne, waking from her reverie.

"Yes. That's why they are so happy. It is very old-fashioned to be in love at all; it is hopelessly old-fashioned to be in love with your husband or your wife; and, if you are so unfortunate as to be so, it is, so I am told, criminally old-fashioned to own up to it. I myself prefer the old fashion to the new; but, then, I'm eccentric—so I hear. Nina! Come off that grass; it's damp. Vane, bring her in at once."

THE END

www.ingramcontent.com/pod-product-compliance
Lightning Source LLC
Chambersburg PA
CBHW011031260626
47153CB00019B/2893